Alvin
&
Grace

James E. Williams

ISBN978-0-9801102-1-0

ISBN0-9801102-1-1

Author James E. Williams

Publisher HenryRetta's publishing

Copy written April 11, 2011

Alvin
&
Grace

By

James E. Williams

James E. Williams

Preface

This book is a work of fiction, but the idea for the story is in relation to a trip I took in1952 from Odessa, Texas to Fort Worth, Texas. I was seventeen years old.

Some of the characters are based on actual people but a few are fictitious. The reader will have to guess at which is one or the other.

Dedication

This book is dedicated to my lovely wife Carol to whom I've been married for forty-eight wonderful years.

She has been my walking dictionary and my toughest critic.

Chapter 1 – Country Boy in the Big City

When the bus finally arrived in the city limits of Fort Worth, Alvin Jackson gazed out the window, overcome with excitement as he tried to see the tall buildings and the beautiful landscape which were almost impossible to see at night. Until that very moment, Alvin had spent all of his seventeen years and a bit among the cotton-fields around the small town of Snyder. Now, for the first time in his life, he was seeing so many neon signs and city lights and headlights from a convoy of cars, which seemed to never end. After a four-hour ride that included a couple of stops along the way, the bus driver finally drove into the Greyhound bus terminal in Fort Worth.

Alvin got off the bus, his eyes still fixed on the tall buildings, which were close enough to see in the dark. He muttered a few apologies after bumping into a couple of individuals, ignoring their occasional exclamations of annoyance. He finally flagged down a taxicab, telling the driver where he wanted to go; the address that Alvin's brother Willie had written in a letter — 1414 Crawford Street. But when Alvin got to the address his brother had written down for him, it was the right street but the wrong number. Alvin asked the driver to wait until he went and knocked on a few doors.

"Now listen, man," the colored taxi driver said to Alvin. "I can't be waitin' around here all night for free, while you go knocking on every door in the neighborhood. It takes time and money to operate a taxi!"

"I don't think it'll take very long," Alvin said, "because I see the icehouse my brother talked about, being right across the street from where the people live that I'm trying to locate." Alvin knocked on a couple more doors. Finally, a tall, slender man wearing thick glasses opened the door. He stared for a moment and then said, "You must be Willie's brother, because you sure do look like him."

"I am," Alvin answered. "And Alvin is my name."

"Well, I don't know whether your brother mentioned my name or not," the thin man extended his hand, "but it's John Lee Bailey. So, come right on in."

"Let me first go and pay the taxi driver." Alvin said. He owed the taxi driver seventy-five cents. "And what is your correct address?"

1

John Lee told him, "1214 Crawford Street. Why do you need to know my address? You're already here, aren't you?" They both laughed, and Alvin explained about having to knock on other doors because his brother Willie had given him the right street but the wrong number. John Lee yelled towards the back of the house, sounding excited.

"Mama! Guess who's here?" From another room, a woman's voice answered.

"Who?"

"It's Willie's brother, Alvin, from Snyder!" John Lee explained. Miss Irene – which is what everyone called Mrs. Bailey – came out of her room, where she had been lying in bed watching television, exclaiming, "Well, you don't say, boy! You sure can tell you're a Jackson, looking just like your brother Willie, but mostly you have your father's features and a bit taller. How is your brother doing nowadays? We sure did like having him around here; he was so much fun to be with! That boy kept us in stitches listening to him telling his corny jokes. Our social life sorter fell apart around here when he left, but one must do what one must do. Myself, I thought he did the right thing when he ran out on this old gal he had been seeing, and went back to his wife and baby. Chullen' always need their father; it makes no difference how strong a woman is. Chullen' need a man around the house. Just like a woman – she too, needs a man. Well, you know not exactly in the same way, but that man's voice is what chullen' need to hear in support of the woman."

"Oh, and by the way," Miss Irene continued, "how're your mama and daddy? You know, we go back a long ways. Your mama was my best friend for years. We used to sit around and talk about different things, and one of the things we'd talk about was leaving the farm and moving to the city. But your mama couldn't seem to make up her mind whether she should stay on the farm or go to the city, so I got tired of complaining and not doing anything about it. One day, just like that, I made up my mind to leave those cotton fields for good. After workin' in that hot sun all day choppin' cotton, with sweat running down my back, I'd look up and see even the cows had enough sense to get out of that blazin' hot sun and into the shade of a tree. Fall – the same thing in reverse; so cold you could hardly straighten your fingers. As my old mama use to say, 'In the summer time it's too hot, and in the winter time it's too cold.' That's why I left them cotton fields and moved to the city. The same thing I kept writing and asking your mama; 'Leave them cotton fields and come to the city and live the good life like I'm doing.'" Then Miss Irene abruptly stopped talking. She stared at Alvin, waiting for him to answer. When he didn't say anything, she looked embarrassed, realizing she had been talking non-stop. Alvin found himself hem-hawing momentarily – not quite knowing where to start, since her disjointed conversation had held him captivated for as long as it did.

At last he gathered his fleeting thoughts and began explaining why he had decided to come to Fort Worth. "When I mentioned to my brother that I was moving to Fort Worth, he told me if I were ever in need of a friend, don't hesitate to call on you and your son. Besides," he added, "just sitting here listening to you talk, I truly understand what he meant." Alvin explained to Miss Irene and John Lee that his stay would only be temporary – just until he could land a job, a job that would afford him to pay for his own apartment.

"You might check across the streets at the ice house," Miss Irene suggested, "They just might be hiring. Of course, the pay isn't that good. I hear the most you'll gross is about forty dollars a week. But that's better than no job at all." At that, she excused herself and went back to her room and bed. Alvin thanked both of them for their hospitality.

The next morning being Saturday, everybody slept late but Alvin. He was up at the break of day. He got dressed and tip-toed out the door onto the sidewalk. He walked back and forth, between the house on Crawford Street all the way down to Rosedale Boulevard. He had no particular place to go, and didn't dare venturing out too far, as he had no idea where he was, or what he was looking for. After an hour of sight-seeing, Alvin sneaked back into the house, and discovered John Lee sitting on the side of his bed, yawning and scratching his head. When John Lee caught sight of Alvin cautiously returning, John Lee called out, "Come on in – you don't have to sneak in and out around here. Walk normal – you just might wake one of us old sleepy-headed people up, and get something done around here."

Irene was in the kitchen making coffee and she called out, "Speak for yourself! I've been awake for over an hour, but I didn't see any reason why I should get out of bed when everyone else is laying around, sleeping their lives away. So I just laid in bed until I finished watching some white minister preach his Sunday service on television. Now that I'm up and made a fresh pot of coffee, would you and Alvin like a cup?"

John Lee turned to Alvin and offered, "Would you like a cup of this stuff my mother calls coffee? But first," he added, "Before I go any farther, I need to ask how old are you?"

Alvin answered, "Seventeen."

"Oh no," John Lee said, shook his head. "You must be at least twenty-one or older before you try drinking that poisonous substance my mama calls coffee. You'll be better off to have yourself a cup of hundred-proof whiskey. That way if you get drunk, at least you can sober up."

"Enough of that kind of talk, you two: Get yourselves to the table and eat your share of the food that I've stirred up for y'all this morning." Miss Irene had set a bowl on the table filled with sausage gravy, a plate of hot biscuits, and a platter of fried eggs and bacon. As everyone sat holding hands, she asked John Lee to bless the food. After everyone had filled their plates, she passed the coffee, but Alvin refused it.

Miss Irene asked, "Did you let John Lee's lies about the way I make my coffee turn you aside from having a cup?"

"No ma'am," Alvin said. "I never got into the habit of drinking coffee."

"Well," Miss Irene answered. "The only thing that's left is milk and water, so take your choice or take both."

"I'll take water," Alvin said. "I've never liked the taste of milk either."

"Are you sure there is nothing wrong with you?" Miss Irene exclaims. "I've never heard of a seventeen-year-old that didn't like milk. Well, suit yourself!" She poured him a tall glass of cold water.

After breakfast John Lee got dressed and invited Alvin to go with him to a friend's house. John Lee didn't own his own car so they had to walk everywhere they went. After walking some distance, they finally turned off into a narrow walkway onto the porch of a ramshackle old house that needed a paint job in the worst way. John Lee knocked on the door and a slender young lady came to the door. "Oh no!" she exclaimed. "Mama, guess who's here?

A distant voice from farther inside the house demanded, "Who?"

The slender lady answered, "You know who!"

Her mama came to see, saying, "Oh! If it isn't the fried chicken man!" At that, the slender girl went back to doing whatever. And then Mama saw Alvin standing behind John Lee, and said, "Excuse me I didn't see you standing there. My girls and I have a habit of referring to John Lee as the fried chicken man, since that's the first thing he asks about, every time he comes to our house."

"Doggone-it!" John Lee said to Alvin. "I thought I told you to stay out of sight – at least until I find out whether Mabel would feel edgy or not, having a country boy like you hanging around her charming daughters. Now that she's already seen you, what else can I do except to introduce you? Miz Trousdale," he added, "This is a friend of mine, Alvin Jackson. You may remember his brother Willie."

"Lord, yes," the woman he called Mabel exclaimed. "How could I forget someone that made me laugh as much as Willie did?" She gazed intensely at Alvin. "Oh yes," Mable continued. "I do see the resemblance. Y'all sure is kinfolks, all right. So, tell me how is that old big-head boy doing? We rather miss having him around here. I know my daughter Bernice did – I think she sort of had a bit of a crush on your brother. But apparently his crush on her wasn't quite as manifest as hers was for him. The last time we saw him – as always – he had everybody in stitches telling us how he hated it that y'alls' daddy had him plowing with this mule that just had been fed oats for breakfast. And there he was, this twelve-year-old boy who stood exactly as tall as the mules behind. After twelve hours of breathin' the mule's gases, he was as intoxicated as if he had inhaled smoke from a half-dozen marijuana cigarettes. After that night, we never saw or heard from Willie, until John Lee told us that Willie had moved to some town in New Mexico." Mabel – Miz Trousdale turned her head and yelled, "Bernice!" The girl Bernice returned, standing next to her mother and asking, "What is it, Mama?"

"I want you to take a good look and tell me who does he remind you of?"

Bernice stood and stared for a minute while everyone stood silent, waiting for what her answer would be. Finally, she ventured, "Except for him being a bit taller, as far as I can tell he could very easily pass for your old buddy, Willie's brother."

"Yes," her mother said. "The only difference between the two of them, Alvin is taller. His height gives him an advantage over his brother, Willie, in the good-looks department. Other than that, they are most definite brothers and handsome ones at that."

Bernice demanded, "Where is your lying, no-good-for-nothing brother? I haven't seen or heard from that bum in so long – I almost forgot he ever existed. One day he was here and telling me lies about me being his best girlfriend, and the next thing I knew he had packed up and sneaked his behind right out of the city. I hope you're not like that. The least he could've done was to tell me that he was leaving town! Shoot, I wouldn't have tried to stop him!"

"Willie came back home a changed man," Alvin answered. "First thing we knew, he had gotten back with his wife and daughter and moved to Hobbs, New Mexico. From what he wrote and told my parents they've got two more li'l girls and another on the way.

"Boy!" Bernice snorted. "He sure didn't waste any time, did he? That man has been gone less than three years – and got two kids and one on the way! If y'all will excuse my French, I'd say he's married to some brainless person that don't know she don't have to have all of those babies. She only needs to take that extra second and slide a rubber over his thingy. Either that or she has this fetish about feeling empty. The instant she shed her placenta, she seduces him into sliding another one in the oven to fill up that vacancy."

"All right, Bernice," Mrs. Trousdale said, reproachfully. "You sound awful trashy using that kind of language. Not only that, but we have a teenage boy in the house."

Bernice laughed – Alvin thought she sounded kinda bitter when she answered, "It might sound a little vulgar the way I put it, but something is kind of strange about a woman that let a man give her two babies in less'n two year, and one in the oven. So, if you wonna tell someone to keep it clean – you need to start with her. And a boy Alvin's age knows just as much about making babies as daddy did, when he helped you to make me and Bobbie Jean."

"Girl," Mrs. Trousdale said. "I don't know what I'm gonna do with that filthy mouth that you wear around on your face every day!"

6

Another voice rang out from direction of the kitchen. "You can send her in here to help me, so I don't have to do all of this work while she standing around, trying to talk her way out of her shares of responsibilities. She could at least finish making the potatoes salad, while I make the Polly-pop. I need to get myself dressed for church – just like she should be doing. John Lee, is you and your friend going to church with us today?"

"Well, not this time. Bobbie Jean," John Lee said, raising his voice. "I need to stick around and tell Willie's little brother where to go and where not to go around this neighborhood."

"That shouldn't take long, Bobbie Jean called from the kitchen. "You can probably explain this old run-down neighborhood to him in about two minutes?"

John Lee replied, "You're talking about a normal person, but that's not the case with this boy. I've been setting here for the last ten minutes, trying to convince him that this old house is not a skyscraper. The tallest thing he's ever seen was a short man on a tall horse, riding behind him in those cotton fields."

Bobbie Jean demanded of Alvin; "Why do you let him get away with picking on you like that?" and Alvin answered, "As soon as I can fin' my way around this town, I'll start treating him the same way the three of you do."

Bernice and her mother finally joined Bobbie Jean in the kitchen; helping her finish making the extras to be served with the chicken which they would fry up, after returning home from church. Then the three women went to their rooms to dress for church. They came out looking like showgirls, smelling as if they'd been drenched in cheap perfume. Claiming they were in hurry, they walked slowly enough to be sure the men observed their luscious and oscillating breasts – not to mention their jutted, but well-shaped backsides. At the same time they scanned the faces of the two men, in hopes of catching the tiniest glimpse of approval in their eyes.

John Lee read their minds. He said, "You girls are looking too good to be going to church. Women that are dressed as pretty as you three ladies are, no'mally use going to worship as a decoy. I'm warning y'all to stay clear of those places where dopes ain't used to seeing such exquisiteness. Someone is certain-sure to reach out and fondle this beauty passing before their eyes. Whenever that happens," John Lee added, "I don't won't to hear about it; otherwise, I'll have no other choice but to come and avenge your reputation by beatin' up on a couple of them jokesters."

"You can count on me to fight to the bitter end," Alvin answered, "Especially over Bobbie Jean. Even if I came along holding her hand, some fool is sure to be bold enough to do something improper like reach out and touch her. If that happens, I'd have me no other choice but to haul off and whip his behind . . . if for nothing more than a potential encroachment on a territory that could eventually wound up being mine some day." The young men chuckled, and the older Miss Trousdale asked, "How old are you boy?"

"Seventeen," Alvin answered, and the girls laughed, as Mrs. Trousdale chided him,

"Um, um, um, you little old mannish thing – boys your age are not old enough to talk that way to my grown daughters. You should be sitting in some corner with your head buried in a schoolbook. How far did you go in school anyway?"

"Not as far as I plan to go," he said. They started to laugh again.

"Not only is he mannish," Miss Trousdale observed, "but he's quick with his answers as well."

In spite of her scolding him about the remarks he made about her daughter, those comments were exactly the words the women needed to hear. It made them feel that they'd been partially rewarded for all of the efforts that went into making themselves smell good and look pretty. Mrs. Trousdale stopped long enough to extend an invitation to John Lee. "I hope y'all ain't planning on leaving before we get back. You know, y'all are welcome to stay and watch television. Maybe by the time we get back, your friend will be hungry enough to sample a few bites of my famous fried chicken – you know – the kind that keeps you coming back every Sunday!"

As Mrs. Trousdale hurried out the door to catch up to her daughters, John Lee asked Alvin, "Did you hear what she just said? What would make her think that I'll be going any place? She oughta know me by now – I'm not about to leave them hungry church folks to eat my share of that golden-brown fried chicken. Man, you ain't tasted nothin', until you eat some of her fried chicken! Let her go right on to church, and I guarantee we'll be right here, when y'all get back. Say, Alvin – have you ever watched a television before?"

8

"Only the once," Alvin answered. "Six months ago, when I was riding with a friend of my father on our way to a town in West Texas, called Seagraves. Standing outside of a service station where we had stopped for gas, I saw all of those people gathered around watching this 'li'l movie screen. Being that I was just a boy, and this being the first television I'd ever seen – I wanted so desperately to squeeze my way past all of those guys with the big hats . . . just so I could hear what I were seeing, standing on the outside. 'Cept those were the kind of people a colored boy didn't dare to shove his way past to get a front-row view. For that reason, I just stood there for the time it took me to get calm. Wouldn't have done – I couldn't have stayed any length of time, anyway. We only had a few minutes to pay for the gas and be on our way again. That was the first and last television that I'd ever watched, if you can call it that."

"Well," John Lee said after a moment, "that either had a profound affect on you – or you spent lots of time rehearsing that unbelievable lie you just told me.

"Well, what differences does it makes anyway? Alvin said, and John Lee shrugged.

"None a'tall," John Lee drawled. "Now, Mama bought our television when they first came out, so I'm use to it. If you don't like what you see on this station, change it and watch something else."

"How do you change from one station to the other?" Alvin asked. John Lee got up and walked over to the television; he turned a knob and stopped at the Amos and Andy show. Alvin was excited to finally see Amos and Andy. He had heard them on the radio, but he had never seen them in any motion picture, and how he was thrilled to finally be able to put the faces to the voices of characters that he had heard on the radio – Kingfish, Sapphire, and all the rest. Around one-thirty, Mrs. Trousdale and her two daughters returned, bragging about the crowd at church service that day, exclaiming, "That was one sermon y'all should've been there to hear! Reverend Halls preached today, and he kept those sisters jumping and shouting, women were passing out all over the place. Girl, did they keep those deacons busy, moving from one sister to the other. Just when they thought that they had everyone under control, Reverend Halls would quote a verse that would send them all shouting halleluiah and fainting, making those deacons to start all over again in their attempt to settle them sisters down."

"Child, I know what you're talking about," Bernice said, "I noticed that it took two deacons, to finally tussle that fat lady who sit two rows in front of Mama, back into her seat!"

"Yeah," Bobbie Jean nodded her head in agreement. "I also saw they had to help Mama up and fan some life back into her, too. Mama was sure full of that Holy Ghost today, honey!"

"If you girls had paid as much attention to Reverend Halls' sermon as you did to those handsome deacons," Mrs. Trousdale answered, " then maybe someone up there would've passed a little of that Holy Spirit onto y'all, too."

"Someone up there oughta tell those brazen deacons the same thing you're telling me and Bernice," added Bobbie Jean. "Didn't you see the way they kept finding excuses to hold onto the younger women much longer than they needed to? All the pretty ones had to do was raise their hands and say, 'praise the Lord!' Girl, and those little slick-ass deacons would come from out of nowhere, with both hands all over them sisters. Now the less fortunate women in the good looks department were a different story. They had to be laid-out on the floor before anyone made an effort to help them up and back into their seats again."

"Yeah," Bernice chimed in, "and did you see the one that grabbed onto Sister Lucille? Now, everybody knows how big Sister Lucille's breasts are, and woo honey! That sweaty little deacon had himself a jolly good time – as if he had no other way to handle her except to grab both hands full of her breast! Yeah, honey, he was fondling around on places that's so restricted even her husband wouldn't dare touch in public. I kept waiting to see if her husband would catch on, an' throw his little immoral behind though a plate-glass window. Oh, he'll catch on all right," Bernice added, "and girl, when he does, I guarantee he's gonna take that little lustful deacon out behind the church house and kick his little wicked behind over into the middle of next week!"

"Did you notice when Mama was shouting and passing out the second time?" Bobbie Jean asked. "That same little deacon was nowhere to be found. But as soon as that young pretty woman – I can't remember her name – all she did was reach into her purse, took out her handkerchief and started to wipe the sweat off her face. Girl, he was there so fast and grabbed both hands full of titties! When I saw that, child, all I could do was just sit there, shake my head, and say 'Lord, Lord, Lord I wish some mischievous kid had a rubber snake and drop it down that horny little demon's back. Believe me you, if that don't take the heat out of his little skinny behind, then I don't know what would.

"Un huh, that's right," Bernice said. "I saw everything you saw – including the second time Mama got happy and passed out. There she was lying stretched out on the floor. Girl, I sat there and watched him skip his little skinny ass right past Mama as if she wasn't lying there! I guess both of 'em thought she was too old and wasn't worth fooling with."

"Haven't you two had enough of that kind of talk for one day?" Mrs. Trousdale demanded, indignantly. "The both of you need to put your aprons on and get in here and start fryin' this chicken."

It only took fifteen minutes to fill the whole house with the aroma of fried chicken, which triggered a slight rumbling from the bottom of Alvin's stomach. He kept hovering and hoping that any minute Mrs. Trousdale would say 'lunch is ready.' Finally, Mrs. Trousdale caught him peeking around the corner and brought him a drumstick on a napkin, and cooed, as if to a small child, "Here you go, honey. I can tell that you're just about starved to death. It won't be long now."

Alvin flushed with embarrassment, feeling like a spoiled brat for not being able to wait patiently like everyone else. Just then, two couples – members of the same church – arrived at the front door. They were also invited for Sunday dinner with the Trousdale'. There was a man named Moody and his wife Juanita, who turned out to be John Lee's sister. The other guests for Sunday dinner were Ralph Mcphee and his wife Effie. Effie was so pretty that Alvin could see why his brother had written in a letter about how Fort Worth was the capital of pretty women. But now Alvin found himself surrounded by a house full of total strangers. Not only was he shy and bashful, but he felt nervous about whether his table manners would be acceptable, sitting and eating amongst the other guests. When Mrs. Trousdale invited everyone to the table, Alvin made sure that he sat next to John Lee, in hope that he would pick up where he left off, before everyone went to church, talking non-stop. That way, all eyes would be on John Lee, and not on Alvin. To Alvin's relief, all the attention fell onto John Lee; he went into his talking mode and never stopped, chewing even as he talked. Every once in a while, Alvin would look up and catch Bobbie Jean's eyes fixed on him. He tried not to pay any mind to her – not because she wasn't attractive, but they had just barely met – the first girl he met since arriving in town. According to his brother Willie, Fort Worth was supposed to be the capital of pretty woman. Bobbie Jean was cute – but as far as Alvin was concerned, she wasn't cute enough to fit into the category of pretty women.

After the meal was over, and the kitchen was cleaned, the ladies gathered around the kitchen table and continued to gossip. They'd say flattering things about the women they saw at church, and liked, while criticizing and saying bad things about those that they didn't like.

The men returned to their seats in the living room and resumed their discussion about politics and baseball. Alvin just sat there in the midst of it all; a tall, shy seventeen-year-old country boy that didn't know anything about baseball or politics. His only interest was trying not to be caught gazing at the beautiful Effie, who unfortunately for him, was married to Ralph. To be on the safe side he decided to alternate between staring at Effie and at Bobbie Jean. He sat there, moving his head from one person to the other, pretending to understand what the older men were saying about baseball and politics.

It wasn't long before his wandering gaze attracted the equally wandering and somewhat lustful glance of Bobbie Jean. She stared until she made it obvious – he was who she wanted. Once she knew she had caught his interest, she asked if he wanted to walk out on the back porch, and visit with her. He followed her, grateful for being rescued from the older men and their political beliefs – not to mention rescue from the possibility of getting his seventeen-year-old ass kicked for salivating over Ralph's beautiful wife. Straight out the gate, Bobbie Jean's first question to him was – did he have a girlfriend? And the second was – had he planned to attend school while he lived here in Fort Worth? Before he could answer, she told him that she didn't have a boyfriend, and the one she had, she had just broken up with him about a month ago.

Then she asked, "What about you and your girl friend. I'm sure you has to have one, as good-looking as you are!"

"That's exactly what she was," Alvin replied, "a girl friend and nothing more. Except for a few kisses here and there, which was so mushy it, turned me off completely."

Bobbie Jean thought that was very funny. "It's an art to kissing," she explained patiently. "And that comes with a lot of practice, which doesn't mean that I'm that kind of girl – I'm just the kind that likes to judge her man by the way he kisses. And I've found that men are no different from anything else, and that one might be interesting in sampling, to some degree. When it comes to kissing, there are bad kissers and there are good kissers. Once a girl gives her lips for a kiss, then it's up to you guys as to how much of it you want and don't want." Bobbie paused, seeing that way of phrasing things was sort of embarrassing to him momentarily. She sighed, "I can see I had better watch what I say around this cute little country boy. I sure wouldn't want to give him the wrong impression about the way us city girls conduct ourselves.

"Oh no," Alvin said, "I don't feel that way about you at all; you have a good way of explaining things to me. I wouldn't mind you using me every now and then as your sculpture whenever you decided to do a little modeling again.

"I'm glad you said that . . . I wouldn't want to make you feel bashful around me the way you were, sitting with those men. You don't know much about what they were talking about, do you? I knew it – that's when I thought to myself, I had better get that boy out of there and get him a breath of fresh air before he have himself an anxiety attack. Don't y'all have movies theaters in the town where you come from?"

Alvin laughed a little, as he answered her. "Now, we're not that backward. We do have movie theaters in Snyder."

"Do you like colored westerns, then?" She asked.

"Colored westerns," he exclaimed! "I've never heard of such thing! The only westerns I've seen was white men dressed up like cowboys and fighting Indians, but never a colored cowboy."

"You mean to tell me you never heard of Herb Jeffery? Bobbie Jean asked, incredulously, and Alvin shook his head.

"No never," he answered, and Bobbie Jean came to a decision. "Well, if you want to go see one of his westerns, I'll take you – there's one showing in the theater that's not that far from where your friend John Lee lives, at Rosedale and Crawford. Can't you drive a car?"

"Yeah," Alvin answered. "I've been driving since I was twelve."

"I think I was about twelve, when I learned to drive too." Bobbie Jean raised her voice. "Mama! Can I use the car to take Alvin to see an Herb Jeffery movie? He says he's never seen a colored western before."

Mrs. Trousdale answered from the kitchen "What's the matter, Alvin? Don't they allow colored folks to go to the movies where you come from?"

"We go to the movies every Saturday night," Alvin answered, with mild indignation. "But I've never seen or heard of any colored man playing in a western movie by the name of Herb Jeffery. And I haven't ever heard of any other colored man starring in a western, as far as that goes. Anyway, I thought all of that Indian-fighting was left up to the white folks, and the colored did nothing but work them fields and grow enough food to keep the white man strong enough to whip those Indians' behinds."

Mrs. Trousdale shook her head and said to Bobbie Jean, "You shouldn't be taking him to see a movie. Instead you should be teaching him the history about our colored heroes. I don't think he know all of our coloreds weren't field hands. There were many of our folk that didn't have to work in the field—not for very long, anyway. There were plenty who got recognition by using their intelligence which made it possible to buy their own freedom. The first thing they did was to educate themselves, and became politicians and representatives, and working for high government official. I guess you've never heard of Frederick Douglass, Dr. William Dubois, Booker T. Washington or George Carver Washington. Not to mention countless of high-ranking colored men that you'll never read about in American's history books. Did your teacher ever tell you about all of the Negro officers and enlisted men alike that fought right alongside General Washington before he became president? The British thought the reason why they were getting their behinds whipped was that the colored soldiers wouldn't stop at nothing to shoot one of their oppressors. So the British officers rounded up a bunch of the slaves and promised to take them back to England as free men if they'd help fight the Americans . . ."

"Mama," Bobbie Jean looked exasperated, as she broke into her mother's lecture, "he's not interesting in hear about the history of all of those colored heroes of yours. All he wants to do is go to the movies and see the colored cowboy I told him about. So I'll ask you again, can't I borrow the car to take Alvin to the movies?"

"I don't know about all of that," Mrs. Trousdale looked dubious. "You know I don't like you driving around town at night in my car. It's too dangerous; nighttime is when all drunks come out."

"Mama," Bobbie Jean said, "Has you noticed the clock lately – as well as looked out the window and seen all of that sunshine out there?"

"It'll be night by the time y'all get back," Mrs. Trousdale insisted. "Y'all get to riding and talking about unimportant things, and before you know it'll be approaching midnight."

At that Bobbie Jean said to Alvin, "Maybe some other time."

"Alright, okay," Mrs. Trousdale yielded. "I'm gonna let you have the car to take your handsome young friend to see an Herb Jeffery movie. But if anything happened to my car to prevent me from going to work on the best job I've ever had, girl – I will wring your neck until it separates from your body. Y'all go on now and have a good time and bring my car back all in one piece."

"Remember, Bobbie Jean," John Lee called from the living room, as everyone laughed, "He's only seventeen."

Alvin thought very carefully about this: He had only had thirty dollars, and he was very careful about how he was going to spend it. He wasn't all that interested in going to the movie with her in the first place. He wasn't going with Bobbie Jean because he liked her; he wanted more to just get away from all of the strangers that he was uncomfortably sitting with. One of the things that helped make it easier to follow her off to the movies, was that he was genuinely attracted by that tiny waist and little cute butterball butt of hers. Other than that, he really wanted to check out other girls before he laid claim on her. Oh, if only there was a way he could put Effie's pretty face on Bobbie Jean's cute little body. His search for a perfect woman would end right then and there.

They drove to the theatre and got their popcorn and soda. In the darkened theater, Bobbie Jean led him to the very darkest corner, where she began to teach Alvin her kissing technique. Suddenly his temperature begun to spin out of control; he pulled away from her lips just long enough to whisper, "I believe you have just shown me how to get the best results out of a kiss. My old girlfriend Gertrude never brought things to life the way you have."

Bobbie Jean murmured in answer, "If you think my method of bringing things to life is exciting, just you wait until this movie is over. I'll take and show you the system I use to sooth that animated feeling of yours."

"If it's all the same with you," Alvin whispered, "I'd rather go home and get a good night's sleep, so that I can be first in line tomorrow morning for a job at the ice house."

"Oh shoot!" she said, "Wouldn't you know it would be just like me to spend all afternoon thinking about having the time of my life – and I wound up with some country-ass boy that can't thank past having enough sleep to be first in line for some stupid job!"

"Well," Alvin demanded, still whispering. "How you know for sure that you want to do this – when you don't even know me and neither do I know you, as far as that goes?"

Bobbie Jean suddenly lost her taste for kissing. She shifted her posture away from him. They sat quietly through the rest of the movie, but he never stopped holding her hand. When the movie was finally over, and they stood to go, he pulled her in his arms and single-mindedly kissed her. When he withdrew his lips from hers, she miserably asked, "Now, why did you go and do something like that if all you wonna do is go home and go to bed?"

"Why don't we let this night be insignificant?" Alvin suggested. "If and when you get to know me, you're gonna find that you're dealing with a boy that has a one-track mind. So if I've disappointed you on our first night out together, it wasn't my intention. It's just I want to feel relaxed and independent when we come to that point. And the only thing is gonna make me feel that way is a job. Okay, sweetie pie?"

"Come on; let me drive your little indomitable-acting ass home." As she drove away, Bobbie Jean glared at him, and snapped, "You ain't no fun at all to be with!" But once she had gotten to John Lee's house and parked outside, she asked, "Do you remember anything I taught you tonight? Or do you need another reminder?"

"I need another reminder," Alvin said. She leaned over and met him halfway and engaged their lips for about three minutes straight. After Alvin got his breath and his lips back, he shook his head, saying, "Girl, if you don't leave me right this minute, your mama is gonna think you've wrestled and lost to a full-grown lion, once she sees the condition of the back seat of her car."

"I would take that chance if I thought you were serious." Bobbie Jean replied. "All you got to do is get in and I'll help you to mess up the back seat of Mama's car." He just stood there grinning but speechless, until she finally admitted, "I'm just kidding. I hope you don't think I'm an awful girl just because you find me to be a little too outspoken. She stared into his eyes briefly, before saying, "Goodnight with your little cute self."

Alvin blew her a kiss and said, "Goodnight, Principal Trousdale."

The first thing he saw, once he went in the house, was John Lee sitting there, waiting to hear whether Alvin and Bobbie Jean went to the movies or went someplace and parked. Instead of Alvin volunteering anything about his first night out with Bobbie Jean, he kept silent and began to undress for bed.

Finally, John Lee said, "Now come on and let me in on what happened. Was she good?"

"Nothing happened," Alvin said, "except lots of kissing, which make me feel like running myself through a car wash with my mouth wide open."

John Lee began to laugh. "Why would you want to go through a car wash with your mouth opened? It wasn't that bad, was it?"

"Not really," Alvin said. "In fact, I'm thinking about marry her just so I could see how long it would take me to bring her down to a mild simmer instead of a boil."

"You don't need to be married to her to do a little snooping around in her underwear," John Lee said. "Who are you trying to be anyway—one of those that believe it's only legal when you're married? How did you know she wanted you to do it to her anyway? She must've said or did something to make you believe she wanted you to tap into her?"

"I may be seventeen, but I'm not stupid," Alvin said.

"Well", John Lee answered, somewhat mollified. "If you're not careful she'll have you so hooked on her that you won't know whose butt belongs to whom."

Alvin shot him a look that gave away nothing but mischief, and crawled into bed. A little past five the next morning, Alvin was awakened by the noise Miss Irene was making while she made breakfast, dressing herself for work in between. Meanwhile, Alvin got dressed and took a seat next to the bed and waited. Finally John Lee's mama yelled,

"You boys come on out of that bed and get yourself dressed." John Lee roused, reached over onto the nightstand for his glasses – and discovered once he put them on that Alvin was already dressed. He shouted back,

"This boy is already up and dressed. I suppose he's just setting waiting for five-thirty to roll around, just to be first in line to be interviewed for the job at the icehouse."

"That's a good sign," Miss Irene said. "It means he won't be asking us to loan him a dollar like his brother did, every time he goes out the door." By the time she finished saying that, Alvin was heading for the door. Miss Irene handed him a key to the house, as he went, just in case he didn't get the job. That way, he wouldn't be locked out until one or the other came home after work and let him in.

Giving him a key wasn't necessary, as it turned out. Alvin was hired right on the spot. It was just as Miss Irene Bailey had said; his starting pay was forty dollars a week, which was just fine with him. That was the most money he'd made and called it his very own. During the first week on his job, Alvin couldn't wait to come home every evening, eat supper, and go join Miss Irene and John Lee on the divan, where the three of them would watch television until the last show went off. Except for the times when Miss Irene's boyfriend, Elmo, came over, and she'd excuse herself and they'd go to her bedroom and do whatever they did behind closed doors. When Alvin got his first paycheck, he offered part of it to Mrs. Bailey to pay his share of his keep. But she wouldn't accept it; instead, she told him to save it until he had enough to afford his own apartment.

That Saturday night, Bobbie Jean came over to ask Alvin if he wanted to take her dancing at this nightclub she called the Zanzibar.

"I would love to," he told her, "but I'm only seventeen, and I don't think I look old enough to pass for twenty-one."

"Oh boy," she said "do you want to go party with me or not? If so, tell me. If not, I won't ask you again."

John Lee said to Alvin, "There's no doubt in my mind that you could easily pass for twenty-five. But if it'll make you feel any better, I'll tag alone just to put your mind at ease."

Bobbie Jean caught his hand and led him out to her car and the three of them piled in for a short drive to the Zanzibar. Alvin and John Lee followed Bobbie Jean to a table in a dark corner of the room. Everybody ordered beer. Once the server came back with their drinks and requested payment, Alvin reached for his wallet to pay.

Bobbie Jean said to Alvin, "Why don't you let me and crazy John Lee pay for the drinks? After all, we invited you, plus you need to save your money for your own place."

"So," John Lee said, "I suppose when that happens, you'll move in with him and leave poor old me to fend for myself. I don't have to tell you about the way it's gonna be for the first few weeks. After he done took you into hiding – and keep you there until you're too sore down there to wear underwear – which means I won't be invited to come over and have a few beers with him ever now and then. And if you're not careful you're gonna have your hands full trying to take on a seventeen-year-old boy that's hotter than a firecracker on the Fourth of July."

"You are right," she said. "You won't be invited to drink with us – and wrong – I won't have my hands full!"

John Lee chuckled, "I could've been more precise and probably embarrassed you – I said 'hand' – so I that wouldn't."

"Alvin," Bobbie Jean snapped, "would you please take me away from this old foul-mouth fool by asking me to dance with you?"

"I never learned to dance very well," Alvin said, "but I would like it if you'd teach me."

"Come on, baby," she drawled, "I would love to teach you how to dance." As soon as he took her hand and led her out on the dance floor, she looked him in the eye, asking, "Would you like it if I told you where to place your hand, you sexy country boy?"

"I think I can handle this part," Alvin whispered at the same time as he drew her close and waltzed her around the dance floor. His one desire on the dance floor was to focus his attention on the beat of the music so he didn't embarrass her as well as himself. After the second dance, he led her out on the dance floor.

He felt relaxed enough that he drew her closely into his arms and whispered, for the first time ever. "I've found myself responding to the sensation of a female's anatomy of which I have held pressed so elegantly against my body." She smiled with pleasure and moved even closer, which led him to believe that the way to her heart was a secret hideaway and she had just handed him the map. After that display of furtive love, they shuffled their way to the middle of the dance floor. They stayed there until the first intermission. Except to take occasional sips of their beer – it was right back to the far side of the dance floor again.

Whether the beat was fast or slow, their rhythm never changed. They just kept gazing into each other eyes, dancing to the beat of their own hearts. Even as they waltzed, it was as if they were two black figurines placed on a wedding cake, stylishly turning in slow motion. Now and again they'd kiss each other lips as they spoke sweet nothings to one another. One of the times when they walked back to their table for a sip of beer, two of John Lee's friends had joined him there. Bobbie Jean knew the both of them and one of them had the nerve to ask her for a dance. She refused, saying, "Man! If you were me, would you change horses in the middle of a stream?" She took Alvin's hand, whisking him back to the dance floor, to pick up where they left off. There she whispered that her excuse for being overly passionately with him was to demonstrate to certain other women who were staring at him with openly lustful eyes – they were wasting their time.

"Not only do I feel that I have to protect you from those women, but I had to tell that silly Gump that asked me to dance to back off as well. I hope I don't make you feel that I'm being a little too domineering." They kept right on drinking and dancing until the band stopped, and the bartender announced the last call.

They left the Zanzibar, clinging so tightly, one would've thought they were joined together like Siamese twins. She hurried and drove to John Lee's home. When Alvin got out he held the door open for John Lee, because of him riding in the back in a two-door car. Alvin made as if to close the door, and Bobbie Joan demanded indignantly, "Where in the hell do you think you're going?"

"Oh,"Alvin said, "do you want me to go with you?"

"You damn right I do!"

He got back into the car; as Bobbie Jean drove away, she scolded him in a passionate undertone. "In other words, what I'm trying tell you, is you can't squeeze and kiss a girl the way you did me tonight – and not expect to be picked to sooth the itch that you started so deep inside of me that's impossible for me to scratch without your help!" By the time she stopped scolding him she had driven within a block of her mother's house. She turned off her headlights, and drove the rest of the way in the dark, parking behind the detached garage, at the back of their house.

No sooner than she turned off the ignition key, she was all over him, saying, "I was woman enough to let you off last week-end but after a whole week of waiting has turned me into a nymphomaniac, so I'm coming at you, baby! Since Alvin hadn't ever slept with a woman before, he hadn't ever seen what was behind their underwear, either. As soon as he reached under her hips, and pulled her panties off, he was overcome with passionate anticipation, and rushed in and lost his virginity in ten seconds flat. He thought if he was satisfied, than she surely must be as well. But when he attempted to get off, Bobbie Jean grabbed his butt and held him there, saying in a stern voice, "Where in the hell do to think you're going!" She lowered her voice to soothing-sweet baby-talk. "It's all right, sweetie. Don't feel bad. Just keep it there, and it'll come back much sooner than you thank."

It came back all right; exactly two more times before she decided that her itch had been scratched to her satisfaction. Afterward she got out of her car raised her dress, squatted until she voided all of his matter, and got back into the front seat and drove away. After she had driven for a while she said, "I believe you now, when you told me you hadn't been with a girl before."

"Why would I lie about something like that" he answered.

"You're a man, and all men lie about their sexual encounters with other women. But one thing I do know for sure, and that is I'm the first woman to ever trip your jack. Not once – but three times, to be exact!" She slapped his thigh and said, "You think I didn't know about the third time, but a woman always knows what goes on inside of her body. That's just one of the many things you'll learn, hanging around with me, baby. You've only spent about two hours with me – and I've already started to teach you about a woman's intuition. On the other hand," she added, "it's just the opposite with you men. I doubt very seriously that you had the tiniest inclination as to how many times I did it – or if I even did it at all, do you?"

"I can't be sure," Alvin said, "since you're the first woman I've had the pleasure of lying with. But if every time you shouted out, 'oh honey are you going with me,' was any indication of the amount of times you did it, then I'm incline to believe I came up a few squeals short."   "Oh, Bobbie Jean answered, "Those little feisty noises I made meant nothing more than a polite way of saying to my man that I've had enough, and be prepared to get his butt off the next time he's told to do so."

"Then which one of those ten-second screams in fifteen minutes told me that you've had enough?"

She grinned. "Now, don't start bragging too quickly about your performance, especially after I had to tell you what to do and what not to do. Before we go patting ourselves on the back, just let us wait until we're not as vulnerable as we were tonight. Then we'll see who's declared the winner in a rematch? Beside," she added, "I have better things to brag about . . . like being the first to ever make love to a good-looking boy like you are. Not only that, it gives me an opportunity, walk around and brag to my friends like I've heard men bragging to their friends about having some virgin girl for the first time." Alvin was unexpectedly silent. Finally, she asked, "What's the matter with you? You haven't said a word since we drove away.

"I'm saddened," he said, "because I didn't wait and save my virginity for my virgin wife, so she and I could brag together about loosing our innocence to each other."

"Now ain't that some shit! I thought you'd be so excited that you couldn't wait to blow your horn to John Lee about what you just did to me. "Isn't that what most boys your age like to talk about, especially after they've gotten their first piece?"

"I'm not most boys." he said. "I only know how I feel."

She said, "I'm sorry, but I can't help you none there, even if I wanted to, which I don't. Plus I sure do hope you're not expecting an apology from me either. Even if I did, it sure wouldn't undo what's already been done. Not after you kept me penned to the back seat for at least one solid hour, if not longer. You weren't nearly about ready to get off me. I had to ask you several times to get off. Even then you acted as if you had something heavy sacked on your back as many times as you domed and slid right back in. Anyway you're a man, and the men I know don't go around feeling that way. You sound like me when I lost my virginity. I was about your age when that lying dirty dog told me that he loved me, until he got what he wanted. Then he didn't love me anymore which made me feel really sad. Except I'm a girl, and girls is supposed to feel that way when they believe that they've been seduced by some silver-tongued devil with a mischievous spirit. It took me awhile to finally get over it, and I suppose in time you will too. Once the feeling of being with a woman soaks in, then you'll start to feel just like I did and you won't ever consider the idea of going back to being a virgin again. You probably won't realize it until tomorrow morning, when you wake up and find that you'll need both hands to handle that miniature baseball bat you used on me tonight. Then you'll wish we'd spent the whole night in the back seat of Mama's car."

By that time, Bobbie Jean had parked in front of the Bailey house. At that, she reached over to briefly fondle his thighs. When he didn't respond, she asked, "Are you too gloomy to kiss me good night, little honey-sweet angel of mine?

He leaned over and kissed her, saying, "Goodnight Bobbie Jean." Inside the house, John Lee was already sound asleep. And Alvin assumed that Miss Irene was asleep, too – which was fine with him – after all, it was past four o'clock in the morning. The best thing about John Lee being asleep was that Alvin didn't have to listen to questions regarding what happened between Alvin and Bobbie Jean that night.

He undressed and went to bed. The next day being Sunday, everyone slept late. Miss Irene Bailey was the first one to get up, followed by John Lee. A full two hours later, Alvin dragged himself out of bed, dressed and took his seat at the breakfast table. John Lee and Miss Irene Bailey were already sitting, reading the paper, and sipping on half-warmed cups of coffee. "Good morning," Alvin walked into the kitchen, and they both looked up.

"It's about time you got out of that bed." Miss Irene Bailey said. "And has you a glass of milk or some kind of liquid to replace what John and I expected you lost, fooling around with Bobbie Jean last night. John Lee said he didn't hear you come in this morning just before the break of day, but I did. I had just come back to bed from the bathroom, and it was past five o'clock. You're hanging out with some pretty fast girls. If you don't believe me, you should ask your brother. Let him tell you how busy her sister, Bernice, kept him. It was in the dead of winter, the night your brother came home with sweat running down his back, and he said to me, 'Miss Irene, you and John Lee will have to forgive me for running out on y'all this way. But if I don't leave this town tonight that girl Bernice is gonna be the death of me.' He went straight to his room, packed his suitcase, and caught a taxi to the Greyhound bus station. I'm assuming once he arrived there, he bought himself a one-way ticket, destination unknown! It was a long time until your mama wrote me, and told me he was living somewhere in New Mexico. The same thing will happen to you if you don't stop giving into her wild imagination. Like I'm about to imagine that you go right now and take yourself a long hot shower, which you should've did before you went to bed last night. Then it wouldn't be so plain to us what you and Bobbie Jean did over those hours that y'all spent from one to five o'clock in the morning." Miss Irene laughed, adding, "Never mind – that smell of cigarettes and perfume you brought to the table with you – that took all the guess-work out of who you were with and what you were doing!"

John Lee muffled his own laugher. "Mama, I wasn't gonna mention it in front of you what he smelled like, when I rolled the cover back to get out of bed, and the scent was fresh. And the only way for you to know what I smelled – you would have had to lay five minutes where I slept while it was fresh. I got out of bed this morning wondering 'when did I get back with my old girlfriend Sarah?' "

When Alvin came back to the kitchen after a long hot shower, Miss Irene grinned, "Now, that's much better – like I said earlier, that's what you should've done before you went to bed this morning. Now that we got my house all aired out, I'll take this instant to ask you boys what you want for breakfast, before I change my mind."

Alvin answered, "I'll eat anything that won't eat me first."

"I hope that isn't retroactive," John Lee said. "Now that we know what, and who attract your sense of taste.

After breakfast, Miss Irene went and took her shower and started to get dressed for church. "John Lee," she said, "you and Alvin will have to fend for yourself today, because after church Elmo is taking me out for my Sunday dinner."

"I'm sure me and lover boy will find something around here to eat. If not, I'll have him to call Bobbie Jean, and asked her to bring over a couple of plates of fried chicken and trimmings. Come to thank of it," John Lee said, "that shouldn't be a problem at all for her. She'll think two plates of food is a bargain compared to what you dole out to her last night." Miss Irene Bailey called from her bedroom. "Go ahead, then, Alvin and call her. If she doesn't, it'll only prove all you did was rebred an engine that took her nowhere.

Shortly after, Miss Irene's boy friend drove up and blew his car horn. She went to the door not yet completely dressed and called, "Give me five minutes to finish getting dressed and I'll be there." She came walking past where Alvin and John were sitting. Alvin didn't stare, but he took a quick look and said to himself, "Not bad, Mrs. Bailey – not bad at all for a forty-eight year old. No sir," he thought, "not too bad at all." She finally came back and passed him and John Lee fully dressed. He watched her through the window as she walked to the car where Elmo stood holding the door open for her, and drove her off to church.

All of a sudden Alvin's feeling for Mrs. Bailey went from a casual to an amorous idea; about what if? It only lasted momentarily before his mind drifted back to Bobbie Jean, which was under discussion before he became interested in dissecting Mrs. Bailey's thingamabob. At last, John Lee changed the subject from Bobbie Jean to the fun he and Alvin had last night – to Bobbie Jean and her sister, Bernice. He considered them to be very nice girls, whom he felt would properly make some man a very good wife – provided of course they'd find one with hormones equivalent to their capabilities.

"How do you know," Alvin asked, "that those girl's motors run on hot all the time?"

"I'm sure you didn't forget so soon about what Mama just told you about how Bernice kept your brother's thingy so depleted, the only way he could replenish was to get out of town and away from whom he refers to her as nymphomaniac. And I won't say who told me, but I've been told that Bobbie Jean have the same problem!

Well," Alvin ventured, "if Bernice is anything like her sister, I can understand my brother's reasons for running out on her." More than ever – if her obsession for him was more aggressive than his was for her. In that case it's what's called 'incompatibility,' which means one is either too hot or the other is not hot enough. Finally, Alvin concluded with all honesty, "If Bobbie Jean wasn't so much older than me, I wouldn't mind marr'ing her. She may not have a Dorothy Dandridge's face, but she definitely has the body and as for as a pretty face goes they're always nice to peer at. But the thing that's more meaningful than a pretty face is what she keeps in the dark anyway. So, when those thing we are so proud of that we keep in the dark, collides with each other, thingamabobs the first thing I do is close my eyes. So the beautiful face doesn't really matter anymore."

"Go on away from here fool!" John Lee said, "I thought you told me you were a farm boy from Snyder, and not this person with a degree that goes around saying who's compatible to do what to who? Mark my words," he added, "that girl will have your ass headed for the bus station the way her sister had your brother Willie doing."

"Well, ain't you being a little too judgmental about my capability to go toe to toe with her – unless you've already did what I did with her last night?"

"All I'm saying is you are not the first one to think that he could latch on to either girl, and have a lasting relationship. Those two women have a reputation as being teasers. Once they get you acclimatize to their sweet 'you know what,' you'll either do what she says – or she'll move on to the next one."

Alvin said, "I feel just like you, when you said all I'm saying is.' I think you've misjudged Bobbie Jean, because I've already felt a sense of compatibility between her and me. Otherwise why was she the first to say 'I've had enough,' after I had spent four hours carving away at her last night, while trying to appease her craving?"

"Well, hush my mouth, an' you go right on ahead. We'll see who cries cruelty first!" That was far from what Alvin wanted to hear, so they both stopped talking and just sat there, staring at the television. Alvin was glad to finally hear the telephone ring, which broke the silence, which had filled the room. John Lee answered the phone, and handed it to Alvin, saying, "It's the lady with the out-of-control hormone problem."

"Hello," Alvin answered.

"Who is that with the hormone problems?" Bobbie Jean demanded. "I hope he wasn't talking about me." Tell me, has John Lee been saying bad thing about me?

"Now, why would John Lee say anything bad about you? He's your friend, isn't he? Friends don't say bad things about each other, do they?"

"Yes," she answered. "John Lee would. 'cause he's jealous for the reason that you're with me, an' that is where he wants to be. Not only with me, he's even tried my sister Bernice and she turned him down as many time as I have. Because of that, we weren't speaking, until you came to town. John Lee's problem is he hasn't figured it out that nobody wants to go out with an old sorry-ass creature like him. Not only is he sorry but he's just as ugly, as my daddy use to say – 'Ugly as green snot on a clean white shirt.'" Alvin couldn't keep from laughing out loud, and John Lee asked,

"Did she say something nasty about me?" Alvin handed him the phone.

"Bobbie Jean," John Lee commanded, into the phone, "you better stop talking bad about me, and hurry up and get over here with two plates of that leftover fried chicken – provided all them hungry church people y'all normally invite over for dinner didn't eat it all?" John Lee chuckled at Bobbie Jean's answer, and added, "Well, are you gonna come and get us?" We're too hungry to walk all the way over to your house. Anyways, you don't want your lover boy out on the streets, exposing him to all of those pretty girls, do you?"

He handed the phone back to Alvin, and Bobbie Jean said, "I'll be right over to pick y'all up and bring you to our house and feed you hungry bombs." She hung up, at that.

Maybe I spoke too soon," John Lee ventured, thoughtfully. "Perhaps she has met her match. Otherwise she wouldn't be so eager to drive all the way cross-town, pick us up, drive us to her house, feed us and bring us back home again. I've never heard of Bernice doing anything like that for your brother. Maybe if he had of stayed and gone toe-to-toe with Bernice like you claimed you did with Bobbie Jean. Instead he forfeited his

27

responsibility and hauling his ass out of town. Otherwise perhaps Bernice may've been feeding him left-over fried chicken too."

Fifteen minutes later Bobbie Jean knocked on the door. John Lee said, "Go on and open it, I thank you know who it is. She'll be very disappointed if your face weren't the first thing she saw when that door springs opened." Like John Lee said, the minute Alvin opened the door, she tried to walk through him. When she saw she couldn't, she latched onto him as if he was a long-lost friend that she hadn't seen in years.

While she was doing all of her tongue-sucking and face-licking, she remembered to ask him about the condition he was in when he woke up this morning, and left off long enough to whisper, "Was I the first thing on your mind the instant you woke up this morning?"

Alvin snickered. "Uh-huh, and how!"

"In a big way baby?" she whispered.

"Yeah."

Bobbie Jean locked one leg around his leg and said, "See, I told you you'd feel much better after the sun came up this morning. Now don't you wish you had spent the rest of the night with me in the back seat of Mama's car?" He grinned, without answering. She said, "You don't have to tell me I know what you are feeling, because I felt the same way about seven years ago."

"Hot damn!" John Lee broke in. "Has it been that long since we been apart?

"Would you please be quiet long enough to let me think about what possessed me to drive all the way across town? You should show me your appreciation for coming to take you home and feed you – but instead you're setting here, lying your sorry ass off about something that you ain't gonna ever do to me?" Bobbie Jean kept hold of Alvin's hand. "To answer your question about what possessed you to drive over to my house should be easy. The first thing is to back far enough away from kissing him, to look down and see what's in your hand, and the rest is easy. But you're so used to blaming me for everything, you let what's in your hand distracted what's in your mind, which caused you to forget your reason was to come and take us home and feed us. Come on Alvin – let's go and take this foolish old night crawler home so I can feed the hungry bum.

"Now there you go again," John Lee said, "blaming me for something I had nothing to do with. Blame the one that kept you out until five o'clock in the morning . . . who I assume did a lot of night crawling during those hours."

"I'm not gonna answer you," Bobbie Jean said, "because I need to hurry up and get out of here and give this house time to air out your filthy remarks before Miss Irene gets home."   Even as she drove, Bobbie Jean and John Lee teased and bickered with each other all the way back to her house. She did feel especially vindicated when she saw how annoyed John Lee was, when he didn't find any fried chicken on the table. Instead she pointed to a couple of pots setting on the stove; one with chitterlings, and the other with collard greens . . . and a few pieces of cornbread.

"Darn!" he said. "How many of them so-called Christian hypocrites did y'all invite over for dinner anyway? Well, I guess beggars can't be choosey. Come on, Alvin – let's dig in." The squabbles ended at that point, this being the only meal they had since breakfast.

In the midst of them gorging themselves to obesity, they paused, after hearing a knock on the front door. Bobbie Jean answered it, and called out to Bernice, saying, "Leon is here."

"Tell him to come on in and have a seat. I'll be there as soon as I can finish getting dressed."

Bobbie Jean said, "Leon, I know you're acquainted with old con-man John Lee, but I want you to meet a friend of his. Alvin, say 'hi' to Leon." Alvin stood and shook hands, after which Leon sat on the divan and engaged in small talk with Alvin and John Lee.

Finally Bernice emerged from her room; all dolled up in a two-piece navy blue suit, over a white blouse, and matching costume jewelry. Seeing this, Alvin wondered if he was hanging out with the wrong sister. Her jacket was short and tapered to fit her tiny waist, and the skirt was perfectly tailored to fit her cute little behind – which was the same shape as Bobbie Jean's. Bernice's face was much better looking than Bobbie Jean's. Leon stood up and extended his hand, and continued to hold Bernice's hand as they left. Alvin, still musing on Bernice and Bobbie Jean's looks, was finally moved to say to Bobbie Jean, "I know one thing if I don't know anything else; without a doubt, you and Bernice is sure-enough sisters!"

"Now, just what makes you say something like that?" she asked.

"Because," he said, "I'll bet anyone five dollars they can look all over the city of Fort Worth and never find any woman with cuter bodies than you and your sister."

"Well, that's very nice of you to say that," Bobbie Jean said. "But in the future, I'd rather you limited your compliments to me. If I'm in a category all to myself, that way you won't get me mixed up with Bernice."

Mrs. Trousdale called out from her bedroom; Alvin didn't know she was there listening. "That kind of talk sounds awful seductive to me, coming from a manly boy like you. Both my daughters are grown women – a boy your age should treat them as such. If it's that important for you to try to tempt someone with your compliments, announce them to someone your own age.

He answered sheepishly, "Yes, ma'am, and I'm sorry—I didn't know you were home."

Bobbie Jean said, "Oh, Mama, he didn't mean any harm. He's just talkative like most boys his age – trying to be all grown up when they know they're not.

"Well, if you stop hanging out with him maybe he won't feel the need to grow up all in one week." Mrs. Trousdale answered tartly.

"With all due respect, I maybe seventeen but I'm not blind." Alvin spoke up. "I thank I'm about the age when young boys becomes interesting in the opposite sex. I'm saying what I said because I haven't ventured out very far since I've been with her. As far as I've ventured, your daughters are more desirable to look at than anyone else I've seen in the short time I've been here."

Mrs. Trousdale chuckled, dryly. "Bobbie Jean you've gone and fooled another one!"

"Now Mama," Bobbie Jean answered, "I haven't tried to fool anyone; I just do what I always do! I try to dress nice and mind my own business. I can't help it if he likes what he sees."

"That's what got me worried about you; minding your own business and doing what you've always done."

"Well,'' John Lee observed, winking at Bobbie Jean, as she sat on Alvin's lap, teasing his lips with her tongue. "I guess I'll have to start leaving this little country boy at home the next time I decide to come to your house. If there is anyone or anything I won't associate myself with – it's a boy that goes around flirting with women old enough to be his mama."

Mrs. Trousdale was indignant. "Now John Lee, let's not get carried away; neither one of my daughters are older enough to be that boy's mama. I'm not asking you to stop bringing him around. I like Alvin. All I'm saying is he should find someone his own age to flirt with. I think the responsibility rests on Bobbie Jean to keep him in his place now – so things don't get out of hand later."

"Well then," John Lee said, responding to Bobbie Jean's wink. "If you think it's all right for me to bring him the next time I come over, then I will. Just as long as he knows I won't let him or anybody come between me and the woman that makes best fried chicken that's ever been served as a Sunday dinner."

Bobbie Jean laughed out loud. "John Lee, you're nothing but a con man."

"Now that we got that settled," John Lee answered, "I don't see any more reasons why I should be hanging around this joint. Unless you want me to stay until I make enough room for the rest of those chitterlings and cornbread."

"No thank you," Mabel Trousdale answered. "We've had our share of foul odors while cooking them chitterlings. Rather than to start all over again, I just as soon to throw them away and invite you and Alvin over next Sunday for fried chicken instead of boiled chitterling.

Bobbie Jean interjected hastily, "Mama, I'm gonna drive them home and I'll be right back."

As the three of them drove away, John Lee said to Bobbie Jean, "If your mama was upset about the flirting remark Alvin made about you and Bernice being desirable to look upon, she would've died if she knew what y'all were doing after the dance was over at the Zanzibar until six this morning?"

"How do you know what Alvin and I did until six in the morning? You didn't tell him anything about us, did you Alvin?"

31

"No way," Alvin answered. "I'm too selfish to share such wonderful secrets with an undeserving soul like John Lee.

"Secret or no secret," John Lee said, "the way y'all was rubbing and kissing while dancing? It was obvious to everyone that saw y'all, what was coming immediately after you two fools stopped dancing. Not only that – I was still standing there, when you yelled at him to get back in the car. What was all of that about? Drive him around the block until five in the morning, listening to him singing you love songs? That alone was a dead giveaway – 'specially after you coerced him back in the car and drive away like a bat out of hell.

"Well," Bobbie Jean replied, "I sure do hope you know when to talk and when not to talk – particularly when you are around my mother."

"Girl!" John Lee snapped, "Don't you know I ain't no fool! If I was going to say something to try to make points with your mama, I would've said it while I was setting there filling up on chitterlings and cornbread. "I know when to talk and when to keep my mouth closed. No one is gonna hear a word out of me about y'all's situation."

Bobbie Jean parked at John Lee's house. Alvin got out to let John Lee out and walked around to the driver's side. She said, "I hope you didn't walk all the way around here just to kiss me goodnight."

Of course not," Alvin said. "This is just my way to punish you for bragging about taking the advantage of my vulnerability last night."

She giggled, answering, "Fool, you scare me half to death. I thought you were about to tell me that you needed to go to bed in order to be the first in line for some interview in the morning. Hurry up and get your ass back in this car so we can do an imitation of what we did last night." She drove back to the same place, behind her mother's detached garage and parked. Alvin got to work on a carbon copy of what they had done the night before.

After a time she asked, "Do you have a handkerchief?" Alvin reached in his pocket and handed it to her. She placed it to her bottom, grunted then scooted back. She wiped and folded it and wiped again. Then she handed it back, saying, "You see, you didn't lose anything. I gave it all back to you."

"Well in this case," he said, "I'll accept it this one time because that's the only one I own. However, in the future when I've spent all of my energy to produce what's on my hankie, don't bother giving it back, just leave in and accept it as a token of my appreciation."

She grinned. "Your comical idea may have entertained me to do just as you suggested if I thought that you were serous about me. But until I know for sure it will always be either your handkerchief or dribble it on the back seat of Mama's car. Because, I'm not about to leave what could be one of your progeny incubating in me between the time I drive you home and back to my house again, before I flush it down the toilet. You'll either have to hurry up and get your own apartment, or buy yourself whole lots of handkerchiefs, because I get the feeling before we're finished with each other I'll be spending a lot of time flushing, your product or giving it back to you on another one of your handkerchiefs."

She had just parked in front of the Bailey house when she got on to a new topic. "I sure do hope you didn't take what Mama said about you this afternoon the wrong way.

"Name something," he said.

"You know – when she told you that you were too young to be flirting with me, including the tone of voice she used to get her point across."

"Yes, I know." Alvin said. "She wants me to save my flirting for someone my own age. As for as I'm concerned, that part of this conversation is over. From now on, I'll make sure I know who's home before I start saying sexy things about you. That way you don't ever have to apologize to me on behalf of your mama – or anyone's behalf. I'm fixing to start using those kinds of words only when the conversation is held in the back seat of your mama's car. Haven't said all of that – now I'm going to say good night."

She didn't argue, but gladly stuck her face out the window, grabbed the back of his head, shoved her tongue to the back of his throat, and held it there two minutes, before driving away, waving goodnight.

When Alvin walked into house, he saw John Lee was sitting on the divan half-asleep watching television. John Lee turned his attention to Alvin with squinted eyes, as if it would clarify his vision to gaze even closer at

Alvin's demeanor. But Alvin ignored his fix-your-eyes-on-me attitude and started to undress for bed. Finally John Lee said, "I hope you're going to wash your nasty ass before you go crawl between those clean sheets. Just to think that she had the nerves to ask me 'how I knew what y'alls been doing?' Well, I wish she was setting here smelling what I smell. But she couldn't anyway; like a dog she too can't decipher her own smell because it's part of her own ass. That's probably why she had the gumption to ask me how I knew what y'all did until six in the morning. And here lately it seems every time you walk through that door, you bring the evidences right along with you." John Lee looked at the displeasure on Alvin's face, and chuckled. "Now, don't go giving me that stern look. I just wish it was me who had just walked in with her sister's evidences spread all over me. Bernice is every bit as fine as Bobbie Jean – she definitely has a better-looking face than Bobbie Jean."

Alvin said, "I understand you wanting a woman but Bernice is not the only girl in this town. There are plenty of girls out there. Why don't you dive in and get yourself one?"

"Well," John Lee answered the tone of his voice suddenly discouraged. "The girls don't take to me like they take to you and your brother Willie. You boys are like magnets when it comes to woman. You were in town just one day, and knew her less than an hour before she had zeroed in on you. I don't have that kind of luck with woman."

Alvin suggested, "What you really need is yourself a car. Girls don't want to take responsibility for getting you to and from places you both enjoying going."

"You don't have a car," John Lee said. "And look how you're being chauffeured all over town and getting yourself a kiss at every stop sign!"

"It's pure luck," Alvin said. "That's all it is; just plain old pure luck." John Lee didn't answer. Alvin shrugged – but he took John Lee's suggestion about a shower.

Chapter 2 – A Place of His Own

During those few weeks of romancing Bobbie Jean in the back seat of her mother's car, Alvin had pinched and saved up his pennies from working at the ice house, until he had enough to start asking questions about different neighborhoods to live in. One Sunday while Alvin and John Lee were visiting at Bobbie Jean's house, Effie and Ralph Mcphee were also there – that couple who had been to Sunday dinner that first day that John Lee had brought Alvin to the Trousdale house. After the traditionally large Sunday dinner, everyone would be too full to do much except relax, lean back in their chairs, and stay awake long enough to make small talk.   On that day, Effie flashed a quick look at Alvin – but she talked to John Lee.

"Every time I see you, John Lee," she exclaimed, "I see your friend Alvin, and I take it to mean that he hasn't gotten his own apartment, yet. That must be getting hard on Miss Irene. Not only does she have to cook and clean for herself and you – but it seems that he's an added responsibility to what she already has."

Alvin felt a bit indignant, but he answered as fairly as he could. "I've been feeling just that way since the hour I moved in with John Lee and Miss Irene. But it's not that I haven't been looking – my problem is that I haven't had the good fortune to find one in the right place."

"I know where there's a place for rent that's in a very nice neighborhood," Effie answered. "The only bad thing, it's not close enough to your job that you could walk to it every day. That is if you still working at the icehouse? If so, there're buses in this city that run twenty-four hours of the day and in all directions. All you have to do is figure out the route that gets you to work on time – then you got it made. If you wanted to see this place, maybe, Bobbie Jean will drive you there and let you take a look."

Even before Effie finished giving directions, Bobbie Jean had already said, "I don't mind driving him to see the apartment." She was already looking forward to getting out of the back seat of her mother's car and into an apartment, with a bed for a change. Since she was a native of Fort Worth, she had no trouble finding the address – the home of an elderly lady with a little two bedroom house for rent, out in the back of her place. The apartment had once been used as maid's quarters, and adjacent to alley at the back of the property.

The area was located at the end of an aging white neighborhood and the beginning of a Mexican new neighborhood situated in the vicinity of Victor and Beach. Bobbie Jean and Alvin got out, leaving John Lee to wait in the car. She knocked on the door, and an old white woman answered the door, asking, "What is it y'all want?"

"Are you Mrs. Nichols? We're here to look at the apartment you have for rent," Bobbie Jean answered.

The old woman nodded, and asked suspiciously, "I am – but who told you that I had an apartment for rent?"

"A friend of mine by the name of Effie Mcphee," Bobbie Jean answered.

"Oh!" Mrs. Nichols said, in a much friendlier voice. "Is she the one that works for my son Ray at the Graystone?"

"Yes ma'am." Alvin said, "She's the one."

Mrs. Nichols asked, "Are you two married or you're just boyfriend and girlfriend?"

"Well," Alvin explained, "we are trying to get to know each other. I'm new in town, and this is Bobbie Jean Trousdale. She's been very helpful at trying to get me settled in the city."

Mrs. Nichols led the way across the back yard, on to the apartment. Bobbie Jean and Alvin examined the rooms as carefully as if they were inspectors, searching for mice droppings in a fancy restaurant, while Mrs. Nichols waited by the front door for them. When Bobbie Jean and Alvin were finished, Alvin said, "We really like the place."

Mrs. Nichols said, "Well if you like it, the rent will be thirty dollars a month. So here is my rule: I won't allow people running in and out at all hours of the day or night and making loud noises. I'll be expecting you to keep the place clean inside and out. I'm an old woman and I need my peace and quiet. So, if it's a deal," she said, taking out a key from her apron pocket," Here it is. If not, then you're free to leave it." Alvin quickly reached into his pocket and pulled out a twenty and two fives. Mrs. Nichols handed Alvin the key, saying as she walked away. "The rent will come due a month from today so make sure you remember what day this is."

The house was furnished, and very clean. In addition to the two small bedrooms, it had a tiny bathroom with a tub, a kitchen, with a combination living and dining room. Overall it was very nice, and Alvin was excited. He said to Bobbie Jean, "I'm gonna go get John Lee so he can see my new home."

"Not before I demonstrate to you one of the things I'll be expecting out of you in the near future."

"What does that mean?" he asked.

She caught his hand and said, "I'll show you." She lay back on the bed and drew him on top of her, grinding her hips against him for a brief but exciting two minutes. "Now," she added, breathlessly, "If you still wonna, you may go and get your friend and show him where he won't be living. This place is only large enough for two people – and he isn't one of them."

This worried Alvin, during the walk back to the car to fetch John Lee; Bobbie Jean believing that she would be taking up permanent residence in his new apartment? All he had in mind with regard to Bobbie Jean in his apartment amounted to no more than the time it took for her to undress, fool around, get back into her clothes, and be on her way to her Mama's house. Instead of him forcing the bothersome issue, Alvin decided to wait and let the newness wear off. Perhaps then she wouldn't feel so bad when it came time for him to say, "No, I've enjoyed your company but it's time to go!"

He waved his hand to get John Lee's attention, beckoning him to come to see the inside of the house. As soon as John Lee did he asked, "When do we move in?"

"Over my dead body!" Bobbie Jean snapped. "You're thirty-some odd years old, and as long as I've known you, you've never lived at any other house except at your mama's. If I were you, I'd keep right on living there – I've always been told that old people can't take to change very well. At your age, you just might jus' die or catch some kind of incurable disease."

"Say what you want," John Lee drawled, completely unruffled, "but I know the truth, and the fact is you're not worried about me dying if I move out of my mama's house. You're worried that you'll die, if I moved in and you don't. Whether, you know it or not, Bobbie Jean, you're fixing to finally get in over your head, taking on a young country boy like Alvin.

Shoot, girl – that boy told me when he was down on the farm, he used to walk out in the barnyard to pee and when the male horses saw, they were so embarrassed that full-grown stallions walked away with their heads down. Now can you vouch for that, or was he telling me one of his country lie?"

Bobbie Jean stared at him for a long moment, and finally answered, "I should be asking you the same question. Since he sleeps with you more often than he sleeps with me, you may've seen as much of his thingy as I have!"

Alvin whooped with laugher, and so did John Lee, except John Lee didn't laugh for quite as long. This was the first time Alvin had ever seen someone embarrass John Lee, who never said another word within the fifteen minutes it took to drive back to the Bailey's house to pack up Alvin's few clothes and things, and thank Miss Irene Bailey for her hospitality. Then they drove back to Alvin's place. When they walked into the apartment, Alvin noticed for the first time that there was one thing missing; a television. He said to Bobbie Jean, "What I'm gonna do when you're not here to keep me company, and I don't have a television to watch."

"You won't be watching very much television for awhile anyway." Bobbie Jean answered, her face set with determination. "I intend to see you get some proper schooling. The very first time I talked to you, I thought you were smarter than the words you used in talking. That's why I'm gonna keep you busy from the time you walk through that door in the evening until you go to bed at night. You won't have time for anything except for reading, writing, and doing arithmetic. You need to have a high school diploma, country boy – the world is moving too fast for those who don't have the education to keep up. Too many colored men are going to be left out in the cold – if they aren't gonna get enough schooling to match their intelligence . . . and then the average colored man will use their energy to blame someone else for their failure. As far as I can see, you're not one of those people. So, I decided – I'm gonna make your life a different story . . . if you're willing to let me help you. Then maybe I'll help you to buy your own television." She pulled open the refrigerator, adding, "We forgot to get something strong enough to celebrate your new residence. Let's go pick a six-pack, come back, lock all the doors, and have ourselves a proper house-warming party."

They squeezed and kissed, while driving all the way back to Rosedale and Crawford to find a liquor store. Alvin picked up a six-pack while Bobbie Jean stood gazing at the bottles on the wall behind the counter. She walked up to the cash register where Alvin was already standing. She sat a half pint of vodka along with two Seven-Ups on the counter. Once Alvin paid the cashier they drove back to the apartment, holding hands all the way like newlyweds.

Bobbie Jean handed Alvin a beer and poured herself a long shot of vodka, topped off with Seven-Up, they went and settled on the divan, lazily kissing and fondling each other, as if they had all the time in the world – which they didn't, as Bobbie Jean still had to be back home by midnight. But sometimes too much foreplay can turn a couple into boredom, especially if you've used up all of your energy the night before . . . and having one drink and then another, and another. They managed to lose all track of time and fell asleep on the divan with her lying in his arms. At about two in the morning, Alvin slid his body from beneath hers in order to go to the bathroom. When he came back and saw her lying there, as if she had no intention of waking up and going home, he shook her once, but nothing happened. After several shakes she managed to open one eye.

"What time is it?" she demanded. He told her the time, and she sat up, angrier than a wet hen. "Why did you let me fall asleep with every stitch of my clothes on? You knew darn well what my intention was before we went to the liquor store!

"What differences does it make, if you fell asleep with your clothes on or not?" Alvin was honestly baffled. "I guess what have you so upset is I didn't do what you had planed we do to celebrate our first apartment. There's other ways – or did you forget I wore myself out doing just that, starting early last evening and ending around midnight? I felt just fine, waking up and seeing you lying in the same place where we both fall asleep last night . . . on top of me in my new apartment."

"You're doing nothing but making excuses! Name me one time that you didn't start foaming at the mouth the minute my dress went over my head? Country boy, your problem is you're too dumb to know a little drink was supposed to lead us up that road to celebrate our new home – exactly the way I had demonstrated to you right after you handed the lady your first month's rent! I wanted us to be hard at work five minute before midnight, thumping like hell when the clock strikes twelve! It's the same as New Years Eve – you don't wait until after midnight to shoot your gun. You fire it at midnight, or else people will start to wonder, like I'm doing, right now

– where was this fool country boy at midnight? This is one time when all of my planning has turned out to be bad luck, which means you'll probably leave me for some fifteen-years-old or the other way around!" Bobbie Jean began to undress, cursing under her breath as she stormed into the bathroom, "I'm gonna shower, just long enough to sober up and drive my disappointed ass home. I can't believe someone your age could lay here beside me and fall asleep, rather than celebrating his first night with me in his new apartment."

Alvin yelled, "Bobbie Jean, I'm totally innocent of all charges – and I'm sorry that I've disappointed you. But you're just as guilty as I am because if I hadn't shaken you – you'd still been asleep! Look, Bobbie Jean . . . can I make amends by scrubbing your back? That is, if you're not too angry to let me shower with you?

"Please do!" she said. "I'm shocked that you would ask without being told. At least I can go home knowing we shower together, if nothing else! " She turned on the water and began to test it for her preferred temperature. She walked under the water, and he followed her. She handed him the soap and just stood there, aroused and wondering what he'd do with it. As the water ran over her healthy young body, Alvin gently began to massage the soap over her skin, until she was lathered all over with soap. He noticed right away that the frown on her face had begun to fade. Presently she took the soap and began lathering him all over as well. When she was finished, she laid the soap on the edge of the tub and turned off the faucet. She began to massage him all over, and as he got the idea, he did the same to her, vigorously lathering each other until they were white all over with soap foam.

Afterward she turned the water back on and they held each other while they turned in circles to rinse themselves off thoroughly. When they both were both free of soap, Bobbie Jean put the stopper in the bathtub, filled it half full of warm water, and laid back in the tub with one leg hanging over the side. Seeing that he instantly knew it was an invitation, an invitation to get into the tub, and pleasure her until the sad look on her face was replaced with a happy one . . . a happy one which lasted long after she came out of the tub. Neither one of them bothered to dry off; they stood outside the tub, hugging and kissing while the water ran off their bodies and onto the tiled bathroom floor.

Finally, Bobbie Jean murmured with gleeful contentment, "Country Boy, I'm taking back every bad thing I ever said about you! You just proved to me that you can make a girl like me get used to this kind of treatment. If only you'd take the initiative so I don't have to beg you for something that should be natural for a boy your age. I bet when I finish teaching you everything you need to know about pleasuring a woman, you'll probably leave me for some fifteen-year-old and have her calling you her 'superman.' How many successful students have you heard praise their teachers for flourishing in society? Country Boy, I jus' know you'll take what I've taught you, use it on some girl, and have her worship the ground you walk on, for something you didn't know jack about until you met me."

Alvin answered, "Bobbie Jean, your face don't match your words. I think you're being contrary about me. You just plain haven't noticed how attached I've become to you, especially now that I have my own apartment. It's gotten to the point that you're the first person I want to see when I wake up in the morning and the last one I wonna see before I fall asleep at night.

"Saying it is one thing, but proving it is another thing." Bobbie Jean looked at her watch and said, "It's two o'clock in the morning; I have to get dressed and get my behind home before my mama wakes up and find that I'm not in my bed. Boy, she'll come all to pieces asking all kind of questions – and the first one will be, 'I hope you haven't been out with that seventeen-year-old boy again.'"

"Why would she say that?" he asked.

"Because she has her suspicions about you and me: She wouldn't mind except she thinks you're too young for me. I don't want to accept it, but I know she's right. That's why I'm tryin' not to let myself fall in love with you. It's not that I couldn't fall for you . . . that part is easy. But when you have people you love and respect keep telling you to get out because he's too young and I'm gonna get myself hurt, you tend to believe them. Country Boy . . . the better you are at fulfilling womanly needs, the harder it is for me to heed other people's warnings. The same way you treat me in the bathtub tonight, as soon as you see how unhappy I was with you . . . I don't have to tell you how you made me feel after that. Times like tonight make me wonna disagree with my mother when she tries to convince me that you're too young for me."

By the time she had finished critiquing his homework, she looked at her watch and said, "All right baby, I've already went past the time where I should've been home two hours ago. So let us hurry and be on our way." It was just before sunrise. They rushed out to her car and he rode with her as far as the Trousdale house, before Alvin decided he'd walk the rest of the way to his job. He didn't won't to keep her from getting home as soon as possible, and he also hoped he'd spare her from being reprimanding for ignoring her mother's difficult-to-keep curfew, especially if her mother thought she was out with him.

Alvin's vigorous stride brought him to the ice house in plenty of time; he wound up waiting on the steps for nearly an hour before his boss came and unlocked the doors. From the time he started his day until the time his eight-hour shift had ended, he felt so overwhelmed that he could hardly think of anything except to go home and rest. Not only was he worn out, but he regretted that he had allowed Bobbie Jean to persuade him to accept her concocted superstitious belief: that it was bad luck for him not to make love to her on his first night in his new home, before the clock struck twelve midnight. But he had gone along with the cock and bull story, and went toe to toe with her   although by early afternoon, he was saying to himself, "The second that clock strikes four thirty, I'm going home and sleep twelve hours straight and hope that Bobbie Jean will do the same thing!" The only time he hurried that day was when four-thirty rolled around, and he didn't waste a second rushing out to the bus stop to catch the bus home.

Just as he reached the bus stop on Rosedale Street, Bobbie Jean drove up behind him and blew her horn. "Oh no, not again," Alvin said to himself as he stepped to one side. She rolled down the window.

"Would you like a ride home, Country Boy?"

"Only if you promise to take me home and leave," he answered.

"Are you for real?" she asked.

"I wouldn't be if you hadn't kept me up half the night. Remember – you persuading me to believe that it was bad luck for you and me – if we didn't make love in our new home before the clock struck twelve?"

"Yeah, but whose idea was it for you to follow me into the shower and work on me long after I had told you I needed to go? I had already accepted the fact that nothing was going to happen. But the minute I lifted my dress over my head, all of a sudden you start foaming at the mouth – and I don't think I need to tell you what happened after that! After I drove home and got in bed, it was three o'clock in the morning before I finally dozed off to sleep. The thought that kept me awake last night has been a bother to me all day . . . right up until you said what you just said! That hurt my feelings, Country Boy! But in spite of it all, I'll drive you home – and after that I'll leave you alone – if that's what you want me to do."

They rode in silence for most of the way, until Alvin finally asked, "Did you go to work today?"

"No," she said, "I took the day off. Why do you ask?

"Because," he said, "I wondered how you could be so energetic after working all day on the four hours of sleep I expect you got last night."

"So" she said, "that's what's bothering you – you can't stand the fact that I got to stay home and sleep, while you went on your job and worked all day. Now," she added. "Can you see why everyone is trying to tell me that you're too young for me? I hadn't seen it until now. So what I saw of you, I saw in the dark, but what my family and friends saw of you – they saw in the light. Since they have no bias against you, they told it like they saw it. You might love what I have to offer as long as it's on you own terms. Now that I think about it, I should've drove here and waited while you rode the bus home. Then maybe you would be more appreciative of me if I'm as inconsiderate of your feeling as you are mine."

Alvin got out, without saying a word, not even thanks for the ride home; he just went into his house and closed the door. A few minutes later she opened the door and walked in. Then she saw Alvin was lying on the divan with his eyes closed.

"So, this is it; I take it, just as I had expected it would be." Bobbie Jean said, "Once I realized you had gone past the time where we were to suppose to honor a belief I've heard all my life: The first time a couple moved into a new home, their first thought should be focused on christening the house . . . by way of making love to each other before the clock strikes twelve midnight. Or what they have won't be strong enough to hold shucks – which is what's about to happen to us."

Alvin opened his eyes and extended his hand, and he drew her on top of him. He kissed her, very gently and begged, "All I'm asking is for you to go away and let me sleep for at least eight hours straight. We both were out of control last night; which is mostly your fault . . . you didn't wait to close the door to the bathroom before you started to undress. So I can imagine how restful your body must've felt all day because you were off. But mine; only I know how exhausted I felt all day. I'm not one to go without lots of sleep. I'm the kind of person that has to have the proper amount of sleep or I can't get any work done proper."

Bobbie Jean laid there for a while. "What about your dinner?" she asked, finally. "You don't have any food in this house, do you?"

"If I'm asleep," he said, "I won't need any food will I?"

She said, "I'll go and pick up something for you to eat and set it on the table, just in case you wake up in the middle of the night hungry. Plus I promise not to awake you when I return." She kissed him, very gently and said, "Bye baby."

At that Alvin said, "Bobbie Jean, honey . . . come here and lay down with me, please."

She came and stood over him, saying, "Are you sure this is what you want me to do?" He caught her hand and effortlessly drew her on top of himself.

"I'm very sure," Alvin said, "and I'm sorry I hurt your feelings. I'm not quite eighteen yet, and already I'm beginning to sound like a grumpy, selfish ol' man. You're always giving and never asking for anything other than a little respect in return. Would you like to undress and lay with me for a while . . . please, baby?"

"I do . . . but only if you really want it."

"I really want you to," he said, "as long as we don't have to leave the divan."

She grinned and said, "Lounging on the divan doesn't bother me none, since that's where I do most of my sleeping when I'm at home anyway." She stripped off her own clothes, and then his . . . and no sooner than they were both naked than Alvin found that he was not all that sleepy. But as soon as they were done, she got up from the divan. She dressed with equal efficiency and headed out the door. He listened, drowsily, as Bobbie Jean drove out of his driveway as if she was in a restricted zone that went into effect at five-thirty and she had one minute to vacate the premises. No need to get up from the divan – he was already on his way to dream land . . . where he stayed that way until about five-thirty the next morning.

He woke up hungry enough to eat a June bug, and saw almost at once that Bobbie Jean brought back a plate of food, which had gotten cold after setting out all night. He looked around for something to heat it up in – but he was hungry. Never mind: he got himself a fork, began to taste it, and tasted until the plate was clean. He had his first meal for the day and saw no reason why he needed to cook his breakfast.

He got dressed and walked out to the nearest bus stop and talked to a couple of the people about catching the right one to work. First they wanted to know where he was going, and when they figured it out, one of the men pointed him in the right direction. This left only the problem of knowing which one to catch to get back home. But, that wasn't an immediate concern of his, since he had eight hours to think about it. When he got off that evening, he was relieved to see that Bobbie Jean wasn't there to pick him up. He walked down to the bus stop where he had been let off that morning, and began asking questions about getting on the right bus home. He was very fortunate to find people who were helpful in getting him on and off at right stop. He went home, sat on the divan, and stared at the walls. He wasn't sleepy because he had slept twelve hours straight the night before.

Alvin said to himself, "I don't know what would suit me better, a television or depend on Bobbie Jean to entertain me." Then he thought, "The latter would be just fine – I haven't felt this lonely since I can remember when. I suppose going home after work and sitting with Miss Irene and John Lee every evening watching television sorter got me depending on some kind of entertainment. So, it's either Bobbie Jean or a television."

At that, he got up and walked outside. He saw Mrs. Nichols, the landlady out on the back porch, sitting in her rocker.

He waved to her, and she called across the back yard, "It looks like you are all alone today. Where is that gal that was with you a couple of days ago?"

Alvin walked over to her so he didn't have to shout. "I really don't know." He said, "She was supposed to been here an hour ago to assist me in getting my high school diploma."

"High school diploma?" Mrs. Nichols looked interested, for some reason. "Ah! Does she have enough experience to call herself a schoolteacher?"

"I do not know," he said. "But when I told her that I didn't go very far in school, she offered to help me."

"Fine," Mrs. Nichols answered, "if she can help you – but she can't if she doesn't have your undivided attention." Mrs. Nichols smiled, knowingly. "Learning takes the right kind of concentration, but if you're boyfriends and girlfriends it might take you a whole year to advance from one page to the next. When you take on something as importance as getting an education, whoever teaches you must have your undivided attention."

"Thank you," Alvin said. It made sense to him in a way. "By the way . . . Mrs. Nichols? You know, we've never been properly introduced. Bobbie Jean just called you Mrs. Nichols –I just supposed that was your name. I'm Alvin Jackson, from Snyder, Texas . . . and I'd like to be able to address you proper."

Mrs. Nichols smiled faintly. She hesitated for a minute and spoke in a voice that sounded like the actress Marjory Maine. "My name is Bertha Nichols, Mr. Jackson – you can just call me 'Mrs. Nichols.' I'm a retired school teacher. I taught here in this town for thirty-one years. It seem like it was just yesterday when I started teaching. I still have a hard time believing that I've been retired almost fifteen years now. My daughter also teaches school . . . Oh!" she added. "I think I see your tutor driving up right now."

Alvin turned around and looked. "Oh, yes," he said. "You're right—that is her. Good night, Mrs. Nichols."

"Good night, Mr. Jackson," she returned, with a look of amusement on her face. Alvin met Bobbie Jean at the door of the little house – as soon as they were inside, he welcomed her with a tight hug and a long amorous kiss. He told her how he'd missed her as he ushered her to the kitchen table. For a few minutes, they sat there, bringing each other up to date as to what went on in their daily work places for that day. Finally Alvin asked, "Are we about ready to get my education up and running on the right road, baby?"

"Not until we get the supplies we need to get this show on the road," Bobbie Jean answered. "We'll need some things – such as pencils, paper, and notebooks..."

"Well," he said, "why don't you give me a list of everything you'll need to get me started and I'll   pick them up tomorrow when I get off work." She began writing and finally finished and handed Alvin the list. He looked and said, "Some of these items I'll need you to tell me where to go so I can pick them up myself."

"Would you like to go alone?" Bobbie Jean asked. "Or would you rather I drive you?"

"It would be easier for me if you'd drive me, but I don't want to take up too much of your time. I know you've worked just as hard all day as I have."

"I don't mind," she said. "Let me help you just this once, and the next time you'll know where to go."

Bobbie Jean drove to a stationary store, and began shopping for the things they needed to get started with. They spent about an hour searching for the best quality for a reasonable cost. It was almost six o'clock when they finished, and Bobbie Jean suggested that they go to a little restaurant located next to the Rosedale Theatre and have a barbeque dinner.

They sat at the table, talked, and told each other love stories, until eight that evening. They concluded that they had the best barbecue dinner in Fort Worth. When they got back to Alvin's apartment, she began laying out the supplies, in order to begin his lessons. But now it was as late as it was, she decided to postpone studies for that night and start fresh on the following evening. About that time she got up, opened the refrigerator, and pulled out the last two cans of beer.

As soon as she handed him one and said, "This is for my sweet man," Alvin knew what was coming next, and thought to himself, "Boy, I don't mind her company, but I'm just not in any mood to accept what she had to offer – not any time soon, anyway." His reluctance had nothing to do with what John Lee had said about Alvin not being qualified to respond to Bobbie Jean's sensuality at any given time. Alvin felt he was very well able to out-last her two-to-one any day of the week, when it came to placating each others sensitive area. But his silent complaint was he didn't like it that he wasn't the one to suggest an intimacy liaison between them at least some of the time. He didn't like it that Bobbie Jean seemed to be the one always doing his job for him, when it came to that particular instigation. By the time he came to that realization, Bobbie Jean suggested, "I just took the last two beers – why don't we go and pick up another six-pack, if that's all right with you?"

"If it all the same," Alvin answered. "I'd just as soon we finish off that half-bottle of vodka you left in the cabinet the other night. Tomorrow after work, I'll pick up a six-pack of beer for me and a bottle of vodka for you."

"Oh?" Bobbie Jean said, "I guess I was so upset about what we should've done and didn't before midnight, that I plum' forgot I left almost a full bottle of booze in your cabinet the other night."

"I still don't understand why you would be so upset about us falling asleep, before we could christen the bed, as you called it. We've been christening the back seat of your mother's car, practically every night since I've been in town."

"I wish you'd stop mentioning that!" She answered, indignantly. "All of that's in the past, except the part when you finally got up enough courage to follow me to the bathroom and unh-huh-honey! I'll take me years to forget about what you did to me that night!"

Alvin's ego was instantly re-inflated: he pushed her over onto the divan and kissed her, thinking how such flattering words of hers could be so very . . . inspirational. He was thinking to himself, "If there are anyone out there that thank they could make me feel better than she does, don't bother to try . . . it be a waste of time . . . Bobbie Jean has taken that position, and it's no longer out for bid."

All the while they were languorously kissing and stroking . . . until Bobbie Jean ventured, "Just think about how much more romantic we could be, if you had a radio or a record player . . . we could dance when we're in the mood we're in. Solitude is nice, Country Boy . . . when there is a purpose for it, like the one we're fixing to use in a few more minutes. But afterward, there is a human need for civilization. Tomorrow," she said, as if she had already made up her mind, "when we get off work, I'll personally take you to the place where we bought our television and co-sign for you either a radio or a television. After tonight, no more isolation for me; we are too young for that kind of life."

"You must be getting tired of me," Alvin said. "Because when we first met, seclusion was the only thing on your mind. Besides – you were the one that said, 'Wait until we have your school situation under control, before we go out and buy a television.'"

"Well Alvin, my precious man," Bobbie Jean explained, "it's very simple and shouldn't be that hard to understand. You only watch television when you don't have anything else to do. With a radio or a record player you can listen or dance to it anytime, and not be distracted like you would be, watching T.V."

At that he stood, took her hand, and began slow dancing around the room without music. "You mean something like this?" He murmured. She smiled as they danced; kissing and holding each other very close. "I'm beginning to believe John Lee – when he told me that you and your sister were very nice women. Both of you would probably make a very good wife for the right men."

"Now, little sweet man – let's not go getting ahead of ourselves if you're trying to propose marriage to me." Bobbie Jean answered, with a grin. "Not until you know what direction you're headed. I'm seven years older than you, remember. It would be foolish of me to give you my whole soul, mind, and body – only to have them torn to pieces. You've already hinted to me about some girl your own age. And I'm not about to put myself in a position to be dropped by the first little fifteen-year-old girls that come along that are ten years younger than me. Not only that but you've been chilly toward me, since you've moved into your own apartment. Surely you can remember that much, can't you? So why don't we keep the thought of marriage out of it, for the time being – and keep doing what we normally do." She pulled herself away from him, and sat down on the divan again. "Like I said earlier, all day long I've done nothing but think about what we did in the bathtub last night . . . and I'm of a mind to have a repeat that's so electrifying that I won't need another jolt for the next few days. Once we buy your television tomorrow night, we won't have time for much of anything – except making notes, reading books, and anything that has to do with education."

"Some of what you said is true and some false, but that was then and this is now, so let me give you my reasons why I want that someone to be you." Alvin answered. "One is so you don't have to jump up in the middle of the night and go off to a different home to sleep. I hate it when we make love, and afterward you get out of my bed and leave. We haven't ever gone to bed, made love, and woke up the next morning with you lying in my arms. The minute we finish, you run out of here like a scared rabbit. I'm tired of not being tired of asking you to 'move over honey' so I can get out of bed and use the bathroom. Afterwards, I want to come back and lay down beside your warm and gorgeous sweet body – because you're still lying where I left you before I went to go pee."

"Man oh man, Bobbie Jean demanded with mild suspicion what brought all of this on?" "A couple of days ago you acted like I was in your way – and now I take it you are trying to ask me to marry you?"

"If that's what it takes for you to stay and not jump up in the middle of the night and run away – Yes," he said, "I'm asking you to marry me. Doesn't that sound good to you, honey?"

"Oh, Country Boy!" she said. "Why the change of heart all of a sudden?" By the time she had finished saying that she was already halfway to the bedroom. He followed her – and they lay together, but the feeling was lukewarm, and the enthusiasm wasn't anything, like all of the times before. In fact it was over for her in nothing flat – odd, as she wound up having to wait for him, when it had usually been the other way around.

Alvin thought, 'Boy, she sure didn't act as if she got her few days worth!' It was as if Bobbie Jean had took him to bed for no other reason than to fooled him once again – and once she had accomplished what she setout to do she couldn't wait to break free, get dressed, and leave. She stood in the middle of the floor, waiting for Alvin to get out of bed and give him her phony kiss goodnight. As she started to leave, he took her hand and pretended to lead her back to the bedroom.

"What are you trying to do?" she asked. "I'm trying to take you back to bed?

Alvin answered, "Why do you think you need to take me back to bed?" I don't think I pulled it off for you – what happened, sugar?

She withdrew her hand and answered, "You pulled it off all right, but if you hadn't, you couldn't do nothing thing about it at this point anyway. Because there couldn't be an once of solidity left in your thingy being that I flushed at least the equivalent of a large egg of your matter right down the toilet, so don't worry about me. You did just fine for me, just like I know I did for you, too. It's getting late. I'll see you tomorrow night."

She walked out the door, on that word. Alvin sat for a while thinking to himself, 'What difference does it makes if a woman is seven years older than a man is? Age shouldn't have anything to do with it; love should be the deciding factor.' He remembered hearing it all of his life, that a man should always be older than the woman. 'If I married her, and take her home to meet my parents, I wouldn't want to lie about her age. So I either tell them the truth about the age difference, and break the tradition, or I could leave things as I had planned in the first place, and wait until I meet the right girl my own age.' After rolling his thoughts around in his head for quite some time, he became exhausted and fell asleep.

The next morning he woke up, with the same thing on his mind as he fell asleep with, which was Bobbie Jean. Even though he may've sensed a touch of uncertain in her demeanor last night but not so disturbing that it altered his thoughts about the time they spent together last night; and especially the night before. To give her the benefit of the doubt he credited her like of enthusiasm regarding his proposal to her who had been so negative with her since the day they met. Suddenly and impulsively switching from being pessimistic about their chances, to optimism might have put her into an uncertain frame of mind. 'I can't wait until she comes by tonight. I'll tell her exactly how I feel about her. I'll tell her that the search for a girl my own age is over . . . And I want to be standing by her side when she makes the announcement to her mother that I've asked her to marry me.'

As he walked out to the bus stop, Alvin began to rehearse what he was going to say to Bobbie Jean that evening. All day at work, he had nothing on his mind, except to prepare what he planned to say to her when he saw her tonight. As soon as he saw his co-workers were walking toward the door with lunch pails in their hands, Alvin immediately came out of his trance and grabbed his lunch pail. He rushed out the door behind them, on down the street to the bus stop. His waiting time was about fifteen minutes, so he raced across the streets to the liquor store, and picked up a six-pack of tall cans of malt liquor, a half-pint of vodka and two Seven-Ups. He rushed back to the bus stop, caught the bus, and arrived home around four-thirty.

Full of excitement, with forty-five minutes before he expected her arrival, he decided to have one of those tall cans of malt liquor. Afterward he went and sat on the divan and spent a lot of time alternating between watching the clock and his imaginary television. When five o'clock rolled around, he didn't think too much about her not being there. But when five-thirty came, he started to worry; what if she had an accident and had no way of notifying him! Anxiety took over, leaving him defenseless. He had no telephone to call anyone to see what might have happened – if anything at all. At that point it wasn't about celebration anymore – it was all about Alvin wanting to know whether she dropped out of the race. And perhaps she hadn't figured out ways to let him down easy. He thought, "Maybe that's why it's taking her so long to get here . . . if she comes at all."

Handicapped without a car or telephone, he had no other choice but to wait and see how everything played out in the end. When he saw that it was seven o'clock, he said to himself, "As soon as this nightmare is over, I promise myself I'm gonna go somewhere and buy myself some kind of transportation, if nothing but a bicycle. I'll never be caught in another situation like the one I'm in tonight." He walked outside, and paced up and down the alley, hoping for a miracle to come his way, with Bobbie Jean all wrapped up in it.

Alvin went back into the apartment and looked at the clock. Nine p.m. Now he was even more worried. This time he poured himself a long shot of vodka, and topped off with Seven-Up. He sipped and worried, sipped and worried until it was all gone, and he had fallen asleep on the divan.

Around eleven-thirty, he was awakened by the sound of a knock on the door. He jumped to his feet and rushed to the door. There stood Bobbie Jean, with a guilty look on her face. He knew something was wrong when she waited to be asked to come in. They stood staring at each other. Finally, she asked, "Can I come in?" Alvin stepped aside, and motioned for her to enter the room. The excitement that once filled his heart had just been replaced with sorrow and dread.

He wretchedly asked, almost in tears, "Where have you been, Bobbie Jean? I've been longing all day long to see you, honey."

She asked in a cheerless voice, "Can we sit down?" I need to talk to you"

He said, "Sure, why not. Is there anything wrong Bobbie Jean?"

As they both sat on the divan, she caught his hand saying, "I don't know where to begin."

52

He said, "Began anywhere where you want to, because I know anything you have to tell me is going to hurt." Bobbie Jean stared into his eyes shortly, and then dropped her head. Alvin's heart sank. "That look in your eyes tells me that what you're about to say, which is you don't want me anymore. Go ahead and fire away, so we can get this mess over with!"

Bobbie Jean moved even closer, with her hand on his shoulder, facing him. "Alvin honey, do you remember last night when I told you not to go proposing to me? Well," her voice steadied, and she continued, "For the last week or so Curtis has been coming by, trying to get me to come back to him. I've turned him down the first few times. Until tonight he told me – he had made the biggest mistake of his life when he broke up with me. Now he's begging me to marry him. After thanking about it I talked it over with my mother . . . and I did mention to her that I had been falling in love with you. When she reminded me that you're seven years younger than I am – that's what tipped the scales in Cutis's favor . . . and I started to remember when you couldn't make up your mind, whether you want to keep me or trade me. Until you told me last night . . . and by then it was too late. I had already told Curtis that I'd give him an answer by tonight, and my answer was 'yes' to whether I'd marry him or not. Alvin honey, you're young and have all kind of opportunities to get yourself a girl your own age. I'd be lying if I told you I didn't love you, especially since I finally taught you the meaning of motivation. And I can hardly bear standing close to you without recollecting how fine it is with you . . . but I'm at the age where a girl needs to know when to take her affections and give them to a man that appreciates her enough to marry and give her security. Curtis is a very nice man. He has his own apartment, and his own car, and a good paying job. So, I was hoping that you'd understand, but it seems that I've hurt you, and I'm sorry. I didn't mean to." She gave Alvin a safeguarded hug and added, "Curtis – he's older enough to know what he wants and that's the only reason I have for leaving you."

Alvin sat there listening, all choked up – he couldn't speak. He walked outside into the darkness of the alley, his back braced against the wall, wiping away his tears.

After a bit, Bobbie Jean came out to where he stood, saying "I really am sorry, honey. I didn't realize my telling you this, would hurt you so much." He wouldn't answer her; he was afraid if he opened his mouth, no words would come out – only sobs – and she would know he was trying to muffle the sound and that would wind up embarrassing him. But she knew anyway; she kept trying to pacify him by taking the skirt of her dress and gently wiping his eyes.

Finally Alvin could bring himself to speak. "I tried to tell you last night that I was in love with you but you didn't want to hear it, and because you wouldn't listen. So your mind was made up long before last night. I waited all day and half the night to tell you that I wanted to marry you. Now you tell me that you and your old boy friend have gotten back together . . . that's a low blow, Bobbie Jean . . . a low blow. Have you slept with him since you and I've been going to gather?"

"No," she said.

"Why not?" he asked. "It seems to me if he loves you, and he was interesting in having you back, and he's definitely no stranger to your screened-off area, then why wouldn't he ask? I would've if I'd been separated from you for more than three months. Don't you thank there're something kind of a strange about that? We just made love last night and twenty-four hours later here I am barely able obtain myself, standing along in the dark with you. So I'm guessing he just broke up with someone else and had his last orgasm the day before he decided to get back with you. That's what you did, with me last night. Remember honey? And tonight you are telling me that it's all over. And he's probably doing the same thing as we speak."

"I didn't ask him about a girl friend, and he didn't ask me about a boy friend." Bobbie Jean said. "The only thing that we talked about was we'd pick up where we left off, and start all over again, and this time we'll be getting married."

Alvin pulled her close and whispered, " I guess you're going back with him; must've got you so distracted that you forgot that you was suppose to teach a class tonight, as well as take and help me to buy my own television, this afternoon after work. Now, I'll be willing to forgive you for everything you promised to do for me tonight, in exchange for five minutes of your time . . . just long enough to get over the feeling that I've had all day from thanking about you. You owe me that much," he added, at the same as he pulled down his pants to demonstrate his readiness.

"Now, Alvin," she shook her head. "You know it wouldn't be right for me to do something like that. I came to tell you that I was going to be married and not to make a slut of myself any more. You'll just have to find other way to get over your feelings."

"There is no other way," he said, "unless you are suggesting I go play with myself. Why should I, when all you have to do is relax and give me five minutes or less? I promise, I'll leave you alone and send you on your away with a clear conscience. You owe me, Bobbie Jean." When she tried to walk away, he became aggressive and penned her against the house and began ramming his genitals against her pelvis. She immediately grabbed it and told him, "Get that thing away from me and move out of my way so I can go home." Alvin grabbed her panties with one hand, and with the other hand he attempted to penetrate her. Being determined to prevent that from happening, Bobbie Jean managed to maneuver it away from his intended target. He realigned in a hurry, and then pressed forward. This time he connected, only to be disconnected just as concisely.

"Please, don't do this to me, Alvin." Bobbie Jean begged, distressed and alarmed. "I'm engaged to be married and it's not right for you to force me to cheat on him. So why don't you stop it!" Her call for a truce was fruitless – Alvin's little man was a carnivorous animal that had just got its first taste of meat, and there was no stopping him until he had itself a bona fide banquet. Likewise, he became that much more determined to reattach and stay until he had achieved his goal. He was nearly there, nearly there ...

"Just one more like this," Alvin thought, "and I'll knock myself a homerun." He forced his knees between hers, and just as he thrust forward for the big feast, she grabbed his member with both hands, which caused him to spill into her hands two seconds before he reached his target. After that, she stopped fighting, allowing him to move against her until he was finished. Then she wiped his secretions off her hands and onto his shirt. Not only did she declare herself a winner, she wasn't worried about being pregnant, either. He followed Bobbie Jean back into the house afterwards. She went to the bathroom where she took a wet towel and wiped the front of her dress as well as the area around her pelvis. She came back into the living room, drying her hands and seemingly not knowing quite what to say or do.

He finally said, "I suppose I made you feel like a cheating slut out there tonight."

"You didn't make me to do anything that I didn't allow you to do. Don't forget that you only got anywhere after you dumped your waste into my hand . . . which I was glad of, since that amount would have gotten me pregnant for sure. So, as far as I'm concern I'll still walk away with most of my pride and all of my self-respect."

"Yeah" Alvin said, "but if I could've held out just two seconds longer, I would've shot your pride and self-respect all to hell and back."

At that, Bobbie Jeans raised her dress, pulled off her torn panties and flung them at him, saying, "You owe me a new pair of panties." She grinned as she walked out the door. "Bye, Alvin. Don't forget to tell your new girlfriend that I taught you everything you know about making love." She slammed the door, and in the next moment, he heard Mrs. Trousdale's car starting up. Just for a moment he felt like calling out to her, asking her to come back, because he felt so empty, but almost at once, he was disgusted with himself for even thinking such a thought. After all she had served her purpose – even if it was for only two minutes. At that, Alvin felt he may've lost his woman, but more importantly he achieved his purpose . . . and Alvin felt even more self-disgust. Why would he want to do an insane thing like run after her when she had confessed to seeing someone else behind his back – even if it was her old ex-beau?

He sat there considering whether or not to have that third beer and maybe a shot of vodka to calm him down before going to bed, and decided against it. It was after one in the morning and he didn't want to go to work, not being able to give it his best. Three hours of sleep ended all too soon, leaving him in desperate need of some kind of stimulant to revitalize his sleep-deprived body and traumatized soul. The only temporary solution for that was coffee, and he didn't own a coffee pot. The minute he got to work, he headed straight for the coffee pot and wasn't without a cup of coffee in his hand throughout the day.

Again, he wished – without results – for that day to end before it ever started. When it did finally end, he didn't shilly-shally around about getting out of there. The minute he got home, he took just enough time to make a sandwich and drink a beer. After that, he stretched out on the divan and slept until he woke up around one o'clock in the morning to use the bathroom. By the time he got back to bed, he was wide awake, his mind filled with contradictory thoughts about why he let Bobbie Jean go. Even with him knowing that she had betrayed him, he still missed her, and from time to time, he would faintly be grieved over her. Before he knew it, he had fallen asleep and slept until six-thirty on the spot, leaving just enough time to get dressed and catch the bus to work. That evening after work, instead of going home he walked across the streets from the bus stop to John Lee's house. Alvin had to wait because John Lee or Miss Irene hadn't made it home from work yet. After about fifteen minutes of waiting, Alvin saw John Lee come walking up the street.

When he came close enough to recognize Alvin, John Lee started to laugh. "So soon?"

"What do you mean by saying 'so soon'?" Alvin asked. "You know exactly what I mean."

"That Trousdale girl – she's kicked your little young ass out. Otherwise you wouldn't spend one minute of your time thinking about coming by to see Mama and me. I tried to warn you about those girls. But 'oh no,' you said, 'I thank I'm compatible when it comes to going toe-to-toe with Bobbie Jean.'"

Alvin said, "The truth is, Bobbie Jean came by a couple of nights ago and told me that she had decided to go back to her old boyfriend and get married while she had the chance. She didn't want to wait around while I make up my mind, whether or not I would marry her, when she had someone that will."

John Lee said teasingly, "Do you want me to go and talk her into taking you back?"

"No," Alvin said. "I want you to help me find a car to buy."

"Buy you a car?" John Lee answered, "What is you gonna do with a car in a town the size of Fort Worth? You have to keep in mind that we have thousands of people and traffic lights that are suppose to protect those people. But not if we have some country jackass driving – like you – that don't know what a red light represent."

"All right," Alvin answered. "So help me, or not."

"I can see that you are not in any teasing mood." John Lee sighed. "So how much money do you plan to spend? And what kind of car are you looking for?" John Lee worked for one of the largest car rental company in the United States. Plus, Alvin thought John Lee would be of some help, since he knew people who might know about good used cars.

John Lee first wanted to know how Alvin managed to save up three hundred dollars in such a short time. "You've only been here about three or four month, you've just rented your own apartment, and now you're trying to buy your own car."

"The reason I could save my money because Bobbie Jean and I had nothing to drink until the weekend." Alvin explained. "I'd buy my six-pack of beer and she'd buy her bottle of vodka and Seven-Ups. After that, we never felt that it was necessary to go anyplace, except to bed."

"I bet you did at that," John Lee said, "And we have all kind of cars makes and models. First, though . . . I'll take you to meet my boss. Maybe he'll make you a good deal on one of our older model cars that we normally sell off this time of year. Now, I sure do hope everything pans out so you can get yourself a car . . . you should come and pick me up on weekends and you can drive me around Fort Worth. Plus – I'll show you where all of the good-looking girls hang out."

"The sooner the better," Alvin said, "because I'm in desparate need of a replacement for Bobbie Jean."

"Well, in that case," John Lee said, "I had better hurry and get you a car before you go grabbing some old hag off the streets that's gonna fill your bed with crabs and your ass full of gonorrhea. Just make yourself right at home," he added, "and watch a little television, while I go cleaned up and get ready for supper. I know you're going to stay and eat with Mama and me, especially since you don't have that someone waiting on you hand and feet."

A few seconds later, Miss Irene came walking through the door. "Well," she said, "Who do we have here? What a pleasant surprise – how have you been, Alvin? You know I've been asking John Lee about you. We haven't seen hide or hair of you since you moved out and got your own apartment. He keeps chitchatting about Bobbie Jean; that girls must've finally realized that she had the best of both worlds. One, she has herself a good-looking man, two, he's ambitious. So when she finally realizes it, she suddenly took you and went into hiding and that's why we haven't seen you around here lately. Although I knew it was a joke, when John Lee talked about her taking you and going into hiding, but to most women that's seen you . . . oh, sugar, you might not think it's a joke. It's more like it would be every woman's dream. It would certainly be mine – if there weren't such an age difference. Every time I see you it's an instant reminder of your daddy. Just when I thought I had gotten him out of my system, you came along looking just like him . . . He was such a good-looking man! So tell me what happened to you and Bobbie Jean – did she go and act a fool and kicked you out? Or was it the other way around?

"The first question you asked was the right answer," Alvin said. "The truth is she came to my apartment and to the conclusion that I was too young to get married. She told me she didn't want to wait for me while I tried to make up my mind. She seemed pretty set on getting herself married. So she and her old boyfriend got back together, and have plans to be married as soon as possible."

"I hope for her sake she did the right thing." Miss Irene said. "Finding a good man these days ain't as effortless as she thinks. More than ever, when she considers that you're the one in a million that works as hard as you do, as well as being as good-looking as you. That alone isn't gonna be that simple for her to replace. She's lived in this town long enough to know that Fort Worth is full of ugly, lazy men. I've always like Bobbie Jean and Bernice. That's why I pray for her sake that she made the right choice. If I were her – I would've given it a little more time." Miss Irene thought for a moment, and then carried on. "I think you loved her but didn't know how to convey the message. And she was too impatience to wait and see. I'm surprised that you haven't already gone out and found a replacement for Bobbie Jean, especially at your age. I'm sure if it affects us women, it bound to works the same for men. Once you've been with the opposite sex it becomes a habit that's almost necessary as food and water. Some things is hard to live without! So you most definitely will go out and find yourself another Bobbie Jean. All you have to do is show a little interest – and they'll come climbing the walls trying to get to you. You got what your daddy's got. According to your mama, Jessie May, your daddy had a lot of problems trying to convince women that he wasn't interested in any of them – including me! As for as I know, he remained true to your mama." Miss Irene laughed and continued, "I'm sure your mama never knew that I was in love with your daddy. But, I think he knew how he made me feel – and most of the colored women around Snyder. I caught a few white women looking too, when they thought no one was watching them. I can remember times in those cotton fields when I would look up, and see him looking back at me with those hazel eyes, and that wavy black hair. Many of times I thought about grabbing that man, an' dragging him off to the bushes, and use him until my 'whatcha macallit' was as dry as a powder house and squeaked like a Pyrex dish when damp hand is being dragged across it." Then Miss Irene laughed, sounding rather embarrassed, and muttered, "Ow wee! I better hush my mouth before I talk too much and get myself all stirred up just thinking about that man." She shook her head and muttered, "Mm, mm, mm," then laughed again. "I should for sure just start calling you Allan Junior. Are you staying for supper? You know you don't have to be shy. You're always welcome at my house. You just rare back and make yourself comfortable and keep watching television while I get supper started. John Lee should be out of the shower in a little bit."

Then she walked into the kitchen. Alvin sat there surprised to hear her talk non-stop about his father and her regret that she didn't have the nerve to lure him into coupling with her in those cotton fields back home in Snyder. He grinned – oh, he shouldn't have been there, listening to her say those things. At the same time trying to listen and see where John Lee was, and hoping that he didn't hear his mother use that kind of language. 'Probably not,' Alvin thought, because she only raised her voice when she mentioned me staying for supper, and everything else she said was spoken in an undertone. 'Miss Irene was listening herself for the water to stop running so she would know when to change her subject and talk about something else other than her regret that she wasn't intimate with my father. Sure enough, when the water stopped running, she stoppeds talking.' That confirmed his suspicions about her being just as cautious as he was about not letting her son listen to his mother's frank style of phrasing things. He was also relieved to hear the only things he referred to was his mother asking Alvin to stay for supper.

John Lee yelled out from the bathroom, "He's got no other place to go, therefore it wouldn't surprise me none if he tried to move back inn."

"Now John Lee," Miss Irene said. "Stop picking on your one and only true friend. Why don't you offer him another beer and stop being so stingy? I suppose he could use one along about now due to the fact that he just lost his bed partner?" By that time, Alvin had finished off his beer and made small talk with John Lee about Bobbie Jean.

Miss Irene said, "I'm only announcing this once: Come and get it you boys." Alvin was the first one to reach the table and pull up a chair.

"Look at him Mama," John Lee said. "That poor boy is starving himself to death. He looks as if he's been on a hunger strike since Bobbie Jean left him."

"Aww, pay him no mind, Alvin," Miss Irene said. "You just go right on ahead and enjoy your supper, and you sure don't look like you've been on any hungry strike either."

Immediately after Alvin finished eating, he thanked Miss Irene for the meal and headed to the liquor store. He had hoped that he could go there, pick up a six-pack of Falstaff, and be back in time to take the bus home. The minute Alvin walked in the door, without delay, he opened his first can of beer. He knew he would feel a slight depression; Bobbie Jean, showing up at his apartment at irregular hours of the night was a thing of the past. As an alternative, he used the six-pack of beer to fill that empty void that she left unfilled. Fortunately, he endured his slight depression until ten o'clock that night. Then he relaxed and slept until six the next morning in time to go to work.

Chapter 3 – Wheels

Once he got off that evening, he walked straight to where John Lee worked, and saw him detailing a car. Alvin asked, "Is this the one?

John Lee turned around and said, "No but I'll show you the one if you'll follow me?" Alvin followed John Lee to the car that he claimed he and his boss had picked for him. Alvin stood by the car, while John Lee went and came back with his supervisor, who told Alvin the price of the car that he was interesting in buying. The car was a Forty-nine blue Chevrolet, and the price was three hundred and seventy-five dollars. Alvin only had three hundred and fifty, and he didn't want to drive away flat broke. The salesperson asked Alvin about his credit and Alvin told him that he'd never had any need for credit. At that, the salesperson asked Alvin to follow him to the office, saying, "We'll see what we can do for you since you're a friend of John Lee." The salesperson promised, "I'll try to give you the best deal possible." After the salesman worked out all the details, Alvin was pleasantly surprised that he walked away with a hundred and seventy-five dollars in his pocket. The rest was to be paid out in monthly payments. Alvin left the place riding on cloud nine, except for wishing that Bobbie Jean were riding with him in his first car. Alvin and John Lee rode downtown to a department store, where he spent more than a hundred dollars on himself. Alvin bought shoes and clothes. Afterward, he drove John Lee back to his house, with the understanding that each would shower at his own house. Alvin promised he'd pick John Lee up later.

John Lee was a man that seldom – if ever – owned a car that would run more than a month. After that he'd either park it or haul it off to some junkyard. The reason was that John Lee was the baby of the family and was spoiled rotten. Miss Irene and all of his older sisters waited on him hand and foot just because they had a little brother. The sisters grew up, married, and moved on with their lives. John Lee never worried about reaching that plateau of maturity like his sisters. He never had a full-time job, and never had to worry about one. His mother had a full-time job, so in John Lee's mind, that was enough for him.

His job working for the car rental company started out as a full-time, but he soon turned it into a part-time job. John Lee was a likeable person; everybody he met immediately loved him— mainly because of the comical ways he possessed. However, it didn't take long for them to catch on. After about the fourth time the server came to collect for a round of drinks, and everyone had paid – except John Lee. Then, his comical act weren't so funny anymore. They found out fast that he was an out-of-work comedian looking to his friends to support his drinking.

Alvin wasn't fooled by John Lee's conniving schemes either; he had advance warning from Bobbie Jean, who had tipped him off early on about John Lee's slippery ways to avoid paying for his share of beer. In spite of John Lee's bad habits, Alvin liked him anyway. He just avoided going bar-hopping with him where he'd wind up paying for his, plus John Lee's share of the booze. But this night was different; Alvin was more than willing to buy John Lee's beer. Alvin needed John Lee's company, which is why he agreed to return and pick John Lee up. Otherwise, he'd wind up spending this night like all the others . . . in depression since Bobbie Jean walked out on him.

John Lee's first suggestion to Alvin was to go to the Zanzibar – the place where he and Bobbie Jean had taken Alvin the first time they went out together. Alvin answered casually, "What a good idea." At the same time, he was thinking, "A damn good idea, I might get to see Bobbie Jean there – whether she's with her old boyfriend or not?" His heart began to pound faster as he walked in and gave the place a thorough look-over, from the bar to the darkest corner. Still acting sporty, Alvin sat there at the bar, talking with John Lee while having themselves a couple of beers, but on the inside his mood was dismal. Alvin paid and tipped the bartender and decided to move on to another bar, about six blocks away.

Again, this was a place where he and Bobbie Jean had spent time dancing and socializing with her sister Bernice, and her boyfriend, Leon. Alvin walked in and looked it over, the same as he had did the Zanzibar, but still there were no Bobbie Jean. After they polished off two beers, he finally decided to call it a night. He drove John Lee home, and returned to his own place. He went and stretched out on the divan, hoping that four beers had just the right amount of alcohol to send him off to sleep that instant, fully dressed and lying on the divan.

The next morning, Alvin drove to John Lee's house. He was hoping that John Lee would ride with him while he circled Mrs. Trousdale's house in hope of seeing Bobbie Jean. Alvin knew Curtis had to work on weekends.

If that were the case, then he'd have John Lee go to the door, whisper and ask her to peep out and see the car Alvin just bought.

He parked and knocked on Miss Irene's door. "Well!" Miss Irene said, when she answered Alvin's knock. "Look what the good lord has sent me. Come right on in here and give me a hug, you young, handsome devil." After she had held him longer than she should have, she sighed and admitted, "If I don't let go of you, I'm gonna wound up embarrassing the fool out of myself."

As soon as she loosened her grip, he backed away and asked, "Where is John Lee?

"He and my old man left here right after eight this morning, with some white fellow, who's suppose to be driving them down to Abilene to pick up a couple of rental cars for the company he works for."

At that instant, Alvin thought, "Now I know why she placed her hands on my lower back and thrust her pelvis against mine. Even with me being as needy as I am I can't see me being entangled with a woman that's thirty years older than me." Out loud, he said, "In that case, I guess I had better get going. I had intended to ask John Lee to go riding with me to see what we could get ourselves into."

With a devious smile on her face, followed by a yearning look in her eyes, she said, "Maybe I can help you to get yourself into something if you're not in too much of a hurry?"

He grinned and asked, "How?"

"Let me show you? At once, she caught his hand and attempted to lead him toward her bedroom. He pulled away to question her meaning, but before he could get the words out, she whispered, "Please don't do this to me, Alvin. You have no idea how long I've been waiting for this opportunity. I'm gonna feel like a fool if you turn me down and probably be too embarrassed to ever look at you the same way as I once did. So, just relax baby. What I want you to do to me is no different than what you've did to Bobbie Jean, except mine is a few years older." At that instant, he knew it was his father that she wanted Alvin to stand in for. Miss Irene continued, "I moved all the way to Fort Worth, thinking I'd left all of those feeling behind until you came to town looking just like your daddy – and gotten my curiosity stirred up all over again. Is you with me so far, sweet baby?"

64

"Miss Irene," he begged, "I don't know about all of that. You know John Lee is my best friend, and how would he feel knowing that I slept with his mother? Besides, he'd probably feel so awful that I'm almost certain he'd never speak to me again."

"How will he know if you don't tell him?

"Well," he said. "What about Mr. Elmo?"

"What about Mr. Elmo?" She asked.

"I think it would be doggish of me to go poking around in something that belongs to another man."

"Elmo is a married man that's caught his old lady fooling around with other men. Rather than leave her he wound up in my bed, looking for gratification for himself and retribution for her or so he thinks. He doesn't know it, but he's doing exactly what she wants him to do. While he's in my bed venting his frustration about what she's done to him, she's filing her grievance with other men . . . men that like everything about her, except a permanent relationship. So, if you're afraid you're infringing in on Mr. Elmo's territories, I'd say 'don't be.' Because I am guessing when we finish with what we're about to do, should put me and Mr. Elmo about even, wouldn't you agree?"

"Well," Alvin said, "that's a horse of a different color. I didn't know all of that was going on between you and Mr. Elmo?"

"Well you hearted from someone who knows. Now," she continued, "Was my answer acceptable enough to persuade you to follow me to my room and satisfy my curiosity?" He reluctantly followed her to the bedroom, where she sat on the side of the bed and watched while he halfheartedly undressed. As soon as she saw his willingness to pursue the matter, she laid back on the bed with this stupid grin on her face, as if she had expected the roof to cave in on her.

It's a wonder it didn't, as many times as she erratically screamed out, "Ooh my sweet lord, Alvin baby! I knew it would be just as I had expected!" At that instant, she burst into tears, with her mouth wide open and panting as if she had just run a twenty-yard dash – so much so that Alvin became distracted. Being that she was an older woman, he thought he was doing something wrong that may have been uncomfortable to her.

"Am I hurting you in anyway," he asked, gently.

Miss Irene locked her arms around him, shook her head from side to side, and grunted, "Uh, uh," and just kept right on crying. Finally, she shivered, squeezing his back and kissed his face. She muttered, "Oh my precious darling, you're too young to understand, aren't you my sweet baby?"

"Understand what?" he asked.

"You've probably never had a woman to cry at the same time as you're making love to her. I can't imagine Bobbie Jean not crying her eyes out at least once, especially if you did it to her the way you just did it to me. Different people are affected by different things. I've had years and years of wishful thinking, and fantasizing. And when my fantasy finally becomes real . . . oh, sweet baby . . . it's enough to make me shed a good few tears!"

"If that's what made you cry," Alvin answered, "then I don't feel confused anymore. You nearly made me cry too. Is that the expected thing, in a situation like I was just in?"

"It sure would've made me feel good to know that I could make this teenage boy burst into tears, even if I am more than twice your age!" Answered Miss Irene

"Well," he said, "if the next time serves us like the first time, we'll both be crying in unison."

Miss Irene laughed and said, "Sugar, I appreciate you making a long-awaited fantasy of mine exceed all my expectations. But there won't be a next time . . . not to say that I wasn't overwhelmed. But at the same time, I'm laying here; thinking about what in the world possessed me to ask a teenage boy to do it to a forty-eight year old woman like me. So . . . I've decided I wouldn't do this with you anymore. I want you to promise you won't mention a word about what we just done." Being that he was still lying on top of her all the while, Alvin refused to answer but kept right on kissing her face and slyly flexing his body. To buy himself a couple of more minutes before he did the inevitable, Alvin whispered, "I want you to know how surprised I was that you'd be as gratified as you were."

She lightly stroked his back, answering, "I'm pretty good at predicting the future and I foresee you being approximately two minutes away from revoking your promise unless you hurry and take that thing out of me." Being naïve and considering her to be his elder, Alvin obeyed. He got up from the bed, and reached for his clothes.

"Wait, baby," Miss Irene asked, "I'm fixing to do something for you that Bobbie Jean never did. I'm not sending you out of my house where everybody and his brother will smell what we've been doing." She got out of bed, went to the bathroom and returned with a wet face towel and made him lay back on the bed. At a snail's pace, she wiped, and flipped his genitals from side-to-side as if she was giving them a thorough examination. Afterward she dusted it with body powder. "Now that I got you all cleaned up and smelling good, only you and I'll ever know what went on in this house today – unless you act a fool and go telling what we did! If that were to happen I'll kill you myself!"

He finished dressing, and started to say goodbye. Miss Irene said, "Wait Alvin, don't go now. Its noon already and I know you must be hungry by now. Stay and have lunch with me. I hate having to eat alone, so just have a seat. Dinner is almost ready. All I have left to do is put the cornbread in the oven – and that only takes twenty minutes." She handed him a beer and walked back into the kitchen.

At the same time, he sat there and watched her as she moved back and forth, shabbily dressed, and preparing her meal. Instantly his thoughts returned to when she led him off to her bedroom, when she reached out and slowly drew him toward her. Their eyes met and Alvin saw the unyielding look on her face. She shook her head, "No, no, Alvin, I thought we promised not to do this again."

He stood up and started toward her while he reached for his zipper. "Alvin," Miss Irene said, "Unless you wonna leave right this minute and go home, you should just stay seated until I put the food on the table. I feel awful enough as it is that I had the gumption to persuade you to lay with me in the first place. So I would love it if you would stay and eat dinner with me. But, with that kind of attitude I don't know whether you'll be able to go back to acting like we're still friends, after what we did. Or else, we might have to sever our friendship, if you keep trying to put me in the same class with your ex-lover girl, Bobbie Jean! All right?" she asked.

"All right Mrs. Bailey," he agreed, and returned to his seat on the divan. He had no intention to go all sullen and leave – not as hungry as he was. Alvin swallowed his pride. Five minutes later, she said, "You might as well come to the table now and start eating, because the cornbread is just about ready." She began piling different kinds of food on his plate and sat it in front of him. "Go on and start eating" she said. "I'm pulling the bread out of the oven right now." She put a hunk of hot cornbread on a small plate and sat it in front of him, and made another for herself. It wasn't to say that his food wasn't appetizing – and flavorsome, but not as enjoyable as it could've been, if he hadn't been so preoccupied with thoughts of what took place in her bed thirty minutes ago. He even tried to make small talk but it wasn't making any sense.

He had only one clear thought on his mind – to repeat the experience. The minute she finished eating, he wasted no time scooting his chair away from the table, and going to where Miss Irene stood next to the stove, covering the leftovers. At seeing him walking toward her with that puppy-dog look in his eyes, Miss Irene realized that he wasn't in any playful mood.

She said, "I'm beginning to think you have an awful opinion of me. The fact still remains, it was a mistake and when I finally realized it, we both were within a few strokes of reaching our intention. At that point I figured the best thing for me to do was to lay back relaxed and let you go on and take us both to the finish line." Then he came even closer and started unzipping his trousers. "Now Alvin," she said, "you didn't hear a word I said, did you?

"Oh yes I did," he said, "but what I heard didn't making any sense to me at all." At that she just stood motionless with a despairing look in her eyes. While she let him back her against the wall, with her hands at her side, not raising them once to defend him off, he lifted her dress and proceeded to vigorously rub his pelvis against hers. He became so involved; he yanked her dress over her head and tossed it aside. Without realizing the wild urgency that existed in him, which passed on to Miss Irene; he picked her up, unresisting, and laid her down on the kitchen floor. This time, he continued at that pace for at least fifteen minutes, until out of exhaustion, he laid motionless on top of her. Although his breathing was as if he had just finished wrestling Dory Funk, he still managed apologized to her several times, as he laid there gasping for breath. What was more surprising was when she began kissing his face as many times with tenderness and pacified him by gently rubbing and patting his back. Finally, she spoke, her voice soft with compassion. "Did you get it all out this time, baby?"

"Uh, huhh," he muttered.

"Then you need to get off me, my sweetie pie, so I can wipe up your mess that's running out of me onto my kitchen floor." With barely enough energy, he slowly rolled off and lay on his back close to her. While they laid there reclaiming their strength, he stroked and embraced her with tentative affection. Finally he climbed to his feet and reached down and helped her up.

Still clumsy with exhaustion, drew her in his arms and began to express his passionate regrets to her, saying, "Miss Irene . . . I'm so sorry . . . I would never have forced myself on you, without your consent, but at the same time I'm chastising you because you left me no choice. All I needed you to do was give me ten more minutes before we left your bedroom and the rest of this would've never happened. I'm apologizing . . . but it should be you asking me for forgiveness for misrepresenting yourself."

Miss Irene never answered him. Instead, she walked over, picked up her dress, and put it on. She repeated what she had done before, going to the bathroom and coming back with a wet face cloth. "Stand still." She whispered, as she locked one arm around his butt while she took the wet cloth and wiped around his pelvis area. Then she sprinkled it with body powder, again. Alvin wondered if that was some kind of . . . strange habit. Then Miss Irene looked Alvin in the eye and said to him, "I know you'll want to visit with your friend John Lee. So, whenever that happens and he's not here, I'd just as soon not answer the door. I think its getting a little too risky for us to be alone together. Just think about it; if I had of resisted you, put up a fight –there're no telling what would've happened to me. One thing I do know for sure: You would've raped me. In fact – you did rape me. I just didn't fight back. I had already said 'no,' but you just kept coming toward me with that bestial look in your eyes. I just gave in and refused to wrestle you over a little piece of tail. I was worried that I could've wound up being hurt – and I don't want that to happen to me . . . nor did I appreciate you slamming me against the kitchen floor and treating me as if I were a prostitute. Above all, I sure don't want the neighbors seeing you coming and going, when John Lee is not here, and having them saying, 'Old Irene is so desperate that she's turning to teenage boys for her entertainment.'"

"Listen, Miss Irene," Alvin answered resentfully, "you started something that you weren't willing to finish, and when I did it for you, and then you accused me of unlawfully invading your private parts. I'm surprise at you for not knowing the different between rape and inevitability. I had my needs for female companionship managed just fine – until that so-called urgency of yours met me at your front door this morning, asking for my help in unlocking something that's been hidden for decades. At this point, I feel so embarrassed about what we just did that I could go for years without seeing you again. And I'd probably do just that – if it wasn't for John Lee being my best friend. When we did it the first time I figured you'd be just like anyone else and I could've walked away feeling completely satisfied. But that wasn't the case with, you" he said. "Because the first time was so exotic – I needed to do it again – just to be sure that the first time wasn't just my imagination. Sure enough," he said, bluntly, "it wasn't that at all; both times felt exactly like a toothless person gnawing on a bone."

Miss Irene immediately began laughing hysterically – laughing so hard that she must lean on his shoulder. When she could speak again, she gasped, "I've heard it called many charming names but never like a toothless person gnawing on a bone."

"I really don't think you know what you have is seldom found on other woman."

"Now Alvin!" she said as she continued to laugh, "Are you sure I do all of that to you?

"Well," he answered, "look and judge for yourself and remember it hasn't been more than ten minutes since it relented to you in defeat. And at this very minute, it's pulsating if it's taking in oxygen and expelling carbon dioxide. Or a better definition to describe it would be like two kids going up and down on a seesaw.

"I'm sorry," Miss Irene said. "I didn't know I did all of that to you. That is, if you're telling me the truth. Maybe you're just saying that because you have some kind of sick uncontrollable sexual appetite. What you've told me is the same thing you'd probably tell any woman, just in order to smooth the progress for your next visit. How many times did you tell this same story to Bobbie Jean? Even if you're telling the truth – surely I'm not the only one that's build like that. There must be millions of them out there, who have the same kind of effects you claim I have on you. Soon or later you'll find her, and I hope for her sake, she'll be young enough to withstand being slammed against the kitchen floor and get herself raped like you did me."

"Well," Alvin said, "if she's anything like you, she'll definitely be slammed against the kitchen floor and raped. Other than that," he added, "there isn't anything that benefits me about what I just told you. Except to let you know why I did what I did to you."

"Well," Miss Irene said, "so far my day hasn't been so dull after all, especially when I think about where I started and where I am until now. We started out in my living room, worked our way to the bedroom, and then we had dinner together. If that wasn't enough, you ravished me on the kitchen floor. And now you're trying to convince that I have that something that no other women have except me. And that's where I draw the line, because I don't believe you!"

He shrugged his shoulders, and reached for the door – then he looked over his shoulder, saying, "You know I don't have a telephone – how will I know when John Lee's not home if, I don't drive all the way over here to see for myself?"

She looked at him, knowing what he was thinking. "Like I said," she answered, evenly. "If he's not here I won't answer the door."

Alvin just thought of something else. "Why did you pick me and not my brother, Willie? He was here long before I was and you'd have had your curiosity satisfied three years before I got here."

"Somehow," she answered thoughtfully, "your brother didn't interest me like you did. Every time I saw you – it was just like looking at a younger version of your daddy. To me, Willie was just another one of those good-looking Jackson boys without the charisma you and your daddy possess." She was hovering close, and Alvin wondered briefly what she wanted – and knowing that – if she still wanted it.

"I sure am glad you chose me, then – because I would've never been able to appreciate that extraordinary talent, which I assume only you possess." She gave a faint smile as she turned her head away as to emphasize that the conversation about her had just ended.

He knew and reached out to touch her in the form of an apology. "Please don't touch me, Alvin," Miss Irene said. "Just say 'goodbye.'"

"Okay . . . but first let me say thanks for a wonderful meal . . . and the other thing, Miss Irene? You make me feel . . ."

She waved her hand, interrupting. "I've already told you 'bye,' Alvin."

He walked out to his car and began to think as he drove in the direction of his home.

'I wonder what was going through her mind when she was doing all of wriggling about and crying like a frustrated baby at feeding time? Maybe she wound up doing it three or four times, and didn't want me to know and covered it up by crying her eyes out. It's very possible that I'm right . . . I was still on top of her – inside her – while she did her crying scene. Who knows – maybe that's why she was so adamant about saying no when I went back for seconds. Maybe she had already had all she wanted and probably more than she needed, which is why she could care less about how I felt. Either way, she didn't get away with it. I got it twice, even if I did have to wrestle her to the kitchen floor to prove my point. But if I'm wrong about her rejuvenating herself each time she's writhing and crying, then I suppose it's been so long since she was seventeen, she most likely forgotten how many times one my age needed it before he's satisfied. Even so, deep down inside I know she did the right thing for the both of us. I'm sure her reason for trying to keep us from repeating ourselves was to prevent ourselves from getting too used to each other's gizmos and becoming to depend on it too much. She was wise enough to know that I could never make a life with someone her age. It would be too embarrassing to be caught walking out in public holding hands with a mother-figure like her. Likewise, she'd probably feel the same way about me. I doubt that she could imagine herself walking down the streets holding hands with someone young enough to be her grandson.'

By that time he just turned in to his driveway. He parked and went into the house, still mystified as to why he didn't tell her before she forced him off – that she didn't have the right to categorize him the same as she did for Mr. Elmo when he went back for seconds. And wrestling her to the kitchen floor would've been avoided.

He tried to let go off all those thoughts, to no use. Sitting on the divan, he began to review those things; seeing Miss Irene pulling her robe over her head, slow enough for him to gaze thoroughly at her pubes and then her breasts, which is the scene that played over and over again in his mind. Finally Alvin took a book off the shelf, leaned back on the divan, and began to read – anything to avoid thinking about Miss Irene's body, being that he had restarted his engine and left it with no place to go. Around six that evening he decided to take in a movie, which turned out to be a good thing. By the time he got home, his encounter with Miss Irene meant nothing more than the equivalent of a stranger he met in a bar and had a one-night stand.

By the time Monday morning had rolled around, everything seemed to have fallen back to normal. Alvin was able to work all day without being distracted with memories of Bobbie Jean to the point of becoming teary-eyed. He was capable of going home, getting into his books, and catching up on those studies that he'd missed, when he had spent so much time thinking about her. It was the best that he'd felt since the night before she walked out on him. He didn't want to, but fair is fair; he credited his new sense of ambition to Miss Irene Bailey for asking him to turn a fantasy of hers into reality. In return, she had banished the loneliness for him, the same as he did for her. Even though Bobbie Jean was out of the picture completely, Alvin still had some feeling of satisfaction, after he'd spent two hours using Miss Irene Bailey as his weapon of revenge. This way, everyone came out victorious, and vindicated.

He began fantasizing; in his fantasy he saw a new dawn, just beyond the horizon, loaded with all kinds of goodness and mercies. In the midst of it all he saw a beautiful woman prepared and adorned for him as though it was her wedding night. He took her away, locking the world outside, and said 'goodbye' to all of the Bobbie Jeans and to all of the Miss Irene Baileys. And Alvin and the beautiful lady of his fantasy became as one and lived happily ever after. He held on to his daydream as long as his flight of the imagination would allow him. But when he opened his eyes, the dream vision fled, leaving him slightly depressed.

"It's a mystery," Alvin thought, "I've seen the girl of my future. I've seen the girl that I'm going to marry. All that is left for me to do is find her, and when I do, I will recognize her." After letting go of his castle in the sky, his old friend John Lee came to mind. Even though it had been four weekends since Alvin had encountered Miss Irene Bailey on her kitchen floor, he still couldn't make up his mind whether he'd be able to keep a straight face around John Lee, after spending so much time probing John Lee's mother's anatomy.

He also had another worry – which he hadn't been with a woman since he was last with her. In any case, he knew no matter how hard he tried to conceal his passionate thoughts about her. His main concern was once he came face to face with her, he worried he'd start to remember what she had under her authority and was certain to loose restraint– especially if Miss Irene Bailey was wearing her Sunday's go-to-meeting outfit – the one which made her look as curvy as an hour-glass.

It was a Saturday morning, about ten-fifteen, when Alvin knocked on Miss Irene's door. John Lee answered it saying, "Well, well – Mama, look what the dog's dragged in. Where have you been, boy? Shucks, I haven't seen you since the last time we went bar-hopping together, about six weeks ago. Me, myself – I didn't worry about you that much, because I knew either Bobbie Jean or someone like her must've put you back into action again. And it took you until just now to come up with an excuse that was good enough to convince her, that it was absolutely necessary that she let you back off long enough to come see Mama and me."

"Nope," Alvin said, "I haven't seen hide or hair of Bobbie Jean – or that imaginary girl that you accuse me of hiding out with."

"What you really need," John Lee advised, "is to find you one of those little girls that haven't been around as many corners as the Trousdale girls. You need a girl with a little decency about her. You weren't in town a day before she had you out on her back porch and went to working on messing up your mind. It took her less than two weeks to finalize her scheme to have you as her appeaser just long enough to get even with Curtis. Even though she may've disappointed you, to some degree but in the end you'll be glad that this callous hearted woman is out of your life. Next time, don't go grab the first train that comes along. You just might be on the wrong one, going the wrong way. Check the schedule before you climb aboard, boy. There are plenty girls out there just waiting to meet you. Don't be in such a hurry. What's the rush – you're only seventeen, with a hundred years of life left to live."

Alvin considered John Lee's words for a moment and answered, "You just might have a point, there. Why am I in such a hurry to enslave myself to an un-appreciating woman? You gotta good point, John Lee – from now, I'll put my thoughts of Bobbie Jean on the back burner and let them melt away into nothing."

By that time, Miss Irene came out of her room, all dressed up and smelling very good. Her voice sounded cheerful, as she hugged and slightly squeezed Alvin. "Well, if it ain't my old friend, Alvin Jackson. Boy, you sure are looking fine! Where in the world have you been keeping yourself? I agree with John Lee – when I heard him say he hasn't seen you in a long while – except when he said that you were probably back with Bobbie Jean. I knew better! Why, I saw Mabel just the other day, and she told me that Curtis were still hanging in there. I figured since you got yourself a car, you just drove poor me and John Lee right out of your life."

"Now Miss Irene," Alvin answered politely. "You've been too good to me for me to just up and drop you just like that. You might not know this – but you and your son had me as a friend for a long time."

"Oh, I know that Alvin," she said, "I was just kidding with you. I know you'd never leave town without telling your only two true friends that you were leaving."

He finally got around to asking John Lee to come ride with him, and relieve a couple of hours of boredom – his purpose for coming there in the first place. After John Lee accepted, he looked into the kitchen and saw Miss Irene standing there, pretending to be stirring a pot on the stove. She caught his eye – and no sooner done so, than she slyly held her hands over her breasts, and wiggled her hips. Flirting with him! Just as he thought, no matter how hard he tried, some way, somehow, she'd bring out the lust in him. Miss Irene Bailey was right about not opening the door when John Lee wasn't home – and her being afraid of him ravishing her. That was exactly what he would have done if John Lee hadn't been home. Alvin assumed – given her last words to him – that she would be hostile towards him, which had turned out to be completely the opposite of what he expected. Judging from the cheerful smile on her face and that secretive flirtation in her eyes, he began to believe she must've enjoyed being ravished on the kitchen floor. Obviously, it seemed to have agreed with her, after all. By that time his rumination on her charms had begun to gravitate toward his sensitive area.

He turned immediately to John Lee and asked, "Are you about ready to go? I sure am."

John Lee replied, "Just let me finish cleaning my glasses, so I can see what you'll be seeing when we drive pass where all of those beautiful chicks hang out.

"Bye, Mrs. Bailey," Alvin said. She kept her hands at her side and responded to Alvin's goodbye in her natural voice because John Lee was standing next to him.

Alvin and John Lee drove away to downtown and did about an hour of sightseeing, just looking at pretty girls and all those tall city buildings that were unfamiliar to Alvin. When Alvin had seen enough of city lights, John Lee suggested that Alvin drive to his sister Juanita's house, so that he could say "hi" to her husband and pay back some money he owed him. John Lee directed Alvin to a street that led to a community called "Stop Six," where John Lee's sister lived. He went and knocked on the door, while Alvin waited in the car, but there was no answer.

After that, they went to a barbecue place, and each ate a platter of barbecue. Instead of going out on the town afterwards, they picked up a couple of six-packs, and drove back to Alvin's house to drink them. Alvin made it a habit to stay close to home, not being quite ready to venture out with the crowds and spend his money foolishly. He was more concerned about other things he needed to buy; he wanted a television, and he needed shoes and clothes. Until he could afford it, he thought his weekend spending would be limited to one six-pack and a plate of barbecue on Saturdays and Sundays.

He drove John Lee home around nine o'clock that evening. It was still early. Alvin began looking at the books that Bobbie Jean had picked out for his ongoing education. He read for quite awhile, until he got sleepy. When he went to bed, he fell asleep almost at once – for the first time without seeing Bobbie Jean's face, which used to keep him awake long after he'd gone to bed at night. The next morning he said to himself, "That advice John Lee gave yesterday was just what I needed to hear." The ache in his heart had already diminished considerably – enough so as to put him back in control of his emotions. Every day after work, Alvin would go home and bury himself in his books; and stayed that way until bedtime.

One evening after he had exhausted himself in his studies, he decided to go outside for a breath of fresh air. He noticed his landlady, Mrs. Nichols, and another woman sitting out on the back porch. He nodded his head to say "hello."

"Where is that gal that was supposed to be helping you with your studies?" Mrs. Nichols called from the porch "I haven't seen her around here lately. You didn't get mad and run her off, did you?"

"Well," Alvin said, "it wasn't quite like that – in fact, it was the other way around. She told me something had come up in her personal life, something more important than being with me. So I've been tackling schoolwork all by myself."

Alvin crossed the back yard, closer to where the two women were sitting on the porch. Mrs. Nichols said, "This is my daughter, Cassie. She's a school teacher just like I was." Mrs. Nichols turned to Cassie, saying, "This here is Alvin, the boy I've been telling you about. He's a good boy; and he's going to be a better boy now that he doesn't have that gal hangin' around and keepin' him up all hours of night." With a sly and humorous glance at Alvin, Mrs. Nichols added, "There were times I worried about you not getting up and getting to work on time, after being up half the night entertaining that gal." Alvin was getting embarrassed, which seemed to amuse Mrs. Nichols. "I know you thought I was asleep every time I turned the light off," she said, "but that wasn't it at all. Sometime I like lying quietly in the dark listening to the faintest sounds of nothing. It seems so peaceful to me some time."

Alvin had listened to more than he had bargained for. He was ready to go back into the house. He turned to leave, but Mrs. Nichols said, "Alvin, if you ever need someone to help with your studies, just let me know. I've been retired for a few years, but I think I still remember a few things about teaching."

He thanked her cheerfully and asked, "How much will this cost me for your help?"

She smiled, answering, "It depends on how willing you are to learn. But I suppose if you weren't prepared to learn, you wouldn't have bothered to ask me the cost. I'll tell you this much . . . it'll be something that you can afford."

Alvin walked away, feeling – for the first time since Bobbie Jean first laid the books and school things on his kitchen table – that he was about to start a new beginning in his own education. He felt a surge of excitement running through his whole body. He still missed Bobbie Jean from time to time, but this business of higher learning was getting to be very important to him. That's where all of the excitement came in; being able to separate business from pleasure. Bobbie Jean laid out a good formula, but she could never have been a very effective instructor for him; his mind would always have been on the instructor instead of the instruction.

He picked up the instructions Bobbie Jean had written out the day before she gave him the ax. He began to look them over, but suddenly remembered that he forgot to ask Mrs. Nichols when would be a convenient time for her to start teaching him. He rushed out the door, seeing that Mrs. Nichols' back porch was empty.

He knocked on the back door, until Miss Cassie opened it. "Miss Cassie," he said, "I forgot to ask your mother when would be a good time for her to start teaching me."

"Whatever time is convenient for you," she answered. "I would say now, except we are having our supper."

Alvin thanked her. "I'll see you tomorrow evening, Miss Cassie, if that all right with you."

Miss Cassie smiled pleasantly, nodding agreement. The following evening, Alvin gathered up his papers and headed to Mrs. Nichols' house. He knocked on the door. Miss Cassie came and let him into the screened porch. Mrs. Nichols offered Alvin a seat at a small table setting against the house wall. She sat at the opposite end, took his notes, and looked them over very carefully. She began to write, making notes of her own. After forty-five minutes of writing, turning pages and making notes, she laid the paper in front of him, then came around, and stood behind him, and looked over his shoulders.

She began going over with him what she had written out and told him what she expected him to bring her tomorrow. "First," she said, "I want you to stay here until you understand the basics of what I'm trying to get through to you. If you need me to answer a question, I'll be in speaking distance. That'll make it much easier; a boy could forget lots, just in the time it takes to go back and forth between my house and yours."

About an hour and a half later Miss Cassie came out with her mother. They both stood looking at his work, and reading in silence. Finally, Miss Cassie said, "He's gonna need a lots of help, but I see the potential, and he's gonna do just fine." As Miss Cassie patted his shoulder, Mrs. Nichols went back into her living room.

Alvin studied non-stop, every afternoon after his shift at the ice house for about a month. One evening around suppertime, Alvin stood up and told Miss Cassie that he was starving and had to go and get something to eat. She told him to let her fix him a plate and bring it out to him. He thanked her, saying, "I think that would be too much trouble ... I'll just go on ahead and buy my own dinner.

"Nonsense," she answered, "you just sit right there while I fix you a supper." A few minutes later she bought him a nice plate of food and a large glass of sweetened iced tea. Alvin felt embarrassed and out of place, because he had never had a white woman to cook and serve him before. It was usually the other way around.

As he began to eat he thought to himself, 'People are people! It makes no difference what color they are. Miss Cassie served me with consideration – and liking, too – just like my own mother would do. Even though I'm colored and she's white ... it makes no difference to her. Woman are raised up from babies, with the word 'servant-hood' in them – there's not a thing they enjoy more than to please a man, no matter what colors their skins are. There is no wonder St. Paul says that the Lord made woman for man ... Miss Cassie and women like her are going about their business to do just that; to serve man. In return, man should cherish and love her. Now, if I were married to a woman like Miss Cassie or even Bobbie Jean, I would be more than happy to cherish someone that made me feel the way they have. Except I haven't slept with Miss Cassie; not yet at least and probably never will. At this point, the only thing I have to compare her to Bobbie Jean is her food.'

Miss Cassie and her mother must have been watching a western on television, because he could hear guns firing and the sound of horse hoofs pounding against the ground. Those sounds made him wish that he was setting in some movie theater, eating a bag of buttered popcorn, and washing it down with a large Pepsi. But he knew that he was on a mission, and no western shootout was going to stand between him and his high school diploma.

Miss Cassie's timing was right when she came and took his empty plate and asked, "Did you have enough to eat Alvin?

"Yes ma'am," he said. "It was very good and I really do appreciate you doing this for me."

She stood behind him, looking over his shoulder and reading in silence. "Oops, that's supposed to be a comma – not a period."

"Oh, sorry." he said. "I guess I wasn't concentrating on what I was supposed to be doing."

"That's why I'm here; to make sure you do it the right way." she said. "It's getting late. Aren't you about ready to call it quits for day?" Alvin gathered up his belongings, excused himself, and went to his apartment.

Every evening after work Alvin would stop at his apartment just long enough to grab his notes and pencil, and head straight to Mrs. Nichols' house. After being around Alvin every day, Miss Cassie had begun to feel relaxed around him. She started with asking questions about his background; where he grew up, were his parents still living, and what kind of childhood he had. Alvin went on to tell her his whole life story, from the beginning to the present. When he told her about the wonderful relationship he had with his parents, it got her attention; she also had a good relationship with her parents. She told him about her father's death, and how she still thought of him, every day, and how much she worried about losing her mother. "The older she gets, the more I worry about her." Miss Cassie mentioned that she had an older half-brother named Ray. "He's part-owner and general manager of a big hotel, downtown."

She told him that she had taught junior high in Waco for the last five years, and she had been married twice. "I guess I spent more time – too much time – worrying about my parents than about those two men I was married to. By the time I figured out what the problem was, it was too late." She smiled, adding, "But I don't have any regrets about them – they were both nice men. They just didn't hold my interest very well."

"Well," At last she exclaimed, "I haven't talked this much to a man since I last talked to my father. I had better leave you alone – you probably have things to do at whosever place you plan to do them at!"

"I don't have things to do or places to go," Alvin answered. "Except to go home and do more homework. Being that I'm a big fan of history, I'm prepared to set here the rest of the night, if I have to, and listen to you talk about the things that took place in your life."

Miss Cassie grinned, widely. "I assure you, it won't be long before you'll have all of the history you can handle."

"Bye, Miss Cassie," he said.

"Bye to you too, Alvin," she replied.

He went to his apartment and thought about the conversation he had with her. He was surprised to hear her talk so freely with him about her personal life, what with him being just an eighteen-year-old colored boy. He figured she must've either been lonely, or just had the desire to do what most woman do best – talk to anybody that'll stay long enough to listen.

Miss Cassie had a beautiful oval-shaped face, surrounded with beautiful dark brown hair. Alvin guessed that most people would call her a brunette woman. She wasn't very tall but she had a tiny waist, which set off nice hips and a generous bosom; she was well-qualified to stand toe-to-toe with the finest of women. It wasn't enough that he was attracted to her, but each time she'd reach over his shoulder to turn a page, it added fuel to the fire. Whether she knew it or not, she was causing his will to refrain from women to waver just a little, even though he knew he must resist – at least until he learned the basics of what she was trying to teach him. Apart from a mild excitement he felt when her breast brushed across his shoulder, he knew his place well enough to not risk a venture over that line. Alvin had a good thing going with his education and wasn't being charged a red cent for all of the hard work those two women were putting, into trying to educate him. Good things were on his side and he wasn't about to mess it up by making a stupidly flirtatious remark to her.

He remembered Miss Cassie mentioning in her conversation that she was only thirty-eight. She must've had her hands full, trying to convince her male high school students that she was too old for them. Most evenings after work when he had no reasons to study at the Nichols,' Miss Cassie would come over and ask if he was hungry. If his answer was yes, she would go and come back with a plate of food and say, "You shouldn't have to cook for yourself, with as much homework as I've assigned you. You have two good cooks living right next door, who'll do just about anything to help you get your high school diploma."

Monday evening after work, Alvin went to the Nichols' house to turn in some paperwork. After carefully going over his homework, and seeing how much he had achieved in the short time she'd been teaching him,

Miss Cassie was very pleased. She was so pleased that she wanted to know what he was going to do with his life when he got his high school diploma. He told her that he hadn't decided yet. He just wanted to first get his diploma out of the way. "Then maybe, after that I should be able to think clearer about what I wanted to do with his life.

"One thing I can tell you for sure," she said, "you're not going any place working at the icehouse. Those kinds of jobs are for people with low self-esteem, which shouldn't be an option in your case. A boy with your talents should go and talk to my brother Ray. You know – he's part-owner of the Graystone Hotel downtown. There is good money to be made in running a hotel. At your age and with your mindset, you could climb the ladder all the way to the top – especially if my brother likes you. If you're interested, I'll ask mother to talk to him about putting you to work and see what he says. Especially with me knowing how much Mama likes you – that should make you a shoo-in, because she can get Ray to do just about anything she ask him to do."

"Well, thank you Miss Cassie," Alvin said. "I'd appreciate if you would ask your mother to speak to your brother about hiring me."

"I'll let you know something tomorrow morning when I see you come out for your breath of fresh air," she said."

The next day being Saturday, Alvin slept late, and got up around nine-thirty. He dressed and walked outside. He didn't see Miss Cassie moving around in her house so he didn't bother to knock. He worried about disrupting something important like her and her mother having their breakfast. He decided instead to just drive over to John Lee's house, and ask him to go with him to buy himself a television.

The first word out of John Lee's mouth when Alvin told him he was going to buy a television was: "How can you afford to buy yourself a television? I thought you had spent all of your savings on this car!"

"That's between me and my bank account. Now, are you going with me to buy a television or not?"

"Okay," John Lee said, "I guess you told me, so I'll either shut my mouth or go with you to an appliance store, and watch you buy your first television." After, spending most of his money buying a television, and a six-pack, Alvin decided to invite John Lee to come home with him and drink beer and watch television until the last movie went off. Being as late as it was, Alvin asked John Lee to sleep on the divan, and he'd drive him home the next morning.

Monday evening after work, Alvin pulled into his driveway and got out. Mrs. Nichols called him over to tell him that he needed to go to the Graystone Hotel in downtown Fort Worth and talk to her son about the job that he had inquired about. "That is, if you're still interested?"

"Oh yes ma'am," Alvin told her. "I do want the job – just tell me, when and where to go and I'll be on my way."

"Well," Mrs. Nichols looked at her watch. "If you leave now you might catch him. He won't leave for another hour." It was four-thirty, the middle of the rush hour. The Graystone Hotel was the tallest building in Fort Worth, the top of it tiered like a wedding-cake trimmed in stone and brick. Mrs. Nichols hadn't finished talking, before he was back in his car and racing down the alley towards Main Street and 6th. He was there in plenty of time before Mr. Davis left.

Alvin timidly walked up to the front desk, and the clerk asked, "What can I do for you boy?" Alvin introduced himself, and told the clerk he needed to talk to Mr. Ray Davis.

The clerk told him, "Mr. Davis doesn't have time to talk to you. What is it you want to talk to him about anyway?" Alvin told him that Mr. Ray Davis's mother sent him.

The clerk asked, "What is her name?"

Alvin told him. "Her name is Mrs. Bertha Nichols."

The clerk pointed down the hall, saying, "His name is writing on the door. Can you read boy? Enough to recognize the spelling of Ray Davis, written on the door?"

Alvin didn't bother answering. He walked down the long hallway and knocked on the closed door that read, "Ray Davis, general manager."

He heard a voice within the room say, "Come in." Alvin opened the door and introduced himself to a tall, medium-build man with black hair and a thin, well trimmed mustache. Like his sister, Miss Cassie, he was good-looking as well.

Alvin said, "Your mother, Mrs. Nichols, told me to come and talk to you about a job".

"I was expecting you." Mr. Davis answered. "My mother told me all about you being such a good boy. She thinks very highly of you. She also tells me how hard you're trying to make something of yourself – not like most of your colored boys. I hear you work hard every day and spend hours at night, studying for high school diploma. It's people like you that I take my hat off to, when I extend my hand. You deserve to be commended for doing what you're doing. I'd like to see more colored people like you, having the will and motivation to stand out from that radical crowd. Every Sunday morning, all you gotta do is pick up the paper and read where a fight broke out over a woman, or about someone losing fifteen-cents in a crap game. Then you read a little further, and you'll see where one, if not both died, from a gunshot or a knife wound. For what, I ask? If they're lucky some of them will spend a lifetime in prison; if not they'll wound up in the cemetery. I know colored folks have it harder than most people do, and there is nothing I can do about that. Believe me, when I say I wish I could do for those people what I'm about to do for you. I would love to give them all a job and warn them it's up to you to keep it. I'm about to tell you that anytime my chefs becomes dissatisfied with your performers – in spite of the good relationship you have with my mother – I want you to know that I won't lift a hand to help you; you're on your own. But I have faith in you that you're gonna prove my mother right. Once she figures you out, she's seldom ever wrong."

Mr. Davis stood up and walked Alvin to the kitchen and said to the chef, "Chef Rittenhouse, this is Alvin, and I want you to put this boy to work."

Mr. Davis started to walk away and Alvin said, "Thanks you, Mr. Ray, sir, for giving me the job, and I promise you I won't let your mother down. I'll make her proud of me." Mr. Davis gave a small grin and went back to his office.

Chef Rittenhouse asked Alvin, "What can you do?"

Alvin told him that he had been advised by Mister Ray's mother, Mrs. Nichols to apply for a dishwasher's position and do well. "Then if it was pleasing to you, you'd probably move me up to a better position."

"When do you want to start?" Chef Rittenhouse asked, with a smile.

84

"Anytime," Alvin said. "Except I have a job working at the icehouse, and I needed to give a few days notice."

Chef Rittenhouse told him that a week's notice was enough. "I'll see you here at eight o'clock Monday morning. There'll also be someone here working with you, and showing you the ropes until you can handle it on your own. By the way," he added. "Did Mr. Davis tell you how much the job pays?"

"No sir," Alvin answered.

"How does forty-five a week sound?"

Alvin grinned. "That's fine with me." He thanked Chef Rittenhouse and drove back home. It was around six o'clock when he parked at his apartment. Full of excitement, he started to walk over to Mrs. Nichols' house, but he stopped and thought, 'Maybe I shouldn't bother them. They might be having supper.' He turned to go back to his house, until he heard Mrs. Nichols saying, "Why did you change your mind?"

He turned around, answering, "It came to me that y'all might be having your supper, and I didn't want to disturb you. I figured I'd just come back later this evening or tomorrow evening, when I come for my studies."

Mrs. Nichols answered briskly, "Oh nonsense! Come in and tell us about your interview with the chef. Did you meet my son?" Alvin came and stood on the step to the enclosed back porch. Miss Cassie opened the door, saying, "Come on in, Alvin." As she walked back to the table where she and her mother were having dinner, she added, "Come on in and sit with us and tell us what happened."

He could see them from where he stood, so he said, "I'm just fine right where I am."

Miss Cassie said, "So tell us about your interview with the chef." He stood there, halfway skeptical and shy about socializing with two white women behind closed doors – despite the fact that he was invited to sit with them. He felt it wasn't the normal thing to do if you're colored, unless it had to do strictly with business. He told her that the interview with Chef Rittenhouse went just wonderful, and he did meet her son Ray – and that he had been very nice to Alvin as well as being a nice man himself.

"So I'll be starting to work first thing come Monday morning." He concluded.

Miss Cassie and Mrs. Nichols congratulated him and Mrs. Nichols asked, "Would you like some of what we're eating? I guess you can see we've made too much and we'll never eat all of this food."

"No ma'am," he said. "I'm okay in that department, so I think I'll go to my apartment and do some homework."

"Fine," they both said, so he left and went to his house. He began to read, following the instructions that Miss Cassie had given him for that day. Gradually he became distracted, thinking about the way Mrs. Nichols and her daughter treated him, almost as if he were a member of their family.

'If I had accepted their invitation to have supper with those two women – who just happened to be white – we all would've sit across the table from each other, eating, drinking, and carrying a conversation with each other. What a difference between those two women and white folk, especially nowadays,' he thought. 'All I have to do is remember what happened in Snyder, five years ago . . . rumor had it that these two men grabbing themselves this colored woman and one of them got her pregnant. Afterward the both of them denied ever knowing her – and whichever one the father was, he was scorning his own fresh and blood. And now – just five years later, I'll be willing to say about ninety percent of those same white folk feel the same as Mrs. Nichols and Miss Cassie do, about people like me.'

After his long silent meditation, he returned to his assignment and studied until late that night. He went to bed – Mrs. Nichols and her daughter still on his mind, and about their attitude toward him. The next morning, Alvin went with papers in his hand and knocked on the back door, to turn in his homework to Miss Cassie.

He started to leave, but she said, "Have a seat and – just let me look at this for a moment." She thumbed through his assignment, until she saw what she was looking for.

She read in silence for a few minutes, before saying, "Very good, Alvin. Your determination has earned you an "A" plus – you can't do much better than that." She ruffled his hair and kissed his face and said, "I usually reward my student with a smack on the cheek when they score as high as you've done."

She went back into the house and brought back a book, telling him to read it and write her a book report on history. He went to his apartment immediately, and started to do as he was instructed to do, while thinking, 'Surely she's not so naïve that she doesn't know that little kiss on the cheek could cause a fellow like me to wonder where her mind is at. Does she think because she's white and thirty-eight, this eighteen-year-old this colored boy isn't attracted to her kissing his face with her lips?'

All of that took place on Friday; being that Alvin was off on weekends, he drove over to John Lee's house to give him the good news about his new job. Before he could open his mouth, John Lee asked, "Why aren't you dressed for the wedding?"

He caught Alvin off guard. "What wedding?"

"Your woman's wedding, that's what."

"Oh," Alvin said, "I bet you're talking about Bobbie Jean. She's going through with it this time?"

"Yes sir." John Lee answered. "Mama and I got our invitation in the mail a few days ago."

"Well," Alvin said, "I'm sure glad I didn't get one since I wouldn't have gone anyway. I'm worried that I might do something stupid like ask Curtis to let me kiss the bride."

"Bet me!" John Lee exclaimed, grinning.

"I'll pass." Alvin said, "I'm lying . . . all kidding aside. Actually," he continued, "I came to tell you and your mother that I'm about to change jobs – yesterday was my last day working at the icehouse. I'll be starting my new job on Monday."

Mrs. Bailey was listening from her bedroom, while she was getting dressed for the wedding. John Lee asked. "What is the name of this place you'll be work at?" When Alvin told him that he was working at the Graystone Hotel, John Lee said, "That's where Effie and her husband Ralph work – you remember meeting her at the Trousdale's, the first Sunday you and Bobbie Jean met. You and I were there when she told you about the apartment that you're now living in. And – I'm not joking around with you. Mama and me really are going to Bobbie Jean's wedding."

"I know you weren't joking from the tone of your voice," Alvin said. "I can also take a hint – you want me out of your way so y'all won't be late for the wedding."

Mrs. Bailey came out of her room all dressed up in black with a pearl necklace and matching earrings. She wanted Alvin to see all four sides of her. She made a few unnecessary trips past him, pretending to have misplaced something that wasn't there in the first place. She stopped just long enough to say, "I heard you tell John Lee that you were changing jobs."

Alvin said politely, "Yes ma'am. I am – and I'm starting first thing Monday morning."

She said as she walked away looking over her shoulder, "Well, the best of luck to you. I hope we'll see you much sooner than it took you this time to come around."

She went and stood between the kitchen and her bedroom, waiting to wave him off in her own covertly flirtatious way. After acknowledging her smile, Alvin excused himself and drove away thinking, 'She's awful friendly today. Maybe Mr. Elmo, as Mrs. Irene likes to refer to him, has been dragging his tired behind back to his cheating wife. And my admission would be free-range as long as Mr. Elmo doesn't catch his old lady creating and come back and shut me off.'

He had nothing else to do but to take in a movie. After the movie was over, he went home, and began studying the book Miss Cassie had given him to read for a history assignment. After a few hours of reading and writing notes, he tossed his book, turned on the television, and watched it before going to bed. The next day was much of the same; searching the dictionary, reading and making notes, and working as hard as he could to get his book report in on time. He also tried to improve his vocabulary, as a means of furthering his education.

The following day was a Monday; the first day on his new job. Alvin arrived a half hour early, making a point to walk over and stand outside of the chef's office until he got his attention, before going to sit at the colored employee table. A few minutes later, the chef came over and escorted Alvin through the kitchen, shouting his instruction to Alvin over the noises made from silverware and china rattling against each other. Chef Rittenhouse took him to an older Negro man named Lee, the head dishwasher. He introduced Alvin and told Lee that Alvin would be his helper. Right away Alvin started to refer to the older man as Mr. Lee.

"So, young fellow, have you ever washed dishes before?"

"No sir," Alvin answered, "But I'm here to learn."

Mr. Lee showed Alvin around, telling him that he would start him on the pots and pans, since he didn't have any experience at washing dishes. "The dishes," Mr. Lee said, "needed more attention than the pots and pans. You need to be fast around here to keep up, because we have a very big turnover. The busboys are sturdy, bringing us those dirty dishes and we're just as sturdy at sending them back clean ones. So let's get started."

Being that Alvin was green when it came to knowing what to tackle first and what to tackle last, his first inclination was to work on the pots that had the most burnt food in them.

When Mr. Lee saw how little progress Alvin had made his first hour, he came over to check on him. "No, son." he said. "You're spending too much time doing nothing. Soak the burned ones and clean the not-so-burned ones first. Then by the time you finish the not-so-burned ones, the burned ones should be soaked enough and ready to tackle. You just keep doing that until Evelyn gets Effie all caught up, and I'll send her over to give you a hand."

Evelyn was a Negro girl who worked between the dishwasher and the pantry lady. It took her and Mr. Lee practically all day to get Alvin started in the right direction. After the lunch rush had died down, and the customers were few, the employees took that opportunity to take their half-hour lunch break. Since it was Alvin's first day on the job, he decided to follow around behind Mr. Lee and Evelyn. He couldn't believe that he had access to so much food and so many difference choices. He followed them to a long table that had been designated for colored employees only. Alvin looked and saw the beautiful Effie Mcphee and her husband, Ralph, sitting at one end of the table having their lunch. Seeing her sitting there, his heart began to beat faster; he had secretly fallen in love with her the very first time he saw her.

She exclaimed, "Aren't you Alvin, the boy that I saw at Mabel Truesdale's house one Sunday, about four or five month ago?"

"Yes," Alvin answered.

She asked, "What kind of work did they hire you to do?"

"They hired me as a dishwasher," he told her.

"Well," she said, "I'm the head pantry person and this is my husband, Ralph – he's the head baker."

"Nice meeting y'all again," he said. "It was also at the Truedale's house where we met and you told me about the apartment for rent, where I'm living now. Its always been at the Trousdale's home where we saw each other. I'm sure you know by now that my visitation rights there don't exist any more . . . which is why I haven't told you how much I appreciated you doing that for me."

"Oh, that's all right," Effie said. "I'm glad that I could be of some help to you. Now, maybe you can return the favor by telling me why I didn't see you at Bobbie Jean's wedding Saturday night – John Lee and his mother was there with all of the other guests."

"I wasn't invited," Alvin said, "so I didn't go."

"And I think I know the reasons why!" Mrs. Mcphee chuckled.

"Maybe not," he said, "so why don't you tell me?"

"Just think about how you'd feel marrying someone for convenience – and the one you really loved were to show up at your wedding? If she's anything like most women, it would probably divert her attention to the one she loved, instead of the one she's marrying – and perhaps wound up embarrassing the fool out of everyone, including her."

Alvin bowed his head with a grin on his face. "How would I know? I haven't seen her since the night I waited for her to come by for a visit, and it turned out to be her last visit. I was prepared to tell her I wanted to marry her and our age difference wasn't a factor anymore. She told me she had a similar thought – except hers was to stop waiting around for me to decide and find someone her own age, who just happened to be her ex-boyfriend. So I just let it go at that."

"She may have told you that, to try and force you to marry her – but it wasn't from her heart, unless Bernice and her mother were lying to me. Otherwise, practically every time I went by the Truesdale's house and I'd ask about Bobbie Jean – 'Well,' her mother would eventually get around to saying, 'I suppose she's out doing what she's always done since that kids

Alvin move to town. I keep telling her all she's doing is robbing the cradle. Not once, but several times I've told her that she shouldn't be fooling around with him. What's going to happened to him if she comes up pregnant? He's gonna drop her like a hot potato and go marry someone his own age.' But maybe not, if you had seen her, I'm thinking age would've been a factor. Because she looked better on her wedding night than all the years I've known her. Now that I think on it, maybe she made herself look so gorgeous because she was expecting you to be there. One don't fall out of love overnight, especially if what her sister Bernice told me is true – she said that Bobbie Jean is still in love with you."

At that, Effie started to laugh, saying "Now she didn't tell me what I'm about to say means – I'm just repeating what Bernice told me. She said Bobbie Jean told her when it comes to the way you treat her, compared to the way Curtis does, is worlds apart. She didn't tell me what the worlds apart meant. She just made me understand the only reason she married him was for security, and let me figure the other out for myself." Everybody around the table was laughing aloud. Effie's husband Ralph saw that Alvin was uncomfortable listening to his wife's suppositions.

Ralph said, "Why don't you mind your business, Effie girl, and leave the boy alone?"

Right away, Alvin thought, 'If only Ralph knew how he wishes those words his wife said about him and Bobbie Jean, would've been Bobbie Jean saying the same words about him and Effie. Then he wouldn't be so eager to jump to my defense – even with him knowing that Effie was a married woman. She's definitely worth suffering the consequences where it says in the bible, 'any man that has a relationship with a married woman, that man I will get.' He glanced over at this nice looking girl named Evelyn who was setting there next to him. She seemed to be about the right age, but he didn't bother with trying to pursue her. He wanted to be sure that he didn't possible wind up with another Bobbie Jean. He decided rather to continue heeding John Lee's advice, and not rush in when there is no need to.

By the time Alvin had finished eating, Mr. Lee said to him, "Come on son, it's about time to get back to work and finished cleaning your station. I just saw the busboy unload a ton of dishes on your station. If you want to leave when I leave, you'll need to snap to it, so the evening shifts don't have to clean up your mess."

After that, he thanked Mr. Lee and Evelyn for helping him through the first day. As Alvin drove on his way home, he felt relieved that he had no reason to cook supper when he got home – he had stuffed himself to the brim with a variety of tasty foods that were laid out on the buffet line in the employee dining room. He had nothing to do but concentrate on his studies.

After a week to ten days on his new job, things started to became routine for him. He began to take on other duties that weren't in his job description, as soon as he'd finish the pots and pans. This took Alvin very little time, compared to the last dishwasher they had. Instead of piddling around pretending to be busy when he knew he wasn't, Alvin would go to the salad department and help Effie to set up her station. At the same time, he'd almost break into a sweat when he would periodically catch her in a narrow place where he needed to squeeze past her and touch her in the process. One way or another, he thought, 'I'm going to be hurt, it'll either be by chopping one of my fingers off or Ralph will catch me working around his wife with the front of my apron propped up and gets his ass kicked.'

All day long she wore her hair in a net, but at the end of her shift she'd let it all hang down, which made her look absolutely adorable. After he finished helping Effie get all caught up, he'd go over to the line cook's station and break eggs or run errands for them. He would do just about anything to keep himself working from the beginning of his shift to the end of his shift. He was even bold enough to go over and give Ralph a hand. In spite of Alvin being obsessed with Ralph's wife, he wasn't about to let a guilty conscience hinder him from impressing the chef. He'd rub shoulders with the devil if he thought it would improve his chances of moving out of the dish tub and to the stove. Eventually all of his hard work paid off for him. One evening as Alvin was about ready to leave for home, Chef Rittenhouse stopped him in the hall and told him that he and Mr. Davis had noticed how determined Alvin was to master the jobs that the chefs had assigned him.

Chef Rittenhouse smiled, saying, "I'm warning you to keep it up and see if you don't work yourself into a better position." Hearing that, Alvin worked even harder and spent more time doing his job and helping other people.

About two month later, Chef Rittenhouse approached him again and asked him about working the evening shift, making salad from three to eleven. "It shouldn't be that difficult," the chef told Alvin, "as much time as you've spent working with Effie. I foresee you mastering it in no time at all." When he told Alvin the pay would be sixty-five dollars a week, Alvin felt like a duck on a June bug. He was thrilled to move out of the dish tub and into the pantry, making salad and sandwiches. The first thing came to mind was Mrs. Nichols; he could hardly wait to go home and tell her about his promotion. He would start Monday afternoon at three o'clock, working into the night.

When he finally settled down from all of his excitement, Mrs. Nichols said, "You must've made a good impression on somebody. Otherwise, I've never heard of anyone being moved up to a higher position in three months, unless an emergency came up and they had no other choice. Thanks for sharing your good fortune with me – I'll let you go home and spend the rest of your excitement alone and when you wake up in the morning, just knock on the door and I'll schedule you for a morning study."

The first Monday morning, Alvin had a lot of time to waste; he watched a little television, but that didn't hold his interest. He was too preoccupied with the thoughts of taking on a new job and doing it well. He walked outside and saw Miss Cassie. "Hi, Alvin," she said. "What's the matter? You look like you're bored out of your mind."

"You're right about that," he said. "Normally I'd be working this time of day, but today I won't start until three. Like you said, I have too much idle time on my hands."

"Go bring your home work," she said, "and maybe I'll help you to find something to tighten that loose screw that has gotten you walking around in circles." He went to his apartment and came back with a binder filled with notes he'd made, in reference to the history assignment she gave him a few days ago. As he sat watching, while she thumbed through his papers, he began to think she wasn't interested in what she was looking at. It appeared to him that she had the same problem that he did; not knowing quite what to do with herself that early in the day.

About that time, she muttered, "Everything looks pretty good. My suggestion to you is until we reschedule your study, is that you read these pages aloud, and explain to me your interpretation of its meaning." He took from her an array of mathematic problems to solve, along with a few pages of things that he had written to be used in his book report, which totaled about forty-five minutes. "Very good, Alvin. If you like, you may be excused."

He went back to his apartment and continued his work and watched the clock until two. With an hour left to get to work by three, and it being his first day in his new position, he wanted to be sure he arrived at work at least by two-thirty. Chef Rittenhouse saw him sitting at the employees table. He beckoned to Alvin to walk with him over to the salad department. The chef introduced Alvin to a tall, dark-skinned man about thirty-five; Toby Mansfield. The chef advised Alvin that he could learn a lot by paying close attention to what Toby did, given that Toby had been an asset in that department for more than five years, with no signs of letting up.

At the beginning, Toby was a bit hostile towards Alvin, mainly because he wanted to establish his authority and hoped that Alvin would respect it early on. Alvin understood this attitude, but also had a way of endearing himself to people. Eventually Toby softened, and took to showing Alvin the way he did things. By the end of the shift, Alvin was doing just fine with the little help that Toby gave. Alvin wasn't depending completely on Toby's assistance to do his job, though. Alvin got most of his experience working for at least an hour a day with Effie, from the very beginning. He had a lot to learn, still – but not as much if he hadn't volunteered to work with Effie.

Chapter 4 – Miss Cassie

One evening, Alvin had arrived at work early. He sat at the employees' table, like most everyone did when they were leaving and coming on duty. Of course everyone ate his or her lunch there too. Effie was the first to sit there on her way out.

She congratulated Alvin on his new promotion, saying, "Boy, you deserved it as hard as you work, but I would never work that hard for no one. They'll let you do all of the extra work for free, and when you decide to stop giving them all the free labor, then the next thing you know you're fired. I do what my job calls for me to do and that's it." She continued, "Now that you're going on the night shifts I guess I won't have to worry about you gazing at my behind every time I look around."

"Who, me?" Alvin said. "I didn't realize I was doing that. I must've been thinking about other things, and you just happened to wander into my line of vision. I'm sure you've misjudged me, but I'll still apologize for making you feel uncomfortable."

"Oh, that's all right," she murmured. "It doesn't bother me, not the least bit. I kind of like it when I catch you looking at me. It gives me something to think about, like wondering what's going through your mind. Of course in your case the word 'wonder' is just a figurative way of saying, 'you want a piece of me.' Other than that, just make sure Ralph doesn't catch you staring at me, if you don't want to see a man come all to pieces."

By the time she chuckled finished speaking, Ralph came and sat beside her, saying, "Woo boy! What a day! They worked the hell out of me!" He said to Alvin, "I heard about you moving up to night pantry. You'll be working with a good man; Old Toby knows his business when it comes to decorating his plates."

Effie said, "I was just congratulating him, and hope they don't do him like they do most of the Negroes that do the kind of work he do around here. When they can't take it anymore, they'll make up some kind of excuse to fire you."

Ralph said, "It's time to go home, Effie. We'll see you tomorrow, Alvin."

After they left, Alvin thought about what Effie said, concerning him looking at her behind, and wondered, 'How did she manage catch me looking when I thought, I was being so careful? I guess I'm not as careful as I thought. Well, that ended that, because from now on I'll be working the night shift, which is opposite of her shift.'

In the pantry, Toby was already prepping for the night's business, when Alvin joined him. They both got their stations all set up and ready to go. As they stood around, talking about different dishes, Toby told Alvin how to put them together to make them look appetizing. As they worked, a young white girl came up to the counter to pick up napkins and silverware to finish setting up the station for the night servers. She spoke to Toby, and then she looked over at Alvin, asking, "Now who do we have here?"

Toby answered, "Oh, Alvin – this is Miss Grace, the dining room hostess."

"Hi, Miss Grace," Alvin said.

"Hi Alvin," she said.

Alvin was genuinely impressed with the sweetness he heard in her voice, no less than the way she looked. He watched her as she walked away and said to himself, "Now, there goes a girl with a name that's fit her perfectly. She's elegant, she's charming, and she's self-assured. The downside for me is that I've let my stupidity override my common sense . . . again. She's only a woman and the color of her skin doesn't matter as long as I stay clear of those good old boys. On the other hand . . . an attempt to pursue a woman as white as Miss Grace would be the same as trying to tame a wild crocodile. But . . . on the other hand, isn't it strange; I've seen thousands of white women and many of them were very pretty. And not once was I ever attracted to any of them, until I met Miss Cassie and now Miss Grace. Two women who just happened to be white and I'm colored and just happened to be in love with the two of them. I wonder – if I were still seeing Bobbie Jean, would those two still be attractive to me? Probably not," he concluded, "Because as busy and dog-eared tired as she kept me, most likely I couldn't even attract flies."

By that time, he and Toby were so busy; he had no time to think about Miss Cassie and Miss Grace. Toby told Alvin that his job called for him and a person from the dining room to go to the warehouse for supplies, and bring them back, every night just before closing. The person they chose just happened to be a girl, and the girl just happened to be Miss Grace. About a half-hour before eleven each night, Alvin would take a flatbed four-wheel cart, pull it across the parking lot, and into a building where they kept all of their paper goods and cleaning supplies. Then he and Miss Grace would load what was written on their requisition list and cart it back to the hotel.

During those trips to and from the warehouse and across the parking lot every night, they never had very much of anything to say to each other, except for Alvin making sure that there were about ten feet of space between them, while they walked to and from the supply house. If not, he could've been reprimanded for walking too close to a white woman, throughout those silent walks he took with her every night across the parking lot. He suffered wordlessly, worrying that if he were to say something sweet to her, there would inevitably be complications. But each time, he'd see her beautiful face glowing beneath the lights that illuminated the parking lot; he'd feel even more inspired to say those sweet words he wanted to say to her between the kitchen and the storage room. Finally, one evening, he ventured in a whisper, "I hope I don't embarrass you with what I'm about to say, but I just have to tell you – there hasn't been one single night since we've been walking across this parking lot that I haven't wanted to tell you how sweet you smell."

She acknowledged by showing a big grin, but nothing in words. Alvin's next question was, "Did you go to the movies over the weekend?"

If her answer was "yes" and they had seen the same movie, then they had a few things in common. Otherwise, that was about the extent of their conversations, which only took place Monday nights. They normally went to the movies on weekends – which gave them something to talk about on Monday. Until one night on their way to the warehouse, Alvin made up his mind that he just couldn't take it anymore. He had to say something to let her know that he was going to explode if another day passed, without hinting to her that he was head over hills in love with her. He awkwardly ventured, "Miss Grace."

"I'm listening," she said.

"Uh oh," he thought. The instant he heard the sound of her voice, he felt sure that she wasn't going to be least bit interested in what he was about to say. However, he had opened his mouth, so he figured he might as well go on with it. "Your boy friend must be very handsome."

"Who told you that I had a boy friend?" she asked sternly.

"Well," he said, "no one told me anything, but I thought if you did he'd have to be very handsome because you're so beautiful yourself. If I was a girl and I was as pretty as you are I wouldn't date an ugly boy – unless I don't know the different. Except I know you are smart and I know you know the difference."

She smiled, a wry and strangely bitter smile, and answered dryly, "Thank you for telling me about something that doesn't guarantee me any more than it does an ugly woman. If that were so, then my mother would be living in a wonderland. I think she's one of the most beautiful women I know. But is hasn't bought her contentment; she drinks, and I'm worried about her becoming an alcoholic. My father is a heavy drinker, and my mother's boyfriend is a nice man, but definitely an alcoholic. With all of her good looks she still hasn't gotten anything better than alcoholic men."

"I am so sorry to hear that your mother drinks too much and all," he said, "and her boyfriend, also. It worries me to think about him being the kind that drinks a six-pack and uses being drunk as an excuse to try to become physical with you. Just tell me one thing, Miss Grace . . . in that event, who would you run to for your defense?"

"Are you asking me if my mother's boy friend molested me?" She asked,

"Now," he said, "I hope my curiosity about you and your family hasn't pushed over a line . . . and you have my utmost apology if it does. In my wildest dreams I could never imagine me going so far to say anything to make you angry. So maybe I should've just kept my mouth shut and minded my own business. But," he said, "being that I've gone this far . . . I would like an answer, if you don't mind."

"You're right," she said. These questions you're asking are really none of your business. But since you were bold enough to ask, I'll be courageous enough to answer you . . . just this once. The answer to your question is no! I'm still a virgin. My father and my mother have only been separated for four years. I was almost fourteen them – old enough to take care of myself. My mother wasn't always a drinker. She started after my father left her and my brother, and me for this other woman. And she doesn't drink so much that she can't go to work every day and watch after my brother and me."

"Miss Grace," he said, "I know I shouldn't be saying this, because it shouldn't be my concern at all – But by you telling me that you weren't molested, I feel as if a load has been lifted off my shoulders."

"There was never any need to worry about J.D. – he's a decent, good man, even if he doesn't have any a speck of ambition." She answered, "But why would you be so concerned about me, to the point of worrying about what happened to my virginity? You hardly know me, and even if I were having that kind of a problem, what could you do about it? Not much. I can just see a colored boy like you coming to our house, trying rescue me from J.D. You'd wind up the victim yourself, instead of the innocent party."

"Well," Alvin said. "You are absolutely right about that. I guess I just got carried away asking so many stupid questions about your personal life. I suppose I sound as if I was some reporter putting a story together for the six o'clock evening news. So – if you don't mind me saying, if your answer had been different, I would have felt different about you."

"Now, Alvin," she said. "Why are you saying all of these things, what make you think that I'm concerned about the way you feel about me?"

"Ma'am," he said, "it's not so much about your feeling as it was about mine, and how disappointed I would've felt to hear that some no-good-for-nothing dog had violated your beautiful body, having no intention whatsoever of caring and protecting you to the fullest. It's apparent that a girl as pretty as you are should never be without those things I'm about to mention – unconditional love, gifts of appreciation, and to live in ecstasy with a boy that's sees no end in sight."

Miss Grace smiled and said, "Boy, you sure do have lots of nice things to say . . . but I find to be unimportant to me. It was you – and not me – that got the impression that I'm incapable of taking care of myself."

"But . . ." Alvin started.

"Please," she said, "I don't want to hear anymore, I've heard enough of your fatherly advice for one night. She smiled, though, as she added, "If I didn't know any better, I'd say you have a crush on me. Come on," she said, "you need to hurry and help me put the supplies away, so I don't miss my bus home."

Alvin kept silent as he pushed the loaded cart across the parking lot to her station. He helped her to unload the dining room supplies, then rolled the cart into one corner of the storage room and parked it.

On his way home he thought to himself, 'What I wouldn't give to be a white boy along about now. One thing for sure, I wouldn't be trying to explain my feeling to her in riddles. Instead I'd be speaking to her in plain English, but since I'm not white, it might be to my advantage to keep speaking to her in illustrations. Just in case I happen to go a little overboard and anger her, then I could always laugh and say that I was just kidding.' He did worry a bit that she might start to remember those graphic questions he kept asking and refuse to let him initiate another conversation with her again based on her beauty.

After that he turned his attention to Effie; recalling her warning him not to let Ralph catch Alvin looking at her behind. It seemed that Effie didn't mind him noticing her beautiful hips – as long as it was kept from Ralph's line of vision. It was a waste of her time to warn him about her husband; Alvin knew the penalty for sleeping with Effie would be the same for sleeping with Miss Grace. The only difference, Ralph would kill him over Effie, and some good old boy would kill him about sleeping with Grace. 'Now on the other hand, Miss Grace isn't married. And not only what other people have told me about what takes place between the colored and the whites after the sun goes down, but I've seen it with my own eyes; white men holding onto to the colored women and the colored men were hanging out with the white women. So with all of what's taking place, here in this state, I'm optimistic that the ban on interracial marriage in Texas could soon be outdated.' He figured if he were allowed to pursue Miss Grace in the manner in which he'd seen other mixed couples do after dark, he felt that their chances of coming together would be very promising – providing he got a little help from her.

The next morning, the first thing he did was start in on his book report and worked until early afternoon and went to his job. He looked through the dining room impatiently, searching for Miss Grace in every corner. Finally, he saw her at the far side, straightening and setting up tables for the night shift.

At last, she was within speaking distance and their eyes met. "Hi, Alvin," she spoke in a sweet tone of voice, "Does the excitement of being on your new job have you rearing and ready to go to work tonight?"

"It's not my job that has me so animated," he said, "but beside that, you're absolutely right. I am excided about being here tonight."

Toby was listening to the tone of her voice as well as he noticed her facial expressions. In a low voice, he asked Alvin, "Have you noticed how that little white gal keeps watching you?"

"What white girl?" Alvin asked.

"Now, don't play crazy with me." Toby said. "I've been around the block a time or two. If you think you're fooling me, you ain't – you're only fooling yourself. My common sense tells me that that little old white gal likes you, and I don't think she cares who knows it either. I tell you one thing; y'all better keep things like that to yourselves around here. They'll do it to our women, but don't you be caught doing it to theirs. That is – if you don't want one those old dumb peckerwoods to catch you and kick your ass all over Fort Worth. And don't think that you're the only one that's piercing them cute little bitches. There is a lots of them niggers out there, that's just as busy spiking them sweet little white devils as much as the white men spikes the colored women. The only different is the colored man can't afford to get caught. I'm just warning you, so don't come crying to me when they hear about you putting the sausage to one of theirs. They'll wind up doing to you like what I heard my daddy tell me they did to a colored man, back when he was a boy. He told me that some old dumb peckerwood caught this colored man dunking his attachment in a white woman. He went and brought back a bunch of his friends, and took this colored fellow out in the woods, tied a string around his nuts, attached the string to a rope, and threw it over a tree limb. Then they started to hoist him up, and the nigger's feet never cleared the ground before they had to cut 'em down. The reason was the poor man died out of pure fright, over the thought of loosing his balls to a bunch of dumb peckerwoods."

"Thanks for the warning," Alvin told him, "but I have a girlfriend, so there won't be any need for anyone to toss a lasso around my balls and hang me from a tree."

"All you got to do is tell me that she ain't colored," Toby said, "so I don't have to disbelieve you're laying black ass." He clasped his hands together and gave a hard five-second laugh. It was funny the way he had phrased that part of his conversation, except Alvin didn't want to laugh. That might encourage Toby to keep talking about him and Grace to the point of overdoing it, so Alvin just kept a straight face.

As usual, around seven o'clock the dining room at the Graystone began to fill up with customers. Toby never had wasted a single minute, worrying about Alvin not being prepared to show off his creative skills; those skills he had learned from watching Toby. A lot of his own pride went into his decorative work, in which he also took delight – in his attempt to be the best that he could. After working eight hours, five of them very hard ones, Toby reminded Alvin that it was time to go pick up the supplies that he had requisitioned. Alvin went ahead of Grace, seeing that she had other things to do before she could leave.

He had half of his supplies loaded when Grace walked into warehouse. "You're late, where've you been?" he asked.

"You were there – you saw how busy we were!" she answered. "I barely had time to do one thing before they called me to do another."

"Well," he said comfortingly, "if you need a shoulder to cry on, use mine it's available . . . as long as you're very slow to return it."

"Alvin," she said. "I think I liked it better when you didn't have very much to say to me. Now, you've done nothing but manipulate me when you think I'm at my lowest point. Last night, it was that long drawn-out love affair you think you have with me. If I was a gambler, I'd bet that my crying on your shoulder isn't for my sake – as much as it is for yours. All the same," she added, "because you have been so persistent – I'll rest my head on your shoulder for five seconds. That would be enough to pay you back for the nice compliments you paid to me, last night." Instantly, he caught her hand, led her out of the light, and gave her a hard squeeze for at least twice the five seconds she allowed him to hold her.

"Please," he whispered, as she pulled away. "May I hold you . . . just until the reality of holding a white girl kicks in?"

"No, Alvin you may not," she said. "You remind me of boys I know, who come to our house with their parents for a visit, who are always asking for a hug. And if you let them, the next thing they'll ask is for a kiss, and the next thing they'll want you to do is undress for them."

"Did you?" he asked.

Not me," she said. "I haven't reached that point yet. I've heard what they say about those girls who let those boys fondle them. They can never make the same comments about me as I've heard them say about those girls that let them. On the other hand, I feel just the opposite about you. I've known for some time that the crush you've had on me was sincere . . . even more so last night. I caught you looking at me, and the look I saw in your eyes gave me a measure of your honesty. Maybe mine doesn't go as deep for you as yours does for me, but the little I have, I'll quickly dismiss it and so should you. We're both are smart enough to know we'll never break the color barrier. It'll take another hundred years – if that – before people will realize that they've been uncivilized for all of those years. Think of all of the innocent lives they've made miserable. Some of those people will have lost their chance to learn how to get along with those who have different ways. Now this next thing," Miss Grace continued, "I promised myself I wasn't going to mention this to you – I'm afraid it might go to your head. But I've changed my mind in order to make my point – you're a very handsome colored man. You shouldn't have any trouble at all finding a nice colored girlfriend who would fit into your life. Now, if I were a colored girl, and knowing the way you feel about me, you wouldn't be around five minutes before I'd scoop you right off your feet, take you home to Mama and tell her, 'This is the man I'm gonna marry.' That's what I'd do if I was colored, but I'm not – and you need to forget about trying to make a relationship out of nothing but trouble."

"I don't suppose there're anything I could say to persuade you to change your mind, is there?" He asked.

"Alvin, listen," she said. "I've said all I have to say on this matter. You need to stop thinking about me in a way that causes you to desire me and your crazes will soon fade away!"

"I respect your thoughts, Miss Grace," Alvin replied, dolefully. "But by you doing so you've left me very little room to express my ideas – before I go, I want you to think about this: If you think life is gonna be difficult for you and me for no other reason than I'm colored and you're white, then you're right. If you think we won't be happy for the same reasons, then you're wrong. Living a life of solitude isn't that bad – if you're living it with someone you really love, the way I love you. The only basis for that style of living – as you well know – is the law. The law makes it illegal for black and white to be married, and walk around out in public like normal people. There isn't any other way except to live a life of isolation – if we want to continue to stay alive in this state of Texas. As far as the good things a man is supposed to provide for a wife? I can work and manage my money just as well as any white boy you may think you need to marry in order to be happy. He might have all of those opportunities that I might not . . . but you could still wound up living a life of seclusion, especially if he doesn't have the motivation to take the advantage of all of those prospects that's available to him. In that case you might as well be married to someone like me. At least you'll have nice house, money to spend, and most of all you'll have a man that loves you. I'll promise you – the only disadvantage between marrying me and a white boy would be solitude. Other than that, I have the incentive, the will, and the staying power to make you the happiest woman in Fort Worth, not matter how much discrimination that I'll be expecting to be placed against me."

"Oh Alvin," she answered sympathetically. "I would be lying if I said I didn't think about you a lot. But I never said or did anything deliberately to give you any reason make you believe that I was in love with you. You brought all of this on yourself. You need to be like me, when I have thoughts about you and me – and see that there was no chance for the two of us. I've made up my mind – I'll keep any sentiments about us having a relationship to myself, and release them out into the atmosphere while I'm sleeping at night. And you should do the same."

Hearing how adamant she was about ending his fascination with her, Alvin felt discouraged for a while, but soon he regained his confidence. He decided he'd give her until the weekend to think about it. Maybe by Monday evening, when she saw him again, she would have reconsidered.

They didn't exchange any more words that evening, except Alvin saying, "I'll see you on Monday," and Miss Grace answering, "Bye, Alvin. I hope you'll have a good time this week end."

"I'm sorry I can't say the same for you," he answered honestly. "I hope you'll be as miserable as I'll be all weekend thanking about me, as I'll be thanking about you." She smiled and gave a feminine wave as she headed for the bus stop.

He stopped at a liquor store on his way home, and picked up his weekly ration of beer. While he sat sipping on his beer, he kept going over their conversation in his mind, wondering if he had said anything different than what he told her, wondering if better words might have inclined her to say "yes" instead of saying "no." 'If not, then I was a fool to think that I could persuade this beautiful virgin white gal to let this black boy be the first to gorge himself on her affections. Like she told me, the time I wasted pursuing after her, I should've spend trying to find myself a colored girlfriend. Who knows – we may've already found each other acceptable, to the point of setting our wedding date.'

The one thing that stuck in Alvin's mind was when she said that she had thought about him a lot, and in a positive way. He meditated on it for a while, concluding that there was still room for negotiation . . . and he would definitely talk it over with her, on Monday night.

At that, he heard a knock on the door and thought, "Who could that be?"

He opened the door and there stood Bobbie Jean. Alvin stood stock still, hardly believing his eyes. "What in the world are you doing in my neighborhood, this time of night all by yourself?"

"Can I come in please?" She asked, in a despairing voice. Before he could answer her, she walked in with extended arms and locked them tightly around his neck.

"Um hum," he muttered with an unhealed heart. "You feel just as good as you did the night you walked out on me and made me cry."

"I came here tonight just for that reason," Bobbie Jean answered, "But this time – not to make you cry but to make you happy. I can't begin to count the times I've regretted not letting you get to where you tried so hard to go. And I thought about me, denying a man I loved a few minutes of pleasure, in order to reserve it for a man I never really loved in the first place. I had only one thought; wait for the first opportunity to make up for what I didn't do, the last time we were along together. I owe you this hug, and anything else you think I owe you."

"You don't owe me anything." Alvin replied. "Did you forget that you were standing there, wiping the mess I made in your hand off on my shirt – and then letting me get my pleasure and access?"

"It was only after you had spilled into my hand that I still let you into to my thingy."

"That part I didn't like," he said. "But it was you whom I loved standing there, holding me and making it feel like teamwork – the way you've done so many times before. I was only disappointed, when you managed to maneuver it away from its intended target which caused me to spill into your hand rather than where I wanted it to go. Yeah, I understood you not wanting to take my stuff back to Curtis, for him to whisk around in. I certainly wouldn't if I were him. Anyway – don't you think you're little late for that?"

"I was told that it's never too late to correct a mistake provided the other party is willing. That's why I want you to take me and make me feel the way you used to. Remember the first time I took you dancing and afterward? I drove us to Mama's house and parked behind the garage. And I don't think I have to remind you about what happened after that!

At that instant, he found himself in an upright position, followed by rapid heartbeats as he reluctantly permitted her to unzip his fly. At the same time as she probed his mouth with her tongue, which weighed very heavy on his vulnerability – but not so heavy that he couldn't catch her hand in time to prevent her one second away from piercing what should've been called "screened-off-area" . . . but she wasn't wearing panties. When she realized he wasn't interested, she suddenly stopped and stared into his eyes. "Why did you do that? Is it because you have yourself a girlfriend?"

"No," he answered. "It was because I didn't want to start, until I ask you to tell me where will Curtis be, while you and me are doing all of this."

"Oh," she answered. "He and his brother and nephew drove down to Summerville to go fishing with his uncle. I'm staying at Mama's until they get back Sunday night, a week from now. If that's what's worrying you, don't let it. I'm so free that I can spend the entire weekend with you, and you can do it to me as many times as you wish."

"You can't promise me anything, Bobbie Jean, honey. Everything you own belongs to your husband. I was doing just fine, until you came and stirred things up for me – to the point of me look for an excuse to go into you, and convince myself that it's my getting revenge for stealing you from me. Except my sense of right and wrong won't allow me to behave like an animal."

"Don't feel guilty, honey – I don't." Bobbie Jean replied, "And if my conscience is clear, yours should be too – since I'm the person who's offering it in the first place. I've already told you I don't love him – so what else is there to do except to make love to me, baby?"

"What you just said doesn't make it any more right for me to go into you, then it was for you to let him get close enough to ask you to marry him. Out of all the men in Fort Worth, he was the one that I was most jealous of. And I was right to think that way since the only persuading he needed, to sucker you back into his arms again was to lie about how much he missed you, and you gave him everything I owned. For that reason I couldn't bring myself to forgive you enough to beg you to stay." His eyes began to tear up, as he continued. "You'll never know how many times I lay awake trying to fight off memories that I had tried to build my world around. Many nights I was so miserable that my only thought was to get out of my bed, come to your house, and drag you home with me."

At that she started to cry. "I wish you had! I've been just as miserable without you, as you say you've been without me. Alvin, honey – all you gotta do is tell me to stay and I'll do it. Make me stay with you, Alvin baby. Please I don't won't to live with him anymore. I promise I'll do anything you want me to do. It makes no different what hardships we may encounter, I'll never leave you again."

"I don't want you to leave me," he said, "but you must. What comes around go around. Haven't you noticed? It's happening to Curtis right now – you want me to steal from him what he stole from me. Honey, even if I asked you to stay and you accepted – that wouldn't be the end of it. Sooner or later someone is going to get me back for what I did to Curtis. I wish I could take you and just run away from anybody that I thought would be a threat, to my relationship with you. But you and I both know better. Bobbie Jean – go before you make me do something that'll haunt me the rest of my life."

Bobbie Jean's eyes were teary. "I drove all the way out here thanking that I would give you some to make up for what I didn't do six months ago and all I get is a sermon. Shit! If I knew that's all I was gonna get, I would've gone to church this morning and got the same sermon from Reverend Hall," she exclaimed sarcastically, as she stormed out the door.

At that instant, Alvin knew that he still loved her. He felt almost as bad watching her walk away as he did the night she walked away the first time. His principle was to never have relationship with a married woman, and Bobbie Jean was no different, which is why he let her walk out the door unscathed. Sad as it seemed, his only option to douse the flame that Bobbie Jean started was to grab him a bar of soap and head off to the shower. Just as he started toward the bathroom, he heard a light tap on the door. He thought for sure it was Bobbie Jean coming back to tell him that she wasn't taking no for an answer. "Fine," he would've told her, "and either am I." At that, he'd take care of Bobbie Jean and most definitely himself, and afterward if he wasn't too exhausted, he'd go back to being moral again.

He opened the door, and to his surprise it was Miss Cassie in her housecoat and slippers. He asked, "Is there anything wrong, Miss Cassie?"

She just shoved right in and quickly closed the door behind her. "I just happened to look out my window and saw that gal hanging around here, and I thought she might be giving you a hard time. I knew y'all have called it quits, so I came as quick as I could in order to see if I could be of any help to you. By the time I stopped stumbling around in the dark finding my housecoat and slippers, I see she had already gone. She's no good for you, Alvin. You shouldn't let her keep hanging around here. She'll do nothing except to keep you from studying for your high school diploma, and that's more important than sleeping around with her – wouldn't you think so?"

"Miss Cassie – do you know her?"

"Not really," she said, "except for what my mother has told me about her hanging around here keeping you up all hours of the night.

"She doesn't bother me at all in particular the way you just described her." he said. "I sent her away because I didn't think it was right for a married woman asking me to get busy with her – especially when she has her own husband to do those things she's asking me to do. Even as dispirited as I was, I still had the strength to tell her 'no.' I'm a firm believer in what's good for the goose is good for the gander, Miss Cassie. Meaning if I did it to his wife, someone will do it to my impending wife, whoever she may be. I figured if anyone should be in dire straits with the opposite sex, it should be me, since I haven't taken the time to get with that someone to alleviate my own insatiable urges. But those desires of mine – that's been tormenting me night and day – that I wish tonight would've become hers. With all of that being said, marriage is the only reason I let her walk out of here without me suffusing her to appease these gruesome womanly thoughts that's been recurring for the past six months."

Miss Cassie was smiling. "Your vocabulary had improved tremendously since the time I started to teach you." In addition to her beautiful smile, he noticed how she had sat on the divan without crossing her legs. That confirmed his belief that she didn't crawl out of bed, and come all the way to his apartment for no other reason than to help him fight off poor little helpless Bobbie Jean. Alvin was certain Miss Cassie had other reasons for being there; she was well aware that the upper part of her thighs was exposed, and she didn't bother to drag the end of her robe over to cover that part of her. She added softly, "I can't ever imagine a man as handsome as you are being distressed for any woman; let long this slut that just left here. Why, I'll bet you could have had the pick of the pack – if you wasn't so busy studying for your high school diploma." With those words, he sensed an imminent storm and he needed to prepare myself. He got himself a beer from the refrigerator. "Would you like one, Miss Cassie?"

"I normally don't touch the stuff," she answered, "but tonight I will, just so you don't have to drink alone." He handed her the beer, sat on the divan beside her, and began stroking her gorgeous hair, telling Miss Cassie how beautiful she was.

She told him how she regretted having to go back to school in a week, especially now that she has sensed this feeling of immediacy between the two of them. Then she lay back in his arms, with one leg straight and the other hanging off the side of the divan. He looked down and saw that she wasn't wearing any panties. He stood and undressed and then he kneeled beside her. Placing his left arm under her shoulders, he gently rubbed her soft breast with his hand. She stared intently into his eyes, she whispered, "I'm not married, so what are your excuses for sending me away?"

"What makes you think I'm going to send you away?" Alvin whispered, passionately.

"I don't know," Miss Cassie whispered, still smiling. "You send what's-her-name away, so I figured this was your night for sending girls away." She mischievously flung open her housecoat, exposing her nakedness to him. Seeing all of that thick brunette hair against her creamy white skin, his mind became distorted. Alvin hadn't ever witnessed anything so appetizingly beautiful, so much so that he wished that an adequate amount of it could've been served to him as a full-course meal and enjoyed it without the aid of metal utensils.

He finally gathered his thoughts and whispered to her, "You can't imagine how many times I've mentally undressed you while lying in my bed at night. Now I can't believe I'm seeing for real all of what I've imagined, and wanted to see and do since the day your mother introduced us." As he continued to gently skimmed the surface of her beautiful white body, he whispered, "Just give me a minute more to appreciate what I'm about to take delight in . . . I bet you had no idea how badly I've wanted to do this to you."

"Of course I did," she whispered, "because I noticed how passionate you became, when I stood behind you – reaching over your shoulders to turn the pages.

"When did you first know I felt that way about you?"

"The minute my breast touched your back." They chuckled softly.

He whispered "Uh, huh."

She groaned. He started with her lips and kissed every inch of her body until she drew him on top and amassed his matter with hers. Being as aroused as she was, climaxed nearly at once. "Oh darn!" she groaned, apologetically, "Alvin baby, I'm so sorry, honey. I couldn't hold back any longer. I hope I didn't ruin it for you, did I baby?"

He grinned sheepishly. "I was about to ask you the same thing, but you beat me to it."

"Oh did you, honey?" Miss Cassie asked.

"Uh huhh," he answered. "I'm surprised that you didn't know."

"What a relief," she whimpered. "I was so afraid I ruined it for you!"

"You didn't, but you will," he said, "if you try to leave before I get things up and running again.

"Oh, don't worry, honey," she said. "I had estimated you'd spend half the night asking me for permission to wait while you re-erect in about ten minutes' increments after each round. In the meantime . . . I suggest we move to the bedroom . . . I'll have room to work, so you don't have to do it alone.

He picked her up and carried her down the hall and lay in bed beside her. Between stroking and kissing, intermittently he'd think to himself, 'How could this lucky country boy wound up in bed with his gorgeous masterpiece of a woman?' Things began re-erecting, just as she had predicted, "Ten minutes right on the nose." Instantaneously, they went into action and fifteen minutes later, they were so exhausted that they carelessly fell asleep with her lying partially on top of him. She woke up around three in the morning. Panicking, she attempted to get out of bed without waking him, but he pulled her back, asking sleepily, "Where do you thank you're going?"

"Not now, honey." she said. "I have to go before mother wakes up if she hasn't already. When she saw how unrelieved he was, she grinned halfheartedly. "Okay, sweetie, but you need to make this one a quick." Still naked, she quickly got out of bed, led him to a chair and made him sit while she straddled him. With her knowing how sensitive his nipples were, she latched on with her lips like a baby on its mother, and in about two minutes flat she had him howling like a coyote and fluttering like a fish out of water.

At that instant, she quickly got off, and began dressing in her housecoat and slippers. "If you want to see me tomorrow, I'll be alone from ten until two," she whispered. "That's when Mama leaves to go shopping with a friend of hers. She brings her back around three in the afternoon and on Sunday her schedule is from ten until two. That same lady comes and drives her to church."

She peeped out the window to make sure the coast was clear. Once she walked out the door, Alvin stood by the window and watched her as she hurried across the back yard to her mother's house. She entered and closed the door, which was about as long as he could restrain himself, still not quite believing that Miss Cassie would submit to him in the manner in which she had just did.

His immediate thought was to compare her to Bobbie Jean; there was very little different between the two women and maybe no difference at all, save for the one that generated the most excitement, Miss Cassie won thumbs down, simply because she was so noticeably beautiful lying beneath the dim light. Her hair – dark brown, on her head and elsewhere, contrasted against her velvet white skin. That alone was enough to give Miss Cassie a huge edge over Bobbie Jean.

'She was the first of her kind that he had been with – and the excitement that came with sleeping with a white woman – that alone made it difficult to make a good comparison between the two. The only problem with all of that," he thought, "I seem to be attractive to older woman, and that's not saying very much for me. Even the way Effie spoke about me gazing at her behind sounded like a come-on rather than a complaint. Now, here I am sleeping with Miss Cassie, which I'm very excited about the needed time I spent with her, and would love to spend the rest of my life with – a woman as pretty as she is – except she's the same as Effie, Miss Irene, and Bobbie Jean. They're all beautiful in one way or another, but they're all too old for me.'

Grace entered into his thoughts, which led him to ask himself, 'Would she be hurt like I would be, if I knew she had done what I've done? Even though she reminded me several times that it was a no-go as far as crossing over the racial barriers, I still, believe sooner than later, she's going to wound up in my arms again, and this time it will be permanent. All I have to do is convince her the reason she rejected my plea was because her sudden thoughts about her mixing with a different races had her so confused, she's couldn't separate her fear of falling in love from actually being in love with me. Then, here I am sleeping with those old women that are old enough to have been my big sisters when I wore diapers. On the other hand, I shouldn't worry too much about what I've possible done to her, because she was very clear about telling me to go find myself a girl my own race. So, I should eliminate any form of guilt that might try to crawl into my conscience and make me feel miserable about what could possibly be a relationship with her.'

The next morning Alvin woke up with the same questions on his mind: 'What if Grace really loves me, and is just slow to accept a mental decision she made in secret and wasn't quite ready to share with me?' As it was a weekend and he had been up half the night entertaining Miss Cassie, he slept late and got out of bed around ten-thirty to use the bathroom. After washing and drying his hands, he turned around to go back to bed. And there was Miss Cassie with a towel in her hand, about to spank his naked bottom. Laughing mischievously, for having startled him, she asked, "Where is your underwear, sweetie?"

"The ones you ripped off me last night? I should be asking you. The last I saw of them, you flung them with so much force, I think they bounced off the wall and stuck to the ceiling."

After a few minutes of kissing and fondling while they lay in bed, she asked, "Do you want me to stop or should I keep going?"

"Take a look," he said, "then you tell me whether you should stop or keep going."

"I thank you'd kill me if I walked away leaving you in the predicament that you're in."

"Maybe not," he said. "If it goes any further you'll use up all of your reasons for wanting to coming back tonight."

"You're right." But she continued lazily caressing him and asked, "Are you hungry, honey?"

"I was just thinking about how wonderful it would be to have a sandwich and something cold to drink. Now I'm thinking if you don't hurry up and let go of me, you may have to hold off on that sandwich and that something cold to drink, until after the enviable."

She kissed him and said, "You just wait right here and I'll be right back."

He got out of bed and followed her to the living room. He waited until she came back from her mothers' house with a bottle of Pepsi and a sandwich—one which she had loaded with baked ham, lettuce, and tomatoes.

She set it on the coffee table in front of him and jokingly said, "While I was making your sandwich I noticed honey on my hand. Apparently I collected it from you, before you got dressed. So I decided to substitute, putting it on your sandwich instead of mayonnaise. And the rest I rinsed off in the kitchen sink."

"Oh, that's what that is." he said. "For a minute I thought it was a new brand of mayonnaise I saw running off the side of my sandwich."

They laughed. When she finally stopped laughing, she offered, "If this isn't enough, come to the house before two o'clock and I'll make you whatever you want. But it must be before two – that's about the time Mama gets back from shopping." At that he stood, kissed, and thanked her for the sandwich, and Miss Cassie took her leave. When Alvin finished his sandwich and Pepsi, he felt he had enough. He decided to drive over to John Lee's and visit with him.

Around three that afternoon, as he was just about to leave, Miss Irene and Elmo came walking in. "Alvin, my boy," Miss Irene exclaimed. "What are you doing here all by your lonesome? I would've thought by now you would've had at least one girlfriend. But the last two times you visited, you come without one. What you really need is to start going to church. That's where you'll find all of the pretty ones. And they are Christian girls, not the kind of girl you'll find, hanging out in those honky-tonks."

"Looking for a girl or not," Mr. Elmo said, "you need to start going to church and serving the Lord. Chasing after girls is a good thing as long as your intentions are good. But you aren't gonna be saved chasing after girls for the sake of committing adultery. When young men like you go after a young lady, marriage should be the first and only thing that comes to mind. After that everything else you're after she'll bring with her at her wedding."

Alvin nodded in an agreement, thinking, 'Boy, I sure could tell him a few things about sleeping with someone that you have no intention of marrying. So, do you think it's okay to sleep with Miss Irene Bailey when you have no intention of marrying? I think you need that same sermon preached to you, before you go around telling other people how important it is to serve the Lord.'

Before seeing Miss Irene dolled-up in her Sunday-go-to-meeting outfit, Alvin was more than satisfied with romancing Miss Cassie from midnight until early this morning. Otherwise he would've responded positively to her flirtatious glance, which Miss Irene always knew inflated his ego. Perhaps he may've returned the gesture anyway – if she had not been in the company of John Lee and her old sinful boyfriend, Mr. Elmo. No, time to go – he had been ready to leave anyway. And he would've missed his movie, which started about thirty minutes, "If I hadn't gotten into this long debate with your son about going with me. As it turns out, I'll be going alone after all. Bye, Miss Irene, Mr. Elmo."

Miss Irene said, "If it ain't free, that boy ain't gonna go nowheres but to the divan and lie around and watch television."

Alvin went to the movie, getting home around seven-thirty that evening. He turned on the television, fell asleep, and didn't wake up until Miss Cassie came, leaned over him, kissed his face, and whispered, "Hi sweetie, I'm here."

"Hi Miss Cassie," He asked, yawning, "What time it is?"

"It's eleven o'clock," she said.

"It doesn't seem like I've been asleep three hours. With that much sleep it'll be hard for me to get to sleep when I'm ready to go to bed tonight."

"If I know you," she said, "sleep will be the further thing from your mind when you see what I have for you." She lay back on the divan and pulled up her robe.

He smiled, enjoying the view. "I've already seen that, last night, remember."

"I was told," Miss Cassie mused, "that when a man looks at a naked woman, it makes no different how many times he sees her that way. He always sees something different than what he's seen before."

"The only thing different that I can see," Alvin answered, "is that I wish I could put it in my pocket, reach in and slip it on anytime I got the urge to do so."

She laughed. "You see I told you – that's something different, isn't it?" They laughed quietly but long.

Finally Alvin asked, "Miss Cassie, are you sure you're a school teacher and not a comedian?"

"I'm yours to be whoever you want me to be tonight. Okay, baby?"

"I'm not going to answer to anymore of your questions. because you might make me laugh again and waste lots of our precious moment giggling . . . when there're much better things to do with our time." At that moment, he initiated a humorous act of teasing in preparation for what was looming in her immediate future. Before his all-out assault on her luscious anatomy, he lay silent, admiring as he admired her beautiful pulsating body. "You know, Miss Cassie – you're not going to believe this, but I think I'm falling in love with you."

She grinned, answering, "Don't let these couple of nights we've spent together be your deciding factor. Just relax and give yourself a little more time to think about what you're saying. You might discover that your passion for me might be nothing more than an overdose of fascination, because I'm your first white woman."

When she said that, he propped himself upon his elbow; this was not what he had expected. At that instant, she rolled on top of him, stretching luxuriously, "I don't doubt that you love me at this moment, but what about a week from now?" She whispered. She dropped a long and lingering kiss on his mouth, and then quickly got up. She pulled on her clothes, and did what was becoming a routine for her, trotting off across the backyard to her mother's house.

The next day being Sunday, Alvin remembered what Miss Cassie had told him about her mother's Sunday's schedule, and that she was available between eleven and two. At eleven-thirty, Alvin walked across the lawn to Mrs. Nichols' back door. Miss Cassie saw him and opened the door before he knocked. Once she had closed the door behind him, she took him in her arms.

"I'm not asking about your cloak-and-dagger because it must be so exhausted that it can barely raise its head." She said, "But who I will ask about is your tummy; did you give it breakfast this morning?

"No," he said, "I was just about to go and get myself a bite to eat; but before I did I decided it was best that I come hold you in my arms, kissed you, and say how much I love you."

"You can hold and kiss me as long as you like, but there is no need for you to go out for food. I had you in mind when I fried those extra pieces of chicken. It would be a shame to let them all go to waste – provided you don't mind having chicken for breakfast."

He pulled her close and said, "Miss Cassie, I'm so sorry to say that I'm not older enough to fall wholly soul and body in love with you. You are everything I'd ever want in a woman. I won't mention the obvious things, like the darkness can't hide your beauty, or the lovely smile you give to let me know you accept my advance when I'm reaching to hold you. I'm talking about things that are not so obvious and are invisible, like knowing what pleases me, and you act accordingly and do all of the small things that help to make my day. As often as you do those things, I'm just as unremittingly falling in love with you . . . with conditions, of course."

She looked him in the eye. "So what are your conditions?

"Well, I love you but I can't let myself fall heads-over-hills in love with you."

"Because," she asked, "there is an age different?"

He said, "So?"

She said, "I'm too old for you to fall heads-over-hills in love with but not too old to fuck me three times Friday night, once yesterday, and twice last night. If my math is right, I'd say this old woman that you can let yourself fall head-over-hills in love with, has inspired you to have intercourse with her six times. I'll bet you if I'd spread my legs right this minute, you'd be on me in nothing flat, making it your seventh time in two days. Now are you going to tell me that a sixteen-year-old girl could make you hard seven times with more excitement than I did in two days?"

"You sound so sincere." he said. "That doesn't mean I don't love you. I'm just stating a fact. And as it seems that my statement of fact has made you feel dejected– so much so that I'd like to take this a step further, and ask you a serious question, and I'd like a serious answer. Forget about what I just said, and think about, what I'm about to ask. Like if I were to say to you right this minute, 'drop everything, pack your suitcase and go to California with me and let us get married,' would you?"

She didn't say a word.

He took her in his arms and forced her to kiss him and said, "All you got to do is say 'yes' and I'll have you on a train to California so fast that you'd think you were having a nightmare." She grinned but still didn't say a word. He put both hands under her robe and massaged her breasts, whispering, "Please. I dare you to answer me 'yes.'"

Miss Cassie laid her head in his chest, squeezed him, and said, "You don't mean what you're saying, do you?"

"I do," he said, "and the sound of your voice tells me that you love me too. And I'll tell you again like I told you last night. Age hasn't been a factor and it never will be. So what if you are not as pretty ten years from now, as you are today? Who is to say that I'll be here, anyway?' Maybe ten years from now I won't be here. Then just think about all of the many wonderful times I'd miss, because I worried about some stupid age differences."

"I would answer you," Miss Cassie's voice was low and languorous. "But I can't thank clearly with your hand under my dress."

They both chuckled, as he attempted to draw back, she caught his hands, saying, "Leave them there until you're ready to exchange it for the real thing . . . unless of you think I'm being a little too greedy?"

"You're not being greedy," he said, "Your hints . . . well; I believe your hits of intimacy coincide with my idea of what an appealing wife would be like."

She took his hand and drew him towards her bedroom. "Wow!" he said. "If we are caught doing it in your mother's house we'll be in trouble, for sure."

"Not me, because I live here," Miss Cassie answered, firmly. "But you will be, if you don't stop fooling around and get down to business."

When Alvin saw her turn back the covers, he told her, "You are really going out on the limb for me – or for yourself. Either way I've always wanted to know what it felt like to make love in a white person's bed. Besides," he said, "does all of this demonstrate a foretaste of things comes?"

She said, "I'll write you when I get back to school. That way I'll have time to think how I'm going to separate facts from fiction. If I gave you an answered right this minute I'd probably say 'yes,' and discover later that I might've given you the wrong answer. Furthermore, I need to apologize, for rebuking you when you spoke the truth about our age difference. Besides, I feel the same way you do, when you told me you couldn't let yourself fall head-over-hills in love with me because of the age differential."

She rolled on top of him, cupped his face with both hands, and said, "Alvin, Alvin, Alvin honey, we could've been so good together if it wasn't for me being too damn old for you. I'm more impressed with you than any man I've ever been involved with. You're lots of fun to be with; you make me laugh a lot . . . and that frees up my mind to see you in a positive and business way. And there're no need for me to mention the gratifying experience I've had since my involvement with you. I could go on and on about the good qualities that I've discovered since I started teaching you. You're smart, ambitious, and energetic, and that alone indicates the industrious person that I imagine you to be. If we could live together I could make things less stressful by educating you so no one would intimidate you as far as education go. Between my mother, my brother, and me, we could open doors for you, and help you to become the man you're born to be. Oh, dear . . . I got carried away . . . we need to hurry, honey, and get this over with. Mama and her friend the judge's wife, will be walking through that door any minute now. Can you just imagine the judge's wife catching us in bed together?

"Yes," Alvin said, "and she'd probably say to you 'move over little dog because the big dog is moving in.'"

"Don't make me laugh," Miss Cassie said, "when I'm about to ejaculate."

"Women don't ejaculate," he said.

She chuckled and said, "Keep going at this speed and watch me." After her climax, he got off, got dressed, and stood by the back door, while she finished wrapping a plate of food to take to his apartment for supper.

"I think I've finally figured out what it is about you that had me puzzled since the first day I met you." Miss Cassie said, as she handed him the plate. "It's those characteristics of yours that are traditionally ascribed to a female's sensitivity, which seems to describe you very well. You are soft-spoken, you are very gentle, and your touch is like a cool breeze on a hot summer day. Your mind is always right in whatever it is you decide to do, if it's with me. That includes giving a simple kiss and put me in the-natural-habitat of an undomesticated female. I think that's how you must've made what's-her-name feel, or else she wouldn't keep coming back begging for more, especially when she has a husband of her own."

"Well," he said, "I'm happy to know that I've made you feel whatever it is you felt, as long as you understand you makes me feel equally as well, or else I would be so eager to keep coming back for more, wouldn't you think?" Miss Cassie seemed so pleased that she wouldn't let him leave until she hugged and kissed him with passion, and sent him on his way.

And away he went, with every fiber of his body being over-taxed, plus very satisfied. All of which was due to the fact that Miss Cassie had presented her time to alleviate his miseries. So much so that he barely finished his food before he had fallen asleep on the divan fully dressed and slept the whole night through.

On Monday morning about ten o'clock, he knocked on Mrs. Nichols's door. "Come on in and have a seat," she said, smiling widely. "I take it you had an eventful week-end? My daughter tells me that you're coming alone very well with your academic studies."

"Where is Miss Cassie?" Alvin asked.

She hesitated for a moment with that curious smile on her face. "I would say she's in the bathroom. Either that or she may've gone back to bed – since I've never known her to stay in the bathroom as long as she has. What's the matter with you anyway?" Mrs. Nichols asked, with a sudden look of concern. "You don't want me helping with your assignments anymore?"

"Oh, no ma'am," he said. "That's not it at all. I asked because she's the first one to answer the door when I come for my studies every morning."

"My son tells me that the crew at the hotel sure thinks highly of you. He also tells me – according to what his chef has told him that there isn't anything that you won't do if asked. I told him I saw that in you the first time I laid eyes on you. And just like I told you, keep it up and before you know, you'll find yourself all the way to the top, working for my boy."

Miss Cassie finally came out and said in a cheerful voice, "Well, how are you doing this morning, Alvin?

"Whoa," Alvin thought, "not so welcoming in the present of your mother, Miss Cassie!"

"Did you have a good weekend?" she asked.

"A very good weekends," he said. "I wish the rest of my weekends could be as jubilant as my last one was. I woke up and in a good mood, got dressed, had breakfast and drove over and visited a friend of mine. After about three hours of chewing the fat with each other, we went into a debate about him going to the movie with me to see my favorite actor Garry Cooper play in High Noon. When I finally left, I rode around town and did a little sightseeing until the movie started and wound up going to a movie all alone. After that, I just happened to stop by another friend's house and I was fortunate enough to finish the day with a plate of food that was given me to take home for my supper."

"Well," Mrs. Nichols said, "it seems you had a very exciting week-end. I'm glad it turned out so well. I'll get out of y'all's way so you can get started on your studies."

As she walked back into the house Miss Cassie glanced over her shoulder to see where her mother was and murmured, "Boy, you've turned out to be quit a bull-shitter!" Miss Cassie continued, "I think I told you that I'll be leaving on Wednesday to go back to work. So if there's anything that I can do for you before I leave just let me know."

He whispered "I think you already know what you can do for me before you leave."

"Okay," she muttered," I can't tell you exactly when, but I'll see you tonight and don't bother locking your door because I won't be knocking." Then she raised her voice and said aloud, "You keep focusing like you've been and it won't be long before you'll have that high school diploma! "Oh, by the way," as she spoke where her mother could hear, "did I tell you that I'll be leaving on Wednesday?"

"No ma'am, you didn't," he said.

"Well, you don't have anything to worry about. You'll be left in very good hands. My mother has more experience at this kind of work than I do."

As soon as Miss Cassie got him started on the right assignment, she went and brought back a glass of orange juice. She took one sip and pointed to where she'd tarnished the glass with her lipstick to demonstrate to him where she wanted him to drink.

He tasted it and muttered, "You must've put extra sugar, because it tastes almost as sweet as the honey that made it?"

She grinned and muttered, "You don't say." After that she told him he could go to his apartment to finish doing his homework. At once, he went and did as he was told and worked vigorously right up to the time he allotted himself to dress and be at work on time. Although he had no reason to feel guilty about his wayward weekend he spent romping in bed and on the divan with Miss Cassie, but the instant he got into his car and drove on this way to work, he become anxious, thinking that he had somehow deceived Miss Grace before she was given another chance to defend her belief about being mixed up with a colored boy. Moreover, he thought if that were the case and her decision was positive, he felt he'd have a lots of guilt to demolish before he'd feel comfortable being in close proximity with a jewel such as she was.

When he arrived at work every evening, he'd always find Grace at the far side of the dining room rearranging and setting up tables for the evening shift. When he finally caught sight of her and saw how beautiful she was, he automatically assumed that it was meant to impress him. However, that wasn't the case at all. Contrary to what he thought, when she came within speaking distance, she said a faint "hello," at the same time she turned her face away, picked up her utensils, and let her persona speak for her. Even though she may've spoke to him in a neutral tone of voice, and a stern look in her eyes, he detected a hint of optimism. Perhaps she planned to reveal her thoughts to him, at the end of their work day, in the supply room. Of course, what he saw of her in the dining room was based on nothing more than wishful thinking. But that evening, when he tried to strike up a conversation with her, Miss Grace seemed to pick her words very carefully.

That's when he withheld his planned flirtatious conversation about him and her, which lessened his guilt about prodding Miss Cassie's doohickey for the last several nights. At the same time he felt that their association was at a dead end; the time he spent trying to get Grace back on track was time he could've better spent focusing on ways to send Miss Cassie back to school with a huge smile on her face. If Grace's intention was to get back with him at a later time, it wasn't like she'd be coming by tonight to check on him. He saw no reason why he shouldn't go on and finish up those two nights and send Miss Cassie back to school with a bang, as well as an indelible smile on her face.

He arrived home around eleven-thirty that night. He showered and stretched out on the divan and didn't worry about waiting up to answer the door. Miss Cassie had already told him that she wouldn't be knocking when she came to see him. An hour and a half later, according to his watch, which was one in the morning, Miss Cassie came in wearing nothing but her housecoat and slippers.

She whispered, "Were you asleep, honey? I'm sorry it took so long. I thought my mother would never fall asleep."

"Are you sure she's asleep," he asked.

"Oh yes," she said. "She's asleep, all right. No one snores while they're awake the way she was a few minutes ago." She wasted no time taking his hand and leading him to the bedroom, discarding her housecoat and slippers along the way. And if one tried to explain in details about what happened once they got in bed together, the things they did would make Hugh Hefner blush. An hour later she slipped into her housecoat and slippers and tip-toed back to her mother's house.

The next morning, Alvin came outside to get a breath of fresh air. Mrs. Nichols called, "What's the matter; you're not lost, are you?

"No ma'am," he said, "I'm just trying to breath in a little of your fresh air."

"My fresh air?" she said. "I don't own this air. The Lord owns it all."

Alvin answered, "That's not the way I see it. As long as I'm standing on your property, I'm breathing your air. This here air where I'm standing belongs to you. Now if you were to tell me to get off your land, then I would have to go some other place and breathe someone else's air. When you bought this house, you bought the air along with it."

She laughed, answering, "Boy, aren't you a funny one this morning. You almost had me going there for a while. I suppose your wit is an extension of you eventful weekend, which you raved so much about yesterday morning."

"By the way," he said, "it seems that asking about Miss Cassie here lately has become a routine with me. So since she's not the first person I see every morning when I've come for my studies. I'm guessing she must be in there packing, getting ready to go back to school."

Still smiling, Mrs. Nichols said, "Maybe you two should be just as specific about scheduling your classes as you are about the things you do to entertain yourselves at night."

He said, "I don't know what Miss Cassie does to amuse herself at night, but the only thing I ever get to entertain myself with at night is more homework.

Instantly, Mrs. Nichols answered, "And she plays a major role in helping you to do that as well?" He didn't quite get her meaning, but he acknowledged her anyway with a pleasant smile, and a shrug. He looked up at the house, and there was Miss Cassie, standing by her bedroom window without her bra, blowing kisses with one hand and fondling her breasts with the other. He acknowledged her gesture with a flash of his smile, thinking, 'Now is a good time for the old lady to take a long slow walk downtown and be slow about coming back. That way Miss Cassie wouldn't have to wait until twelve tonight before she's reprimanded physically for flirting without her bra.'

That evening on his way to work, he stopped by a drug store and picked up an alarm clock, just as Miss Cassie had asked. The purpose of the clock was to be set at a specific time, which she would designate; depending on what time she could get away from her mother. Instead of Miss Cassie leaving immediately, she would be able to lie beside him until she had fallen asleep, lying in his arms just as he had requested she'd do. With all of that on his mind, he had very little time to be concerned about what Grace might play in his future. He had no other choice but to turn his thoughts back to Miss Cassie. Like Grace, Miss Cassie too, was about to exit his life. He began examining his feelings about how he'd handle being without her nursing and rocking him to sleep every night as if he was her baby. Her leaving him certainly wasn't going to be something to celebrate, nor would he cry over her the way he did over Bobbie Jean. Bobbie Jean's goodbye was deceitful, but Miss Cassie's departure was out in the open. She told him in advance. This gave him time to acclimate reality of her loss. 'Since this is my last night with Miss Cassie, I mustn't waste anymore time worrying about what Bobbie Jean did and what she didn't do. The minute the clock strikes eleven, I'll be on my way home, fully prepared to gratify whatever her wishes may be.'

Immediately after work, he drove home, took a shower, and just as he came out of the bathroom, she miraculously came in the door smiling. "Are you surprised to see me here so soon?"

"I am." he said. "What happened?"

"There wasn't anything on television that held Mama's interest so she lay down on her bed and fell asleep. So here I am. Take me and give it your best, because this is going to be it for me until next summer, and it better be for you too."

She stood motionless, even as he unbuttoned her robe and let it fall to the floor. They walked naked to the bedroom. She saw the clock, picked it up, and asked. "Do you think from the time I'm finish with you until three a.m. Is enough time to satisfy your crave to have me fall asleep in your arms? I'm suggesting . . . anything beyond that could become catastrophe, in case my mama wakes up and fine her daughter is not in bed."

"You should know me by now that three hours of you sleeping in my arms, or otherwise will never be enough time to spend with you."

She set the clock at three anyway. "What I'm about to do to you will put you in such a deep sleep that you was remember jack shit when the clock goes off at three. Don't expect any mercy from me and I won't be expecting any from you either." After a few minutes of jostling and kissing, she whispered, "Enough of this more-ado crap. Out with the repartee and in with revelry." It was a celebration, all right; which so exhausted them both, they fell asleep on a whim, with her lying on top of him.

It was as if they had only been asleep for a short time before the clock went off. In a daze she quickly got off and out of bed. He got out right behind her, grabbing her panties and robe. He went and braced his back against the wall and asked her to let him put her panties on for her in order to have that something special to remember her by. She came and leaned back in his arms and waited patiently while he put them on one leg as a time. Then he picked up her housecoat, wrapped her in it, and held her tight for one last time. She became teary eyed as she embraced him as well, saying, "I can't remember when I've enjoyed a vacation so much in such a short time as I have with you. It's too bad, Alvin honey, that we couldn't have planned a future together. I think you love me and I know I love you too. But, even if you asked me to stay, I wouldn't because it's not fair to you. Young boys don't go around marrying older women, but old men marry young girls. What a shame that it had to be this way and not the other way around. I'll truly miss you Alvin." she said as she walked out the door with her head down, wiping her tears.

He walked out behind her, whispering, "Bye Miss Cassie, I love you, more than you'll ever know. I meant what I said when I told you I wanted to marry you."

She broke into tears, turned around, and whispered, "I love you too, Alvin, but you don't want to marry me, honey. Five years from now you'll leave me for a girl your own age. So just let me remember you as always being the best thing that ever happened to me, and we should just leave it at that." He held her again for one last time and went back into the house feeling very sad and let down – knowing that he'd probably never see her again under those conditions. In an instant, he went from pessimistic to optimistic, thinking, 'Who knows what this time next year will bring? Maybe I won't have a permanent girl friend. Perhaps Miss Cassie and I could pick up where we left off and start it all over again. If that be the case, we won't wait until the last week of her vacation. We'll start at the beginning and spend the whole summer doing what we did in those few days we spent together.'

He went to his bedroom, wrapped himself in the sheets where they spent their last electrifying moments, and inhaled her sweet perfume mixed with their pheromones. He then fell into a very satisfying and peaceful sleep.

Chapter 5 – Miss Grace

The next morning, about ten o'clock, Alvin went and knocked on Mrs. Nichols' door for his tutoring. She came out with a book in her hands, saying, "It's about time you got out of that house and start moving around. I had expected you would've been here an hour ago. Beside that," she said, "you look as if part of your life has gone missing. Yep, my daughter – Misses Cassie – certainly leaves an impact on people that love her when she goes away."

"Is it that obvious?" Alvin asked, sadly.

Mrs. Nichols looked at him very keenly. "Like I just mentioned, I had expected you'd be here at nine, to at least tell her goodbye when she left this morning."

"Well," he said, "I'm sorry, now, but not half as sorry as I was when I woke up this morning. I got out of bed, got dressed, and started to come and tell her goodbye. But at the last minute, I changed my mind when I thought about how childish it would've been of me to come to say 'goodbye' to Miss Cassie and burst into tears like some prissy little thin-skinned girl?

"You should've come anyway; you may've been just what she needed to see to send her off in a good mood." Mrs. Nichols answered, "She seemed sorter strange, when she came out of her room, just before she left. I don't think she ever slept in her bed last night. I asked her if everything was all right. She answered, 'she was just fine except for a slight depression.' I'm guessing, she's not too bent on going back to school dealing with all of those rowdy students, especially after she's taught an individual such as you, who's eager to listen and learn."

"How could I have done otherwise when she's giving me something as important as a free education? When you write Miss Cassie, tell her I'm sorry I didn't get here in time to say goodbye to her. Don't tell her the reason why I didn't; I don't want her to know that her 'bright young student,' as she calls me – is this little sissy, afraid of becoming too emotional to tell her goodbye."

Mrs. Nichols smiled and gave him the math book she held in her hand. "Why don't you take this and go to your apartment and study there, and I'll start tutoring you at this time tomorrow. One sad face is about all I can handle in one day. And I wouldn't want to catch whatever virus that has you and my daughter walking around like two stir-crazy prisoners that's been given a death sentence."

Alvin took it and went to his apartment, but before he started his studies, his thoughts went back to Mrs. Nichols making the remark about him and Miss Cassie both having sad faces, on the day of her leaving. 'Was that just a harmless thing to say, or was it my guilt that started my imagination to run wild? Or was Mrs. Nichols trying to make it clear that she knew exactly why we both were walking around with sad faces? If that's true, she wasn't asleep at all but played opossum every time Miss Cassie came to my apartment. If that is the case, it doesn't seem that the old biddy is in any hurry to put me out for doing such thing to her daughter. In fact she seems rather pleased with whatever secret she thinks she might hold over me. Then again," he considered after a little more thought, "Maybe I'm being paranoid about the wrong thing. It could be that the old lady has had a crush on me all along, and now that Miss Cassie is out of the way, perhaps Mrs. Nichols has been thinking about – is a sixty-five year old woman too old to ask an eighteen-old old to lubricate her apparatuses just for the sake of revitalizing her memory of the way it once was...'

After that, he worked on his book report until time to go to work. As he and Toby went through their regular routine prepping for the evening rush, Toby began to tell Alvin a few jokes that he had heard over the weekend, which he thought were very funny and kept the both of them laughing most of their shift. When it was time for Alvin and Grace to pick up supplies, on the way to the storage room, Grace surprisingly said to Alvin, "I take it you found yourself a girlfriend."

"What makes you think that I have a girlfriend?" he asked.

"Because," she said "I've never seen you so happy and full of laughter since you and I stopped speaking to each other."

"You mean, since you stop speaking to me?" he said. "I've always tried to striking up a conversation with you, but you had nothing to offer but a cold shoulder, decorated with lots of animosity. I took your advice and tried to do what you told me you did – releasing your thoughts about me into the atmosphere while you slept at night. That might've been easy for you, because your feeling for me doesn't go as deep as mine does for you. If that were so, then you'd   know how difficult it is to erase the memory of someone that's left an impression on you the way you've left on me."

"You sound awful sincere," she said. "Are you sure you don't have a girlfriend, Alvin?"

"I'm sure and very sincere," he said. "Otherwise, I'd be busy making an arrangement with her parent for our wedding day. You're probably wondering why an eighteen-year-old boy would be in such a hurry to enter into to a permanent relationship when I have the better part of my life to choose. The answer is that I'm on a mission to fulfill a dream with little time to waste. I've gone past the age where my daddy told me that I should put aside foolish things and start thinking about the future. 'First,' my daddy said, 'you must find a good job, and then you must establish a good rapport with not only your superior, but as many as those of who will accept you for who you are. Secondly,' he told me, 'to scout the community in such of a good woman in my youthful years. You should not wait until you've hoist every dress and plundered what's under every skirt before you decide to think about marriage. And when you find such woman, then you must do like it says in the bible, 'cherish your wife.' He went on to tell me, 'create good memories of each other in your formative years, store them up, and reminisce about them in your elderly years. Save your money in your youthful years and spent it in your senior years. Likewise seek the Lord while you're young and have someone to lean on as you and your wife travel through this ungodly world we live in.' All of those things make a lots of sense to me. I want you to know how pleased I am that you listened without interrupting while I explained those ideas to you, which was passed on to me by my father. All that's left to do is to persuade you to become the final piece to my puzzle. At the same time, we can begin storing up the things that I just mentioned. I'm a person who's a firmly believe in the saying, 'a bird in hand is worth more than ten in the bush.' Why waste time on trying to separating the good women from the bad and white women from colored when I have the perfect example walking next to me?" By the time he had finished talking, they were in the supply house.

Grace answered, "Alvin, I know this may sound pretty awful, and it makes me sound like I don't know my own mind. I know I told you to find yourself a girl friend. But since then I've had a change of thought. Those few days of silence between us have given me time to think about what you tried to explain to me. And I've missed your out-of-the-ordinary way of saying how much you love me. Just the way you're saying it to me right this minute makes me feel kind of exceptional. What I'm about to say to you might surprise you – I think I'm falling in love with you. If I'm not, then you tell me why have I been so worried about you having a girlfriend?"

"The only way that I could answer your question would be to say what you feel 'is an example of the way I feel' after you stopped me from talking to you. Except mine may've been more intense, because of me feeling so dejected that I started asking myself, 'why is it that a man will become so obsessed with a specific woman when there are so many others to choose from?' Instead he'll spend most of his awakening time concentrating on building his imaginary walls around her, which he'll restricts to all intruders other than himself. At last, he'll say to himself, as he takes her home and becomes her guardian angel, 'There is no doubt in my mind that my attraction and persuasion, has brought us to this point. And from this point forward he must protect her from the slightest disturbance, even if nothing more than a bad dream. Even then, his patience with her will never cease to be nothing more than enthusiasm. He'll comfort her and tell her not to worry, but 'rest peacefully, my darling, because you're lying in the arms of her defender.' The wall that I just mentioned is around you, Grace, my darling, and it started to construct the very first day I saw you. Now," he said, "I wanted to know if you would accept my imaginary wall as real and strong enough to hold you, until the idea of escape are no longer in your memory. At the same time you'll never again stop me from telling you how much I love you."

Just as she turned her head away, she smiled and looked him in the eye, saying, "If that's what you want of me, Alvin honey, then I'll be that girl in your imaginary walls and consider me as being practical. All I'm asking in return is for you to be sure that I'm who you think I am, and not some short-lived fascination. And I'll use one of your saying, where you made reference to a love between two people, 'which should be from everlasting to everlasting.' Otherwise I would be afraid to have any more to do with you; especially with all the odds we'll have against us, once we are involved."

As soon as Alvin heard Grace admit that she wanted to give herself to him, whole heart and soul, he became deeply ashamed of what he had done with Miss Cassie, the last four or five consecutive nights in a row. He thought, 'Why now, Miss Grace? After giving me up just long enough to spoil everything, now I feel that I'm not worthy of standing in the same room with you. I wish you had remained hostile toward me at least until my filth was old muck. That way, I would be feeling so disgusted about my behavior with Miss Cassie.' Then he thought, 'Maybe I shouldn't think of it; what she doesn't know shouldn't hurt her. I have no other choice, because I can't afford to tell her and take a chance on losing her forever. So, with any luck she'll never find out about my short-lived promiscuous lifestyle.' He got hold of himself and tried to act as confident as had, before she confessed her love to him. He took her in his arms, "Now that you've admitted to me you're mine, and we feel the same way about each other, shouldn't we seal it with a kiss?"

She threw her arms around him, as she looking at him and said, "What took you so long to be asked?" He took her tongue in his mouth for the first time, and it was incredibility sweet. His kiss seemed to have the same effect on her, because she wasn't in any hurry to retrieve it.

He said, "Miss Grace?"

"Why do you keep calling me 'miss'? You may call my mother 'miss' – that is, if you ever meet her, which I doubt very seriously – but not me."

"Before I was so rudely interrupted, I was about to ask you another one of my stupid questions."

"Don't let this glee in my eyes stop you. Keep talking."

"I was downtown a few days ago to buy myself a new pair of shoes, when I saw the most beautiful dress draped over this manikin in the store window." Alvin said, in all seriousness. "I said to myself, 'that dress is definitely all Miss Grace needs to bring her natural beauty to its peak. Now, all is needed is for you to let me buy it for you as a token of my appreciation, as well as a mini-celebration for myself?"

"Alvin," she said, "you never cease to amaze me! I guess that's why it only took me two weeks to surrender my precious life into the hands of a boy that's so willing to please me. But you don't have to buy me a dress to prove you love me. You've convinced me of that with your sweet poetic sermon, and if you meant it like you said it, then that alone is worth more than ten dresses."

"I'm asking you again, please say 'yes' and stop rejecting what I'm trying to offer you."

"How much does it cost?" She asked.

"A little more than thirty dollars," he answered.

"Oh my Lord, Alvin!" She exclaimed. "Have you lost your mind? You can't afford to pay that much for a dress on my behalf; that's almost a week wages for you!"

"Are you trying to tell me that you are not worth thirty-five dollars to me?" he asked.

"What will I tell my mother when she sees me in a beautiful and expensive dress that caused thirty-five dollars?"

"Just tell her that you brought it on credit, and you're going to pay it out in monthly payments."

"I don't have any way of buying anything on credit," she said.

"I'll give you the money; then you'll be in debt to me. In that case you won't be lying to her."

"And how do you expect to be paid?" she asked, as she stared into his eyes, waiting for the wrong answer to come out of his mouth.

He said, "By admitting that you'll marry me." Her color came back into her face as she became excited.

"Alvin," she said, "that sound so sweet it just makes me want to take you up on it, but what kind of things would we do and where would we go, especially living in Texas? But the reason I'm willing to follow your lead is because we haven't been . . . involved with each other, and intimacy is supposed to be the ties that bind. If I already feel that I've bonded with you, just think of the way I'll feel once we get married! I'm thinking the only way we'll do all of those things is to move to California. For something as serious as going to California, I hope you'll excuse me for asking for a few days to be sure this is what I want to do. I should warn you, leaving my mother is going to be the hardest part, between my brother and me – mostly me – is all she has to depend on, since my daddy left her for that other woman."

"In that case," Alvin answered, "we'll just take her with us."

"That's very sweet of you to include her," Miss Grace said, "but you don't know her the way I do. She'll never accept you as being her son-in-law. If we move to California we'll be going alone. Then again – who knows? Maybe she'll give in and move to California, once she knows how wonderful you are to me, and realizes that hers and my inseparable relationship is at stake. Once she's in California where it's legal to marry out of our races, she'd have no other excuse, except to fall right in line just like the rest of the people in California." By that time they had loaded and on their way back to the hotel.

"Grace, honey," Alvin said, "I'm so relieved that I won't be going home tonight with that sad look on my face – the one that I took on, the instant you stopped me from speaking to you."

"So am I." she said. "And we'll talk more on this subject tomorrow night, okay, Alvin?" she said as she rushed out to catch the bus home.

The next morning he went to Mrs. Nichols to ask to be excused from his studies and drove downtown to the dress shop where he had previously seen the dress that he had described to Grace. He asked the store manager for a credit application to open a charge account. In filling out the application, he made sure to print her name as "Grace L. Jackson." At the same time, he signed his as "Alvin Jerome Jackson" with a three-hundred-dollar line of credit. He asked customer service to notify him by mail as to whether he was approved or not. After that, he never wanted to show his face in that dress shop again. Anonymous was what he wanted to be, as he didn't want the staff to realize that a white woman was using an account that had been opened by a colored man. He looked around and saw other items that he thought would add a touch of decorative enhancement to the dress; shoes, earrings and a pearl necklace. Alvin was very frugal with his money. He could've paid cash for it all, except his reason was to make her feel committed by opening the account and purposely adding her surname as "Jackson."

It took three days from the time he applied for credit until it was approved. Alvin told Grace that he had opened an account in his and her names, and wanted her to go and buy the dress that he had spoken to her about. He reminded her that she should sign her name as "Grace L. Jackson," since that was the way it appeared on the credit application.

"You know we are not married yet, Alvin. So, why are you doing this?" She asked, nervously.

"Remember what they say about practice makes perfect?" He answered. "This is just the beginning of the way you'll be signing your name to certain documents for years to come. I've heard about colored men and white women living together; not openly, but behind closed doors. They're just waiting for the day when the law on interracial marriage won't be an issue any longer. If they can do it, so can we. I've even been told that there are white men living with colored women and they too, are secretly waiting for that change in the law which states segregation is illegal in the State of Texas."

She said to him, "How long will we have to wait? Will it be five, ten, or even fifteen years? Maybe it'll never happen in our lifetime. But if you are willing to put your life on the line for me, I'm willing to do the same thing for you. Hopefully it won't come to that, but if it does, I'll be there for you, just like I know you'll be there for me."

He said, "I believe very seriously, honey. Nothing is going to happen to us. My reason is that we are two nice people that are in love with each other. If we just happened to accidentally wind up on the wrong side of the tracks. I believe people will know by the way we conduct ourselves, that we're not out trying to provoke anyone to wrath. Once they see that, they're more apt to forget about race and kindly help us to find our way back to where we came from. On the other hand, there is always room for error, just in case I'm wrong about our safety here in Texas. And things start to look a little scary; we need to keep in mind that California might be our only alternative route of escape. What I'm more concerned about right now – than people and their bigotries – is whether or not you're going and buy the dress I picked out for you . . . and the other accessories I mentioned that would complement the dress. I'm dying to see you wearing it all."

She smiled and said, "That was a sudden switch from tormenting yourself over our survival to my personal appearance."

"That was my original point, so go ahead – don't worry," he said. "Just charge it to your account, and when the bill comes, I'll pay for it by giving you the money, and let you pay in person. The only restriction is you mustn't let a certain older black-haired woman assist you in buying anything – she was the one that assisted me in filling out the credit application.

Chances are she might remember that it was a colored man that filled out the form, and along comes a white woman, signing a document bearing the same last name as the colored man who filled it out in the first place."

This was Friday night, and with the both of them being off on weekends, they didn't see each other again until Monday evening. As soon as Alvin got to work, and the instant they made eye contact, Grace didn't need to mention a word about her buying the dress. He already knew – the look in her eyes revealed her secret and the wide smile on her face told him that she had bought the dress. Since she didn't know that her smile and the flashing of her eyelashes was a dead giveaway, she finally worked her way around to his station and whispered, "I got the dress, honey."

Throughout the evening, they covertly, spontaneously, flirted with each other, waiting impatiently for the clock to strike ten. He had planned to listen while she talked about her beautiful dress, as they walked to and from the storage room. She did just that, the minute they walked out the door on their way to the warehouse. She began describing the dress, the shoes, and the jewelry, in every detail, and how well she thought it looked on her, standing in front of the mirror at home before her mother came home. Sandwiched between each word was a volley of kisses, which she released upon him when they entered the storage room, saying, "Before you ask me again the answer is 'yes, I'll do something stupid and marry you. I think we'll be okay, don't you? We'll live together, love together, and we'll die together if necessary – for the reason that we love each other so much."

Afterward she said to him, "I hope you're giving me these things because you love me, and not because you're looking for some sexual favors in return, are you? If you are, as much as I love the dress, the shoes, and the beautiful jewelry, I wouldn't hesitate to take it all back. You need to know before we get too far involved. I'll never let those clothes or anything else serves as a tool to degrade myself. So if you say you love me and it's for the right reason, then I have no other choice but to take you at your word."

"For whatever its worth to you, when I confess that I love you, it's unequal, because I believe I love you much more than I think you love me. Just to prove my point, if you tell me right now that you wanted out of this relationship, but you loved the clothes so much that you'd rather not leave them behind, I wouldn't think twice about telling you to take it all and be on your way. Because there isn't any gain for me by dealing in a one-sided love affair with you. I believe if I willingly deceive you without just cause, someone will do the same thing to me. I suffered a broken heart when you stopped talking to me. Given the fact that I had experienced a broken heart and knew how bad it hurt, then why would I impose the same punishment on someone that means as much to me as you do? You need to know that I'm not a revengeful person. Even if I did have a vengeful kind of attitude, you were well in your rights to take the time to make up your own mind as to whether you wanted to except me or reject me. Sure it hurt me when I thought I had lost you, but the feeling I have since you've came back in my arms again has more than made up for the hurt I endured those two weeks of estrangement between the two of us. As I've promise you before, and I'm reiterating again those same statement, if you'll just be patience and trust me, you're gonna know that I'm going to make you a very happy woman, and I can't do that worrying about whether you trust me or not."

"I do trust you, Alvin," she said. "I just want to hear you say it repeatedly mostly for my reassurance. I'm a young and inexperienced girl as well as being open to possible risk, as I'm about to put my precious life in your hand. So I'm asking you to please don't disappoint me. I'm just a poor little innocent and defenseless girl that just happened to fall in love with a boy of a different race. I hope for my mother's sake that you'll be kind to me and take care of me, and I promise to be kind and with the little that I know, I'll use to take care of you too. Now," she said, "give me a kiss so we can go and put these supplies away."

"I will," he said, "if you'll promise to wear your new outfit to work one evening. Mainly, because I'm curious to know whether or not you're in any competition with the manikin that wore it before you did."

She teasingly said, "The day I took the dress home and looked at myself in the mirror, I instantly knew the manikin that wore the dress before me was childish compared to the way it look on me." Then she said to him, "Give me a little time and I'll come up with a plan to sneak out of the house without arousing my parents' suspicions. My mother doesn't know yet that I have the clothes, and that'll be the hardest part, getting out the door without her noticing."

"One way or the other, around this time tomorrow night, hopefully I'll have something positive to tell you about what my plans are." After their discussion, he walked away with the feeling that his mission to monopolize her attention had begun to take effect.

"Now all I have left to do," Alvin thought, "is to continue to look for things to keep her committed to coming over and modeling her outfit for me. Then the final step would be to secretly induce her to sleep with me, which should obligate her to maintain our relationship, at least until she finishes high school. By that time she'll be so hooked on the feeling that she can't wait to go to California and get married."

This was his first relationship with a woman that he felt bound with. The possibilities of a short-lived liaison with her were not acceptable. He hadn't had a sexual relationship with her, but he had already begun to take on responsibility for her that was beyond the call of duty. The dress he bought her, as well as the jewelry and all the rest – that was just a few of the many things he'd planned to take delight in doing for her, once he persuaded her that it was safe to move in with him. Alvin was not anything like the dog that chases after cars, and when he catches one, doesn't know what to do with it. 'No sir,' he thought, 'I've done too much persuading to get to where I a,m just to get so fainthearted that I'd forfeit a banquet and go back to having a bologna sandwich such as Bobbie Jean and Irene.'

After examining his thoughts about a solidified relationship with his new-found love, he saw that his chances of winning Miss Grace were good. Exhausted, he fell asleep shortly lying on the divan. In the morning, he was knocking on Mrs. Nichols's door by nine-fifteen, turning in his assignments, picking up new ones. He waited while she thumbed through his report. He saw that her way of teaching was an annex of her daughters' progression; Mrs. Nichols proudly scored him with high marks for good works and sent him on his way.

He went back to his place and worked on his assignment until time to go to work on his job at the hotel. Grace's excitement about her reunion with Alvin last night was still with her on their way to the storage room. She said to him, "What a coincidence, I won't have to lie to my mother after all. I was prepared to, if Earline hadn't told me that they had booked a party here at the hotel on Saturday night. Now that I know for a fact that they are having a function here on Saturday night, I'll tell Mama that they're expecting me to work. Instead, I'll come to your place and model the dress for you."

"That's fine with me," he said, "except I hate the fact that you'll still be lying to your mother, by avoidance. But I'm pleased that you don't enjoying lying to her. A good relationship like the one you have with her is very important. It shows honor and respect. In the Bible somewhere in the Proverbs, it says 'children that makes their parent happy, their wishes shall be granted.' That's why I'm careful not to sway you away from the bond that you have with your mother. In our predicament we'll definitely be depending a lot on that verse in Proverbs, while pleading for our wishing to be granted. You and I may not prove to be so successful if we've dealt deceitfully with your parents."

Grace laughed, as she parted from Alvin, to catch her bus, saying, "I'd loose my grant for sure, if Mama knew I was coming to your apartment this weekend. I'm laughing – but I feel a little nervous about it. But I'm going to do it anyway – because I know what I'm about to do is the right thing. I know something good is about to happened to us."

The day of their rendezvous finally arrived; a Saturday. Grace and Alvin normally were both were off on weekends. Alvin woke up the next morning excited – and worried – as he thought, 'What would it be like to be alone behind close doors with someone that meant more to him than a few rolls in the hay?'

He finally got dressed, drove down to the little café and had breakfast and a lots of coffee. For no other reason but to kill time, he got back in his car and drove past the Truesdale's house, in hopes that he'd catch a glimpse of Bobbie Jean visiting her mother, and sitting outside on the front porch. That would definitely take his mind off Miss Grace, and he'd rid himself of a lot of anxiety. Whether he saw her or not – which he didn't – he had planned to visit John Lee as another way to take his mind off Miss Grace. Alvin and John Lee talked and told jokes until they ran out of things to say – and Alvin thought up yet another excuse by inviting John Lee to have lunch with him at the same café where he had eaten breakfast that morning.

By five that evening, they finally ran out of things to talk about. Alvin drove John Lee back to his house. By the time Alvin returned home that evening, he had relaxed – but to be sure he stayed that way, me made himself a double shot of the vodka from the bottle that Bobbie Jean had left behind. He mixed it with Seven-up, turned on the television and sipped his cocktail until he noticed the dusk had begun to dominate over daylight. He opened the back door and stepped into the alley – just standing and nervously waiting, like a singer on stage before a crowd of thousands without a band. He finally saw a pair of headlights beaming down the alley toward him, traveling at a slow speed. She was looking at every house, trying to read the faded numbers, with most of the signs hanging crosswise, or on just one nail. Finally, Grace caught sight of a figure standing at a distance under the light that illuminated the back porch to his apartment. She increased her speed, recognizing the figure standing beneath the light as Alvin, and at the same time, he knew it was Grace driving the car. His heart began beating rapidly, his knees became weak. He motioned to her to park very close to the back door. He wanted to conceal as much of her as possible. As it turned out, she only took three steps, and she was in his apartment. He immediately closed her car door as well as the door to his apartment. She seemed to be very relaxed; yet he could hardly stand on his own two feet.

His unease and nervousness in greeting her was so apparent that she put her arms around him, saying, "Honey, don't be nervous; we are not doing anything wrong. All I'm going to do is model the clothes you bought me, and I'll be on my way before either of us even realized it happened." At that, he reached into the refrigerator and offered her a beer.

"Seriously Alvin," she said, "I never liked the taste of alcohol, and anyway I've seen what it does to people." They both sat on the divan. She began to look around and said "I'm surprised to see that you have such a nice apartment. I didn't expect this at all."

"That's a relief," he said. "I was afraid you wouldn't like it."

"But I do." she said as she grinned. "What an ideal place for some newlyweds." They made little small talk between coddling each other, until Alvin had began to relax.

Finally, Grace asked shyly, "Are you ready to see what I look like in my new outfit?

"Well," he said, "I was hoping to be more relaxed than what I am, when I saw you in your dress for the first time. Due to the amount of time you've allowed yourself to model your dress, I guess I have no other choice but to lie back, relax, and let the show go on. All the same," he added, "I must warn you – if the dress looks half as good on you as it did on the manikin, you might have to give me mouth-to-mouth resuscitation. It's been documented that too much beauty may well cause me to have a seizure."

She smiled, blushing in pleasure, "Ah, you won't."

Silently, he pointed her the way to the bedroom, while he remained sitting on the divan. It took her about ten minutes to change into her new outfit, including putting on her lipstick and her hair up in a bow. When she came back into the room, he sprung to his feet, fumbling for words. "Oh Grace, my darling," he exclaimed, "You look magnificently beautiful! You're a star that hasn't been discovered by the outside world. Now that I've seen you in all of your splendor, you're a constant reminder that I must do everything in my power to keep you committed until you're out of school, or else I risk loosing you to the highest bidder."

She didn't answer, but she continued to smile as she turned from side to side as a professional model would do – except she had all of the curves that professional models don't normally have. Grace had the curves of a Marilyn Monroe. Women who possess such bodies are referred to by colored men as "stone stallion." Alvin thought to himself, 'This poor innocent white girl must not have any idea what she's made of – if she did she could've easily married herself a rich white man, instead of wasting her time with a three-hundred-dollar-a-month salad boy.'

The dress was a black sheath with a bold diagonal swath of white from her left shoulder all the way to her right hip. Her shoes and purse was as black as the dress she was wearing. He reached out and straightened her pearl necklace which matched her earrings. He stepped back and gazed into her beautiful white face, which contrasted stunningly against that black dress, and her head of thick brunette hair.

Once she saw how impressed Alvin was with the way she looked, she asked in a soft sweet voice, "Now tell me – do you really like the way I look?"

He hesitated for a moment. "Are you bold enough to asking me to describe someone as beautiful as you?" He finally replied, "You are the most indescribably beautiful and sexiest woman in the whole wide world." Her face lit up even more as her eyes sparkled like a Christmas tree, as she was just as pretty or even more than a well decorated tree at Christmas time.

He took her hand and led her back to the divan and began kissing her fervidly. She finally whispered, "I think I'll take these nice clothes off before I get them all wrinkled and get back into my jeans."

He whispered, "Can I help you to take them off?"

She whispered, "Do you want to?"

"Yes," he said. At that, they stood and continued to kiss at the same time he slowly unbuttoned her dress. Eventually it slid off her shoulder and slowly over her curves onto the floor. At that, he carried her to his room and genteelly lowered her on the bed. Even after he lay in bed beside her, he continued to kiss her everywhere; she became momentarily flustered, and frantically demanded, "Do you have anything on to prevent me from being pregnant?"

"Yes," he answered.

"Can't I see, to be sure?" At seeing, she smiled shamefacedly and said, "Okay." At that time, she drew his arm across her as a hint to roll on top of her. Instantly they initiated the task of intoxicating each other at full force and coincidently attain satisfaction simultaneously. Not only did she lose her virginity, but she momentarily lost sight of reality, as well. Once her eyes rolled back in her head and her mouth flew open as she began to pant like an overheated dog on a hot summer day.

When she finally came back to reality, the first thing she said to him, "I'm not a virgin anymore. I gave you my virginity – I hope I gave it to the right man." She seemed saddened at that point.

"Of course you did, honey. I'm your first and I'll be your last if you'll let me . . . all right, sweet baby," He crooned comfortingly as he kissed and stroked her hair." She didn't answer, but just laid there flush-faced as well as flustered, with her hair all a mess and waiting for her breathing to subside. She finally looked into his eyes in deep thought, as if she was sorry for what she had just done. Then she said in a quiet voice, "You're also the first one to ever see me without any clothes on. If you really love me, Alvin, you won't ever let another man see me this way."

"Oh, honey . . . I promise you, you'll never have to undress for any man due to my lake of response to your needs. Likewise," he added, "what you expect from me, I want the same commitment from you as well."

"I promise you," she whispered, "and also I want this night to be the example which we must always follow. Case-in-point . . . you're Alvin, and I am Grace. There is no one else in this bed except the two of us. It must always be just like this for the two of us. We'll adopt this as our slogan 'as long as we live, what you have belongs to me and what I have belongs to you.' "Furthermore," she continued, firmly, "the declarations we just agreed to must serve as an interdiction to all outsiders for all time. It's important that we keep all invaders at bay – that our children don't have step-parents, like I have." She smiled as she finished. "Would you like to do it again before I go?"

"Would you?" he asked.

"Yes, I think so," she answered after their second emotional liaison.

She got out of bed, and when she finished dressing, she took her new dress, held it to her chest, and humbly asked him to let her leave her new clothes with him. "That way, I won't have to worry about hiding them from my mother.

"By the way," she said, "this purse you saw me carrying? I charged to your account also – given that you mentioned everything except a matching handbag. So I thought a beautiful dress like this should not only have matching necklace and earrings, but a handbag as well. I hope that was all right with you."

"It was," he said, "but I'm sure you meant to say I charged it to my account. Or did you forget that the account is as much in your name as it is in mine, especially after what we did tonight. From now on, the accurate way of saying it is to say – what I charged to our account. And even then, it's only to alert me so when the statement comes, I won't have any surprise. If you agree with what I just said and you have no alternative, let what happened between you and me tonight be accepted as a makeshift wedding, until we are actually married – practice saying in an undertone that your name is no longer Adams, but Jackson; in my opinion, the instant we united, it automatically gave us a do-it-yourself certificate in matrimony without the few words of some clergyman. From that moment forward, it makes no different what your problems are, I'm the one you bring them to. Even though you still live at home with your parents, you're still my responsibility, and I take my liabilities very seriously. Now," he finished, "with all fairness to you, and just in case you're having trouble feeling what I'm feeling, I'll give you the rest of the weekend to thank about continuing to be Mrs. Jackson or revert to being Miss Adams again."

"Oh, Alvin honey," she said. "Why do I need the rest of the weekend to tell you that I accept Jackson as my last name? Not only will I allow it, but the name Grace Jackson had a very sweet and sophisticated ring to me. To be more to the point," she said, "I am no more disingenuous about the way I feel about now then I was when you were on top of me. All of this inspired me to make my declaration of fidelity to one another." About that time she was so anxious to leave that she could hardly wait to finish her sentence, so he walked her to her car and kissed her goodbye.

He walked back into his house, still not quite believing that he had actually had intercourse with this beautiful girl that he thought a few months ago was out of his reach. Yet, tonight this same girl stood completely still, 'while I undressed her right down to her bare skin. Am I a bona-fide seducer or am I just plain old lucky? Whatever it was, it all boils down to the fact that I swayed her to accept not only one jab but two of my blocked insinuation, due to the fact that she made me wear a condom. So," he thought to himself, "I will not shower and wash away the sweet aroma of my first virgin. Instead, I'll wear it until the coat she smeared all over my body turns pungent.' He went and got into bed, and laid there staring at the ceiling with nothing on his mind except Grace. And nothing on his body except a hormonal excretion, which was produced by their bodies. Being that the next morning was a Sunday, he woke up with nothing to do but lounge around and mirror back to last night. At which time he found himself reliving that blissful encounter, which instigated an urge within him that he had no way to satisfy. He got dressed and drove to the hotel where he worked. He went and sat at the employees' table, and by the time he had finished his fourth cup of coffee, Mr. Lee, the dishwasher, saw him sitting there. He came over and asked, "What's the matter, son? You look as if you have been caught cheating, and your woman kicked you out. Now, you got no other place to go except right back to the place you've already worked for the last five days."

"I have a place to go," Alvin said. "If only I knew how to get there."

"It's that bad, huh?" Mr. Lee said

"Yeah," Alvin said, "it's that bad."

"What you really need," Mr. Lee said, "is for old Randy, the cook, to fix you a big plate of ham and eggs, which should head you off in the direction to whomever dress you're looking forward to get under." Even though Alvin ate an enormous breakfast, which satisfied his stomach, a meal had nothing to do with filling the emptiness he had to endure until Monday evening – the earliest that he could see Grace. He had no friends, other than

John Lee and his mother. He certainly wasn't in any mood to see Irene secretly brandish her breasts, and move seductively while she watched to see whether his reaction for her was still sharp, or gone dull. As an alternative, he drove around town, sightseeing for a while, then came back home and turned on the television. He read until he became exhausted and fell asleep on the divan.

Monday evening when Alvin got to work, Chef Rittenhouse came out of his office saying, "Alvin, I need to talk to you." Alvin walked over to the office. "Sit down," The chef said. "Let me get right to the point. "First of all, I wonna know how do you like it here, so far?

"Oh just fine," Alvin said.

The chef said, "I'm glad to hear that since I like the way you carry yourself around here. You are always doing constructive things that are good for the Graystone; I've being noticing it and so has Mr. Ray. You don't have to give me your answer now, but I want you to think about how you'd feel, if I moved you out of the pantry and promoted you to work the front as a line cook. The pay is a little better, about twenty-five more dollars a week better."

Alvin was so ecstatic with the offer he could hardly speak. He looked down at the floor and became slightly emotional. "Mister Jim," he said, "why did you go and ask me a silly question like that? You know perfectly well I would love a chance at filling that position, and I promise that I want let you down."

Mr. Jim laughed as he patted Alvin's shoulders and asked, "When do you want to start?"

Alvin, being full of excitement said, "Right now!"

"Now hold on," the chef said. "Breakfast was over four hours ago."

Alvin said, "Just kidding, boss."

The chef said, "Why don't you come in Monday morning from six to two; how does that sound?"

"Anything you say, chef. I'm just so glad to have the job."

When the chef finished, Alvin walked around the corner filled with so much excitement that he couldn't wait until Monday morning to inspect his imminent domain. He just barged right on in amongst the busy cooks with the intention of inspecting his new workplace. But Randy, the head line cook, made short work of his inspection when he asked Alvin to come back when they weren't so busy. All the while, Alvin kept thinking to himself, 'what a miraculous event that his fifty-five a week paycheck had suddenly advanced to eighty dollars a week, just when I committed to being Grace's provider.' He could all but imagine a colored person such as himself coming right out of the cotton fields and to this town, landing a job, making three-hundred and twenty dollars a month. His excitement inspired him to walk over to his workstation to tell Toby that Friday was his last night working with him, being that he had been promoted to line cook and starting Monday morning.

Toby's response was, "You go right on ahead and flip all the eggs and burgers as you want. As long as you don't include me, I'm very happy right where I am." He said, "If you're taking over Lowell's shift, you'll be loosing your Saturdays off. But with the way you love making money, I'm sure when you get your first check and see the additional take-home pay; all your memories of Saturday being one of your days off will fly right out the window."

Alvin continued his excitement – until he told Grace on their way to pick up supplies at the warehouse. After the speech she gave suddenly had him believing that he had made a bad choice. "Six AM to two PM!" She instantly became indignant, "Why would you go and do something so stupid as to leave me to work the night shift while you work the day shift? Don't you realize how awful it'll be for me to have to wait seven whole days before we can touch each other? Even on my days off I did nothing except think how nice it would be if we didn't have to wait until the weekend. Because I know of such opportunity in the past when we were all alone and could have made love that way. I wouldn't have to put myself in jeopardy with my mother, because my emotion had caused me to spend half the night with you. Why can you tell him that you've changed your mind so we don't have to wait a whole week to be along together?"

"First of all, my darling," Alvin said, "just let me say that you have no idea how wonderful it makes me feel to hear you demand my presence – it assures me that our relationship has bonded more sudden than I had expected it would be. You spoke as if you had a legal right to demand what I do and what I don't do – which you do to a certain point. Besides all that, I want you to tell me how I will fulfill not only the promised I made to buy your house but to keep buying beautiful dresses. Sooner than later you're gonna need your own car. Honey, this sacrifice that I'm making is going to be as advantageous for you as it will be for me. And that is about as far as your authority over me goes in that direction. You, of all people, should know how much I'll miss secretly flirting with you at the opposite side of the counter; the same way we do crossing the parking lot on our way to the storage room. I don't have to tell you what happen, once we enter the building where we try to cram a whole days worth of holding and kissing into five minutes. I'm gonna miss all of the things I just mentioned – but I'll miss much more if I don't take this opportunity to create, more so I can give you more. Isn't that's what a man is suppose to do when he accept responsibility for the woman he loves beyond anyone's imagination? I'd rather not have the liability of having you, if I'm not capable of taking the very best care of my impending spouse."

By the time he had finished his argument, they had just entered the supply house. He reached out to pull her into his arms to kiss her. She pulled away, saying, "The only reason you could walk away and leave me alone to work with some stranger is because you got what you wanted and now you don't care anymore. I feel like I've been betrayed . . . and you never really love me in the first place, did you Alvin?"

"Oh please, Grace, honey, my darling," he said. "Did you not hear a word I said? Surely you know how crazy I am about you, so why are you questioning my credibility after what I just told you?"

"The same reason you didn't ask me before you went and gave the chef your answer. It's not like you can pick me up in your car in broad daylight and ride down the streets together. In our case, nighttime is the only time we can be along together. Even so, it only last fifteen minutes, and we won't even have that much time if you take the morning shift."

"How well do I know that," he said. "I'm trying to make you understand what I'm trying to do is not just so I can move above being a salad maker. My plans are to take every opportunity that's presented to me. Each time I get a new promotion, I get new money. In turn, it brings me one step closer to being a serious contender in the world of business. Think about this – beginning Monday morning, we'll be going from a measly two hundred and twenty dollars to a not-so-measly three- hundred and twenty dollars a month. That's just the beginning of the advancement I plan to accept and share with the girl I'm going to marry as soon as time permits it.

146

Otherwise, the commitment you made lying in my bed Saturday night was no more than a fragment of your imagination. Then again," he added, "I'm not going to criticize you anymore over a little spat such as this, and falter on our plans to succeed in life. Otherwise how could you trust me to deal with a major problem if we can't transcend a small one? All I'm trying to say – if what I've said is contrary to your way of thinking – now is the time to bail out. Or else, you'll soon find out if I'm gonna be responsible for someone that gives me the authority to decide what's best for that person. You'll have your hands full trying to make me do otherwise. So one last thing," he said, "let us show the chef our appreciation by accepting his offer, so I can do the job without worrying my little sweet responsibility into frenzy."

"Mercy me, Alvin," she said, "there're more to life than just to make money. I could never imagine a boy your age with so much determination to succeed in whatever you set you mind to do – which leaves me defenseless. It brings me to the point of asking myself why did I said anything – except to say I'll miss you on the night shift! So now," she added, "do you still want to kiss me?" Instantly he took her into his arms, squeezing half the life out of her: he was so pleased that he had been able to talk her around.

"Will we see each other before you start your new shift?"

"Tonight is as good of a time as ever; all you gotta do is making up a story to tell your mother, without arousing her suspicion that you're gonna be an hour late."

"I didn't mean now, Alvin, you naughty boy." I was thinking about maybe this weekend."

"Absolutely," he said "if we're talking about the same time as last time."

As they came out of the storage room and headed back to the dining room, a few drops of rain began to fall. Grace looked up at the sky and said to Alvin, "Just look at how dark those clouds are. They must be carrying enough water to flood the entire city of Fort Worth. They hadn't got halfway across the parking lot, when it began to thunder and lightning, and it wasn't too long after that it began to rain.

"You see what I told you," she said. "We need to hurry and get inside. Otherwise the paper goods are going to get wet, and we don't want that to happen do we?" They raced across the parking lot, into the storage room in the hotel and began putting the goods away. By the time, they had finished and walked to the back door to peep outside to check on the rain conditions.

When they saw that it had turned somewhat torrential rain, she said to Alvin, "It's raining too hard for me to be standing out there waiting for the bus. I'll go and call J.D. and see if he'll come and drive me home, or unless you want to."

"Now wait a minute," he nervously said. "Isn't that a little too dangerous for us to attempt to do something so juvenile such as riding with a white girl, especially at night?"

"Not really," she said, "but first I'll call Mama and see if J.D. is sober enough to drive in the rain. If not, I'll tell her that you'll be driving me home."

"Well, does your mother know who I am?"

"Oh yes," she said. "I've already told her and J.D. all about you – even my little brother John knows your name."

"I didn't know you had a brother," Alvin said.

"Yes – I think I told you, but you were so busy sniffing my perfume, you probably forgot that part of the conversation. Nevertheless," she said, "he's two years younger than I."

She went to the phone, called her mother, and came back all excited. "Mother said it'll be all right for you to drive me home."

Alvin grudgingly allowed, "If I'm gonna be driving you home, you'll need to go get in the back seat. I'll come a couple of minutes later. Otherwise, if we're seen riding off together, we could create a episode so devastating that the progress that's we've already made would set us back so far that I might as well give up and go find that colored girl you suggested when I first came on to you." She grinned and brushed him off as being a jokester. At that she held a piece of cardboard over her head to protect her head from the rain and raced across the parking lot and sat in the front seat.

Alvin gave the parking area a visual examination, and when he didn't see anyone, he ran to his car, and saw that Grace was sitting in the front seat. "Grace, baby," he said, "you can't sit up front with me. You'll have to ride in the back, while I'll act as if I'm your chauffer – without the black suit and cap."

She chuckled and said, "And don't forget the limousine."

"Go ahead, honey – get in the back seat like I asked you to do."

"I heard you the first time," she said, "and I will, after you park," as she pointed to the dark side of a building over there. He was guessing that the pouring rain had brought out the tigress in her. As soon as he parked, she slid as close to him as she possibly could and began a passionate, and frenzied kissing of him, like the torrential rain that were falling for at least five minutes. Finally she retrieved her tongue and halfheartedly climbed over into the back. Lucky for the both of them, Alvin's instance on her riding in the back was warranted, because as soon as he turned on to the street leading to her house, he saw flashing lights at a distance.

When he drove up to the checkpoint, there were two police officers standing and directing traffic. One of the officers approached his car with a flashlight in hand. He told Alvin, "There is a low spot in the road and the water seems to be rising too fast to try to cross. So you'll need to turn around and find a different route to wherever you're trying go." The cop never shone shown his light in the back seat. Even if he had, he may have had a hard time seeing Grace, being that she sat frozen into the right corner of the back seat.

Alvin turned around and took an alternative route that she suggested that he'd take, to get to her house. He finally drove up to this small trailer in the Polly Tack district where many of the poor whites lived. Grace got out and asked him to wait while she went and talked to her mother's boyfriend, J. D., who was standing outside under an awning and out of the rain. He held a can of beer in one hand and a cigarette in the other hand. Grace raced back to the car still holding the almost soggy piece of cardboard over her head. She opened Alvin's door, "Come on!" she excitedly said. "I want you to meet my mother."

Although Alvin had trusted Grace with his life, he still felt nervous, about following her over to where J.D. stood. Grace said to him, "I want you to meet Alvin, the boy that I've been telling you about."

J.D. put the cigarette in his mouth and extended his hand. "Howdy, Alvin," he said. "I've heard a lot of good things about you, boy." He was a burly man of about middle age, with a shave two or three days old, and a decade or two of old grease embedded in his hands. Curiously, Alvin sensed no hostility from him, only that he was being sized up.

Grace was at her limits with excitement, but she was cautious enough not to let it show in front of her parents. "Come on, Alvin," she said. "I want you to meet my mother."

He followed her into her house where he saw her mother setting on a dilapidated old cushion-seated chair, watching television and drinking a can of beer. "Mama," she said, "I want you to meet Alvin, the boy I told you about everyone likes so well, because he's not hard to get along with, like most of those cooks. Alvin this is my mother, Maggie Adams." Alvin stood with difficulty for a moment looking sheepish; not knowing quite what to say; as if he thought she was about to ask if he had slept with her daughter.

He timidly walked over to her and shook her hand and said, "It's nice meeting you, Miss Adams."

"Yeah," she said, "and thanks for bringing my little girl home, so she didn't have to drown standing out in all of that rain waiting for the bus."

By that time J.D. came back inside. "Are you old enough to have a beer, Alvin?"

"No sir," he said, "I'm not; I'm only eighteen going on nineteen."

"Now," J.D. answered, "don't tell me a boy your age hasn't had a beer before, especially if you're like them truck-driving colored boys I served with in the Army – France, in the big one. That being the case, hell – you've already drunk your share and half of mine too."

"Sir," Alvin said, "if you're asking me if I want a beer the answer is yeah, but by law I'm not old enough."

"All right," J.D. said, "let's cut the horse shit. Do you want a beer or not?"

"I do, but only if I can take it with me," he said as he flashed Grace a quick grin. She averted her face from her parents to hide the sparkle in her eyes, which she knew would be there as soon as she made eye contact with Alvin.

"Hell," J.D. said, "You can have a seat and drink it here if you want to. My daughter has told her mama and me all about you being one of the few decent colored boys that work at that hotel. Let me tell you something about myself, boy. I served with some damn fine colored boys – trust some of 'em better'n' some white folk I know. I got nothing against colored folks, as long as they stay on their side of the tracks." He stared at Alvin momentarily, then added shrewdly, "From the looks of you, it seems that you ain't all colored; there must have been some white-mixing going on in your family. Who do you favor – your mama or your pappy?"

"Most folks tell me it's my father that I take after."

"Well, is he white or just one of those high yellow niggers?"

"My father's father was white," Alvin said. Again he flashed Grace a look, and this time he saw her flushing with embarrassment; Alvin guessed that she felt that J.D. was out of line for mentioning such a distasteful thing, after Alvin went to the trouble to drive his daughter home so he didn't have to. Especially with his level of alcohol consumption which Alvin smelled the instant he opened his mouth to say, "Howdy Alvin."

A few minutes later, a tall boy with dark-brown hair like Graces' came into the living room. Grace said, "Alvin, this is my brother, John." Alvin stood up and shook John's hand and he set back down, trying to think of something intelligent to say.

He finally turned to Maggie and said, "Did Miss Grace tell you that I've gotten myself another promotion?"

"No, not yet," she said, "but she'll eventually get around to telling me. She keeps me pretty well informed about what goes on around that hotel. She's said some very nice things about you too. That's why I thought that it was safe to let you drive her home tonight."

J.D. asked, "What do they pay a boy like you for doing the kind of job you do?"

Alvin answered him, "Three hundred and twenty a month."

"Now that's not bad money for a colored person," he said. "In fact, if you want to know the truth that's pretty darn good for a white person too. What do you have do to make that kind of money"

"I'm a line cook." he answered.

"Well I'm a waitress," Maggie said, "and the line cooks where I work don't make that kind of money. Those people over at the hotel sure must thank highly of you."

"We all do." Grace said, "The waitresses are always telling each other, 'if you make a mistake, tell Alvin and he'll make it his priority so no one gets in trouble with the boss, as well as the customers.'"

Alvin looked over at Maggie and assumed that those three beer cans he saw setting on the coffee table were empty, because she had a full one in one hand and a lit cigarette in her other.

Alvin continued, "The chef and most of the kitchen crew thinks that I'm doing a very good job. Obviously, the same is true with the chef as well, because he just keep moving me toward the top every chance he gets. And that's a plus for me, because I'm not going to settle with just being a line cook. I'm going as far as I can go in mastering the culinary arts, European style – and when I reach that point I plan to have my own restaurant."

J. D. said, "I wouldn't think you'd need European training to cook pig's parts and black-eyed peas with cornbread."

Alvin laughed and said, "You're right – I don't need European training to boil pork and black-eyed peas. But I will, if I'm going to open a restaurant that serves gourmet food."

Alvin was so anxious to see if Grace's idea of beauty was equivalent to what his assessment of beauty was. He tried not to stare too hard, but from what he saw of Maggie, Grace was right; she was a beautiful woman. She had gotten into too much of a desperate hurry when she hooked up with J.D. Otherwise how else could a raggedy assed white-trash beer-drinker like him wind up with a beautiful woman like Maggie?

Once he had exhausted his thoughts about Maggie and J.D. being such a mismatch, he suddenly realized he had overstayed his time. He stood up and turned to Grace and said, "Good night Miss Grace – hopefully I'll see you tomorrow." Then he turned to Maggie, "It was so nice meeting you Mrs. Adams, and you are just as beautiful, if not more, than your daughter described you to me."

She answered in a slurred voice, "It's nice of you to say so."

He said to J. D., "Thanks for the beer, Mr. Granger, and goodnight to you too, John." As Alvin headed for the door, he heard a dull sound

152

coming from J.D. "Why don't you stay long enough to have another beer? I'm beginning to enjoy your company." Alvin didn't answer him.

He got into his car and drove away in the rain and began to analyze every minute he'd spent with Grace that evening. The first thing came to mind was seeing how attractive she was, racing to his car with a piece of cardboard on her head, trying to keep her hair dry in the pouring rain. Somehow she managed to do just that. He went on to recalling the adoring look in her eyes when she coaxed him to park behind the building, in order to express her love with tender kisses. He remembered seeing her gorgeous face in the rearview mirror and how her eyes sparkled each time they made eye contact, followed by her beautiful smile. The sadness of it all was when he mulled about how dreadful he felt when he saw her standing motionless with the alarmed look on her face when he walked out the door.

It was obvious that every fiber in her heart wanted to cry out in defiance against her parents. But she couldn't. She knew if she followed her desire to walk him to his car and kiss him goodnight, it certainly would've been in opposition with her parents' beliefs. How wonderful it would've been if he could've told her mother that he was in love with her daughter without some sarcastic threats, followed by a barrage of racist remarks. If the opposite were the case, he would've told her mother that she was losing her daughter, only to gain a tried and proven, true son-in-law, but one whose affection for her daughter would never cease, till time indefinite.

He finally drove into his driveway, turned off the engine, and sat there with his mind still on Grace. The one thing that he dwelled on while sitting in his car was the loving look he saw in her eyes when she introduced him to her family. However he detected just the opposite when he said "goodnight." He saw a devoted girl, weighted with a damp spirit, just waiting for a time where she could openly announce to her parents that she had a steadfast relationship with the boy who drove her home one rainy night. In view of the fact that her feeling for him was steadfast, along with her assertive way of questioning his reasoning for changing his shift from evening to morning without consulting her – that was a good indication that his worry about keeping her inspired until school was out – wasn't warranted anymore. Now he was having second thoughts about quitting his job and moving out of state, just for the sake of keeping her committed. But even that wasn't a priority anymore either. That being the case, he was able to discard those negative thoughts, and concentrate on work; at the rate in which he was climbing the ladder working for the hotel, and realizing more money each time they moved him up, he figured it would be to his best interest to stay in Texas. Not for that reason only, but because Grace's lack of enthusiasm wasn't a concern of his anymore.

He got out of his car and hurried in out of the rain and changed his specific thoughts about her, to his experience of meeting her family. Other than Grace's lack of independence to walk him to his car and kiss him goodnight, as well as J.D.'s sharp eyes and their living conditions being a mess, he felt that it wasn't that bad at all . . . provided one could overlook the old, wide-opened toolbox with tools scattered about on the living room floor, the clods of mud on J.D.'s boots – some of which had dried and scattered down the hallway. The place was messy, but everybody seemed to be contented living in a cluttered-up house. At the same time, he felt confident that Grace would be much better off being married to him. Besides, he couldn't wait until tomorrow to tell her so.

Chapter 6 – The Letter

Mid-morning the following day, Alvin walked across the back yard to where Mrs. Nichols was sitting in her rocker, to tell her that he had gotten another promotion.

He asked, "Would you be willing to let me start coming to you in the evening again, instead of the mornings?"

"Of course," she answered, and congratulated him on his advancement in the world. He finally got around to asking her about Miss Cassie, and if she had heard from her lately.

"Yes," Mrs. Nichols told him. "I got a letter from her on Saturday, I believe. She asked about how you were coming along with your schooling."

"Mrs. Nichols, "the next time you write to Miss Cassie, tell her that I said 'hi' and I'm still trying to get to the point where I'm not missing her as much'"

For an assignment that morning, Mrs. Nichols first assigned him several mathematical problems, which he spent an hour solving. Next, she handed him a newspaper and pointed out an article to read for a report to be turned in by Friday. With four days left to turn in his book report, he turned to reading and gathering information for that assignment. He studied hard for an hour or so – until the thoughts of Grace came to mind and cost him his concentration, which slowed him down a bit. By the time he regained his focus, it was almost two o'clock, and he felt that he had done enough research for one day anyway; time to do something even more constructive, like preparing for eight hours of work, to earn him food and shelter. He got dressed and drove to work. Before he changed into his uniform, he walked around the corner to the dining room just so he could get a glimpse of his Miss Grace. As usual, she seemed to always be at the far side of the room. As she wove her way in and around tables, preparing them for the evening meal, Alvin dawdled, waiting for her to finally work her way to the counter.

She raised her eyes to him with a smile on her face that couldn't be wiped off with a scrub brush. All of, which activate every part of his being, which wanted to just reach out and lick every trace of lipstick right off her tender, ruby-red lips.

As soon as the dinner rush was over, he summoned Grace to wait for him by the back door. He would meet her there, once he brought out the cart they used to pick up and haul supplies back to the hotel. She must've been thinking the same thoughts as he had been thinking all day; the instant they headed out across the parking lot, the first thing she told him was how remorseful she felt that she couldn't walk him to his car last night and kiss him goodbye – just one of other things she regretted not doing. He told her his plan; how they should continue their routine until she was out of school, go to California only to get married, and return to Texas to live as man and wife in seclusion. Hearing him say that they'd be staying in Texas, had her feeling so gratified; the only thing that kept her from announcing her last name as Mrs. Jackson was a marriage license. The following evening she drove to his apartment with such exuberance.

Even as she extended her hand to him in order that he could escort her to the divan, they were diverted, using the divan to pile their clothes, impulsively undressing each other, right down to their bare skin. Unlike the first time when he was so panicky that he didn't remember what she looked like without her clothes, this time he looked while he undressed her. He stroked here gently, all over, including her thighs and the little triangle of curly hair where they came together. That led him to her reason for being at his apartment in the first place – several times, without a brief intermission, and were about to go for a third, until Grace noticed what time it was.

"I've overstayed my time, honey. I have to hurry . . . get dressed and be on my way home . . . and I may have to think of a different excuse to tell Mama, just in case I have to." She began rushing around picking up her clothes in different places, and putting them on. She found her shoes, and with them in her hands, she kissed Alvin, saying, "I'll see you on Monday, honey."

"Wait." he said. "Don't you want me to walk you to your car?"

"No," she said, "I'll be just fine."

"Meanwhile," Alvin said, "I'll go and jump in the shower. You be careful going home. I love you, honey."

Grace sat on the divan to tie her shoes, and something crinkled, as she did so: an envelope, an opened letter, stuffed between the cushions. With idle curiosity, she pulled it from between the cushions – it was addressed to Alvin Jackson, and it looked like a woman's handwriting. Grace had already begun thinking of herself as Mrs. Jackson – who was this woman, writing to her husband, and what business did she have . . . Grace opened the letter, and began to read. The first few lines were enough.

"Alvin!" Grace screamed, as she began to cry. She was nearly incoherent. "What have you done to me, Alvin? Alvin, you've lied to me!"

Hearing only Grace's hysterical screams, Alvin ran out of the shower stark-naked, in a state of panic, water and soap-suds running off his body. He instantly feared that some white person had found out about them, and was there to kill them both.

He rushed into the living room shouting, "What is the matter, honey?"

She threw the wadded-up letter at him. Alvin was aghast with horror. He knew instantly what had caused Grace to cry out that way.

He picked it up, smoothing out the folds, pleading, "Oh my Lord – Grace, honey – please let me explain to you. It's not what you think. She wasn't my girl friend!"

Grace cried, "Stay away from me! Liar! I don't ever want to see you again! You lied to me Alvin! You lied to me! Tears rolled down her face; she jerked the door open, letting it bang back against the wall, as she left, still repeating furiously, "You tricked me Alvin!"

Alvin ran after her, as naked as a catfish without fins, begging "Please! Grace, honey – just let me explain!" He did not go very far; with Grace making so much noise, he was afraid the neighbors might hear her, call the police, and get himself hauled off to jail . . . or something even worse. He decided that he'd wait until Monday night, when they were going to the supply house to explain to her about the letter. His imagination suddenly began to terrify him; what if the noise Grace made had awakened Mrs. Nichols, or other neighbors? What if someone had called the police? He'd be out of his apartment and into a smaller one, a single room with bars on the door.

"More than ever," he thought, "if they saw a naked colored man chasing after a screaming white woman, they'd accuse him of rape, for sure." With that fear, he scrambled into his clothes and left the apartment as quickly as he could. He drove over to John Lee's house and parked out front, thinking, "Even if Mrs. Nichols or her neighbors did call the police – they wouldn't know where to come to find him." Coming to that conclusion, he lay back in the driver's seat, to relax and try to sleep, but his sleep never came. He tossed about until around six that morning.

Still worried, he drove back to his house, intently watching the back of Mrs. Nichols' house, until he entered his own apartment. He was afraid Mrs. Nichols would be waiting to tell him that he had to leave, without giving him a chance to explain himself. He waited a while, before realizing that if she planned to throw him out, she would've done it by now. He relaxed, to some degree, until he began to think about how he had been put into a no-win situation, with regard to Grace. The thought of losing Grace forever brought him to tears. The more he thought about his ordeal, the less control he had over his emotions.

Someone knocked on his door. He quickly came to his feet, hoping that it might be Grace – she had come back to tell him that she was wrong for running away before he explained, and that she wanted to continue their relationship. He found himself scrambling for something to dry his tears, and to straighten his face before he answered the door. It was not Grace – he was face-to-face with his landlady. His voice quavered as he invited her to come inside.

Mrs. Nichols opened the screen door and saw him crying. "Boy, you look a mess!" She observed. "What happened with you last night? You and that gal were making a lot of noise around here – so much so that I was afraid she'd alarm the neighbors and get us all thrown out of this community. I suppose you lost another girl friend, did you now?"

Alvin just made a pure fool out of himself, even to the point of losing control of his emotions. He finally managed to answer, "Yes ma'am. I think I've lost her for good."

"You know, I told you when you first moved in here, I didn't want a lot of loud noises. I'm an old woman – I need my rest, and not being awakened in the middle of the night by a bunch of noisy people. On top of it all, she was a white gal. Don't you think you are getting a little too big for your britches? Boy, you are wading in deep water now. I think you had better get back to sticking with your own kind and leave them white gals alone. They could cause you a heap of trouble in more ways than one."

Alvin was still trying to talk without crying. He answered, "I know that, Mrs. Nichols, but please won't you bear with me, for a while longer? Our plan was that when Grace graduated from high school, we would go to California and get married, and that's only six weeks from now." He had collapsed onto his knees, holding his face in his hands.

Mrs. Nichols' voice softened. She patted his shoulder, observing with gentle pity, "Love is nice when the both of you are in agreement, but it's a mighty worrisome thing when you've lost control of it. Now, tell me what made her run out on you the way she did."

"It was a letter that I got from a woman that I used to know. After I read it, I forgot to destroy it, and it somehow worked its way between the cushions on the divan . . . where Grace found it. She read enough . . . and that's why she ran away from me."

"So" Mrs. Nichols answered, "Grace is her name . . . I'm assuming she did all of the screaming and yelling last night?"

Alvin nodded, "Yes."

"Well," Mrs. Nichols observed, "I suppose if she didn't care for you, the letter wouldn't make any difference to her, now would it?" She added, "May I ask – who wrote you the letter."

"I'm sorry; Mrs. Nichols," he answered, "but I can't tell you that."

"No," she said "and I didn't think you could either." She asked "Where did you meet this girl? At work, I suppose?"

"Yes ma'am," he said, "but please don't tell your son anything about what happened here last night – we might be fired. We need to work and add to the money that we've already saved for our trip to California. We have plans to make a new start there."

"Do you think you can get her back after the way you broke her heart last night?" Mrs. Nichols asked.

"I don't know, Mrs. Nichols," Alvin answered, incoherently, tears still running down his face. "But I'm going to try . . . this coming Monday night. That's when we go for supplies from the storage house. I'll try with all of my heart to get her to talk to me again."

"Aren't there enough colored gals you could've chosen from, rather than to get yourself mixed up with a white girl that you can't even take to see a movie? This is a terrible mess you've gotten yourself into, Alvin ... do her folks know about your involvement with her?"

"No, ma'am," he answered.

"Well," Mrs. Nichols continued, "if you're sure this is what you wonna do, and you think you can get her back, she's welcome to stay her with you. Once her folks find out about the two of you, she won't be welcome at home anymore. She'll have no other choice but to live here with you ... unless she's got some responsible friend whose place she could live. Otherwise she's too young to be left to live on her own."

Mrs. Nichols went on to say, "That gal of yours, did you tell her who wrote you the letter?"

"No ma'am," " he said.

"Well, if you're counting on getting her back and let her stay here with you for any length of time, you shouldn't tell her. My daughter will be coming home every year after school is out, and you wouldn't want to make any more trouble for that little gal of yours than you already have," Mrs. Nichols answered, calmly. Alvin wiped his eyes, and looked at her in shock, wondering if he had heard her right. "And don't give me that surprised look. I knew my daughter was having an affair with you." Mrs. Nichols continued. "But it didn't bother me none, she's a woman and you're a man, and as far as I'm concern she got what she wanted and I suppose you got what you wanted. If the both of you were happy about it, then it shouldn't be anybody else's business but the two of you. Those silly discriminatory laws should be done away with. Then those that don't like it, you can tell them to mind their own business and leave people along to marry whoever they please. Now you and that gal are going to be all right, staying right here in Fort Worth. I have a feeling that this racial things is fixing to change."

"You see that house over yonder with the tall fence around it? You ought to think about saving up your money, and buying it for you and that gal. That is – if you're serious about keeping her. I'll take a loss and let you have it for three thousand. Give me three hundred down, and I'll carry the

160

note myself. You're good boy Alvin. I like you, my son likes you, and my daughter is moderately in love with you – you've got my whole family behind you!" Mrs. Nichols patted his shoulder again – and Alvin felt as if she had lifted the weight of half the world off his shoulders. All was left was for Grace to lift her half off, and put some normality back into his life. He wanted to hug Mrs. Nichols, but he decided against that. In spite of her words, he didn't know how a proper lady like Mrs. Nichols would take to having a colored boy wrapping his arms around her in gratitude. So he just thanked her and got into his car and drove to a small cafe and had lunch.

Then he drove slowly by Grace's house, hoping to catch a glimpse of her standing at a window or walking around outside. He circled her house a few times, wishing he could magically turn white just long enough to get Grace by her beautiful hair and drag her outside, so he could tell her how much he loved her. He didn't see her; disappointed, he drove back to the apartment. The letter that Grace had found was still lying in the middle of the floor. Alvin picked it up, smoothing out the crumpled paper, the pages scribbled over with Miss Cassie's handwriting.

"Dear Alvin, I'm writing to you to tell you the things now that I wanted to tell you while I was with you, but couldn't because our time together was so limited. After I left your apartment that last night I spent with you, I walked back to mother's house. I decided not to lie in that cold bed after leaving your warm, almost hot, body. Instead, I sat up the rest of the night, bawling my eyes out. At first, I couldn't find any reason for doing that. Sitting alone in the dark, I began to think rationally. I realized you had filled a vacancy in my heart with merriment, which you gave so freely; the tears I cried were tears of joy, not sorrow. I believe your feelings for me were genuinely ecstatic and I loved every minute of the way you spent proving it to me. In turn, I gave it all I had to keep you in that state of mind the only way I knew how – which was to let you continue take delight in what I had to offer. I even went so far as to imagine how wonderful it would've been if you and I could've gone to some nice restaurant for dinner, where the lights were dim and the waiter was serving us imported champagne. I imagined that we were sitting across the table from each other, staring into each others eyes with intense love, after each sip of fine champagne. When I come back to reality, it's such a huge letdown! I become depressed and I cry sometimes. I have been wishing for the first time, that my skin was black, or yours were white. I have seen many Negro men, even good-looking ones – and never thought twice about a relationship with those men. I guess, after meeting you, I remember the saying, "to know him is to love him." Whether or not I see you again, I hope that you will have met a nice girl your own age, and give your all to her like you gave to me. And if in return she does likewise, then I know you will have a lasting relationship. I know how much my mother loves you, so feel free to go by and say 'hi' to her, she would really like that. Alvin, you must destroy this letter the moment you finish reading it!

Love always

Your Miss Cassie!"

He threw the letter on the floor and stomped it. Then he picked it up, tore it into tiny little pieces, cursing himself for being so stupid as to leave it lying around when he knew good and well that Grace would be spending a lot of time there. 'Furthermore,' he thought, 'what could Miss Cassie have benefited from, in writing such stupid letter anyway? The last thing she told me before she left was that there wasn't no future for her and me.'

He grieved until he fell asleep, getting up early enough on Monday morning to go to work, so that he would be there in enough time to get himself set up. At the hotel he situated himself so he wouldn't be such a burden to his co-workers – especially on his first day in his new position. When the rush started, the experienced cooks took the lead in doing the heavy cooking, while Alvin watched and ran errands for the veteran cooks. They'd let him flip a few eggs every once in a while; mostly Alvin kept the lines stocked. When all was said and done, Alvin quickly found out that cooks also – like everyone else – liked working with him.

At two o'clock, Alvin had cleaned his station and went to the pantry, killing time talking to Toby, while he waited in hopes of giving Grace a sign when she showed up for her shift. He didn't want to seem too obvious standing around, so he talked with Toby for about thirty minutes. Grace didn't show up. Alvin left for ten minutes and came back to see if she had come in, but when she didn't, he became worried. There was no reason to remain at work. He drove home, grieving over the thought that he may never see her again. He sat around half-heartedly until late; until he finally fell asleep. The next day was pretty much the same.

After the third evening and she still didn't show up for her shift in the dining room, Alvin began feeling depressed and sorry for himself. He bought himself a bottle of vodka and a large Seven-Up at the liquor store. At home, he mixed himself a potent drink, which sent him that much further into depression. Around nine that evening, Alvin decided that three days of dejection was enough for anyone to bear. He was to the point where he either had to stop procrastinating and go after her – that or find himself another consenting white girl, and let bygones be bygones as far as Grace was concerned. Except he wasn't ready to let this disruption with Grace be his deciding factor. No, this was temporary, he decided. emboldened, Alvin told himself, 'She doesn't have the authority to arbitrarily end a relationship. Not when there is more than one person involved.' The more he thought about the declaration she made the first night she came to his apartment, the more he wondered if she might breach those vows by involving herself with some boy, just to get back at him. His own survival could be jeopardized, in going after her. He weighed the options carefully. If he chose to go after her and prove his love, he also feared she wouldn't come back. Possibly he would lose her forever. No, an asset such as Grace was too valuable, to dear to him – well worth a gamble, rather than to lose with no recourse. 'The only thing left for me to do is go to her house and make her tell me to my face that she really meant what she said when she told me she didn't want to ever see me again.'

He drove over to Grace's house, and apprehensively knocked on the front door. J. D. answered the knock, asking, "What are you doing here this time of night, Alvin?"

Hesitantly he answered. "I need to talk to Misses Grace."

"Talk to Miss Grace about what?" J.D. answered, with a look of suspicion on his face.

By that time, Grace also came to the door. Right away he could see the uncertain look in her eyes – mostly fear, but excited nonetheless that he had cared enough to risk coming for her.

"Alvin!" she spoke with nervous force. "What are you doing here? I told you I didn't want to ever see you again."

"What in the hell is going on around here?" J.D. looked from one to another, suspicion hardening.

In a deliberately casual tone of voice, Alvin repeated, "I need to talk to Miss Grace, please."

"Oooh shit!" J. D exclaimed, "Maggie you better get out here! I think there're something going on between our little girl and this here nigger boy, Alvin!"

"Mr. Granger," Alvin said patiently, "I'm sorry I don't mean to bother anyone, but when I didn't see Grace at work for three days, I became afraid that I wasn't gonna ever see her again." He turned towards Grace, pleading, "Please – won't you just listen to me, so I can explain to you that I'm innocent?"

"I told you I never want to talk to you again! Leave me and my family alone!"

Maggie emerged from an inner room, demanding, "What in the hell are you doing here, boy – meddling with my daughter?" She rounded on her daughter. "Grace! Have you been sleeping around with that sorry nigger?" Grace, cornered, looked from Alvin, to J.D., and then to her mother – it was obvious to Alvin that she feared her mother the most.

"Never!" Grace insisted, on a voice of rising panic, and Maggie shouted fearlessly,

"Then get out of here and leave us alone! Get your black ass out of here right now! J. D, you pick up that tire iron by the toolbox and cold-cock that nigger with it!"

By the time J. D. had picked up the tire iron and drew it back, Alvin dropped to his knees begging, "Mr. J. D., please don't do this. All I want y'all to do is to allow me a few minutes to talk to Grace."

"Get out of here nigger, before I break this tire iron over your damn head! Don't make me be responsible for having a dead nigger bleeding all over my living room floor!" Although J.D. was making as if he wanted to obey Maggie about hitting him with the tire iron, Alvin saw something in the uncertainty in J.D.'s eyes that made him doubt that J.D. really wanted to hit him. Was he putting on airs to impress Maggie? And Grace wasn't his biological daughter. In the midst of his crying and begging, he constantly keep an eye on the tire iron in J. D's hand, and was ready to defend himself from it, in an instant if need be. But Maggie still sounded hysterical – a mother lion, defending her cub.

Now she was demanding of her daughter, "Why, Grace? Tell me – why is he here if you haven't slept with him? Are you afraid to tell me that you got yourself hooked up with some no-good god-damn sorry nigger! You got so much going for you!" Grace didn't answer, and Maggie turned her fury back on her common-law husband. "I told you to get that nigger out of here! Use that tire iron you have in your hand!"

"Mrs. Maggie," Alvin said with both hands extended, still on his knees, "this don't have to come to this – if y'all will allow me the few minutes I've already ask for, and I'll be on my way. Please, Mrs. Maggie!"

Grace looked between them, her lip beginning to quiver. "Stop it mama!" She whispered, but Maggie paid her no attention. "Get that nigger out of my house! Give me that tire iron, J. D.," she screamed, like a mad person. "And I'll show you what to do with it. John!" she yelled to Grace's brother. "Call the police and tell them they're fixing to have a dead nigger on their hands. I'm cracking me a got damn nigger's head wide open!"

"G'wan," J.D. added, in a slightly lower voice, "She ain't gonna calm down, lessn' you leave now, boy."

Grace repeated herself, only this time louder, confidence and decision growing in her voice. "I said stop it, Mama! Please stop it!" In a quieter voice, she commanded her brother, "Hang up the phone, John," as she hugged her mother's waist, her head pressed against Mrs. Maggie's chest. The tears were rolling down her face, and she spoke between sobs. "Mama," Grace pleaded, "Alvin is here to take me home with him, because he's in love with me, and I'm in love with him, too. Alvin, honey," she added, "I'm sorry for the trouble that I've caused, but I'll go home with you . . . okay, honey?"

"Oh my Lord," Maggie cried. "John! Come over here and talk to your sister. I think she done gone and fell in love with a no-good-for-nothing got damn nigger! She has just disgraced her folks! How could you do this to your family?"

Grace continued to cling to her mother's waist, crying, "I'm sorry I lied, Mama!" John came and tried to help his mother to pull free from Grace. Meanwhile J.D. scowled, still gripping the tire iron. Grace abruptly loosed her hold on her mother, and scrambled to stand between Alvin and her stepfather. "Stop it J.D.!" she screamed, furiously, "Tell him to stop it, Mama! I said stop it! Put that iron down J.D.!" She dropped to her knees next to Alvin, leaned against him and begged him, in her normal voice, "Stand up, Alvin!"

Alvin answered in a shaking voice, "Grace, honey, I'm sorry to tell you this, but you can't get away with yelling at your mother in that tone of voice. You'll need to fully apologize to her, especially if you expect our plans we made for the future to materialize." Silence fell, as he stood, helping Grace, as they clung together. "Please, Miss Grace," he said, "all I'm asking of you is that you come with me, and let me talk to you. If after you've heard my side of the story, and you still don't like my explanation, I promise I'll bring you back home and leave you alone, once and for always . . . even to the point of never speaking to you again if that's what you want me to do."

Maggie, with John's arm around her shoulders, began to cry. "Let her go, J. D." she sobbed.

J.D. scowled. "Maggie, I don't wanna let our girl run off with some no-good nigger that's gonna turn her into some kind of white trash – can't you talk some sense into her?"

"I said, 'let her go!'" Maggie answered. She drew Grace away from Alvin, taking her in her own arms. "Grace, honey . . . you done gone and broke your mother's heart. I never expected anything like this from you. Honey, I thought I knew you better than that."

Alvin anxiously reached out and took Maggie's hand, and speaking through his own tears, "I'm sorry for the trouble I've caused y'all. If there had been any other way around this mess that I've just made, I would've taken it. Except there wasn't – I did the only thing I knew to do to keep my heart from breaking – and that was to come and bring her home with me, where she belongs."

"Yeah, but –" J. D protested, but Alvin noticed that he had lowered the tire iron.

Alvin answered, "Please – I have something else to say, if you'll allow me. In spite of my unintended incivility, I want you to know what I did was out of desperation. Otherwise I wouldn't have had the nerves to come unannounced, and cause a ruckus in your private home, like I just did. I also want y'all to believe me when I tell you whether she accepts my explanation or she rejects it – I promise you whatever her decision is, I'll support her in it. If her answer is 'no,' I'll immediately bring her back to you, as safe as she is right this minute. On the other hand, if she accepts my explanations, I promise you I'll take the very best care of her. Love covers

166

over a multitude of imperfections . . . I'm a beginner in the realm of matrimony but I'm promising to strive to do my very best."

Grace cleared her throat, sniffed, and said downheartedly, "I'm sorry too, Mama . . . I feel responsible for things turning out the way it did. I refused to stay and listen to Alvin explain to me what really happened . . . our plans would've remain a secret until after my graduation."

Alvin took Grace's hand to leave, just as J.D. added, in a low warning growl, "Don't be surprised nigger, when someone takes a gun and blows your goddamn head off for fooling around with a nice white girl, when you got all of those nigger whores out there to choose from!"

Alvin and Grace ignored this; they left the house in silence, and went to Alvin's car. He had her ride in the back as she had done before, as he drove home. Still shaky from the encounter with Grace's mother and stepfather, they huddled together on the divan, embracing each other for comfort and reassurance. Finally, Alvin ventured, "Grace, Honey, I feel really bad about what I put you and your family through tonight. Believe me when I tell you – I did what I did out of love and desperation; three miserable days and nights I spent waiting to hear from you. I was afraid you would do the very thing that we agreed not to do, apart from each other. Finally, I didn't care one way or another; if I would be in danger for coming after you . . . I couldn't bear to think I might never see you again. Now that I've succeeded in rescuing you out of the hands of a potential stranger, and into a life of temporally immorality, I want you to know that I had no intention of living with you before we were married. If you decide to stay with me – and if I'm right, then it has to bean affirmation – we have to consider this night to be our wedding night. We may not have a certificate that says it's legal, but you're definitely my wife. I also want you to believe me when I tell you that the official document will be provided as soon as time permits. Until then, I sure do hope you're in agreement with me. I don't want you to feel as if you're being used. At this point we have no other choice but to live together, unless you can think of something else. Please tell me now before I start up my engine with no place to go. And you gotta promise, Grace, honey – don't go back to your mama and stepfather, and make me repeat what I just did!"

She answered, her voice still sounding uncertain, "I want to be wherever you are, go where ever you go, and that should be enough assurance that this night doesn't repeat itself."

"I'm glad you said that," Alvin sounded relieved. "Because this is one time I would've lied to you if your answer had been different. I wasn't about to let you go anywhere without me. After all I went through to get you away from your parents, then turn around and send you back again? Not on your life, baby."

"And I'm glad you said what you said too." Grace giggled. "I would've been disappointed if you allowed me to go anyplace other than to the bedroom –which is as much mine now, as it is yours."

"Now," he promised solemnly, "I want to make it up to you and your family by trying my best to get y'all back together as soon as possible. Until that time, I'll be here to help anyway I can. All you gotta do is ask. With all of what has been said, and all the promises I swore I'd keep, I'm in hope that you'll continue to hold me accountable for them, and not derail our plans, when I finish explaining to you what really happened."

"Oh, please honey," Grace answered, "don't tell me anything I don't want to know. Anyway, you've more than proved to me tonight how much you love me and nothing else matters. I'm sure you wouldn't have done what you did tonight if you didn't love me more than yourself, or anyone else that I don't care to hear about. It wasn't the act that made me run away, I suddenly thought you were deceiving me, that I shouldn't trust you. I was so convinced that I had gotten myself snared by a deceiving, silver-tongued devil. I figured since I was young and naïve that you had picked me out as one of your harem of women. I don't feel that way about you anymore, after what you did tonight on my behalf, as well for your benefit." She smiled as she caught his hands in hers, "On one hand, I am so happy to know that I'll be sleeping in our bed the whole night through. And on the other hand I'm sad about the way in which I arrived in our little patch of utopia. Anyhow, I don't have to worry about getting up going home to Mother, prepared to lie the moment I walk through the door. That first night, I wanted so badly to stay and spend the entire night lying next to you. It would've been so much fun – just holding, kissing, and loving each other until we tired ourselves out. Then I imagined we'd drifted off to sleep and wake up in the middle of the night, and the next morning and start all over again." Grace's eyes brimmed again with tears. "I'm just so sorry about hurting Mama . . . somehow I'm going to make it up to her, because my Mama and I are close. She didn't mean what she said to hurt me when she used the kind of language. She only used it to try to get her point across to you. I'm sure you can imagine someone coming out of nowhere to take your teenage daughter away – and the sudden shock to your system would cause any parent to react the way she did. Once you get to know her, you'll see that my Mama is a good woman that doesn't normally act the mad person that she did tonight."

"I definitely understand your parents not wanting you to go off with me," Alvin replied, sympathetically. "Because they don't know me the way you do – if they did, they would've had you all dressed up and waiting for me to take you home when I got there, instead of calling me those bad names. Apart from that –t hey will know me, and they'll know me in a good way once they know how well I'm providing for you. Maybe though – you shouldn't be too eager to contact her, not anyway soon, and even at that it should only be by phone, just enough to let her know you're still alive and kicking. Then, next week call her and say the same thing. She'll get use to hearing you say how contented you are. Maybe then she'll stop feeling so hurt, and we can invite her over, so we can all began to reconcile some of our differences."

"Boy, Alvin," she sighed, "I sure do hope so, because living without visiting with my family is gonna be very hard for all of us. I know one thing that's going to make Mama unhappy, and that's if I drop out of school. That's going to really make her feel bad, knowing that I want be getting my high school diploma this year."

"Why do you think that you won't graduate this year?" he asked. "Honey, all you got to do is take the car. Drive yourself to school, and I'll take the bus to work every day until you're out of school. You only have six more weeks of working and going to school. Six weeks is a small sacrifice for a high school diploma! I wish I was getting my high school diploma in six weeks under the same circumstances."

Grace's face lit up. "Boy, you're trying to tell me that you're willing to give up your car and ride the bus just so I can get my diploma? That is the sweetest thing I think I've ever heard you say to me. I had already accepted that I wouldn't be graduating this year."

"Honey," he answered, "haven't you realized yet that we're in this thing together; as man and wife? That's what I was trying to explain, when I told you we must consider this night as our wedding night. We are no longer one individual, but are two personalities that has become one, in union with each other. Whatever affects you, affects me also. For you to have to ride a bus with the kind of schedule you have would affect me in the worst way. A man should always be willing to give his wife the benefit of the doubt under all circumstances. Tonight, you've earned that right. Why? When you decided to leave your family and come with me, all of those things went into effect. And that reduced my ownership in the car to half-ownership in the car. Everything else I have interest in has been reduced to half. You see, honey – it all boils down to one thing – and that is we're in this mess together, split right down the middle."

Grace answered, "I'm not surprised that you would do such thing as giving me the use of the car, just to make life easier for me. You've just validated what I've suspected you'd be to live with, the minute I made up my mind to come back to you, after these last two weeks! Now, I won't have to worry about telling Mama I had to drop out of school. But even with me driving the car," she added, "it'll still be eleven o'clock before I get to see you again. But the main thing is, I'll be getting my high school diploma and spending my nights sleeping in our bed!"

"One other thing you should know," Alvin said, seriously. "You're my responsibility, now, and my job is to provide for you. Let me support you, until you feel up to going back to work again – it would be careless of me, if I didn't at least let you know how worried I am about you going off to school, and then to work, when you are still upset form all this that you just went through."

Grace smiled, "I can't help seeing how persuasive you are, when you're explaining your ideas to me. You just said 'we're in this mess together,' and so far I love the mess I'm in. If I didn't, then everything we endured this night would be all for nothing. We wouldn't be fair to ourselves, if we didn't do something spectacular to impress those who would speak ill of our association. Alvin, honey – I have no other choice but to keep working and help you to succeed at whatever project you come up with."

"Well in that case," Alvin said, with a touch of relief, "That way, we can keep to the course that I've mapped out for us – and I can buy all those things that I had promised buy for you. One thing in particular, though – amongst other pledges I've made and intend to keep – we'll need to start making plans to buy a house for our own selves, that's big enough to hold all those things – and furniture too, with as many rooms in it that your

Mama and family can come and visit overnight . . . Provided that they are forgiving enough to set aside their anger and extend the family to one that would include me. What would you think about us owning our own home?"

"It sounds wonderful, Alvin," she answered. "But that will take awhile, even if we start saving our money right now. As much as I know about things like that, I'm guessing it'll take us about six months from now before we should have enough for a down payment. I think that's the way they do it. Am I right?"

"In some cases, yes," he said, "but not in ours, because tomorrow I'm going to show you something that's gonna take your breath away."

"Having my breath taken away," she said, "shouldn't be that much of a problem—after all I've had enough practice in the last two hours to be dead right along by now." After that, she was quite for a minute, and then she said, "I'm so happy to be sitting next to you, knowing the only curfew that'll be imposed on me, will be done by you. That makes it obvious that I've accepted the fact that I am a married woman, Alvin . . . with the freedom to do whatever married women does that pleases her husband."

Alvin picked her up, and carried her to the bedroom, where he laid her on the bed, and stood looking down on her with his heart full of passion. He said, "Miss Grace, I hope I'm not out of line for asking you this – especially with me knowing how hectic your night had been. If you're not in the mood for my idea, just tell me and I'll understand."

"Now, Alvin" she answered, "if you're thinking what I think you're thinking, I'd say don't be so ceremonial about your desires because I'm your wife. I don't have any clothes on and either do you – and I am assuming that we're sleeping in the same bed tonight. So of course you're out of line, but not for very long, once you tell me where you keep our condoms – unless you want to start a family on our first night together."

"First night together?" He asked.

"Yes." Grace answered, firmly. "Those other two nights don't count – they were only a test of your sincerity. Tonight, my darling, your honor was proven to me, when you came to rescued me from a dire situation such as I was in." They loved each other just the once, that night; there was no reason to cram one week's worth of love into a single evening, the way they had done before, not when they had the rest of time for each other. And too,

Alvin and Grace were exhausted, over what had taken place, and the discussion about what would come next for them both. And yet one more reason for withholding enthusiasm on their makeshift wedding night – that they both had to be at work the next day.

Even so, he still had to stay awake and listen to her talking for at least an hour about how glad she was that he loved her enough to come and bring her home with him. She talked about other things until she noticed that her lively conversation with her subject had begun to elicit blurred answers: it wasn't until then that she finally realized not only had she exhausted his virility, while jointly allied with him, but her parent's combative attitude had added their lot to his being dog-eared tired as well. She tenderly kissed his lips and rolled off him before she drifted off to sleep. This time when they finally fell asleep, they stayed that way until the clock went off.

He got dressed, came back silently to the bed, giving her a long kiss goodbye, and left her lying in bed as he walked out to the bus stop in time to catch the bus to work. Once he climbed aboard, he headed to the back of the bus, selecting a seat in an empty area, which meant he rode alone, and began to think how pleased he was that he had accomplished the two most important things in his life. The first was his job that he was so happy to have. And the second – his mission came to its completion when Grace agreed to live with him permanently.

All of which just goes to show what a little faith will do in a devoted situation. From the time he woke up, realizing that Grace was actually lying there next to him – and wasn't his imagination – his happy mood never departed him. It lasted throughout his entire eight-hour shift, and even longer – for the instant he finished his shift, he walked over to his old station where Grace normally began her day. He saw her out in the dining room, talking with one of the other waitresses.

He waved at her with both hands until he got her attention. Having gained it, she walked towards him with a beaming face. "How do you like your new job Alvin?" She asked, in a cheerful voice.

"Just fine," he said. "I'm looking forward to mastering it just as I've mastered all of the other ones. I guess I had better be moving toward home."

"I'll see you soon," she said, followed by a dazzling smile.

On his way home he stopped by one of the bank branches and picked up a form for Grace to fill out, so that her name might appear on the checking account. When he got home and he went to talk to Mrs. Nichols about the house, the first thing out of her mouth was, "I take it you got your girl friend back?"

"Yes ma'am," he said, with a big grin on his face. "I got her back! From now on, everything is going to be all right."

Mrs. Nichols said, "Well, did you come to talk about purchasing the house? Or would you rather wait until you're able to afford it?"

"Oh, no, ma'am," he said, I'm as ready as I'll ever be." He pulled out his checkbook, and started to write out a check.

"Don't you want to see it first?" she asked.

"I trust you, Mrs. Nichols," he said.

"Well, what about that girlfriend of yours? I'm sure she'll want to see it before you go to the trouble of writing out a check, just in case she doesn't like it."

He handed her the check, saying, "She'll like it. I know her pretty well by now."

"Tell her that she won't have to buy any furniture anytime soon. The old lady that rented that place from me died, and left the house full of furniture. No one has come to claim it. Until they do, it belongs to her."

Mrs. Nichols went back into the house and brought out a key and handed it to him and said, "I'll get these papers drawn up as soon as possible so you and that little gal of your can sign them. I'm assuming you'll want her name to appear on the documents, or don't you?"

He grinned cheerfully and replied, "Yes ma'am, I sure do." Afterwards, he went back to the apartment and waited anxiously for eleven o'clock so he could surprise Grace when she came home. "Look honey," he'd say. "We've only been married less than twenty-four hours, and yet I've gone out and bought you one of the things I promised to buy for you."

Chapter 7 – New Hearth and Home

With nothing much to do but wait until Grace came home, he decided to turn on the television and perhaps rein in his anxiety about Grace being absent the first day of their honeymoon. As soon as he reached for the knob to turn on the TV, he remembered the book that Mrs. Nichols gave him to read for an assignment due on Friday. Three days late! Without any more ado, he set aside his be-in-a-funk over Grace and feverishly began writing his report on Hemingway's The Old Man and the Sea. He became so involved that he lost track of time and just as he remembered to check the clock, Grace came walking in the door.

After he had kissed and told her how much he loved and missed her, he asked, "Where did you park the car?"

"In the same place I found it this morning," she answered.

"Come with me," he said "and let's be sure you didn't park in the wrong place."

"I don't understand," Grace was baffled.

"Come on and I'll show you where you'll be parking from now on." She followed him to the car, they got in, and he directed her to drive straight ahead up the alley for a half a block, and then stop. He opened the gate and motioned for her to drive through. It had the same set-up as Mrs. Nichols house, with the same detached two-bedroom apartment out back. He took her hand and led her to the back door of their new home. He took out his key, and opened the door. He picked her up and carried her over the threshold.

Alvin brandished the key triumphantly, saying, "This is the key to your new home!" He pointed to the car and added, "And there is where you'll be parking from now on."

Half excited and not knowing quite what to say, Grace asked, "How much rent will we have to pay for such a large house?"

"Pardon me!" He answered. "Didn't you mean to ask how much will our payment be for such a large home?"

"Alvin Jackson!" she said, "Are you trying to tell me that you and I own this house?

"I thought you would never figure it out!"

"Alvin," she whispered, "I can't believe you did all of this for me, honey!"

"Well I did, and this is just a partial payment of what I owe you for saving my life last night."

"Oh darling, this is too much. I don't deserve all of this. And by the way" she asked, "What did I do to make you think you owe me for saved your life last night?"

"It's simple," Alvin answered. "You did as I asked – to come home with me. Otherwise, I wasn't about to go nowhere without you, and your parents would've killed me for sure."

"It could've been just as easy me as it was you," Grace answered, "Being that you didn't know that if you hadn't come for me, I was going to grieve myself into bad health and eventually dying a slow death."

"Well in that case," he ventured, "Why don't you let me do a little poking around and afterward we'll call it even, whatta ya say?"

She smiled, saying, "If I know you, your poking around to call it even will last the rest of our lives." She caught his hand, and he followed her as she led him from room to room, admiring their completely and well-furnished home. Finally he reached into his pocket and handed her the form from the bank, telling her to fill it out, and sign it Grace L. Jackson.

"Assuming of course you want your name to appear as a co-signer on our checking account?" He added, and which she gave him a delighted grin.

"Of course I do, aren't that what married people are supposed to do? Mama would be astonished if she knew how far I've come in the few days we've been together. I don't see why I should wait to invite her, until after we accumulate other possessions – just to prove that I'm not hooked up with some looser like she thought you to be. I've gathered more in the two days I've been with you than she has in the four years she's been with J.D., and not to mention the sixteen years she was married to Daddy."

"Your point is well taken," he told her, "I understanding you are missing your family and all – but it's better to be safe than sorry. Don't think about facing your mother just yet; give her time to get over her bitterness, which you caused her the instant you walked away from her to come live with me. "

"I caused them?" Grace exclaimed. "It wasn't me that came to your father's house in the middle of the night and took his son away. If I'm not badly mistaken – you were the one that took their daughter away in the middle of the night." She grinned as she continued, "Our house was filled with peace and quiet, until you came in, firing up your engine and acting as if I were your lawful wife who had decided to call it quits and you decided differently."

"Let me put it this way," he said "I blame you for forcing me into a dangerous situation like that. You should've known after our first night together I wasn't gonna ever think about letting you go. You could've saved yourself as well as your entire family a whole lot of trouble just by staying and listened to what I had to say. Whither you knew it or not, we were and are invisibly as well as physically linked to each other with no possible way for you to escape. Wherever you go I'll go also, or better yet, wherever you go I'll come after you and bring you back. I yield to no circumstances even to the ends of the earth. I'll come searching, fighting and cursing wild animals all the way there. Just to hear you say "I don't like it here I want to go home. Like the fool I am about you, I'd turn right around and follow you all the way back home or wherever you decide to lead me." She smiled and added, "Alvin Jackson tell me what did I say to get you to talk about something that's gonna never happen? When I have everything I need right here in my own beautiful home. As you just said 'we are invisibly linked to each other without the possible of escape.' Now, when do we move into our new home?"

"Anytime you like." he said.

"Then," Grace answered, "We should do it now, before it gets any later." It was already almost midnight, and very dark along the alley. They left the car parked in the driveway, and walked back to the apartment for a few necessary things, such as clothes to wear to work the next day.

"We've barely been together twenty-four hours, and just look at what you've done for me." Grace observed, with deep contentment, as they walked. "It would be a shame if either of us let someone ruin what we've accomplished thus far. I'm constantly being filled with amazement as to how this nineteen year old boy could manage to take a seventeen year old girl, and move her into this four-bedroom house. You tell me how long it would have taken me to find a phenomenal boy such as you – of any race – with the determination to do what you've done. You just said the magic word 'determination to please.'"

The darkness and the shelter of the alley gave them the freedom to walk holding hands, and to stop and kiss out in the open. It didn't matter to them what time it was; it was better to kiss under the stars, after always having to do such things behind closed doors. After he locked the apartment door they slowly returned to their new house, holding hands and gazing up at the stars, and now and again looking over the back fences of the houses along the alley. They left the clothes they had brought on the bed, and went back outside, to sit in the garden at the back of their new house, talking about their plans for the future, before they went off to bed. The next morning, Alvin woke up, slightly disorientated in these unfamiliar surrounding. He stumbled around in the dark searching the wall for the light switch – something that he should've familiarized himself with, before going to bed with his new bride. Dragging his hand across the wall a few times, he finally located the switch. He walked back to the bed and lay next to Grace, with the bedcovers between them. Alvin kissed her and told her how happy he was to have awakened a second morning, seeing her lying there next to him.

"You should see yourself," he whispered, "so you can see what I see. She was barely awake, just enough to answer, "I feel the same way about waking up next to you in our new surroundings. I suppose it's just like being on our honeymoon except we have to go to work today." Alvin kissed her again, lifted himself from the bed, and reminded her to go by the telephone company, on her way to school. She should ask them to have the phone turned on, and the number listed as belonging to Alvin and Grace Jackson. She nodded and smiled tenderly, still half-asleep, with her gorgeous brunette hair fanned over her pillow. Alvin stood looking over his shoulder at the clock, trying very hard to resist the temptation to call his job, and telling his boss that he had a problem at home needing his undivided attention. He thought about getting back into bed with her; at the last minute he changed his mind, wrapped his arms around her, whispering, "You are definitely the definition of the word they call love." As he left the bedroom,

Grace called out, "Alvin "I am so glad we're together; you've made me so happy."

He blew her a kiss as he walked out to catch the bus to work. He spent the shift working in a happy daze. When he had finished his shift, he sat down at the employee table for a Coke and a few minutes of relaxation before walking out to catch the bus home. Effie and Evelyn were setting there too, having a glass of ice tea and sighing lamentably.

"Well, well," Effie commented, "if it ain't Mister Chef himself! I heard about you moving up to line cook. So tell me – what does a person have to do to be promoted as often as you have, without even having been here a year yet?"

"I suppose hard work and doing what I'm told to do," he answered.

"No, no," Effie replied. "There are a lot's of us people that do what they're told and work just as hard as you do and they're still in the same spot as they were five years ago."

"He's lucky that I'm not his boss," Evelyn interjected, "or else I would've promoted you the very first day you came to work here. But not for the reason you think!" Both women laughed knowingly, as Evelyn added, "I know exactly the job you'd give him which has nothing to do with food."

"Girl, what took you so long to read my mind?" Effie muttered, "I'm a woman – and all women think alike when it come to evaluating men plowing skills. And if I ever got my hands on him, I'd keep him so busy plowing he'd feel as if he had gone back to being a sharecropper again!"

"Huh, huh honey," Evelyn shook her head, "Not you're field – but mine, since you have Ralph to plow yours anytime you need it. I broke up with my boyfriend about six weeks ago, so you can imagine how bad my field need plowed, so much so that it had become an emergency, honey!"

Effie answered, "If you really want to know about his farming skills, all you gotta do is ask Bernice – his old girlfriend Bobbie Jean's sister – and she'll probably tell you what she told me. One afternoon while Bernice and I was talking, she said to me that Bobbie Jean told her what she misses mostly about Alvin was the way he till her field?"

"I won't accept hearsay from no one," Evelyn said, "I only go by facts that are privy to me and me alone."

"You heard her Alvin," Effie answered, and looked across the table at him. "What you gonna do about it?"

"Not much of anything," he answered, with an expression of mild regret. "Except to be sorry that I can't demonstrate my – as y'all call it – plowing skills on Evelyn, since I already have a girlfriend."

Fortunately, there was no more need to discuss this topic, as Mr. Lee the dishwasher, Toby, and a few other employees came over to the table, to shake his hand and congratulate him on his new position. Then he walked around the corner to see Grace and wave goodbye to her, before walking out to the bus stop. When he got home, he went straight to his new house, and sat down to put the final touches on his book report. He went and knocked on Mrs. Nichols back door, presenting it to her with an apology for turning it in two days late.

"I'm surprised at how determine you're on turning in your book report in, especially in the midst of your makeshift honeymoon." She said, as she took it.

"You wouldn't be," Alvin answered. "But Grace and I work opposite of each other, and so I have the time for schoolwork."

Mrs. Nichols smiled. "I guess I hadn't thought of it that way."

He told her that Grace really loved the house, and both of them appreciated her for all of her kind deeds – especially in accepting their reasons for being together. "We also owe you our gratitude for tolerating us, the night Grace and I raised a ruckus outside the apartment. Selling us this house is solid evidence that you're not against her being white and me being colored. Instead you're helping us both get ahead."

"Well" Mrs. Nichols answered, "I'm glad I could be of some help to you two. Grace seems to be such a nice and caring young woman, and you two deserve each other. The reason I sold you that house is because I believe you both are going to do just fine, living right here in Fort Worth. Y'all have to go to California for your marriage to be authenticated – but just you try to be patient a little while longer. As fast as things are changing you and that wife of yours will soon be able to walk out in broad day light together. I wish that girl of mine wasn't too darn old for you, or else I would've made you marry her while she was here. That way I wouldn't feel jealous when I think about Grace moving in with you next door instead my girl, Cassie.

Since there is a shortage of men like you, my girl's chances of finding such a good man are next to nothing."

"Now that you know all about Miss Cassie and me," he said, "Age was definitely a factor between us. I told her more than once that I was in love with her, but she wrote it off, saying it was nothing more than a case of infatuation, brought on only by the color of her skin, and it would pass as soon as she left, but she was wrong."

"Well," Mrs. Nichols exclaimed, "I'm so relieved to hear that your parting was full of civility and not rudeness. That morning she left here she made as if to walk out the back door but each time she'd stop as if she were confused. It looked to me as if she needed to tell you something that she forgot to tell you that last night. I was at the point of telling her to go on and say to you what was on her mind – except I was afraid I'd embarrass her and give her the shock of her life. Or maybe she couldn't remember what she needed to say to you, being that the two of you were so busy hugging and kissing and crying on each others shoulders. In fact," Mrs. Nichols added, "it nearly breaks my heart in two as I stood by my window watching you both."

Alvin put a hand on her shoulder, saying, "I'm so sorry Mrs. Nichols – not about my being committed to Grace – but I'm sorry about Miss Cassie not being where she's should've been. If she had only taken me at my word, when I asked her to marry me"

At that, Mrs. Nichols reached into her apron, for a handkerchief, to blot her teary eyes. Alvin figured it was time to change the subject. He felt bad seeing her cry for her daughter's missed fortune. He wanted bygones to be bygones, but bygones wouldn't be bygones, if he kept telling her sweet things that happened between him and her daughter. His sworn duty now was to focus his attention on Grace. He told her that he and Grace had spend the night in their new home, even before they had signed the papers, and he hoped that it was all right with her. She told him to do as he pleased; regardless of what papers they hadn't signed, she had his check and the house belonged to them.

"I'm going to pro-rate your rent and credited to your first payment." Alvin was electrified and nearly speechless; all he could say was, "Mrs. Nichols you never cease to amaze me. You are the most wonderful woman in the world!"

"Now Alvin," she smiled and said, "let's not get carried away!" He thanked her and walked back to his old apartment to gather up his belonging. He didn't have many things of his own to move and nothing for Grace, except the outfit he bought for her and the clothes she wore the night she came to live with him. Lucky for both that the hotel furnished uniforms for all the restaurant workers. As a result he only made three trips on foot, and he had finished moving everything they owned. After that, he hooked up the television and scanned the channels, looking for a western to watch. When he did find a Hop-along Cassidy western, it didn't hold his attention for very long. His mind dwelt on his mixed happiness and disbelief that Grace would come and sleep in the same bed with him tonight. To think that it was the second day of their honeymoon and here he was in one place, horny as a horned toad and Grace was in another, getting her high school diploma.

With nothing else to do except to try not to be bored, he stretched out on the divan and watch television until he fell asleep. He didn't wake until she came home shortly after eleven, dog-tired, after a sixteen hour day of work and school. Her obvious exhaustion led him to ask her a second time to quit her job, at least for the remaining five weeks she left before she graduated.

Grace answered, "No, Alvin honey. My role now is no different from the way it was when I lived at home, except to spent time with you before I go off to sleep. The good thing about me loosing those two hours of sleep is because I'm spending them visiting with my husband. Trust me – five weeks of sixteen-hour days isn't going to kill anyone. Relax and trust me, like I trusted you when I ask you not to work the morning shift." Alvin moved to the end of the divan; he'd taken off her shoes and began massaging her feet.

"Well, he said, "Since you're so dead set on working yourself to death, let me add another burden to the ones you already have . . . can you be here at two o'clock on Friday to let the phone man in to turn on our phone service. And use one of our checks to pay the deposit; I just want to see what Grace Jackson's signature looks like on our check carbon."

"Boy," she answered, "You are just full of surprises, aren't you? I didn't realize we'd be getting a phone so soon I thought it took longer. I like the idea of having a phone. I can call mama, and if she's still sensitive about my shacking up with you, then I won't have to see her reaction – I'll just listen to it on the phone. Now," she added, taking his hand. "I want us to take another tour of my beautiful house, since I was too tired to see much last night."

They started out in the living room; they took their own sweet time going through every room, studying the floors, the walls, and the ceiling. They finished up back in the living room, Grace yawning and insisting that she was more impressed with what she had seen than she had been the night before. Very shortly after that, they went to bed; Grace falling almost instantly asleep, after the long hours she had spent at school and work – hours that he didn't approve of, to no avail. He lay there; his elbow propped up on a pillow, his face in his hand and just watched her adoringly while she slept. He reached over and gently took a few strands of her dark brown hair; between two fingers. As he tenderly stroked it, he wondered, 'Will there ever be a time when I could tell her how committed I am to her, and to a degree that she'd understand – it to the depths of my perception – even when I'm telling her how much I love her? And can I determine her sincerity and accept it as fact, when she tells me she understands . . . and the depths of her feeling for me are felt in the same degree in which mine is for her? Perhaps not,' he thought, 'Since it's obvious that mankind wasn't programmed from the beginning to dig into one's heart and measure the depth of one's love. If that was the case, then the secret of love wouldn't be a secret anymore. It would be established abundantly even in the heart of the dim-witted ones, the same as in trinkets that sparkles. So is true love, it too, is a secret jewel that very few are able to find its true significance.' He wiped away the few heart-felt tears that slowly slither down his cheeks; he wanted to kiss her but was afraid of waking her. In its place he gently blew her a kiss goodnight, then fell back on his pillow and dozed off to sleep, utterly content.

On Friday the telephone man came. Grace was there to let him in to hook up the phone. She left Alvin a note:

Alvin Darling, I suppose you know by now that the phone man has been here and turned the phone on. I did what you told me to do. I used one of our checks and if you look on the kitchen cabinet you will find a carbon of it. Oh yes – while you are looking for the amount of the check, don't forget to check the signature. Love, Grace L. Jackson

The phone rang, as he finished reading the note; he picked it up. "Hi honey!" Grace asked. "Did you see the note I wrote you?"

"How could I miss it?" he answered, jokingly. "You had it attached to a string that ran from the front door all the way to the kitchen sink."

"Liar!" Grace answered, fondly. "'Bye, honey – I have to go now, I'll see you tonight, love you."

Grace would be off from her job on Saturdays as well as out of school. Because Alvin had been promoted from pantry to line cook, he would have to work on Saturday. On that day, she got to stay home and sleep late, as well as having the car. By that time it was nearly a month since she left her mother's house and moved in with Alvin. It was difficult for Grace to take Alvin's advice – she should wait for at least two weeks before trying to call her mother: he figured by that time Mrs. Maggie's anxiety about her daughter's after living with this colored boy would be such that she could hardly wait to hear from her daughter. Grace had made several attempts by phone to invite her mother over for reconciliation. The last two weekends, she had called and tried to persuade her mother to go shopping with her, to no avail. Grace figured this Saturday wouldn't be any different.

"Well," Alvin said, "From the look in her eyes for you, when she told J.D. to let you go with me, I'd say she just playing hard to get. Maybe this time will be different. If you do, get her to change her mind . . . You should take her and buy her a nice dress at the shop where you got your outfit. And, "he added, "Provided you get your mother to go shopping with you, wear the outfit I bought you. I want her to see you at your very best and not dressed the same way you were the night you left her to come with me." He kissed her, and walked out to catch the bus to work." When he got home from work that afternoon, Grace had left him a note:

Guess what, Honey – you're not going to believe this, but Mama has finally invited me over and agreed to go shopping with me. Hopefully we'll be back by the time you get home, Love Grace.

Excited, Alvin poured himself a long shot of vodka, and topped off with Seven-Up, and thought to himself, 'Hopefully this will have calmed me down by the time Grace and her mother came home from shopping. That way I can be just as submissive and polite to her today as I was the night she had J.D. brandishing his tire iron at me.' He turned on the television, picked up a book and began to read, with no concept whatsoever of what he was reading, or of the movie that he was half-watching on television. He would soon be face to face with his to-be-mother-in-law, which filled him with remorse and trepidation. He would need to find the words to explain that his living with her daughter was only temporarily.

Every word went straight of his mind, once he saw Grace walk through the door, with a smiling joyously, with a dress-shop bag in one hand and leading her mother with the other. Maggie carried a bag also – a grocery bag, filled with the kind of food that Grace and Alvin normally snacked on while setting around on weekends watching television. The smile on Maggie's face was somewhat uncertain. Alvin rose up from divan; his heart feeling like it would jump out of his chest, he kissed Grace, saying "I was just starting to worry – I've missed you so desperately."

"I know you have – and I've missed you as much, even so." She added, in a nervous voice, "I'm sorry to have given cause for worry . . . after Mama and I did our shopping we stopped off at this little café where we had a long discussion over lunch, which lasted until a few minutes ago. But, anyway" as she took a deep and shaky breath, "I want you to say hi again to my sweet and wonderful mother Maggie."

"I am so delighted that you would come, and be with your daughter who loves you exceedingly more than the normal." Alvin spoke from the heart. "I'm also anxious to know whether or not my Grace has told you how sorry I am for all of the trouble I caused everyone. If not, then I'll tell you how sorry I am . . . and I understood how you might have been a bit hostile, towards me, trying to save her from a person that you knew very little about."

"She told me that and many other things about you," Maggie answered.

"Good, he said. "In that case would I be right to assume, that Grace has made it understood that John and Mr. Granger will be coming over later to join us for a bite to eat?" "Now that –I don't think she has," Mrs. Maggie answered, and Grace chimed in.

"Oh please, Mama – call John and J.D. – tell them to come over, if for nothing else to see my house. That way, we can all have dinner together and maybe settle some of our differences." Maggie looked doubtful. "I don't know about J.D. – he's still pretty sore about Alvin showing up uninvited and taking you from us. He's not likely to forget something like that." She paused, adding, "But I guess it won't hurt to call and see what he says." She went into the kitchen and picked up the phone. Alvin could hear her argue back and forth – he assumed she was talking to J.D., saying, "It was him that invited you – and they don't live in nigger town either. They live in a nice neighborhood and you'll be amazed when you see the house they live inn . . ." after a moment, Mrs. Maggie called out to Grace, saying, "Sugar, they need your address so they'll know how to get here." Alvin heard her give him directions, "If you're coming over, it shouldn't take no more than twenty minutes to get here."

Taking her mother's hand, Grace insisted, "Come and let me show you the rest of the house, Mama." She led Mrs. Maggie throughout the house; her arm around her mother, as they went from room to room with Alvin following closely behind. He was curious to see what her mother's reaction would be – if any at all. She had a reaction all right, she was impressed and had many favorable comments, but all directed towards Grace. Never once did Mrs. Maggie mention Alvin's name, in reference to the house or anything that she admired as they went from room to room. Alvin thought, 'I bet Mrs. Maggie sure do wish it had been some white boy that did these nice things for her daughter. As nice as this house is – in the instant she walked through the door she'd probably already showered him all over with love and affection.' When Grace realized that her mother hadn't acknowledged Alvin's part in acquiring such a wonderful house, she said, "Mama, I think I told you Alvin's reason for buying such a large house – it's not just for the two of us, but so there's room for you and the family, anytime you choose to stay over. Otherwise we would've been happy to stay in the little rented apartment."

Alvin put in his two cents' worth by adding to Maggie in a calculating manner, "Grace is so appreciative for the littlest things I try to do for her. In the short time we've been together, she has come to know me as a staunch believer in her – every bit the accomplished woman I believe her to be – a woman that would never be caught living in a disgraceful, rundown neighborhood. She's a woman that will always have the very best of everything – and she will have it all, as soon as I can fulfill all of those promises I made to her."

"Well," Mrs. Maggie's voice already sounded more cordial. "You seem to have a head- start on accomplishing just that."

Grace and her mother sat at the kitchen table, where he assumed they were reestablishing their former closeness. Alvin sat on divan in front of the television, listening while the women talked. He couldn't help noticing again how inviting Grace looked, and it pleased him that she took his suggestion and wore the dress he had asked her to wear. Surely, Mrs. Maggie must have seen how stunningly beautiful her daughter looked, now that Grace had gone from living in a small trailer to a four-bedroom house, from wearing blue jeans and hotel-furnished uniform to a closet of fine clothes and shoes, not to mention driving her own car. With all of what he had acquired in the face of adversary he felt that he had earned the right to walk into the kitchen, place his hand underneath Grace's chin, and tilt her head back for a kiss on her mouth. He said to Mrs. Maggie, "I'm sorry for the interruption, but what I just did has become a routine, happening about this time every evening. The compliment that I'm about to give, you'd probably rather I didn't give. But I'm gonna give it anyway, because if you and your ex hadn't produced such a darling of a daughter, then my hunger for her wouldn't have driven me to invade your house four weeks ago."

"Alvin" Grace protested sheepishly, "You're embarrassing me, saying these things about me in front of my mother."

"It's true" Alvin insisted, "and I'm gonna embarrass your mother as well. I saw the resemblance the night I drove you home in the rain, but I was afraid to tell her. But now that I'm on my own turf and have an opportunity to say it openly – Ma'am, you're almost as pretty as your daughter."

Maggie smiled, for the first time, open and frank, answering, "I haven't heard a compliment like that since before your father left me for that trashy old whore he wound up marrying."

Grace got up from her chair, and leaned over her mother, to give her a hug. She whispered, "I know, Mama."

Meanwhile, Alvin stood straight, and mimicked a stage master of ceremonies. "Ladies and gentlemen," he intoned solemnly. "May I have your attention please; you're now looking at the two most beautiful women in the whole state of Texas!"

Those few silly words were all it took to break the ice. After that, Maggie seemed more able to speak up, instead of in a voice so soft that only she and Grace could understand, knowing that Alvin held no grudge against her and J.D. Apparently she took his play on words to mean leniency for her and J.D., after insulting him so, on the night he took her daughter away. 'And now she's beginning to act like an innocent mother who's taking delight in her daughter's accomplishments,' Alvin thought, with deep satisfaction, as Maggie began showing Grace the way she would've arranged things if she owned the house. She walked around, suggesting how best to place the furniture, and finally asked if Grace would like help putting things in order throughout the whole house. Then she asked, "Grace, honey, – do we have enough food in this house to feed five hungry people for supper?"

"I don't think so, Mama" Grace answered, "Alvin and I mostly lay around on our days off, eating sandwiches and watching television."

"Then" Maggie commanded, "We had better go back to the market and pick up something for supper . . . do y'all have the money to pay for enough food for a good supper? I understand that y'all just bought this beautiful house and all. So I just thought that y'all might be running a little short on cash."

"Not at all Mama" Grace smiled, answering, "Old Mister Penny-wise setting over there is going to make sure that we have at least enough money to buy most of what we need as well as his impending in-laws."

Alvin chimed in, "While you're at it, get enough food for breakfast in the morning. I'm thinking when we finish eating, drinking and talking half the night. I'll suspect that you'll be too exhausted to do anything except to go to one of those bedrooms and spend the night."

Maggie grinned widely, as she turned to Grace. "Did I hear him right when he mentioned something about us spending the night?"

"This is just one of the nice things I told you about him over lunch today." Grace answered, "He's not a begrudging person – he understood perfectly well what you and J.D. did was for my own protection. He has nothing but high praise for you, Mama – because he knows how much I love you."

"Well," Maggie said, "In this case, I had better bring back a couple of six-packs for J.D. because that's about what it takes to get him through the evening." She looked at Alvin and asked, "I'll buy you one also, if you want me to."

"Yes, that'll be all right," he said, "but let my lovely Mrs. Grace pay for it." They both chuckled, as they walked out the door. Grace and Maggie hadn't been gone more than fifteen minutes before there was a knock on the front door. Alvin knew it was J.D. and John; he opened the door, inviting the two to come right on in. Alvin extended his hand to J.D., who walked past Alvin as if he weren't there at all. J.D. took to studying the furniture, the walls and just about everything else, except Alvin. Alvin held out his hand to John and John shook it, politely. When J.D. finally finished casing as much as he could see of the house from where he was standing, he took a seat on the divan, and without any preamble, asked, "Where are the gals? Shopping for groceries, I take it?"

"They are, sir," Alvin answered. "They've been gone no more than fifteen minutes." J.D. didn't respond to Alvin's remark, but continued to look around the room. Alvin decided that as much attention as J.D. was paying to the living room, maybe he wanted to see more but still too angry to ask. Alvin took the initiative as a host, offering to show J.D. and John from room to room, so they could see the rest of the house. J.D. never broke stride; but he continued to study each room they came to. When they finally wound up back in the living room, and J. D still didn't have anything to say, Alvin decided to try something different – like offering him a beer.

Surprisingly, J.D. answered, "I don't mind if I do – hell, you've drunk mine when you came to my house."

Handing J.D the beer, Alvin asked John, "Would you like something cold to drink? Like a Coke or Seven-Up?"

"Yeah – a Coke," John answered.

Alvin said to him, "Here is how I want you to act when you're at your sister's house. Let's pretend you remembered back when you and your sister were kids, and your best friend came over to play a game that you just had to take part in. So the ham sandwich and Coke your mother sat out for your lunch – your sister swiped it, lit out and she was gone to the movies a half hour before you came back in to claim your sandwich and Coke. You being a man of fortitude, you waited for the precise moment when she decided to go out and do something constructive . . . like picking up food for supper. Now is you're time to get even! So, the point of the story is – whenever you come to your sister's house, pretend she owes you and raise the Coke in one hand and the sandwich in the other and say, 'Hey sis, payback is hell isn't?'" He grinned and wasted no more time, opening the refrigerator, and grabbing him an ice-cold Coke. Even J.D. chuckled, as he got up and helped himself to another beer from the refrigerator.

He sat back down on the divan, saying, "Boy, this is some cold beer, just the way I like it!" Alvin still felt somewhat ill at ease, sitting there with a man who just a few weeks ago wouldn't have shown a scrap of remorse for threatening to use a tire iron on his head. Alvin could hardly wait for Grace and Maggie to return, hoping their presence would ease some of the atmosphere which had filled the house the minute J.D. came in.

"So how did things turn out for you at work today?" Alvin ventured, just to fill some of the silence.

"About average," J.D. replied, curtly. At least, he did have an answer.

Alvin carried on, undiscouraged. "It sounds like you and I have lots in common – because that was about the way my day turned out, too." The only response he got from J.D. was a grunt, which made him realize that J.D. was a long ways from forgiving Alvin for upsetting Maggie the night that he took Grace away; and he was there because his wife told him to. Finally, Grace and Maggie came back, carrying bags of groceries.

Setting them on the kitchen counter, Maggie observed to J.D., "I see you two made it all right."

"Yeah, about twenty minutes ago," J.D. replied, sounding a little less surly.

Grace gave John a big hug, saying, "I've really missed you my little brother."

"I've really missed you too, Sis – and I've been worrying sick about you. Is everything gonna be all right with you?" John asked his voice anxious.

"Of course it will, John," Grace replied. "Don't you have any faith at all in your big sister? I know what I'm doing. Alvin is a very nice person that's extremely concerned about my well-being. Haven't you noticed how he went out and got me my own beautiful home? If it wasn't for him being so in love with me, I doubt very much that he would've made the effort. He was plenty happy, living as a bachelor in his small two bed room apartment." Maggie stood listening to Grace tell her brother John how caring Alvin was for her, with an approving look in her eyes. She put her arms around the both of them, and squeezed them.

"Isn't it wonderful to be a family once again?" Maggie looked the happiest that Alvin had yet seen her. She turned to J.D., saying, "I would offer you a beer but I see that Alvin has already taken care of that."

"Yep." J.D. answered. "And it's good and cold just the way I like it." He already sounded much more cordial towards Alvin.

"Can I get you a beer Alvin? Maggie asked, and Alvin answered, "I want one, but I'll get it myself. I don't want you waiting on me."

"But I want to," she said, as she took and opened the beer. "Do you mind your mother-in-law having the first sip? It's sorter like a small endorsement, until I get to know you better." "Not at all," Alvin replied. "Be my guest and have as many sips as you'd like, because I'll certainly be striving to get your approval."

Alvin and Grace's eyes met, mildly surprised, and gratified to have Maggie's approval. Grace went to her mother, put her arms around, and murmured, "Thank you, Mama – for including Alvin as part of the family. Even though you've accepted him on the basis of what you've seen materially, and what I've told you about him over lunch today . . . but what you've seen today, compared to what I know about him, is nothing more than a drop in the bucket. His idea of being a genuine husband is set in stone – and he keeps telling me the best of him is yet to come." Hearing this praise of him, Alvin noticed that J.D. and John seemed to have become much more at ease.

"Time will tell," Maggie said, briskly. "But with what I've seen so far, I'm very optimistic that he will do everything that he has promised to do, and more." She reached for one of Grace's kitchen aprons, hanging from a hook just inside the kitchen door. "Come on, Grace darling," she said, with a cheerful voice, "show your mama where you keep everything, so I can get started on the meatloaf we'll be serving my dear family for supper."

Grace was watching and listening to her mother's instructions on how she should manage in the kitchen, now that she had taken on the responsibility of preparing meals for her husband. In the few minutes it took Maggie to finish making the meatloaf and into the oven, she was on her second beer. She said to Grace, "Pull up a chair, and have a beer that is if it's all right with Alvin. It might sound a little unusual for me saying this, but you're not my responsibility anymore. Alvin took on all of that when you chose him over me and the rest of your family."   "Mama"   Grace answered, "You know I don't drink"

"There's a lot's of things I thought I knew about you and come to find out that I didn't know you at all." Maggie answered. "As it stands right now – as far as I can tell – it's not a bad thing, that I didn't know you. Or else, I wouldn't be setting here telling you how very happy I am to say that you've choose very well for yourself." No one said a word. Grace was expecting the worst to come out of her mother's mouth, but Maggie took another sip of beer, sat the can on the coffee table, and leaned back on the divan. She said, "I haven't mentioned a word to J.D. regarding what I'm about to say. I'm speaking for myself – and if J.D. wants to say something then let him speak for himself. I suppose I owe my daughter and her soon to be husband – my soon to be son-in-law – an apology. Based on what I've seen and heard about your association with Alvin, puts my thoughts about him the night he took you away from me worlds apart from the way I felt about him tonight. It's obvious that you knew exactly what you were doing. I can't ever remember when I've seen my little girl so happy, as if she doesn't have a care in the world. How hard I tried to prevent something so wonderful from happening, between two people that were willing to die rather than to be separated from one another! It was obvious! You spent all that time listening to my yelling, crying and cussing, until I ran out of thing to say. An' you two were so brave, clinging to each other and defying J.D with his ol' tire iron cocked and ready to use in an instant if push came to shove. What I saw when you two walked out the door was obsession for each other. But now I believe I saw a combination of craze and investment; Alvin, in less than a month, you're already earning dividends on your wager. I'm a proud mother, but I want to be modest as I can possible be. I can't ignore what I have witnessed the immense affection you have for each other; any more than I can ignore that what you've accomplished to this point is nothing less than phenomenal. Grace has always talked about having a beautiful house, and that I would live with her and she would take care of me for the rest of my life. Now that I've seen what she fantasized about has crept into the realm of reality . . . maybe I ought start fantasizing about my future, and apologize to her for telling her not to let your imagination get the better of her. I've been in and out of marriage for twenty-one years, and I've never had a man to buy me a nice house and beautiful clothes, the way Alvin have done for you in the four weeks y'all been together. One of the things I think about that bothers me the most –

what if Alvin had just gotten discouraged, given up and left without you? Suppose I found out later that he had found another wonderful girl, and fallen in love with her like he loves you – and was doing for her the same thing he's doing now for you? I would probably never forgive myself for blocking a wonderful future that you have now with Alvin. And with you knowing what you already knew about him, you'd probably never forgive either. What I just said was a compliment. Now it's the apology I owe the both of you that I'm ready to talk about." Alvin," Maggie continued, "The night you drove my girl home from to keep her from being out in that awful rain we had that night – I saw something in your manner towards each other that sorter alerted me – but I just thought to myself, 'I know my little girl well enough to know she wouldn't ever go so far as to do something as stupid as letting herself get involved with some nigger boy when she's got so many white boys to choose from.' That's what I called you at that time – but now I know better. Anyway, the night you came and begged for her hand in makeshift matrimony, it proved my suspicions. And I was just devastated, knowing I could've prevented it before it went as for as it did – just as I am embarrassed now because I ranted and raged against something I knew nothing about, except that you're a colored boy. According to what she told me over lunch today, she didn't just cave in because of your good looks. She listened to every word you said, each night, as you went back and forth from the supply house, until she had your trust and you hers. Grace didn't dare to bring you home, and let her ill-informed mama and step-father analyze the boy that she was so madly in love with. She knew I'd rule against her. I'll be honest and tell you I'm so glad she didn't. Otherwise, she might have wound up like her mother never owning her own home nor having a nice car and beautiful clothes to wear. I sat there for at least two hours, listening to her tell me all of the good qualities that she had discovered in her Alvin and what he means to her. And for all you've put yourselves through, in order to be with each other – not only am I apologizing for the harm I may've caused y'all, but I give y'all my blessing. And please, please – ignore those as I once was, and keep doing what you're doing, and listen to no one that tells you, you can't." Having finished, she sat silent, and looked across at J.D.

J.D. scratched his head and asked, "Do y'all own this house?"

"Yes" Grace answered. "Alvin bought it especially for me"

"Hell!" J.D. exclaimed, "I thought y'all were just renting, so how did y'all go about buying something as nice as this and either one of you are twenty-one yet?"

"I'm nineteen, going on twenty." Alvin said "But I don't consider this house to be anything special, compared to the expectation that I've set for myself, concerning the things that I'll be presenting to her in the not-too-distant future."

"If I owned this house," J.D. said, "it would be plenty good enough for me and Maggie, and John, too – except, he don't have many more years at home before he'll be leaving us and going off with some little old gal that he'll follow her to where ever she decides leads him." He stood up and looked all around and said to Grace, "I'm really impressed with what you've did with your life so for."

"So am I," John spoke up. "It just proved what Mama just said – old Alvin sure must really love you a lot. Not only did he buy you a nice house but the clothes you're wearing, really looks pretty on you, especially the dress – you're what's called a real knock-out."

"Just give him a little more time," Maggie said. "And there no telling what he'll do for her. You've heard the saying about love brings out the best in people. In Grace's case she seems to be its beneficiary."

"I think you're right, Mama." Grace said. "And think you, John – for mentioning my dress. Which reminds me – after supper, Mama and I are going to model our new dresses for you three handsome men."

"A new dress huh?" J.D. said to Maggie "I hope you didn't spend all of the money on some damn old dress that's going to hang around in the closet until it rots, since you never go any place to wear a nice dress anyway."

"If my boyfriend would ask, I would." Maggie replied. "Besides – you don't have to worry about me spending my money on clothes. My daughter had strict orders from Alvin to buy me my dress. I forgot to tell you that Alvin has opened for Grace her very own charge account – at one of the nicest dress shops in Fort Worth, with a three hundred dollar line of credit."

Maggie walked into the kitchen, and from the stove, she called, "Grace, honey – come over here and let mama show you what a meatloaf is suppose to look like when its cooking at the right temperature. The meatloaf I cook at home doesn't look like this, because my oven isn't as nice as yours. You need too pay close attention to what you see your Mama do – that way, you'll learn everything there is to know about cooking the right way." Maggie lowered her voice, and continued. "That craving y'all get for each other isn't gonna last forever. You'll need other things to keep Alvin happy, and good food is going to be the key." Saying that, she raised her voice. "Y'all come on now, supper is ready." She ushered Alvin at the head of the table, and Grace at his left.

After Alvin gave thanks, he caught Grace around the neck, and kissed her in the mouth, saying to John, "I do this before each meal; they tell me it's good for my digestion. They laughed; even J.D. Maggie took upon herself to become Alvin's personal server. She made sure that he didn't want for anything, as far as food went. Alvin felt that she was going a little overboard, but he understood she was trying to make up for her bad behavior as well as but J.D.'s. After everyone had finished supper, Grace took her mother's hand and led her off to the back bedroom. They both changed into their new clothes, and emerged looking like movie stars. While Grace kept looking to Alvin for his immediate approval – which she usually got when she'd walk into living room all dressed up. This particular time was different; he couldn't give his instant evaluation, since he had two beautiful women to appraise. Like her daughter, Maggie put a lot of tension in her dresses, especially the hips and breast. She may have been twenty-some years older than her daughter, but as far as Alvin could tell, old J.D. still had a whole lot of eventful nights at his disposal.

As the two women made half-turns and shifting their weight from one hip to the other, flaunting their sexy bodies in their new dresses, Alvin went to Maggie, saying, "Ma'am, you look so beautiful tonight – it would be heartless of me if I didn't ask to have this dance with you!"

"Of course you may," Maggie answered with a gleeful smile. She extended her hand, and began what Alvin thought was a whirl around the living room floor – which turned out to be a sophisticated three-minute waltz, to the music of a tune playing on the radio. Maggie surprised Alvin that she was such a polished, dancer. Not only was she a refined dancer but she had no sense of restraint when he'd whirl her and she'd land in his arms, breasts first. This happened several times, although Alvin was sure that Maggie was unconscious of this; her style of dancing was as innocent as a morning sunrise. But he felt self-conscientious, and somewhat reluctant to dance with her again. When they danced together again, he was very careful to whirl her at arms length, to save the both of them from the embarrassment of being misinterpreted.

It was late when everybody had tired themselves out, danced and drinking themselves into exhaustion. Maggie told John that he should've already been in bed by now.

"I don't want to leave and go to bed before the bride looses the gleam in her eyes." John argued back, and Maggie answered,

"That want happen any way soon, so you might order go on and go to bed, because the gleam in your sisters' eyes will be there for years to come."

Alvin asked Grace to come and sit next to him. "Mrs. Maggie and Mr. Granger . . . you too, John . . . I have a confession of my own as well as an apology to make to you folks. "Let me just first say that I'm truly sorry, knowing how awful you must feel, knowing that Grace and I are not married but we're living and sleeping together in the same bed every night. I want you to know that this wasn't our plan at all. When Grace and I knew we had fallen in love with each other, we agreed to continue as we were, until she was out of school. Then, we had planned to sneak away to California and get married. Depending on how y'all would have handled it, we might even have chosen to stay there. But I was advancing at the hotel, making more money each time they moved me up. Between my job and the money that Grace would make once she's out of school, we saw no reason why we should go to California – except to get married. So, after we got married, we'd return to Texas, since we're so well established here. Provided we'd stay clear of the police and the authorities . . . but we needed to figure out ways to deal with your feelings. But things got a little out of hand over a misunderstanding that caused Grace to mistrust me . . . and she was so upset. I tried to explain to her that I was innocent; she refused to listen to what I had to say, and ran away. I was afraid, straight out, to chase after her – I'd just give her the weekend to consider her options, and Monday night on our way to the storage room, I'd tell her my side of the story. But I didn't see her on Monday night, or for three days after. And I started to worry that I would never see again. I remembered the agreement we made the first time we were alone together, where she promised that no man would see her the way I had, just like no other woman wouldn't see me the way she had. The more I thought on that, the more that I worried about those promises we had made to each other being irreversibly null and void. At that point my imagination began running wild . . . so wild that I chose to sacrifice our secret, when I showed up at your house that night, begging for her to come home with me. I figured once I made you aware of my association with her, and me being a colored man, she wouldn't be welcome at your house anymore. So, I had no other choice but to bring her home, rather than to leave her to face y'all, who might have made her feel disgraced. I didn't intentionally set out to hurt anyone. It wasn't my plan at all; it just turned out that way. Prior to y'all knowing about us, Grace and I agreed – even though she still lived at home, I would take full responsibility for her consider myself her guardian. My responsibility is to put her above all others, no matter who they are or what they are to her." He paused to take a sip of beer, smiled and continued, as he squeezed and kissed Grace's hand. "And actually – one other thing that stands out in my mind – I thought I was going to die from hyperventilation. My heartbeat was so out of rhythm it scared me half to death. I figured if I was going to die anyway, it might as well be in the presence of someone I loved beyond anyone's imagination. It was my landlady, Mrs. Nichols – she heard me crying. She came over and knocked on my door, she asked what the matter was. I couldn't stop crying long enough to make any sense to her at all. She understood what I was trying to say, because she knew what happened between Grace and I, that one night when she ran out of my place." He chuckled, and continued, "Miz Nichols told me, 'If my crying was any indication of the way I felt about Grace then I shouldn't waste anymore time setting around bawling.' She said, 'If you love her like you seem to be, lamenting over her won't do a thing to bring her back. You need to know that love doesn't always come so easy. Sometimes, you'll have to be bold enough to fight for what you think is important to you.' She knew Grace was white – and that was even more of reason I took her advice, because Miz Nichols was willing to take a chance on getting herself in trouble on account of mine and Grace's problem which was no benefit to her whatsoever – except she likes me. Therefore, I said to myself, 'Who am I waiting on?' At that moment I stood up straight, took a deep breath . . . even though my thoughts were directed to the Lord, it was still a scary request because I didn't feel that I was good enough for instant gratification. I'm happy to say that I was wrong. My prayer was answered – the proof is setting here next to me. We had no other choice but to live together. She's in school, too young and inexperienced to live alone, which meant she had no other place to go but to come live with me. So, I'm admitting to you that we are sorry if we've embarrassed y'all, but I'm glad I did what I did. If I hadn't, I may have lost my credibility with the Lord, because you don't ask unless you have faith and the little I had paid off in hundred-folds, whatever that means." Now, Alvin looked very earnestly at Maggie and J.D. "If you'll just let me use a phase that I've heard a few low-life people use, when they're living with a woman with no intension of marrying her; 'Why buy the cow when you can get the milk free?' I want y'all to know – that's not me at all. These four weeks that we've lived together has been an inspiration in our lives. And I give you my word – as soon as she's out of school – without fail; we're going to California to be married. You're asking yourself 'will it last?' and my answer to that is – it will last until time indefinite. It will last! And finally," Alvin said, with a grin. "The other thing that I want to apologize to you about – is that I'm sorry for causing you and J.D to use up your ration of the word 'nigger' on me, which was suppose to last y'all at least a week, instead of using them up in about ten minutes or less." Everyone laughed enormously at that, even J.D.

Maggie put her arms around Alvin, and tenderly said. "I'm so sorry to have put so much emphasis on my words, but I fought the only way I knew how. I suspect that's normal for any mother, trying to save her baby from what she thought at the time was a monster."

"You don't have to explain anything to me, I understand," he said. "If it had been the other way around – as much as I love her, there would've been a killing for sure before I would've let her go."

"That is so reassuring to me – you truly love her and not just some animal that's going around, preying on innocent young girls." Maggie hugged him again. "Please take care of my girl – be nice to her and she'll be nice to you." Then she said "I think I'm gonna tuck it in for the night. Come on J.D. –You've had enough beer for one night. Save at least one for breakfast in the morning."

Alvin followed Grace, as she showed Maggie and J.D. to their bedroom, and let them familiarize themselves with their surroundings. Maggie kissed Grace, then Alvin goodnight, and then they went to bed. The guest bedroom she picked for J.D. and Maggie was next to hers and Alvin's bedroom. Alvin and Grace had just descended from their world of euphoria, into tranquility, lying there waiting for their hard breathing to lessen, when they heard a sound like that of a bullfrog, signaling to females that he was available.

Alvin turned to Grace and whispered, "Are they doing what I think they're doing?"

"It sounds like it," Grace answered.

Alvin ventured, "Do you think it was us that caused them to carry on in such behavior?   "No I don't think so," she whispered, "Because this is one time I tried to muffle my fits of hilarity to be sure I didn't make any loud noises."

"Was I making loud noises?" Alvin muttered

"Not as far as I could tell."

"Well something turned them on!" he said.

"It wasn't necessary us that turned them on," Grace said, "Because this is the weekend and both of them been drinking – and that's when I hear those embarrassing noises they make."

Around seven-thirty the next morning, she was fast asleep, lying face down with her head resting on his chest. Alvin had barely fallen asleep, after a brief trip to the bathroom when he heard a light knock on their bedroom door.

"Grace, honey; are you awake?" Maggie had already cracked the door to their bedroom just wide enough to peep in, with one eye. "Can I come in?" She spoke in an undertone, "Are y'all decent?"

Alvin whispered, "Come on in."

Maggie tiptoed in, slowly, as though she didn't believe Alvin was telling her the truth – it was all right for her to come in. She went to Grace's side of the bed, seeing her sleeping on Alvin's chest and whispered, fondly, "Now isn't that a beautiful sight? She's laying there drooling on your chest and you're letting her get away with it." She laid her hand on Grace's back, and shook her. "Honey" she said, "It's time for you to get up and stop drooling all over Alvin. Mama can't teach you how to cook if you're going to sleep all day. Come on now . . . show Alvin a little appreciation for doing such a fine job of taking care of you."

Grace barely opened her eyes. "Oh Mama, do I have to? Alvin and I were up late last night talking about inconsequential things, so we need our rest, please, Mama."

Alvin whispered, "Can we delay breakfast just for a few minutes longer? My baby is still trying to finish out her sleep."

"No" Maggie said. "She can sleep when there is no one here but the two of you. Plus I have a lot I want to talk to her about."

"Mama!" Grace groaned, "You might have to leave the room, so I can get dressed because I don't have any clothes on."

"Oh mercy me, Maggie said, "I'll do just that. "I never imagined that you wouldn't be sleeping without a gown or at least a pair of panties on. I seldom ever go to bed without at least my nightgown!" As she left the room, Alvin thought to himself, 'She may've gone to bed with her gown on, but after all the noise she made last night, I bet she and J D woke up this morning naked as a jaybird.'

Presently, the aroma from freshly-brewed coffee had spread throughout the house. A few minutes later frying bacon and sausage added their aroma. At that point, Alvin decided he couldn't take it any longer. He washed up, went, and sat on the divan in front of the television. Right away, Maggie poured him a cup of coffee, asking, "Do you like cream and sugar in your coffee?

"Yes ma'am" he answered and Maggie gave the cup to Grace, saying, 'Take this to your husband – I think he'd like it better if it were you that gave it to him."

"You're spoiling me, Mrs. Maggie," Alvin said, "And there is no need for it."

"I'm not spoiling you," Maggie answered. "I'm just teaching my daughter how to spoil you."

"That's what a mother is supposed to do with their daughters?"

"Did you ever hear your mother explain to your sisters about how they should treat their husbands?" Mrs. Maggie said, and Alvin answered, "I suppose so . . . but I never actually heard her go in to any special details about how women should treat her man. Apparently she did, though – their husbands are just as crazy about my sisters as I am about your daughter. So that should give you some comparison between the way you're tutoring Grace how to treat me, and the way my mother taught my sisters to keep their husbands pacified."

"People have a tendency to carry on the tradition. My mother taught me and I'm teaching my daughter the same thing. Servitude just seems to be something that runs in my veins. I guess that's one of reasons why I choose waitressing for a living, just so I could see that satisfied look on people's faces."

She set down a platter of bacon and sausage on the table, and went to the guest room where J.D. was still sleeping, and told him to wake up and have coffee. She knocked on John's door, and told him breakfast would be ready by the time he washed up and came to the table. J.D. and John came out of their rooms, still yawning. They sat at the breakfast table, Grace had sat a platter of fried eggs, with a pan of the most wonderful tasting biscuits, and a bowl of gravy – all of them the very best-tasting that Alvin had ever eaten.

After they had all finished eating, Alvin complimented Maggie. "Before I ate this, I was a little reluctant having you teach Grace to cook my breakfast. Now that I've tasted your cooking, you're welcome to come and teach her as often as you like until she master's your technique for making biscuits and gravy. I've never had anything that was so scrumptious since I had the first taste of my mother's milk as a baby."

Maggie beamed proudly. "They should be. My mama started me making 'em when I was just knee high to a duck."

"Speaking of mamas," Alvin said, "I sure would like to see my mother along about now. Being that you and Grace are mother and daughter again. I hope that you would spend a weekend with her, so she doesn't have be left alone while I'm away down at Snyder visiting with my folks."

"You just tell me when," Maggie answered, "And I'll stay with her to make sure your Miss Grace is here when you get back."

Around mid-morning, Maggie suggested to J.D. "I think we should get out of these kids way, so they can get rested up for their long journey back to work tomorrow morning?"

"Y'all aren't bothering me none," Alvin said. "What about you, Grace?

"By all means," Grace answered. "Stay as long as you wish Mama, and that goes for you too, John and J.D. – Mama and I will drive to the store, and bring back something to make sandwiches for everyone. After the two women came back with the food and made sandwiches, the three men were served theirs, as they sat in front of the television. Grace and Maggie ate at the dining room table, and talked nonstop for two hours. The three men spent that time watching westerns, except Alvin would look over from time to time, and see the enormous love between a mother and daughter, which pleased him very much. He decided suggest to Grace that she rent the empty apartment to her parents. He figured that a mother and daughter with that kind of affection for one another shouldn't be any further than a child's throw away. And Maggie and J.D. and John would have a nice clean place to live, instead of the dilapidated trailer. When her family left that afternoon, Alvin laid out his idea to Grace about renting the apartment to her parents.

She thought it over, for a bit, before answering thoughtfully, "I appreciate you for suggesting such a lovely idea – but I would rather not have them move in until after I finish school. I spend six hours going to school and six hours at work, and then there is where which you need my undivided attention. Right now, it's not closeness with my mother I need – its solitude. I need in order to concentrate on my studies, if I'm gonna graduate on time. Besides all of that," Grace added wistfully, "I'd like to know what you think of my family, now that you've met them under different circumstances."

"I was pleasantly surprised to see that everyone was so readily to forgive. Your mother is just the way I remembered you saying she'd be, once she knew her daughter was safe and secure. I think she was genuinely impressed with your decision to choose me as your mate."

"I gathered the same thing you did," Grace said, "And I'm so pleased that things turned out the way they did. With one exception, mind you," Grace added. "She was so excited – I still think she drink more than I would've liked to have seen her do. What about your parents, Alvin – do they drink?"

"Occasionally," Alvin answered. "Neither one of my parent have an alcoholic tendency in their blood. They are very quick to condemn excessive drinking as well as overeating. Folks that let themselves be dragged down by those things are disgusting to my parents. Not that they want take a few every once in a while – it's just that they know when to put it down. I like drinking myself, but I have an obligation to fulfill, a promise I made to you, and I can't do it drunk."

"Oh Alvin," she said. "I know I'll never have to worry about you drinking to that extent. Because you know I don't like it and you love what pleases me."

A week before Grace's graduation, Alvin lift work that evening and rode the bus from his job down town between main and commerce to Crawford Street and Rosedale. He got off and walked the rest of the way to John Lee's house.

"Well come right on in here, Mr. Long-time-no-see!" John Lee said after he answered the door. "So what brings you back into my neighborhood?"

"I want you to be on the look out for me a nice used car, no more than two years old, preferably a Chevrolet. If all possible I'd like it if you could have it ready by Thursday evening about this time."

"I think we got just what you're looking for," John Lee told Alvin. "A nice clean 'fifty-three Chevy Bellaire that has a beautiful two-tone red and beige paint job. So," John Lee squinted at Alvin. "Where is your 'forty-nine Chevy? Don't tell me let me guess – did you loan it to some girl that promised to go pick up a six-pack and she keep driving?"

"The girl that's driving it – I know where she is," Alvin answered.

"So," John Lee said. "I take it you are buying this one for yourself?"

"You've got it partly right, except it's the other way around," Alvin replied.

The following Thursday after Alvin got off work, he rode the bus to Hertz's rental car lot to choose between several makes and models, of cars that they sold off each year to replace them with new ones. It happened that Alvin dealt with the same salesperson that sold him the 'forty-nine Chevy earlier. When they came to an agreement on the price and payment arrangement Alvin took out his checkbook, and wrote out a check, paying half down. John Lee was standing there watching and listening during the whole transaction.

"Boy!" he exclaimed, "Where did you get that kind of money? I've been in this town practically all of my life, and I ain't ever had that much money at one time!" Alvin had only paid hundred and seventy-five dollars which didn't seem like very much to him. He thanked John Lee and shook hands with the salesman, then took the keys to the car, and drove around for an hour, just to get the feel of it. All the time, he was imagining what it would have been like, being at his wife's graduation, watching her accepting her high school diploma. Due to the severity of the segregation laws in Texas, it made it impossible for him to attend.

By the time he parked in his driveway at home, in time to see Grace and her parents getting out of her car, and Grace waving her diploma, and exclaiming, "Thanks to Alvin for letting me use his car – I graduated at the top of my class!"

"Congratulations!" Alvin replied. "This calls for a celebration – starting with a salute for all of the hard work that went into accomplishing your achievement. I'm a firm believer that any newlywed who would sacrifice being away from her husband sixteen hours a day, just to get their high school diploma deserves to be stoned. Not with boulders or any other stone as far as that goes, but with a nice glass of wine." He filled four glasses full, and a fifth half way, giving the half-glass to her brother John, adding, "This is symbolic only. Grace, darling – before we toast I want to apologize for buying a graduation gift that's not small enough to bring inside the living room. Is it too inconvenient if I were to ask everyone to celebrate your accomplishment outdoors?"

Everybody stopped laughing and began to listening, as Alvin he caught her hand and led her out back. He pointed at the car. "There is, your graduation gift that's too big to bring inside."   Seeing the car and realizing that it was for her, Grace just lost control of her emotions; she turned to her mother with tears rolling down her face. "Mama, would you just look at what my Alvin has bought me for my graduation?" she hugged her mother and danced around her in circles. "Oh, Alvin honey – when are you going to stop it? I didn't expect this at all, I had expected a lovely card, followed by congratulations maybe ... but nothing like this."

"I thank you deserve it and much more," Alvin answered firmly. "Now, why don't you let me dry those eyes so you can see how to drive your new car?" He turned to Maggie and J.D. "Y'all are too old to be hanging out with us teenagers – why don't you'll stay right here and wait your turn?" They looked on, as Alvin climbed into the back seat, while Grace and John rode up front. In those days it was customary that a black man like Alvin ride in the back, if a white woman was riding up front, or visa versa. To defy that custom might bring down a tragedy to mar Grace's graduation day, should anyone chose to make an example of Alvin. After they rode around for thirty minutes or so, she came back and took her mother and J. D. for their ride, leaving John to stay in the back seat with J. D., while Maggie rode up front with Grace. She spent about the same amount of time driving her mother and J.D., as she did Alvin and John. She only parked long enough to let J.D. and John off. Then she and Maggie drove out and brought back food to finish celebrating Grace's graduation. After everyone had eaten and Maggie had her last glass of wine and J.D. his last beer, the both of them figured they'd go home and sleep it off.

Being that John was out of school for the summer, he asked for permission to stay behind and spend the night with his sister Grace. The three of them started a conversation that lasted right up to the time Alvin decided to go off to bed. He asked Grace to bring John and their mother to the hotel for breakfast in the morning. And he reminded Grace and John that tomorrow evening after work was as good of a time as ever for Alvin to make that trip back to see his folks in Snyder, which he had mentioned to Maggie.

"Then it's all settled," Grace answered, "I'll have my brother John to stay and keep watch over me while you're away." Alvin went off to bed, and left her and John to visit with each other.

When she finally came to bed, she shook him and asked, "Where is my graduation present? Even though she brought him out of a deep sleep, he immediately knew what she meant, but he acted as if he was disorientated, and mumbled, "I bought you a car, what more do you want?

"Why don't you use your imagination?" Grace whispered, and twenty minutes later he was still following his imagination.

Nine o'clock that next morning, Grace gave one of the waitresses a dollar bill, to give to Alvin and to tell him that it was for a wonderful breakfast. Alvin clearly understood what the dollar bill meant; a signal to let him know that she, her mother and brother had been there. As usual, as soon as Alvin finished his shift, he'd change into this street clothes and head for the bus stop. Except that day he had walked halfway there, before he remembered that he had his own car to drive. He turned around walked back to the parking lot, got in his car and came home to find that Grace had already packed his suitcase, for the trip to his parents' house. The thirty minutes he allowed himself to shower and dress was cut to fifteen. The other fifteen minutes he spent holding and kissing Grace until he finally persuaded her to say goodbye. Otherwise her tempting behavior was gonna cause him to delay starting his trip by about an hour.

Chapter 8 – Back to Snyder

With no time to wasted, he headed west out of Fort Worth on Highway 80 through Weatherford, then on to Abilene, and through Sweetwater, taking Highway 84 on to Snyder. He was racing against time, to reach his father's house before everyone went to bed. When he arrived at nine that evening, though, everyone was setting around the radio listening to Amos and Andy. He surprised everybody as well; as they were flabbergasted when they saw him walked in the door. It had been almost three years since they'd seen him, a reason for an exuberantly excited welcome home. It never once crossed their minds to ask him why he didn't take the time to buy them each a souvenir or a present from the big city. So Alvin had a few minutes to consider – should he give them money, or promise to send them gifts once he return to Fort Worth?

Before Alvin could finish making excuses for why he didn't bring anyone a gift, his father Allan said, in an undertone, "Our worries were not about you bringing us all a present; we were more worried about you having enough money to get back to Fort Worth. If you have something to give us, that's fine and I'll accept it as a bonus. But more than that we're so pleased that you would come home to see your family – that's all the bonus we'll need."

Alvin got out his checkbook, and pen. As he wrote out two five-hundred dollar checks for each of his parents and twenty-five dollar checks to each of his two brothers, he observed, "You're going to be glad that you choose the word 'bonus' because there is no way I'd spend this much on presents for four people!" Once everyone saw the amount, they were as mesmerized with his generosity as they were happy, to see him. Allan Jackson looked sternly at his son, saying, "I want to be sure you can afford to give away so much money all at one time; did you save some for yourself?"

"Yes sir, I did," Alvin answered. "And there are lot's more where that came from, as long as I show up every morning for work and collect my paycheck every week. Meaning," he explained, "that I have a very good job, which has enabled me to buy two cars . . . and my own house."

"Boy," his father said, "If you can afford a house and two cars, you're really doing all right for yourself. Almost makes me want to quite farming and start doing whatever it is you're doing to make this kind of money!"

Alvin's mother Jessie had heard him say that he was hungry, which was why she rushed around the kitchen trying to find enough leftovers to put together in a hurry. She called from the kitchen, saying, "Unless they have cotton fields in Forth Worth you've waited a little too late to think about looking for a new way to make a living!" It was very hard for Jessie to get a word in edgewise, with everybody trying to talk and ask questions at the same time about his life in Forth Worth. Alvin's sixteen-year old brother, Allan Junior, couldn't wait to show off his big brother to his friends. He asks his father if Alvin would agree to drive him and their younger brother Freddy to a little dinky place where all of the colored teenagers hung out. Would he permit them to go?

Allen Senior didn't finished answering, "Yeah," before they were out the door, and on their way. One of the first people Alvin saw was his old girlfriend, Gertrude Cox. The second thing he noticed was that Gertrude had herself a boyfriend – which Alvin figured would exempt him from answering questions about why he hadn't written and kept in touch. Contrary to what he thought, it didn't turn out to be the case at all. Her eyes fixed on him so intently that he felt that he had no other choice but to ask her to dance. Even though the both of them were aware that her boyfriend was watch her slow-dancing with her old flame, Gertrude still managed to tell him that her relationship with this boy wasn't anything serious.

"If you're interesting in talking to me some more, maybe we could get together tomorrow evening? That is if you're still in town at that time." Gertrude ventured. Alvin's response to her suggestion was a pinch on the back and a word of praise, telling her how beautiful she looked and that three years of absence had allowed her to fill out in all of the right places. Once the record stopped playing and they parted, she walked away from the tiny dance floor with a big grin – but still confused as to whether he did want to see her the next day. In Alvin's assessment of her – and other women – Grace was at number one, Effie a very close number two; so far, Gertrude and the others didn't even register. Eventually Allan Jr. and Freddy took Alvin around to all of his old stomping grounds in Snyder – which only amounted to a couple of dinky little cafés, where most colored teenagers went to dance, drink Cokes, eat French fries and hamburgers. When Alvin had seen and shaken hands with most of his old friends, he decided that he had seen enough of seeing nothing, so they drove back to the house. There, his father Allan was sitting up, waiting to get the lowdown on what was going on in cow town. Allen Senior began telling Alvin where the rest of his brothers and sisters were, in case he didn't know and hadn't heard from them. Allen Senior went down the list, of what they were all doing and how long they had done it. Alvin's older brother Willie was living in Hobbs, New Mexico, with his wife and three girls.

Alvin's father eventually got around to saying that things were not going so well with him. "Unless we get lots of rain," he said, "the farmers in this part of the country are going to be in big trouble. Gettin' too old to handle much of that, son." Allen Senior squinted down at his son, and said, "Getting' too old to remember much – like your age, boy."

"Nineteen, almost twenty," Alvin said, and his father asked if he had a girlfriend yet.

"I do," Alvin said to him and ask his father if he could keep a secret.

"A secret?" Allen Senior asked. "Why would I have to keep a secret about you having a girl friend? But if that's what you want that's what it'll be."

"Well," Alvin explained, "My girl friend is white, and we are living together . . ." before he could get any farther, his father stood up. "Whoa," Allen Senior muttered, "Let's you and me go outside." They walked out into the darkness and away from the house. Finally, Allen Senior stopped. "Now, I want you to tell me again what you told me in the house."

"You heard me right the first time," Alvin answered. "My girlfriend is white and we are living together and are going to California to get married as soon as I get back and start making all of the arrangements. Oh yeah," Alvin added. "While we're on the subject of going to California, I would appreciate it if you would notify your sister and my aunt Ellie May that we'll be there the latter part of July."

"Boy," Allen Senior finally said. "Has you gone and lost your mind? Surely you could be satisfied with just sneaking in to do your business, and go back to your place, rather than put yours life in jeopardy, because you ain't so stupid that you don't know sooner or later they'll catch you. And when they do, they'll take a branding iron and stencil 'nigger leave our women alone' all over your ass! Make me understand why you would risk your life for their woman – when you can get the same thing from your own race and less likely to be killed over her? Those people can get away with having our women, but you had better not be caught doing it to their women if you ain't ready to leave this world? And son, its not to say that I haven't ever thought about what it would feel like to wrap my arms around one of those delicious pretty things that I've seen walking the street on Saturday evening, doing their weekend shopping. But not so much that I'd put my life at risk over a pig in the poke – no matter what color she is. In fact, as much as I know, the color of skin and the difference in hair are the only things that differentiate between the two women. Otherwise, why is it that you see so many white men who can't wait for the sun to go down so they can work their way into some colored women's bushy you-know-what? I'm hoping when I stop talking, you're gonna tell me that this is all a joke and you're fixing to take it all back."

"I'm afraid not," Alvin said. "I'm in love with her and she feels the same way about me."

"What about her parents? Sooner or later they'll find out about it, and as soon as they do you're dead man."

"In that case," Alvin answered. "I've been dead about three months, now because that's how long it been since they've known about us. Grace and her mother were inseparable until I came along, and she had to choose between me and her mother – naturally, she chosen me. The way I'm telling it to you now, sounds easy in comparison to the way it actually was the night I showed up at her parent's house. I'm not going to tell you the danger I encountered to get Grace to choose between me and her family, especially her mother. All I'll tell you is, inside of a month, she and her mother were on the phone every day, crying their eyes out over how much they missed each other. And now, they're spending the weekends with her while I'm here, visiting with my family. When Grace finally persuaded her Mama to come over and see how we were living, she could hardly wait to see the kind of neighborhood we lived in. Grace's Mama was so impressed; she couldn't wait to reconcile their differences. Afterward, they wound up spending the night with us at our house. I have to admit that since that time, our social life has been less stressful, especially for Grace. Otherwise we lived like hermits, which was all right with us because all we did was work, come watch television, make love, go to bed – then the next morning, we start all over again. But once Grace and Mrs. Maggie made up, now if we're not at their house, they are certain to be at ours. She seems to be completely contented to have her mother as her companion. Grace has even accepted the fact that her best girlfriend, Peggy – whom I've never met and probably never will – Grace told her she was involved with a colored man. It wasn't Peggy that had the problem; she was afraid her parents would find out that she was associating with a girl who lived with a colored man. The nice thing about it all she and Grace severed their relationship on good turns. With all of that being said, I strongly believe if we stay clear of the public, we are safer in numbers, white numbers in this case."

In a calmer voice, Allen Senior asked, "Is she pretty, or is she some fat stringy-haired girl that her own kind want have anything to do with . . . and perhaps out of desperation they were willing to pawn her off on a colored man, rather than to have her marry some old white man, that' gonna die and leave her with a house full of children?"

"No sir," Alvin answered. "She is about the most beautiful white woman you'll ever see."

Alvin Senior grunted, and let out a short laugh. "Well, if you're gonna have to die over a woman – which I hope will never happen – make damn sure she's worth dying over. Even with her being as pretty as you say she is, I still think you're headed for big troubles, provide you keep carrying on with her. Son, you might be putting your life at risk, for other reason except for the color of her skin and the texture of hair. On the other hand, if your mind is already made up to stay the course, then I won't bother to tell your Mama about your involvement with this white woman, until long after you're gone. I promise you, once she hears about you being involved with that white gal, she's just liable to have herself a nervous breakdown, worrying that you might get yourself killed. Now, the other thing I wanted to say to you, before you threw me off-course telling me about this white gal you is living with – I appreciate the money you gave me and the rest of your family. Now I know which of my children have money, it'll make it easy for me to ask, when times get to be a little too rough."

"Anytime," Alvin told him. "Don't wait to write but call."

"I appreciate that," Allen Senior said, "and you'll be blessed for doing that, because the Lord takes care of children that are good to their parent."

Alvin jokingly asked, "Is that a bribe, Dad?"

"No son, it's not," his father answered. "I've watched people come and I've watched people go, and those that showed kindness toward their parent got along fine. Those that didn't got along poorly. Pay attention to these words – and see what the future has in store for you."

It was late and Alvin was tired, so he asked if his father would excuse him so he could go, and go to bed. The next morning after breakfast, Allen Senior asked him to take a walk with him, to show Alvin the conditions of the crops in the fields. As soon as they had walked some distant from the house, his father asked, "Do you and Miss Grace plan on having children, or have she already decided against having a mixed babies?"

"We haven't given that part of our lives very much thought, not yet anyway." Alvin answered. "I suppose we've been too busy thinking about getting enough money and wealth for ourselves – there hasn't been much of anything else on our minds but that."

Allen Senior looked out, across the field. At last he said, "It's nice to have money, because I sure could use a lot more than you've already given me. A child is a blessing. You're getting to the age where you should be thinking about receiving that blessing, by asking Miss Grace to bless you with a son and me a grandson. Of course," Allen added, "I'm sure it'll depend on y'all doing it, without a bunch of white folks noticing a white woman with a colored baby. I've always thought babies that are made between white and black are some of the prettiest children you ever wonna lay eyes on. The only thing wrong with that – it's always the white man and the colored woman. It's a known fact that the colored man has been given a whole lot of slack here lately by the white man, especially in the last few years. That being the case, you and Miss Grace might be the first to break that tradition. 'Specially since you have her folks behind you and their daughter. If I were you, I wouldn't waste anymore time. I would hurry up and get that white woman pregnant, and let it be you that give me my first mixed grandson. Otherwise you'll fool around and let one of your brothers grab him some white girl, and beat you to it."

"If you feel that it's that important that I be the first to give you your first mixed grand child, then that's what I'll do," Alvin answered. "Although my original plan was that I would send Grace off to college this fall. Once she graduates with a degree in business administration – only then can I even consider getting her pregnant."

His father asked, curiously, "How have you kept her from being pregnant in the first place?"

"How? A danged old condom until I'm twenty five – that's when I plan to have enough money to support a wife and three or four children."

"First of all," Allen Senior mused, "If she is as pretty as you say, I certainty wouldn't wait until I'm twenty-five before I discard that thin piece of rubber that says you haven't had real sex at all. It's more like a man having his feet washed with his socks on. It may've felt good at the time, but there're still that little something that says it would've felt better without the socks.

"Maybe so," Alvin agreed. "But there're so many things life has to offer Grace and me, besides tossing the rubbers and having lots of babies. I have a woman that's willing to carry her share of the load every step of the way, but not if she's pregnant. Then again," Alvin added, "Maybe I ought to talk this over with Grace and see what she says. If I know her she'll probably love the idea of being pregnant – she's mentioned several times to me about us having a baby."   His father put his hand on Alvin shoulder, saying, "Son, you do whatever feel is right between you and that girl. I'm just an old selfish man that didn't get very much out of my life. Maybe if I had used condoms when your mama was in her susceptible years, I wouldn't have struggled as much as I did to feed those hungry mouths that worked me ragged all of those years. Unlike your father, you have a plan – and in order to execute it, you need to be at the right place at the right time."

Alvin was relieved, after the long talk he had with his father last night and again this morning, concerning his involvement with Grace, all of which led him to believe that his father had accepted his relationship with Grace. The only other request that Allen Senior had was for Alvin to drive him over to a neighbor's house.

"I want you to take a little time to share with them what you've accomplished before you head out for home," was how Allen Senior put it. "The reason being – they have children your age, still riding around in junky old cars and getting into trouble on weekends.

His first stop was at his friends the Millers. "You remember my boy Alvin, don't you?"

"I sure do," was about all Mr. Miller got to say before Alvin's farther continued. "Yes sir, my boy Alvin lives in Fort Worth now, and does he make a lot of money cooking for them white folks! He owns a house, two cars and a whole lot of other stuff. Out of all of my boys so far, he's the only son that's a real trailblazer and being as modest as I am, I'll have to say he takes every bit of it after me. As you well know, opportunity for colored folks – back when fellows like me and you were coming up – wasn't the same as they are today. That's why I got stuck in these cotton fields. The important thing is that I'm so grateful to say that it all stemmed from the fruit of my loins. I passed an unlit torch onto him, and he set a flame that will pass onto his children, and hopefully his children will pass it onto their children, and into a Camelot of elite Jacksons."

Allen Senior had Alvin drive him over to another one of his friends named Jonas Wilson, and told him pretty much the same story. Pretty soon, Alvin got anxious; he was missing Grace, and he wanted to visit with his mother, before he headed back to Fort Worth. He reminded his father of those things, at which they abandoned the rest of his father's intended visits and returned home just in time to see the boys helping their mother to put the food on the table.

As soon as everyone took their seats and began to eat, Alvin's mother Jessie came at him with all kinds of questions, concerning his time away from home for almost three years. One of which was about having a girlfriend, and before he could answer, she told him that he needed to come back to Snyder and marry Gertrude. Jessie's reason was that Gertrude had turned out to be such a beautiful young lady. She came to church on Sundays, Jessie insisted, and in addition to that she was a Christian girl and it was unlikely that he would find one like her in a city the size of Forth Worth.

"I know she still love you," Jessie insisted. "Practically every time I see her, she never fails to hug and kiss me, and ask 'when do you think he's coming home?' I told her the only communication you and I have is through Miss Irene Bailey, and I've had her address some fifteen odd years, but not yours. I didn't have a clue as to where you live or how to get in touch with you except through Miss Irene."

"I saw her with her boyfriend last night," Alvin replied. "And with all the attention he gave her, I don't think she'll be missing me too much longer. Anyway, I've met a girl that I'm interested having a resolute relationship with."

"Before you go being too resolute with her, just make sure she's a Christian girl that understands – one woman and one man, and not Tom, Dick and Harry." His mother insisted, eventually changed the course of her questions, and began talking about what had gone on since he had left home. She admired him, saying how well he must be doing especially if he could give eleven hundred dollars all at one time. "And only the lord could've sent you home with this money when he did, because he's the only one that knows how much we needed it. I'm sure your daddy has already told you how bad our cotton crop was last year, and if we don't get some rain soon we're gonna have ourselves a repeat of last years!" By the time she finished asking questions and thanking him over and over again for his generous contribution to the family, it was two o'clock in the afternoon and Alvin was missing Grace something terrible.

He reluctantly said to his mother, "I'm sorry that I came so late and have to leave so early – but I must, since I'll have to make up for the sleep I lost last night driving here." They all got up from the table, and walked Alvin to his car, and after his mother hugged and kissed him, they all waved him goodbye. Alvin headed back to Fort Worth. Before he left on Saturday evening he told Grace that he would be home around six-thirty on Sunday evening. She went and changed into her silk robe, about fifteen minutes before he was due to arrived. The instant that he walked through the door she rushed into his arms, and clung to him adoringly, as if her staying alive depended on his love and affection.

When they finally detached, Maggie was standing there next to them. She handed Alvin a cold beer, saying, "I know you haven't had one of these since you left Fort Worth – I've heard about how those hypocrites down there won't let y'all drink anything stronger than a coke."

By the time Alvin had finished off a couple of beers and told everyone about his trip, J.D. and Maggie was about ready to go home. It couldn't have happen too soon as far as Alvin and Grace were concerned. One night away from each other was swiftly causing them to lose their restraints and to wait five minutes longer was almost unbearable. The instant the front door slammed shut they headed towards the bedroom, with different thoughts on each of their minds. His first and foremost urgency was intimacy; and hers was conversation first and urgent intimacy later.

Alvin had his work cutout for him, staying in control, while answering her many questions about his trip to his family's house. Contrary to what she thought was important, his need was to get things pacified, and then talk about his trip to his parent's house. But that wasn't the case as far as she was concerned; it was more important for her to hear him gossip about his trip rather than diminish her urgency, which he had a lot of. Since he didn't want to overreact, he took the time to tell her about his father's reaction, when he told him about being involved with this white girl. "I admit," Alvin explained. "It took me some time to calm him down and when I finally did – he is asking me to tell you that he wants you to give him a grandson."

"I think that would be a wonderful idea," Grace answered. "I would take great pleasure in giving your daddy a grandbaby and so should you – if for nothing more than to save a trip to the bathroom to dispose of something that could have created one."

"It may not be as easy as all of that," Alvin said. "I haven't gotten around to mentioning this to you yet, but I had intended talking to you about going to college this fall. We might be flushing in down the toilet for years to come."

"Well Mr. Alvin Jackson," Grace exclaimed. "You're just full of surprises aren't you?" Tell me – when did you come up with this plan?"

"The very first time I noticed how uniquely intelligent you are . . . and I think you are intelligent far above normal. I saw that you had the potential to become a famous lawyer, or a doctor or anything – even an Indian chief."

Grace began to laugh. "Now I know you're kidding me, aren't you?"

"About you being an Indian chief," Alvin hugged her closer to him. "But not the other two professions – I'm serious about you going to college and becoming anything you wish to become. But," he added, "now that I think about it, I should go ahead and impregnate you anyway – that way I won't have to worry about some good-looking college boy encroaching on my territory. Most boys don't want a woman if her tummy sticks out further than her tits, unless he caused it himself."

"You're being silly-jealous, if you think I'd get myself involved with some immature college boy who doesn't know the first thing about responsibility. I might be young but I'm not stupid. As far as me going to collage this fall – if it's all the same to you, I'd rather work with you on the morning shift as a waitress for another year. Then I should be able to concentrate on my studies, instead of always wanting to rub tummies with you every evening after work. That should tell you how interesting I am in going to college this fall!"

"In that case," Alvin answered, "You'll probably be in your thirties before you decide we've rubbed tummy enough . . . if you're anything like me, I'm afraid the closer you get to the one-year mark, the more you'll want to add a another year . . . and that might wind up in double digits. Even so, I can't imagine either one of us saying, 'Well I've rubbed tummy with you every night for a solid year. Now it's time to move on to better things.' Then we'll ask ourselves – isn't it better than to stick to the things we know best?"

"I hope you really mean that," Grace said. "Anything else I don't worry about."

"Well," Alvin ventured. "How's about me giving you something to really worry about – making plans for a train ride to Los Angeles? I thank the time has come to show our Lord, as well as our parents a little respect, for letting us go on living in sin for as long as we have. Less than two weeks from now, not only will we be on our way to Los Angeles to be married – we'll finally know what it feels like to walk the streets holding hands, without the fear of being shot by some bigoted policemen like we have here in Texas."

"That sounds wonderful," Grace sighed, "Except I don't know what part of this conversation I've missed that makes me believe I have something to worry about . . . what?"

"Married couples do it more often, and I'm worried that you won't be able to keep up."

"Is this your way of telling me to stop talking and roll over on my back?"

"Something to that effect," Alvin answered, and there was no more conversation for some time. Afterwards he said, "Now that you've solve that riddle, I have another mystery – not as urgent as the one you just solved. This one I need your input to help me to figure out. Can we afford to have your mother and John to come with us to California, and celebrate our wedding? The reason I haven't come right out and mentioned it, is because they would not only feel obligated to come along, but they'd feel responsible to buy their tickets as well. I don't know whether we could afford ours and their expenses for two weeks, and still stay on course."

"What course you are talking about" Grace asked, sleepily.

"I haven't gotten around to telling you this," Alvin answered, after a moment. "But I've saved a little over seven thousand dollars to invest in real-estate as soon as we're back from California."

"Seven thousand dollars!" Grace suddenly did not feel so sleepy. "Are you saying that we have seven thousand dollars in the bank? How did you do that?"

"By saving my money – I made up my mind before I met you, to never become just another car and homeowner. I heard so many people say, 'Lord if I can only pay for this house and car, then everything else is gonna be all right.' And that is as much as they get out of life because that is as far as they can see. I've set my sights much higher than a house and car. You can bet I won't be spending the rest of my life saying 'once I get this old house and car paid off everything is gonna be all right.' When I make my first million – and it won't be until then that you'll hear me start saying 'everything is gonna be all right.' But that doesn't mean that I won't do a foolish thing from time to time . . . like spending half my savings on a dress for a certain girl who never pay me a dime for what I went through to get her the dress."

"Bet me," Grace replied. "That dress was paid for – ten times it's worth, the first night I came to your apartment. I distinctly remember you calling out to some girl several times by the name of, 'Oh honey baby please' long before you reached satisfaction! And then afterward, you smacked her butt and said, 'Your dress has just been paid for in full, honey baby!'"

The next evening when Grace got to work, she gave her notice to quit the night shift, and applied for a waitress job on the morning shift. She made it known to Earline that if she was hired for the waitress position, she wouldn't be able to start until after her two-weeks vacation in California with her family and boyfriend. Meanwhile Alvin had already asked for his two weeks off to begin on July 24, the same as Grace had requested. All that was left to do was to wait until the time to ride the train to California. His father had already consulted his sister Ellie May about making the arrangement with her pastor to marry him and Grace. Aunt Ellie May also agreed to accommodate her nephew Alvin and his guests, and provide hospitality. Aunt Ellie May was a widow whose husband was killed in a work-related accident; she had children, none of them living at home. They were all grown and married, living in Los Angeles. Two days before Alvin and Grace were scheduled to leave for California; Alvin came home from work, and saw Grace and Maggie had just gotten back from shopping. One of the things Grace had had picked up was her wedding dress. Alvin had previously seen it and approved.

In the middle of Grace and her mother's conversation, Grace asked him, "Did you decide whether or not we can afford to pay for John and Mama to come with us to California and back?" Before Alvin – caught off-guard – could answer, Maggie said, "I will not let you and Alvin pay my way to California. Between J.D. and me, we'll have enough money to pay John's and my way there and back. J. D. can't go because his job at the garage won't allow him, but not me . . . and anyway, there're nothing in the universe that's gonna stop me from missing out on a once in a lifetime event such as witnessing my daughter walk down the aisle on her wedding day."

Alvin, upon, hearing Maggie's put so much importance on going to her daughter's wedding with barely enough money to do it with. Alvin felt a surge of compassion for his mother-n-law to be. He suggested to Grace, "Why don't we do this in the form of a ritual? I'll give you the cash for their tickets as your wedding present; in turn you give the money to your mother as a token of your appreciation. In that way she'll pay hers and John's way to California without spending a dime of her hard-earned money. If you were marrying a white boy, there wouldn't be any reason for her to spend her money going California. How does that sound to everyone?"

"Good," Maggie said, her face showing her relief. "Then I'll buy all the food for the four of us, going to Los Angeles and coming back to Texas, too."

218

Chapter 9 – The Promised Land

July, 1954:   The four of them – Alvin, Grace, Maggie and John boarded the train to California. It was midmorning the following day when they finally arrived in Los Angeles.   Grace, Maggie and John had already exited the train through the front, and wait some time for Alvin to exit the train through the rear.   Once Grace caught sight of Alvin, it was as if she had just crossed over the Sinai desserts into Beulah land. They felt quite demoralized, as they had to travel separately, those two days from Fort Worth, Texas, to Los Angeles.   Their feet barely touched the ground as they raced toward each other at what time they were necking and kissing in public with no inhibition whatsoever. Every now and then, they'd glance over at Maggie to see what her reaction was. As soon as they saw that Maggie positively approved of their open affection for each other, Alvin and Grace went from casual to deliberately turning themselves into public spectacle for everyone to see. A few minutes of them flaunting their new-found freedom was about all Maggie could tolerate, as she finally flagged down a taxi and told them that they needed to get in and be on their way to Ellie May's house. She told them if everyone would hurry, it was possible they might have time to do a little sightseeing. As far as Alvin and Grace was concerned, they had all of the sightseeing they needed: As they wove in and out of the crowds of people to where Maggie had flagged down her second taxi, because they had taken too much time to catch the first one. They laughed on their way to Aunt Ellie May's house, about all of the stares they got – but it didn't matter to them. Integration was legal in California. They murmured to each other that the same laws were needed in Texas to protect people against intolerance, and where biases ran rampant in favor of the wicked ones. It's was not so much the public as it was the law itself; a handful of lawmakers did all of the thinking on racial matters for the whole state of Texas – almost a police state, when it came to protecting the minority. Since Maggie had all of the directions, she did all of the talking, telling the taxi to drive them to Seventieth Street and Broadway on the South Side.

Alvin's Aunt Ellie May came to the door, with extended arms. "Oh," she exclaimed, "My nephew Alvin! Come on in here, boy, and give your Aunt Ellie May a great big hug!"   Then she looked over at Grace, adding, "And I know who you are, you have got to be Miss Grace!" She gave Grace a hug. "Now, Miss Grace, this lady, she has to be your mother?"

"Yes Aunt Ellie May," Grace answered, "This is my mother – Maggie Adams, and my brother John Adams."

"Y'all come right on in, here and make yourselves right at home!" Aunt Ellie May offered. "It's about noontime and I was just about to fix myself a bite to eat. Would y'all like to join me?" Everybody was hungry, and answered eagerly. "I'm making vegetable soup, and there's cold ham and cheese sandwiches – I sure do hope y'all like cold ham and cheese sandwiches and hot vegetable soup because I sure do, it's one of my favorites. Now . . . ." Aunt Ellie May continued, "after we all finish eating, and y'all are ready to go, I'll give you the name and address where you're suppose to go and get y'all's marriage license."

Grace suggested to Alvin, "Why don't we allow ourselves an hour or so to take a stroll up and down a few blocks before we decide what we're going to do next?" By the time the three of them, including John, had walked to Slauson Street and back to Aunt Ellie May's house, an hour or so had passed. Maggie called a taxi; the four of them rode downtown to the courthouse, and waited while Alvin filled out documents and signed for their marriage licenses. After that, Alvin and John trailed along behind the two woman as they shopped for souvenirs to take back home. They were very surprised to return to Aunt Ellie May's house in the late afternoon, and see so many people there. Alvin got the distinct feeling that it wasn't him that all of these people came to see. It was all about that white girl that he was about to marry, which brought out all the cousins and kin-folks.

Not only had Ellie May's kin and friends come out in droves but they bought enough food to feed a small army – and an assortment of liquor as well. Eventually, everyone realized it was near eleven o'clock at night, and they had been eating and drinking for four hours. That's when most of them started to yawn and complain about being tired, wore out from working all day. When Alvin heard the kinfolks complaining about being so fatigued, from working all day, he attributed it to a whole lot of booze and too much food. He had another thought – about the men being exhausted – which had nothing to do with booze or food. He attributed their exhaustion to the fleeting and flashing of their overworked eyeballs which they secretly stole glances at Maggie's notable figure. Probably got themselves all charged up and couldn't wait to get their wives home and do the inevitable, while their memories tried to hold onto the last image they saw of Maggie's curves. But if Maggie was willing to call it a night, as much as she loved socializing – especially after she had a few drinks under her belt, then just maybe the kinfolks had a legitimate reason for complaining about being tired.

Maggie came right out and said to Alvin, "Hurry up and find the four of us a hotel, or anything with a bed in it so I can shift my weight from my feet to my back. It's been a fine party, but I've had about all of this night that I can possible handle."

Aunt Ellie May spoke up. "Honey, you ain't going nowheres. I have plenty of room right here in my own house – I thought it was understood that y'all were to stay at my house – I ain't about to let y'all travel, all the way from Texas to California, and then going to some hotel and pay some outrageous amount of money for a room when you have one that already paid for. No ma'am," she said emphatically. "I've spent all day washing and changing sheets and cleaning up around here. So y'all don't have to go nowhere but back yonder and go to bed. I only have three bedrooms – since I'm up every morning around five thirty I'll just sleep on the sofa. If y'all think you is putting me out – don't be, because I've slept here many of nights when there wasn't a soul in this house but mine. I know y'all are used to better living conditions – but like I just said, what I got is clean and I keep it that way."

Alvin listened to Aunt Ellie May make excuses about her house not being nice enough for her guest, and he wanted to tell her that she'd be surprised to know that her house was much nicer than where Maggie lived, that time he drove Grace home. Aunt Ellie May's daughter Pauline – who was Alvin first cousin – was married to a man by the name of Juan Gonzales. Juan being half-Mexican and half Negro, he had a low toleration for alcohol, which meant they were about the last ones leave. It took Pauline half dozen attempts before she finally got Juan onto his feet and stagger out the door to the car. She drove away pretty well miffed. The very next day, Grace and Maggie took Aunt Ellie May grocery-shopping and came back loaded down with all kinds of food and supplies, which bought a joyful smile to her face. Alvin was sure that the reason she was so excited about all the food Grace bought was because she didn't work full-time. The little money she got every month was from her husband's pension, which wasn't enough to feed many extra mouths. Of course there was a settlement from his accident, but according to family rumor, she didn't get enough from her insurance to amount to a whole hell of a lot.

The next day, Alvin and Grace, Maggie and John, all went to the movies. Every day thereafter, the four of them did something different and exciting. They even rode the city busses in different directions – another way to amuse themselves while anticipating their real reason for coming to California. Finally the appointed time arrived; a Sunday afternoon. Maggie spent all of it, trying to make sure that Grace and Alvin looked their very best, before marching down the aisle to say 'I do.' It wasn't until Maggie was certain that her darlings met her standards as to what a bride and groom was suppose to look like, that she allowed Frank and his wife Stella to drive Grace and herself to the church where the wedding was to beheld. Alvin and John rode with another cousin of Alvin's – Trudy and her husband, Rufus Smith. When the bride and groom arrived at the church, they were each escorted to separate rooms, to wait until the evening service was over. Finally the time arrived for them to march down the isle to take their vows.

Grace entered the aisle, escorted by John and their mother Maggie. Grace looked like someone who had walked out of a big Hollywood movie screen. She was amazingly beautiful after all of the effort her mother put into making sure that every stitch of clothing was perfect and every hair on her head was in place. She left no doubt in anyone's mind about the way a bride should look at her wedding. She wore a beautiful ivory silk mermaid style gown. The off-the-shoulder style displayed her glowing golden skin. With unerring taste she had selected a simple yet form-fitting dress that showed her gorgeous figure to best advantage. The beading and lace embellishment on the gown was her only accessories save for elegant satin pumps, in the exact same shade of ivory. The veil was short in the front and gathered in the back to flow down past her shapely shoulders. Alvin wore an Italian black pin-stripe silk suit with a pale silver-gray shirt and tie. The flower he wore on the lapel was the same deep pink color as the blossoms Grace carried in her hand-held bouquet.

The preacher began to say a prayer for Alvin and Grace, regarding their safety once they were back in Texas. He said that there were no place in the Bible or any book he'd ever read, that said it was unlawful for two peoples of different races to be married. "Except in those southern states of the United States of America – I declare to you this day that people urgently need to get together, change those laws, and give people the freedom to marry as they please. Now," he continued, "we got lots of racial tension right here in Los Angeles, California, but what do we say about that?" The congregation must have rehearsed it several times because they all answered in unison, "Sticks and stones might break my bones, but talk doesn't bother me!"

He continued, "So as long as nobody physically touches you – what they say shouldn't bother you. Let it go in one ear and out the other! Can I get an amen?" Everybody said "Amen!"

"Now, before I get started here, joining these two people together in matrimony, I just want to say one thing to the people here tonight – I ain't never in all of the weddings I've performed since I've been a preacher – seen a couple that look more beautiful than these two people standing right here in front of me tonight. Now son," the preacher continued, "I just want to ask you one simple question; how in the world, did you wind up with someone as beautiful as this young lady you're about to be married too? Whoo-wee mercy, mercy, mercy me!" He exclaimed, as he wiped his face with his handkerchief, "I tell you the truth – you must've done something that pleased the Lord! Only a chosen few ever gets the chance to be in the position where you are, with such a pretty woman as she is! Can I get a witness?" Everyone applauded, rising and standing in the pews. At that point, Alvin and Grace finally got to speak their vows, and Alvin was told to kiss the bride. When that happened, Maggie rushed over, clinging to Grace and weeping uncontrollably; while she tried to tell Grace how happy she was to have finally seen it happen. "Now," she exclaimed, between her tears. "It's all legal – you are a married woman. This is your real husband, not some illegitimate roommate you've been living with for the last six months. I'm so proud of you, Alvin, for keeping a promise you made to me the first night I came to your house. You've finally relieved my grief and worry about you letting some woman come between you and my baby before this day arrived!" At Maggie's emotional outburst, some of the colored woman standing nearby began to cry, right alone with her. They put their arms around her and Grace.

One woman said to Maggie with sympathetic words, "You need to stop your crying before you start all of us to crying, too. Your daughter is gonna be just fine! She done married herself a fine young man. And he'll make her just as happy if she had gone and married herself a millionaire!" Those women escorted Maggie and Grace to a side room where they set up a surprise wedding reception for the bride and groom. They served punch and assortment of hors d'oeuvres, cake, ice cream – and jelly beans for good luck. Before the wedding, Alvin had asked Maggie to make reservations in advance at the Belmont Hotel. He had promised Grace when they first moved in together that he would take her to a great hotel on their wedding night, and the morning afterward he'd have her breakfast served to her in bed. The Belmont didn't discriminate against colored people who wanted to stay there, but the management didn't go around advertising it, either. Upon entering the hotel lobby, Alvin and Grace noticed a few hostile stares from other guests, which didn't intimidate them the least bit. Maggie and John's room was adjacent to Alvin and Grace's room. It was something that neither one of them had ever experienced before, a once and lifetime adventure for them all. There were two bottles of champagne included, compliments of the management, since Maggie had already told the clerk the room was for a honeymoon couple. Maggie popped the cork on one bottle, the minute she walked through the door. At first, no one was drinking champagne except Maggie and Alvin.

Alvin kept after Grace, urging her to try just a sip. "Think of it as being medicine subscribed by your doctor. The only way you're going to get well is to drink it. Honey, everyone knows except you that we're supposed to celebrate our wedding with a bottle of champagne. Once you taste it you're gonna be preoccupied with trying to figure out if its medicine, and then why in the hell does it make me feel so good? All the medicine I've ever taken has always wound up making me feel even sicker."

"Okay," Grace agreed. "You've made your point –I don't want to hold up the celebration, so go ahead and pour me one."

The four of them made a toast and touched glasses, Maggie commanding, "Bottoms up everyone!" Everyone obeyed, even John – making it his first taste of alcohol as far as anyone knew. After Grace's second glasses of champagne she became more than usually amorous, which finally prompted Maggie to suggest, "John, we'd better move out of these newlyweds' way so they don't keep dancing on my feet. They started out in that corner of the room and now they are tripping all over us."

The two smiled and just kept right dancing even closer, dancing to the soft sound of music which Alvin had noticed was piped into theirs, and every room in the hotel. They slowly moved their feet to the sound of music; now and again they'd pause long enough for a sip of champagne and it was back to caressing and tasting each others lips as they slowly moved around the room. When Maggie and John finally realized that the bride and groom were in a world all to themselves, they stood up to say goodnight. Grace stopped just long enough to hug and thank her mother for making a fantasy of hers come to full flowering.

"I didn't do anything" Maggie answered. "It was you that made your own dream come true, the night you left me for Alvin, remember?

"You can say that now," Grace said. "You weren't aware of the guilt I carried around for the first few days after I left. I'm not quite sure, but I think if you had asked – I believe I would've caved in, came back and been miserable for the rest of my life. Except you didn't; I believe that my anxiety to rekindle loving relationships with you, Mama, actually caused me to accelerate my efforts to contact you. Once you gave me your approval of Alvin and me marrying . . . well, that was just settled. I have other choice but to credit you for all of the wonderful things which have happened to me. This jubilant night might never have happened if I had done otherwise."

"That was another one of your secrets that I didn't know about," Maggie answered. "And I'm glad I didn't, because I could have messed everything up for you. Now, it's just the opposite, if you ever decide to come back home without Alvin, I wouldn't let you. As long as you have a husband who treats you the way Alvin does, you don't really need me anymore. You are no longer dependent on me, and I am no longer responsible for you. Your accountability to Alvin went into effect the moment you walked out my door, and into his house. Your name is no longer Grace Adams; from now on people will refer to you as Mrs. Grace Jackson. I was so worried that something would happen to cause you and Alvin to break up, and all you'd be to him was a roll in the hay! Now if something goes wrong – lord forbid and y'all split up – I can always say she was legally married to him with good intentions, and not just someone he'd use for just a good time." As Maggie started out the door, she added in a whisper, "While y'all are celebrating your wedding night, why don't you let Alvin squeeze in a grandbaby for me, I would just love it if you'd do that for your dear old Mama."

Grace smiled, waving her hand, "Good night, Mama," and kept right on dancing.

The next morning, Alvin was awakening when Maggie knocked on the door. He reached for the covers to cover Grace's nudity; he remembered that the covers had been flung off on the floor, the instant that Grace fell into his arms. They had a lively night, Alvin attempting to recreate that most memorable night, the first night they slept together. He spring to his feet and tossed the covers over her, then slipped on his trousers and opened the door.

"Boy," she exclaimed, "What took you so long? Y'all weren't still at it were you? I'm going to order up coffee – and I was wondering if y'all want me to order you some too?" Coffee was the farthest thing from their minds, but since Maggie was on cloud nine with excitement, they didn't want to hose down her cloud by letting her drink her coffee alone. At that they both said yes. Alvin wouldn't allow Grace to get out of bed, except to go to the bathroom, since he had promised that he was going to serve her breakfast in bed the morning after their wedding.   When   the   room server bought the coffee, he asked everyone if they were ready to order breakfast. Everyone answered yes, and told him what each of them wanted. When room service returned with the food, Alvin had the waiter to serve Grace her breakfast in bed. According to tradition, they locked arms and gave each other their first bite, followed by a kiss and washed down with a swallow of fresh-pressed orange juice. Then he went and joined Maggie and John at their table and ate his breakfast.

After Grace had finished, Alvin peeled back all the covers, except a sheet which he wrapped her in, lifted her, and carried her around the room, telling her to repeat after him, "My last name is no longer Adams. My surname had been changed to Jackson." They fooled around for most of the morning, before taking a taxi back to Aunt Ellie May's house. The next morning after breakfast Aunt Ellie May suggest that they take a tour of Hollywood, and possibly catch a glimpse of some famous movie star. They did and visited many places they thought they'd find movie stars hanging out. Hollywood and Vine, was one of the many places that they visited that day, which included looking at hand and footprints of some famous Hollywood movie stars. permanently planted in the sidewalk in front of Graumann's Chinese Theater. They came to a hotdog stand and ordered each one a large chilidog with French fries and Coke. They sat there eating their hotdogs, just watching people as they walked by, and hoping that at least one of them would prove to be a famous movie star. But none of them was anyone they recognized as being a movie star.

Finally, Alvin said, "According to my watch we should be headed back to Aunt Ellie May's house. We've got to be at the train station no later than three forty five."

They barely had enough time to finish packing and kissing Aunt Ellie May good-bye. As they rushed out to the awaiting taxi, which Aunt Ellie had already called while everyone was running around making sure they didn't leave anything behind. Once they exited the taxi and headed for the ticket counter at the train station, the good life was over for Alvin and Grace. He warned Grace, even before they reached the train station, to act as if she didn't belong to him. He was afraid that someone boarding the train destined for Forth Worth would notice their affectionate behavior and cause trouble for them once they got off the train. It wasn't like Grace didn't already know, but she listened anyway and boarded the train with her family through the white section. Alvin boarded through the colored section, and rode back to Texas the same way he rode to California – segregated. The moment Alvin boarded the train and took his seat, he realized that their few days of freedom over – and now he and Grace were reverting back to that former feeling of furtiveness and unease, when they were in public together. The freedom of walking the streets, holding hands, and kissing in broad daylight had suddenly become a thing of the past. Not only must Alvin ride segregated from his new wife in those two days it took to travel from Los Angeles back to Fort Worth, he had to take a separate taxi home. Otherwise he might have given away their secret; sharing a car with the same two white women he boarded the train with in Los Angeles. To be absolutely safe, Alvin waited twenty minutes before flagging down a taxi. By the time he came home everyone was well into talking about their visit to Los Angeles. The minute he walked through the door, conversation came to a sudden halt. Those two days of traveling separately was as if they had spent months apart from one another, even though they had lived together for six moths before the wedding. Something about the legality of being married that inspired them to openly fall into each other's arms and suck lips in the presence of her family.

J.D. drawled, "It must be nice to be young and in love, or else those two days y'all spent apart from each other would've had such an enormous impact. So Alvin – was that any indication of how y'all conducted yourselves on your wedding night?"

Alvin answered, jokingly, "If you could compare what you just saw, to what took place on our wedding night, every one of us would be calling you 'baldy'. By now you would've pulled every strand of your hair out of your head, right down the middle and probably looked just like Larry from the Three Stooges. Anyway, Alvin continued, "it was phenomenal experience for me – and everyone. We could have spent our honeymoon in Paris, France, and it wouldn't have been any better than the time we had in Los Angeles."

"J.D.," Maggie exclaimed, "You would have to have seen it for yourself. Alvin and Grace – they were magnificent, radiant – from the time their feet touched the streets of Los Angles, until the time they boarded the train back to Texas. I think hey tried to cram one solid year of solitude into the two weeks of freedom we spent in California. I admit they got quite a few gawks, from some curious-minded people, but the important thing no one tried imposing their biased behavior on them, like it would've been if they were here in Texas. Knowing that – they didn't allow anyone or anything to trespass on their freedom to move freely in the crowds at the train station – they reminded me of two skilled figure skaters! The embarrassing part of it all was when the preacher announced to them you're now man and wife – I became so emotional that I wound up in the arms of a bunch of nice strange colored ladies. It seems more often than not nowadays, that I find myself secretly apologizing to people of color. First it was Alvin – six months ago. I was willing to kill him, not so much for taking my daughter from me, but for the color of his skin. But it would be a waste of words if I were to say I love him now as much I hated him back you know when. What really made Alvin acceptable to me was my first visit to his home – that's when I saw that he could transform my baby from a person of peasantry to a princess, living in a castle! And I so liked Alvin's Aunt Ellie May, her daughters and their friends. I never knew much about colored people, but they were some of the nicest people I had ever met. They all treated me as if I were some kind of royalty. Why does everyone always show colored folks in movies and on TV as undomesticated without a right to live amongst civilized people? I was one of those naive people who believed such nonsense until Alvin became part of my family, and his Aunt Ellie May showed us her hospitality. I am just so sorry that I've been so ill-informed all of these years."

J.D. interrupted, saying, "Now, you're not gonna find Alvin's Aunt Ellie May, and her daughters in every colored person you meet. There're some of those black bastards out there that would as soon to cut your throat as to look at you. It all right to be friends with them – just make damn sure that when you leave you take your head with you – alive, that is!'"

"He has a point there," Alvin agreed. "There're times when I'm around certain people? I'd check from time to time to make sure that my head is where it supposed to be. The only difference between your fear of the colored man's threat and my fear of the white man's admonition – the colored man will talk big, until the white men shows up wearing the big Stetson hats. Then the colored men and all of their big talk flies right out the window. Whereas, when a white man threatens to take a colored man's head off – he'll do it because he has no one to answer to, since he has the law on his side. Let me put it another way; if Grace and I were to accidentally stray out of our domain and wound up in the wrong district? It's more dangerous for me and Grace to be caught in a white neighborhood than it would be in a black neighborhood. A black man will try and take your woman but a white man will try and take your life over a white woman – even if she doesn't belong to such."

Maggie spoke up, "You can say what this one does on this side of the tracks and that one does on the other side of the tracks – as far as I'm concerned it's wrong, and doesn't make a lick of sense, now that I've mingled with people like Alvin and his Auntie Ellie May and her relatives." That brought everyone to silence for a minute or so, and Maggie and Grace withdrew to the kitchen, where they spoke in undertones, of their lavish excursion. Eventually Maggie and Grace ran out of things to talk about, so Maggie summoned her family together and went home, while Alvin and Grace went off to bed.

The next morning Alvin went out to get a paper, mainly to collect information for his book report. Usually after he'd collected the material he needed for a book report, he'd give the paper over to Grace and she'd hand him back the classifieds. Then he would browse through the real-estate section, looking for property to invest in. One which caught his eye was a twenty-unit apartment building, for forty-thousand dollars. Alvin got all excited over this: he asked Grace to call the real estate office to see how far seven thousand dollars would go toward purchasing a forty-thousand dollar apartment building? The real estate broker whom Grace spoke with told her that she would be happy to show her the building. If Grace liked it, then the broker would take her back to the office and work out the details – including how much she needed to deposit in escrow as earnest money, to start the ball rolling. Immediately Alvin called Maggie, and asked her to go with him and Grace to the apartment building to do a walk-through. Alvin asked Maggie to act as her inexperienced daughter's representative, and he would pose as their maintenance person. Maggie came right over, and the three of them looked over the building very carefully. Alvin loved it at once; so did Grace and Maggie.

When he said, "If it was me I'd buy it in a minute," that was his signal that he approved of purchasing the building. Maggie let the real estate lady know that she had made the first step in selling her the building. At the real estate office, the broker worked out all the details, and Grace wrote out a five-hundred dollar check for the earnest money. Then, they went home and began studying the numbers; if they raised the rents on the apartments by just a little, the rents would leave them about eleven hundred and some odd dollars a month profit. This was contingent upon all units being occupied, save the on-site manager's two-bedroom apartment. Ten days later the real-estate broker called Grace to tell her that her loan had been approved and she could close escrow in three weeks or less. After Grace hung up the phone, she called Maggie to tell her the good news. Excited, Maggie told Grace that she and J.D. would be over, bringing a bottle of inexpensive champagne to celebrate their accomplishment. The instant Maggie came through the door with the champagne, she went straight to Grace, wrapping her arms around her and exclaiming, "You are so lucky to have latched on to Alvin when you did! Just look at what this colored boy has done for you!" She shook Alvin by his shoulders, and said, with a happy smile, "Thank you Alvin for being the unique person that you are!" Everyone raised their glasses and J. D. also made some corny but flattering remarks, and they gathered around the kitchen table for a conference, for Alvin had an important request to make of his in-laws.

"Grace and me are about to ask y'all to do something for us – something impossible for us to do for ourselves, without revealing us as a mixed couple. Not only would that send our tenants moving like rats from a burning barn, but once they saw their landlord was colored! They'd be out of here so fast that they wouldn't bother to ask for a refund on the unused rent. But if you two where to move into as managers, then things should go off without a hitch . . ."

That was as far as he got before Maggie was on her feet saying, "Yes we'll do it and what a loving and honorable thing to ask me to do for my two babies! It would be my pleasure to move out of that old beat-up trailer and into a nice place, just the right size for the three of us! J.D. – you and John will just love it as much as I do." She turned her attention back to Alvin and Grace. "You two" are so thoughtful to offer me the opportunity to work for my very own daughter and son-n-law."

"You are quite welcome," Alvin answered. "Though, there are a couple of things required of you two – you two must keep the place neat and clean. Don't bring along those old beat-up cars that have got your old place so junked up – and I also noticed that old trailer was cluttered with car parts and a tool-box, sitting in the living room. The point I'm trying to make – y'all have to keep the apartment clean inside, as well as the outside. This way the tenants will appreciate it, and it will hold its value much longer. The other thing . . . and it wasn't my idea, but Grace came up with it . . . she'd be willing to match whatever your take home-pay is from your job, plus she'll let y'all live in the manager's apartment rent free."

"Oh!" Maggie exclaimed, "Just letting me live rent-free is more than enough, I wasn't making that much anyway. My job was only part-time and was just about enough to cover the rent. J.D.'s paycheck is enough for the three of us to survive on."

"I'm sorry Mama," Grace spoke up firmly. "But Alvin and I had already figured your salary as being one of our expenditures, and we don't plain on wasting a lot of time refiguring our budget."

Maggie kissed Grace, said her goodbyes then her and J.D went home. They were very well aware that Grace and Alvin's vacation and honeymoon was over. The next morning they were both back to work again. Grace had secured the waitress job, working the morning shift, the same time as Alvin's shift, but they still had to ride to work in two separate cars. She was white and he was colored – and that made it illegal for them to ride in the same car together.

Grace's first day on her new job as a waitress was chaotic for the first few hours. It would have been a lot worse, but she had studied the breakfast menu, and she had the experience of working in the evenings. In addition to her keenness to persevere, she also had the assistant manager watching her back to make sure she did it right in the first place. By midway through the breakfast shift she was still a little slow, but she was handling her station all by herself. In spite of her lack of experience in the breakfast rush, tips poured – which Alvin credited to her being more attractive than ever.

Two weeks after Alvin and Grace had return to work from their honeymoon/vacation, Alvin had just finished his shift and was about to leave for home, when he encountered Mr. Davis in the corridor leading out to the parking lot in back. Mr. Davis spoke, telling Alvin how nice it was to have him back. Alvin politely thanked him, and then Mr. Davis continued, unexpectedly. "Did y'all have a nice vacation?" Alvin stopped to answer him, thinking that Mr. Davis did really want to know if he had a nice vacation. Alvin answered, "I sure did – I really enjoyed my first-time trip to California."

Mr. Davis looked all around, and seeing that no one was close enough to overhear, asked, "Did y'all get married?"

Alvin's knees trembled, and he replied, "I don't understand what you mean – did y'all get married?" Mr. Davis only remarked casually. "She's catching on to this waitress business pretty fast. She's made a lot of improvement since the first day she took the job as a server."

At a loss for words, Alvin couldn't think of a way to lie out of it. Now he knew how a deer must feel, caught in the car headlights, only he – unlike the deer – had a stupid grin on his face. Mr. Davis looked knowing. "You've got yourself a nice girl," he observed. "So you take good care of her. Y'all are going to be just fine as long as you're able to keep it on the down-low, and not attract any attention. I'm sure I don't have to tell you that most of those old boys aren't so nice when it comes to seeing a colored man mixing with white women."

Mr. Davis walked back to his office, leaving Alvin flabbergasted over the fact that his boss had somehow cracked his and Grace's secret-code of conduct designed to hide that they were married. He was rendered absolutely speechless, realizing that not only did Mr. Davis accept his being married to this white woman, but he allowed them to continue to work together at the Graystone. 'This is not normal,' Alvin thought, 'and if this isn't a nightmare, then Ray Davis is ahead of his time. Better yet, maybe the Lord approves of our marriage, and installed some kind of invisible regulator in Ray Davis's conscience to minimize his animosity against mixed marriage.' It did puzzle him – how did this man know about Grace and him being married? It had to have been his mother, Mrs. Nichols. He had told Mrs. Nichols that he and Grace were spending their vacation in California, but he never mentioned anything about them getting married. Alvin wondered that if Mrs. Nichols had gone so far as to tell her son about his and Grace's affair – had she said anything about his affair with his sister, Miss Cassie? 'Probably nothing,' he thought, 'Very unlikely – that a normal mother would discuss her daughter's sexual behavior with her son . . . and since the subject was a colored perpetrator and a minor at that.'

Alvin's first reaction was excitement; he couldn't wait to tell Grace that Mr. Davis knew all about him and her going to California and being married. But the down side – he would have to tell her that it was Mr. Davis's mother who must've told him about them going to California to get married. And that wasn't what he wanted to do at all; Grace might believe that if he was still close to Mrs. Nichols, he might also still be in touch with Miss Cassie – who had written the letter that caused her so much pain. It saddened Alvin that he couldn't honestly share that kind of news with her, without distorting the facts. He thought about it for the rest of the day, and came up with the idea of telling Grace that a friend of Mr. Davis had been riding the same train to California. That friend had told Mr. Davis that he saw this nigger boy and white gal hugging and kissing the minute they got off the train, in Los Angles. And when that friend was boarding the train in Los Angeles bound back to Forth Worth, he saw this very same colored boy and white gal boarding the train, too. Moreover he saw a woman that could've been the girl's mother and a young boy that could have been the girl's brother.

"Mr. Davis had noticed that you and I had taken our vacation on the same day and returned to work the same day." Alvin explained, "So he agreed with his friend's assessment concerning the mixed couple. He told me 'We came up with only enough letters in the alphabet to spelled honeymoon.'"

Grace was just as mesmerized, listening to Alvin lie as he was in listening to Mr. Davis tell the truth. As soon as he finished, she went and called Maggie to tell her mother all about Mr. Davis knowing. Not only was the news heartwarming for Maggie to hear – that Grace's and Alvin's boss approved, but Grace had a bit of good news for her and J.D as well. Escrow had closed; they were free to move into their new home anytime they wanted to.

At the conclusion of their second investment – counting their home as their first – Alvin and Grace had less than four thousand dollars left in the bank. But, based on Grace's tips and salary from first week as a waitress, she had brought home more than two hundred dollars. Their combined salaries and the rent from the apartment building brought their total income to just under eighteen hundred a month. When both of them had finished calculating the numbers several times to make sure their math was correct, they went off to bed feeling that they had just entered into the world high finance and industry.

When Grace and John's father, Walter Adams, separated from their mother Maggie he moved back to a place in Oklahoma called Muskogee – the same small town where he grew up, with his two brothers and one sister – as well as their widowed mother. Each year during the last two weeks of August, Walter would drive from Muskogee to Fort Worth to pick up John. Walter would take John home to Muskogee with him to spend those last two weeks of summer before going back to school in September. Grace wouldn't have anything to do with her father. She could never forgive him for leaving her, Maggie and John to take up with another woman, whom he eventually married. This had happened when Grace was barely fourteen, and John not quite twelve. Eventually, their father had two children by his second marriage.

After picking up John at Maggie's house, Walter Adams would turn around and drive all the way back to Muskogee, straight to his mother's house to let her pour out all of her affection on her favorite grandson. Grace wasn't her favorite granddaughter anymore, because Grace didn't like what grandma's son – Grace's father had done to Maggie. Grace really didn't want to have anything to do with anyone who's last name was Adams, outside of her mother and John.

After visiting with his Grandmother Adams, his father would then take him home and let John bring his father up to date about what went on between the last times they'd seen each other. During this year's visit between father and son, discussion was centered mostly on progress John had made in school. Now and again Grace's name would come up, but each time John was careful with his answer. He wanted to avoid making any mistake that could lead to self- incrimination.

Walter Adams finally got around to saying, "I heard that your sister was supposed to graduate this year; if that was the case, did you go? How did it turn out, or did she graduate at all?"

"Oh yes she did," John answered. "She had a beautiful graduation."

"I'm proud to hear that," Walter Adams answered. "I want you to tell her that I'm sorry I couldn't be there to see my first child graduate from high school. I don't want this to get back to your sister – but I didn't go was because I knew it would've been a waste of my time. She is so bent on making me the bad guy that she won't allow me ten minutes to try to reconcile our differences. Now that she's done with school, though, I expect she'll follow her mother's example, and go out and get herself some good-for-nothing bums like J.D. He's nothing but a drunken old bastard, sitting around on his day off, drinking himself into oblivion. Your mama doesn't know that she's sitting a bad example for her daughter to follow. She thinks if it's good enough for mama – it's good enough for daughter. With you being the age you are, you have no choice except to associate with those low-class bums that she'll go on bringing home when opportunity presents."

"Just to put your mind at ease," John answered with some indignation. "The man that Grace is involved with isn't a bum or a drunk. He's a hard-working man that takes very good care of her. An' ol' J.D. is as square and as honest a man that ever lived – even if he does drink. He looks after Mama, leastways."

"So," Walter said, completely ignoring John's defense of J.D. "I take it she's already got herself a boyfriend – are they living together? And if so, how long has she been fooling around with him?"

"They got together about a year or so ago," John said. "As for as I know, she isn't pregnant – not yet anyway – and from what I've heard, they planned it that way. They both say they wanted to hold off on having a family, until they reach some goal they set for themselves. In the midst of his money-saving scheme, he was still generous enough take Grace, me and Mama on a train ride to Los Angeles. We spent almost two weeks vacationing there; we even spent a night at this beautiful hotel called the Belmont. The next day we took a taxi and went to Hollywood, looking to see if we could spot any movie stars. And we visited the famous

Graumann's Chinese Theatre; it was a real vacation. I just wished that you could've been with us, so we all could have enjoyed it as a family."

"So why would someone just pack up and take the three of you off on a free train ride to California?" Walter asked, curiosity sliding into suspicion.

"I suppose," John answered, "Because he's so in love with Sis." John went silent, suddenly afraid that he had given something away.

His father said, "There's something you're not telling me, son. It sounds to me like she's living with this old boy and you don't want me to know. What is it that you're trying to keep me from knowing, about your sister and her boyfriend?"

"Daddy," John answered. "I don't know whether or not you can handle the truth."

"Try me and let me be the judge of that!"

No use farther evasion; John said in a quite voice, "His reason for taking mama and I on the train ride to California was so we could be with Sis for her wedding."

"Are you trying to tell me that your sister went and got herself married without hinting a word of it to me? What else are you trying to keep me from knowing about your sister's situation?" Walter demanded, and John answered reluctantly, "There're not too much more to say, Daddy. He bought her this four-bedroom house and a car – and lot of beautiful shoes and clothes." John refused to add any more details, and finally Walter Adams got tired of beating around the bush.

Finally he said, "Since I can't get you to come clean with me I'm assuming that he's either an old geezer or a well-to-do young man. A train ride from Texas to California for four people is not just a gust of wind –You need a few dollars to take a trip like that, plus having the leisure to do it for two weeks. But since you're so tight-lipped, I'll just leave it at that, until you decide to tell me the whole truth. I blame her mother for not teaching her different; but if she can't help herself, she can't help Grace. The blind can't lead the blind, without the both of them falling off a cliff." John made no comment; he just left it at that. Now and again, Walter would come up with something else to question John about, but all he got from John was evasion.

About half way through the second week Walter loaded up his family and John and headed back to Fort Worth, so that John would have time to get ready for school. When they got back to the old trailer where Maggie and J.D. lived there was no one home; it seemed obvious that Maggie and J.D. had moved out, during the weeks that John was in Muskogee. John hesitantly asked his father to drive him to Grace's house, so he could find out where his mother had moved. Walter agreed, as long as he didn't have to face his daughter Grace. He knew very well he wouldn't be welcomed, and he didn't want to meet whoever his daughter claimed to be married to, insisting that his feelings were hurt upon finding out that Grace had married without inviting him.

However, Walter suddenly changed his mind, upon seeing Grace and Alvin's house from the street. "Very nice," he said. "I'm not gonna be bad-mannered – I might as well to say hi to your sister, and perhaps that'll give me an excuse to see for myself the kind of looser she got herself involved with."

John was shaking in his boots, terrified nearly out of his mind. He had stuck to his guns all during the journey back, by refusing to open his mouth about Grace's husband. John figured he had chucked the ball to a runner in the clear – now it was up to Alvin and Grace to score the touchdown. At that very moment, Grace and Maggie were all dressed up, ready to head out the front door to shop for groceries and other things, while Alvin and J.D. watched television. As Grace reached for the doorknob, there was a knock; Grace opened it, and there stood John and her father. Walter had left his wife and two girls waiting in the car. Grace suddenly found herself in a state of panic.

"Mama," she said nervously, standing with the door opened partway. "It's Daddy and John."

"Open the door and let them in." Maggie answered with careful control. Grace stepped back from the door, allowing it to swing farther open. Walter walked over the threshold and stood in the middle of the living room. Grace took a place beside Alvin on the divan, as if she was looking to him for security. It was obvious to everyone that she was very nervous, even with Alvin at her side.

John said, very calmly, "Daddy, I want you to meet Grace's husband Alvin." Alvin had already gotten up, after squeezing Grace's hand in reassurance. He stepped forward to shake Walter's hand, but Walter exclaimed, "This has to be some kind of a joke, and I'm not in a joking mood. Where is the man that your sister is supposed to be married to?"

"Sit down Walter Adams," Maggie commanded. "Your daughter has something to tell you – and the story is so long, you might want to have your wife and kids to come in before they suffocate in all of the heat – I certainly wouldn't want it said she died of a heatstroke, because her guilty conscience wouldn't allow her to face the woman which she stole her husband from!"   "My wife and kids is not your concern!" Walter snapped, and now he turned to Grace and demanded, "Now what is it that you're about to tell me? Is that nigger standing there – that's supposed to be my daughter's husband? If it is, I'm fixing to knock his god-damn head off! No daughter of mine is going to be married to a nigger for very long, once I find out for sure it's true. Someone better tell me what in the hell is going on, before I kill myself a black boy!"

Alvin boldly put his arm around Grace, and Maggie came and stood by her other side. John took up a place by his mother. J.D. never budged anything that belonged to himself, save those muscles in his face; his expression seemed to read, 'I can't wait for you to do something stupid so I have a reason to kill you, you son of a bitch.'

Walter stood six-two, with broad shoulders – built very much like Alvin, save that Alvin was thirty years younger and without the beer gut. Alvin said, with enormous calm. "Mr. Adams, I'm Alvin – Grace's husband. I hope you'll accept what I just said as fact, and that you will have to respect this house and everyone in it. These people are my people and I'll do whatever is necessary to keep them safe – including myself.   Take Mrs. Maggie's advice and listen to what she has to say. You're ramping and raging isn't intimidating me – or my family. All you're doing is provoking me – and if I take you on, it will be as if you're fighting a windmill in a windstorm."

"A young black buck like you ought to think on that for awhile, before you come after me!"   Walter snarled. "You just might be the victim of an old fashioned ass-kicking."

"I've had the same thought about you too," Alvin said, still calm and controlled. "But only in reverse and I've said all I'm going to say on this subject. It's all up to you to take it or leave."

"Hell I'll just leave," Walter said, disdainfully. "I don't want to be in the same house with a bunch of god-damn nigger lovers anyway!" As he turned on his heel to walk out the door, Grace yelled, "Daddy! Come back here and close that door! You're no different now than you were the day you walked out on your family to be with some other woman. You knew Mama was right when she asked you to answer a plain and simple question. Otherwise you would've turned and walk away from your family if her accusation was false. The truth was known long before your two daughters ever came into existence, but now that they are a way of life. All of which are overwhelming evidence that Mama was right. You did have the affair – which turned out to be with the same woman mama accused you of having affair with – this same woman bore you your two daughters. So if you could walk out on your wife and children four years ago, who am I that you won't walk out on me too? That is if I decide to let you but I won't. You're gonna stay and listen to me, if I have to have my husband knock you down and hog-tie you." Walter flashed Alvin a quick look as he sized him up again, and then turned to Grace, surprised that his little girl had that kind of anger tied up in her. Grace continued, "This is my husband, and we are happily married."

"Honey, you don't know the meaning of the words 'happily married.'" Walter insisted. "You say that because you've gotten yourself in a no-win situation, and don't know how to get out of it. If you'll let me, I'll do everything in my power to end the nightmare you've gotten yourself in – there are millions of white boys out there, they would just jump at the chance to marry you. Just look at you, honey! Do I have to remind you that you are a young beautiful white lady and there's no reason why you should feel committed to stay married to some nigger that fed you a line of bullshit in order to take the advantage?"

"Please!" Grace began, but her father interrupted her again. "Will someone explain this to me and prove me wrong? I don't think you can. I've never seen you when you looked so beautiful, and it's all wasted on some no good for nothing nigger."

"That's your opinion," Grace recovered her voice. "But it's my opinion that counts in this situation – all the more reason that I didn't have you in mind when I decided to marry Alvin! I might have married a man like my daddy, who never did a thing for my mother except to cheat on her. This man that you're so judgmental of – he did more for me with in our first two months together than you did for Mama in the seventeen years you were married to her. My husband bought this house for me; my husband gave me my first car for my graduation present. My husband brought me my twenty-unit apartment building – and my husband is the one that stopped my mother from working. See if you can find me that white boy that you think is so deserving of me and takes care of my mother like Alvin does – then I just might give your idea some consideration, but until you find him I'm going to stay where it's safe and that's with my husband, Alvin!" She went back and stood beside Alvin, who put his arms about her, and murmured, barely a breath above a whisper, "Good job, honey!" Reassured and heartened by his approval, Grace continued, "Now that you've heard what I had to say, you're welcome to walk out that door anytime you want. Or you can stay and be my friend, but you will never be my father again. I once loved you more than anybody in the whole wide world! It used to be that I could hardly wait for my heroic father to come home, and tuck his little girl, into bed before I went off to sleep every night. But not any more, not after listening to Mama, crying her eyes out, night after night, over you – I came to hate you, for all of the hurt you caused Mama, and to John and me."

Walter watched, as she turned and laid her head on Alvin's shoulder and began to cry. At last he begged, "Would it be wrong for a deserting father to ask his little girl for a hug before he leaves?" Grace hesitated for a moment, until Alvin whispered, "Go on then, Honey." She walked to her father with some reluctance, and allowed him to put his arms around her, but he got no response. Grace looked towards Maggie, who nodded just the once, her face expressionless. She returned Walter's embrace, and he suddenly let out a deep sob, and began to weep as he told her how sorry he was for hurting her and Maggie. Grace started to cry again, and Walter whispered, "No, no, punkin', don't you start crying too – why the both of us could dampen this floor pretty good, with all the tears we've held onto for all of these years." Then he held her a little way from himself, saying, "Just look at you! You are so beautiful – I wasn't aware that I had a daughter who looked like this. You're not the same little girl I knew four years ago!" as he took her in his arms again. Those words seemed to have cleared the road. Grace locked both arms around him, and they both began to cry. Finally, Maggie took Grace's hand, and led her off to the bathroom to calm down, and to wash her face. Once that was done, she sent Grace back to the living room, but Maggie stayed, once she knew that Walter's wife and two children were sitting in the living room. Even though she had asked Walter to invite them to come in out of their hot car, Maggie couldn't bear to be cordial to the woman who took her husband. Meanwhile, Walter introduced his wife and kids. Grace slightly bowed her head but she did not shake hands with Walter's wife, or did she show her any particular welcome. She clung to Alvin – which made it clear to Walter's new wife, Maurine, that her step-daughter was involved with the colored man whose arms she were clinging to.

Walter had no other choice, but to say reluctantly, "This is Grace's friend Alvin – they work at the same hotel." Alvin acknowledged the introduction with a slight nod, and suggested to Grace that they offer everyone something cold to drink, and Grace recovered her composure and her good manners.

"I'm sorry," she said, as she stooped down, picked up the smallest girl and walked over to the refrigerator to get a Coke for them both. Alvin took two beers, offering one to Walter. Walter answered, with a fierce look. "No, I'm afraid if I were to have one at this point I might become a little too aggressive for you, and who knows what may happen after that!"

"Good point!" Alvin said, and Grace offered Walter's Maurine a Coke, which she accepted. Seeing that everyone had pretty much calmed down, John asked, "J.D., where did you and Mama moved? Dad and I stopped by the trailer and there were no signs of life there."

"We moved into your sister's apartment building," J.D. answered, "And guess what – she stopped your Mama from waiting tables – now, all she does is collecting rent for your sister. Not only do we get to live rent-free, but your sister and her husband are paying your mama to make up for what she lost in wages working at her old job. You tell me, how can you beat a deal like that?"

Walter looked at least a little impressed, asking Grace, "What kind of work does your friend do that he can afford to do all of the things that I just heard J.D. say he does for you and the family?"

"Alvin?" Grace answered, "My daddy needs a translator and I'm not very good at that kind of thing. Will you please do your best to make me understand so I can tell him what you do for a living?"

"With pleasure," Alvin said. "I'm a cook, at the Graystone Hotel – that's where you and I met, shortly after I moved to Forth Worth."

"What a shame," Walter said, still not looking particularly pleased. "Even so I suppose you must make a fair amount of money, or else you couldn't buy the things that you are buying, according what I've been told."

"I do pretty well for myself," Alvin said.

J.D. chimed in, almost for the first time. "How about eighteen hundred a month up to this point sound?"

Walter's astonishment was written clear on his face. "god-damn, boy – how in the hell did you go about making that kind of money? They can't pay you that much money for cooking!"

Grace explained, "That's a combination of mine and his salary, plus the rent from the apartments."

Walter shook his head, saying, "Boy, what are y'all gonna do with all of that money?"

Alvin replied, with an absolutely straight face, "I'll get drunk, beat my wife, and gamble some of it away. And then I'll kill somebody and go to jail on week-ends. Ain't that's what we're supposed to do with our money?" Everyone but Walter snickered. "Don't laugh," Walter insisted, "that's more typical than you know regarding his kind of people!"

Alvin sighed. "All right; to cut through the horse play and be sincere about answering your question – we'll invest in real estate. Don't worry; we'll make sure that Mrs. Maggie is well taken care of. Other than that, I suppose we'll be spending a lot on trips to Los Angeles where we can freely do as we please."

Maggie emerged from the other room, saying, "Grace, honey I think we had better do our shopping another day," as she walked towards the front door. Alvin reached out, catching her hand as she passed, and said, "Wait, Mrs. Maggie." Alvin led her back to the bedroom and motioned for Grace to follow. "Grace, we need to send your father and his family away – I'm not about to let your mother go out that door with her head down. When she goes, I want her to go with her head held just as high as it was when she came through that door. I want you to do what you set out to do in the first place – take your mother shopping."

Maggie answered, "That's her father, Alvin. She hasn't visited with him for over four years. Therefore, I'm willing to let this afternoon go, for as long as she won't forget who took care of her and loves her more than anyone else – except you, Alvin." Grace hugged her mother and whispered, "No one will ever change mine and your relationship." Maggie walked out and told J.D. that she was ready to go, but John stayed behind to listen to his sister duke it out with their father. After Grace had discussed – sometimes vociferously – her marriage to Alvin for nearly two hours with her father, she felt civil enough to invite him and his second family to stay for dinner. "If, she added, "you promise you'll stay and eat with Alvin and I, and to behave yourself."

"Hell," Walter answered, "I might as well – I've had worst things to happen to me." Grace invited her father's wife Maurine and the two little girls to come along with her to pick up a few things for supper. While they were gone, Alvin talked Walter into drinking his first beer – he saw almost at once, that Walter was rather like J.D., in that he loved drinking that ice-cold beer. Walter also had many questions for Alvin, but could barely bring himself to ask them directly. He used John as an intermediary: Instead of asking Alvin directly, he would say to John, "So how does Alvin get alone with J.D.?" or, "He and Grace don't drive to work, together do they?"

While Grace and Maurine were out shopping for groceries, Maurine confided in Grace that their financial condition was very bad. Hearing that, Grace immediately felt quite sorry for them. She reached into her purse and gave Maurine fifty dollars to buy each girl their school clothes. Maurine thanked Grace, begging her not to mention to Walter what she had told Grace about their condition. She asked Grace to let the children tell Walter that the money was Grace's idea. As soon as they returned to the house, the girls rushed to their father, saying,

"Daddy – look what Grace gave us, fifty dollars! That's a lot of money isn't it, Daddy?" "You're god-damn right that's a lot of money" he answered, "You can buy lots of things with fifty dollars. Did you thank your sister?"

"She's not our sister," the younger girl insisted. "She's too big and to old to be our sister, out sister is supposed to be little like us."

Everyone was momentary amused by the little girl's statement, which briefly interrupted John and Walter's small talk conversation. They instantly picked up where they left off – still without including Alvin. This didn't bother Alvin in the least; he wasn't the intruder. He lived there and he wasn't about to let Walter's undignified behavior make him feel belittled.

And who would want to be in a conversation with a person who needed only two beers to start slurring his words? By the time the women got supper ready, Walter was feeling no pain. He looked over at Alvin, saying, "Boy, if anyone had told me this morning that I'd be eating supper with a nigger eight hours later, I'd have jumped up and beat the hell out of him. But, as the old saying goes, one never knows what an ill-supervised child might bring home and asked their parent to sit and eat with – especially if child's mentor is too stupid to know that she's more dire need of a teacher than her pupil is!"

Alvin laughed, to soften his own words, but there was little humor in them. "Well, I guess Mrs. Maggie's folks can say pretty much the same thing about you."

Walter scowled. "Now, you don't know a god-damn thing about what you are saying. This happened between two people who just happened to be white – one of them is me, and the other my ex-wife, whom you call Mrs. Maggie!"

Grace interrupted what her father was about to say, "Daddy, I invited you to have supper with me and my colored husband, but it was you that come to my house, not the other way around. And as for being ill-informed about the man I married, I studied him very carefully. Between his assurance and the insight I gained about the kind of person he is, I rolled the dice and look what it's got me to this point? It could've easily gone the other way, Daddy, if I hadn't caved in when I did."

"How so?" Walter asked, and Grace explained, saying,

"Alvin and I had this little misunderstanding, and he decided to let me cool off for a while, but when he tried to prove how much he loved me, it almost got him killed. He came to Maggie and J.D.'s house uninvited and demanded that I go home with him. I never saw Mama so angry, until I heard her used language on Alvin that only a slave master would use. She kept screaming to J.D., 'get that nigger out of here.' She pointed to a tire iron lying next to the toolbox, as she yelled, 'use that tire iron, and crack that nigger's head wide open.' In the midst of all the commotion, he became even more persistent – he saw that he wasn't making any progress standing on his two feet, so he dropped to his knees, and started crying and begging me to come with him. I was obstinate about breaking up with him, because he hurt my feelings, until I thought J.D. was about to hit Alvin with the tire iron. That's when I dropped to my knees beside him and told him that I would come home with him because I was in love him too."

"In love my ass," Walter said, "Why in the hell did you go and do a fool thing like that? They were well with in their rights to kill any nigger that comes walking into your house and try to take their daughter away. If you haven't stopped them we wouldn't be having this discussion!"

"Why am I not surprised to hear you said what you just said?" Grace said, sadly. "You have just sent me back to the time when all of your excuses for failure were to place blame on the niggers and Mexicans, for taking an opportunity that could've been yours. You ought to know by now; you're not going to sway me against loving Alvin. I know you're an intelligent man, Daddy, but Alvin doesn't. Just try to be nice, show him that you're not as stupid as you act?"

Walter had the grace to look at least a little ashamed. "You can take what I just said as a joke," he finally mumbled.

Grace answered, "I think you should have waited until you've known Alvin a little better before you go joking and running down my husband. I was gonna tell you that we have plenty of room if you'll want to spend the night, but now I don't know!"

"And I don't know whether or not we should be sleep under the same roof with you and old Alvin," Walter admitted. "It'll be just like I'm giving him permission to sleep in the same bed with my beautiful daughter."

"You are a little late, to be concerned about that," Grace returned, "Alvin and I have been sleeping together and doing married things in the neighborhood of almost two years. Accept or reject it – I've said all I needed to say when you attempted to walk out the door."

"Surely" Walter answered, after a long moment, and a look across the table at Maurine and his daughters. "You don't expect me to pay for a room when my daughter has three unoccupied rooms that I could stay in for free?"

With an expression of exasperation, Grace went to the telephone, called her mother, told her that her father was going to spend the night with her, and she would see her in the morning. Grace pulled up a chair next to Alvin. She kissed him and spoke softly, "Are you going to be all right with them spending the night here, honey?"

"Of course I will," he answered, "I'm used to hearing those kind of insults – heard them before. 'Sides that – I also rather understand what his concerns are. Now that I'm actually involved with you – and you being his daughter – that gives him a valid reason to questioning his daughter's future with a man of a different race. Especially if he's a colored boy; lots of us coloreds are qualified to go all the way to the top, but most are too intimidated to approach the people in authority. They'll give up before they even start, and their pessimistic attitude will force them to fall by the wayside. If you were married to a white boy, your father wouldn't have to be faced with that kind of dilemma – he knows that most white boys don't have to worry about having doors slammed in their faces. Now, there is nothing offensive to anyone about what I just said – I say this to make a point to your father. I'm not one of those boys that are going to fall by the way side. I know where I am and I know where I'll go from here. Take all your troubles and worries about Grace's future, tie them up in a bag and toss them between here and your home back in Oklahoma. I promise you that Grace is going to be better off being with me than any white boy that you could ever think about introducing her too."

Grace spoke in an undertone. "He's already set his heart against you becoming a success; he doesn't believe a word you say. Being my father, I can tolerate him. If you can't, then I'll have to ask him to leave."

"By all means," Alvin said, calmly. "Don't do it on my account, I'm beginning to think he likes me. It's just that he hates the idea of me having access to his beautiful daughter's embrace."

Walter and Maurine were listening, and now Walter said, "Well. I think it's a waste of time, worrying about you and my daughter, anymore – I'm a little late, trying to keep her anatomy out of the hands of the wrong person – I'll just have to wait and see what comes out in the wash. Now, I just listened to you explain to my daughter concerning my thoughts about you. You sound intelligent, and I guess you are at that, or you wouldn't have my daughter and these other people so darn crazy about you. Still and all, I could care less about the money you claim to have. I'd much rather seen her marry someone her own race. This mixing crap between the races just doesn't cut it for me."

"With all due respect, Daddy," Grace answered, "It's been more than four years since I was concerned about your opinion of me. My one concern was making Mama understand that what I saw in Alvin was love and compassion for me – the same as I feel about him. It may've taken me four weeks to convince her that Alvin was the person I told her he was, and I don't think I have to tell you that I've never seen her so happy, since before you started to treat her bad. Now she's laughing again and it all stems from the way Alvin treats her daughter."

Walter admitted, grudgingly, "It's plain enough to see he takes good care of you . . . maybe we should just leave it at that."

Hearing this, Alvin went to the refrigerator and got Walter and himself a beer to secretly celebrate Walter's capitulation. Grace's celebration of her father's reprieve was by doing what she had waited to do all evening; to gather each of her half-sisters to sit on her lap and become acquainted with them for the first time. "If I'm not badly mistaken," she said, "you two little rascals are going to see lots of your big sis and be loaded with all kinds of goodies." Eventually, Maurine asked Grace to come show her what room she'd be tucking them in for tonight. Grace gave Maurine and Walter a tour of the house; they both claimed to be genuinely impressed. Walter became especially interested when Grace took them out back to show them the vacant apartment.

He asked, "What are y'all gonna do about renting out this apartment?"

"Not much of anything until we find the right people," Grace answered. "We don't want to rent to colored – even if they were good tenants. We figured too many colored coming and going around would attract attention. The neighbors might get curious – and then everyone would know that Alvin and I are living here together. "We're holding off until we find the perfect white person, who would accept us as being a mixed couple – and wouldn't go and turn us into the authorities. We are so paranoid about our neighbors watching us, that Alvin never uses the front entrance to the house during the daytime. He always uses the alleyway."

As they walked back to the house, Walter wrapped his arm around Grace's shoulder. As he hugged her, he said, "You've done very well for yourself in the short amount of time y'all been together. How old did you say Alvin is?"

Grace answered, "Not quite twenty yet."

He's a hell of a lot's different from the colored folks I'm use to being around." Walter observed, with the smallest touch of respect. "They'll work all week and draw down a paycheck and they'll wound up borrowing on a paycheck that they'd never earned yet. All they want is enough to buy a bottle of hooch to give to some little old gal, make her drunk, knock her up, and go on to the next one. On the other hand, here y'all are racking down eighteen hundred a month, and work as if you don't have nickel to your names." He smiled as he patted Grace's shoulder and added, "Shoot, y'all ain't doing badly at all. Maybe you're not as crazy as I thought you were."

"When it comes to someone other than Alvin judging my sanity," Grace answered, "I look at them as being pretty foolish, especially when Alvin is constantly telling me how fortunate he is to have me as his wife. I wish we hadn't put the kids to bed, or I'd ask y'all to ride with Alvin and me to take John home – then I could let y'all see our apartment building."

"Take 'em anyway," Walter said, "They're sleep and don't know any different."

She and Maurine gathered the babies; everyone loaded into Grace's car and drove to the apartments. She parked and pointed out to John the apartment where Maggie and J.D. were living, where he would be living now. Afterward, Grace drove slowly around the building a couple of times, letting her father and Maurine look at it all, and perhaps be just as impressed with the apartment as they were with her house. Finally, as they were returning to the house, Walter mentioned to Grace in a deliberately casual manner, "That apartment in the back of your place would be just right for me and my family."

Grace answered, "Are you asking me to let you move in?"

"Well," he said, "I would be just that much closer to my other two children, being that it's vacant and all. If you are going to be renting it anyway, I would as soon to rent it from y'all. At least, you'll know who your tenants are. That is, of course, if you have no hard feelings toward me for mistreating you as I did."

"Daddy," Grace said, "I would love to have you and Maurine and the girls move in out back. But it'll be up to Alvin – but I'm sure once we put our heads together and figure out how we're gonna do it without Mama being too uncomfortable coming to my house. Other than that, the ball is in Alvin's court and he has the first serve."

Walter said to Alvin, "Well . . . you're not still sore at me for calling you all of those choice names, are you?"

"What choice names?" Alvin said. "Those bad names you used towards me, I accepted as part of a debt I owed you and your ex-wife. No one should be able to walk away from such a fine woman such as you two produced without having some kind of a penalty imposed on him. Except for a formality that Grace and I have adopted – never sign to off on anything unless we discuss it behind closed doors – other that that, the apartment is yours."

"Let them move in anyway," Grace said, "It'll only be temporary – just until we find our next income property. We're going to need a manager for it, and when we have bought it, you and your family can take up residence there. We'll have to get it as far away from Mama's apartment as we can afford, and still stay in a decent neighborhood. I don't think it would be a good idea for you and Mama to be operating in the same region. If all of this sounds confusing to you, don't feel alone – sometimes I'm just as confused as you are now. My husband has never given me this much responsibility, since the night he made me choose between living with him and Mama. There is one thing I can say now that I don't have to wait before we're behind closed doors – and that is, you'll have to pay rent. I'm doing the rent-free thing for Mrs. Maggie only, as Alvin calls Mama."

"We don't have very much to move, mostly pot and pans." Walter replied. "And our furniture is not as nice as the furniture in your apartment back there. We'll just hang around here until y'all know for sure what ya wonna do. I might be out of work for a while, but it shouldn't take long to find a construction job – hell, there are always buildings going up, in a town as big as Fort Worth."

Grace walked over behind him and began massaging his back. "Now, Daddy" she said, "You don't worry about anything, my husband has a big heart – meaning, he won't take care of you – but he'll do everything he can to help you, and your family until you get on your feet." She turned to Alvin, asking, "Did I say it right, honey, or would you like to add something to it?"   "Honey," Alvin answered, "I couldn't have said it any better."

They all went off to bed, and when their bedroom door closed behind Alvin and Grace, the first thing out of Grace's mouth to Alvin was,

"Oh, sugar – what a mess we've gotten ourselves into, just because we've tried to do the right thing. And now we'll need to come up with something good to tell Mama and J. D tomorrow . . . before we fall asleep tonight! Knowing how much she hates Maurine, I'm gonna need a good reason for letting Daddy move his family this close to my house."

Yawning, Alvin answered, "The only thing that I can come up with is to either make your dad wait until we buy the next apartment building, or have Mrs. Maggie make an appointment before coming over. Or you might have to visit with her at her own apartment – just until we get everyone settled in his or her own domain."

Grace snickered, "Honey, maybe I should've let him leave when he started to! Then we wouldn't be having this discussion . . . but I couldn't have let him walk out the door, not after I had waited for four long years to tell him how badly he hart his family . . . and for what? He's worst off now then he was before he left Mama and John and I."

The next morning Alvin was awakened from the noise of Maurine, busy in the kitchen as she tried to locate what she would need to fix breakfast. He knew one thing for sure – she had found the coffee and the coffee maker. After about thirty minutes of noise in the kitchen, there came the smell of fresh brewing coffee. By the time Alvin finished washing up; he could even smell biscuits baking and hear the sound of bacon frying. The minute he walked into the living room, Maurine poured him a cup of coffee, followed him to the divan, and sat it on the coffee table in front of the television. She smiled and asked, "Would you like me to bring you cream and sugar?"

"Yes please," he answered, wondering how on earth how a nice, sweet woman like Maurine could stay married to a jackass like Walter. After she set the cream and sugar on the coffee table, she went into Walter's bedroom to tell him that coffee was ready. Walter washed up and dragged himself to the kitchen table where Maurine had already poured his coffee. The little girls were already up drinking orange juice, with crisp pieces of bacon in their little hands. Grace emerged from their bedroom, and sat beside Alvin, all dolled up and waiting for the time to drive over and pick her mother up so they could go do the shopping that they should've done the day before. She sat, drinking her coffee and gazing fondly at the little girls as they ate – very clearly enjoying every bite of breakfast. Grace was definitely finding favor in being their big sister; she could hardly wait for them to clean their greasy hands, so she could cuddle with them.

When Maurine put breakfast on the table, she asked Grace, "Do y'all normally bless the food before y'all eat? If not, Walter and the girls are going to start digging inn."

"Alvin normally does," Grace answered, "but he's on his way to work. I'll just leave it up to Daddy as to whether or not he wants to say a blessing."

Alvin stood up, kissed Grace and said his goodbye as he left for work at the Graystone. Grace joined her father and his family at the breakfast table. Over breakfast – biscuits, sausage, and scrambled eggs – she began to discuss with her father how he and Maurine and the girls would move into the back apartment, since it was an all-but-settled question.

Suddenly she glanced as her watch, and interrupted their conversation. "What in the world happen to the time? I should've been at Mama's house fifteen minutes ago!" She rushed over to the phone to call Maggie and tell her she was on her way. She called to her father as she rushed out to her car, "Think about what we talked about – when I get back; we'll come up with a solution to this problem." She drove at high speed trying to make up for lost time. The very first thing out of her mouth when she arrived at her mother's apartment was "I need to discuss an important matter with you and J.D., concerning the apartment behind our house – would you believe after all of the ruckus that man made over Alvin being my husband – now he tells me that he's interested in moving into that place?

"Doesn't surprise me," Maggie answered. "He's always been a man without a conscience."

"Alvin is at work today, "Grace began, "but he and I discussed it after we went to bed last night – about letting Daddy and his family move in out back. We decided not to confirm anything with him, until I had talked it over with you and J.D. It's important to Alvin and me to have yours and J.D.'s opinion. And if it's not agreeable with you, it won't hurt my feelings none. I'll just give him a few dollars and send him on his way – not tomorrow but today."

"Again," Maggie said, "I must remind you that he's your father, so do whatever pleases you and don't worry about me. You can come to my house until he has his own place." She turned to J.D. and asked, "What do you think about all of this?"

"If I had my way," he said, "I'd send his wife-deserting ass back to Oklahoma and leave him there where he belongs. But I don't have that authority; Grace does – she's the boss."

Grace said, "Since he's down on his luck, as well as being that he's my father, I'm inclined to let him and his family move in . . . in spite of his lack of consideration for his first family."

"If that's the case, just make sure you remember that I'm your mother – not that tramp that your father is married to." Maggie said, somewhat grudgingly, and Grace hugged her.

"Now, Mama – you know you're irreplaceable when it comes to being my mother."

They got into Grace's car and went shopping for groceries among other things. Normally they would stop off at their favorite café and having lunch together. Then Maggie and Grace would browse from one dress shop to another – and depending on what was showing, from time to time they'd even take in a movie. After more than three hour of shopping, Grace dropped her mother off at her apartment. She drove home and parked out by the apartment, with enough groceries for her father's family to last more than a week. She went and got her father and took him out back, and told him to start unloading the groceries.

"This is where you and your family will be living for the next few months." She said to Walter. He hugged and thanked her, and told Maurine and the children to come, and see their new home. Besides the necessities, Grace had also bought a variety of foods that kids love to snack on between meals. She was so taken with being a big sister that she kept one or the other in her arms at all times. When Maurine had put all of the dry goods away, she unwrapped the various packages of meat until she came to pork chops. She took them and everyone followed her back to Grace's house, where she served up a dinner of fried pork chops with potatoes and vegetables.

After supper, John said to Grace, "As soon as I see Daddy off, I'll need to be driven back to Mama's place," and Walter replied, "Y'all don't have to bother with driving him home – I'll drop you off on my way back to Oklahoma – provided you'll look after my wife and girls until I get back, probably around the weekend. I hate to keep asking you for favors, but it's out of the question for me to take them with me, and still move everything in one trip in that old car of mine."

"We can't do very much more than we've already done," Grace answered, "Except to lend her one or the other of our cars, in case she wants to run to the store to pick up a bottle of milk or a loaf of bread. Other than that – Maurine and the girls will be kept safe, under the watchful eyes of your daughter and son-n-law. Oh – and one other thing," Grace added. "Will you have enough money to make the trip?"

"It'll be a little close but I think so." Walter said, and Grace slid a hundred-dollar bill in his hand, saying, "Since you'll be gone for most of a week you might need this."

He looked at her with pleased surprise, and promised, "I'm going to give it back to y'all, as soon as I get back and find work." Kissing his wife and children and goodbye, Walter looked at his watch again and said to John, "I've had second thought about dropping you off at your Mama's place."

Hearing that, Grace urged him, "Go ahead, Daddy – I'd rather drive him home anyway, because I have some unfinished business I need to talk to Mama about. Maurine, honey, will you feel comfortable staying here with Alvin while I'm gone? If not, you can take the children home and I'll check on you the first thing when I get back."

When she told Grace she'd rather go home, Walter kissed his family once again and headed out on the highway to Oklahoma. Grace returned home around seven-thirty that evening, and went straight to the apartment to ask the kids to come over and watch television with her. Maurine at first refused, saying, "No, I don't want the kids to be a bother to you and Alvin." But with Grace's influence and the girl's persuasion Maurine finally said relented, as long as she could come to make sure that they stayed out of trouble. The three of them came, and had cookies and ice cream while they watched television.

"Tomorrow," Grace promised, "you're gonna be watching television in your own house." "You know why," Maurine said to the little girls, "because your big sister is going to buy it for you."

The next day was Monday morning – back to work for Alvin – and for Maggie too, although she went to work only to give her notice. Maggie went straight home, right after she announced to her boss that she was going to work for her daughter, managing an apartment building. That afternoon she called Grace to tell her how grateful she was to her for giving her the opportunity to quit a job she'd hated since the day she took it.

"Fantastic!" Grace exclaimed, "So, now let me asked you a silly question. Would you think I was awful if I asked you to ride with me over to pick up a television for the little girls?"

"I don't see anything awful about that," Maggie said. "They are your father's children and that makes them your sisters."

Later that afternoon, Grace came home with the kid's television set, and gave it to Alvin to hook up for them. Having done that, he asked Grace, "What would you think about me inviting my old friend John Lee and his mother, Miss Irene over for dinner Friday night? With your approval you'll get to meet the people that I've told you about for the last two years."

"Can we trust them enough to keep our secret?" she asked. "If you think so then I would like to invite Mama over to kelp because she's so good at that kind of stuff."

"Good." Alvin answered, "As far as old crazy John Lee and his mother are concerned, they're as trustworthy as a morning sunrise and as faithful as I am to you."

She grinned and said "if that's your opinion of them then bring them on we are sure to be safe."

Chapter 10 – Moving On Up

The next evening after work Alvin drove straight to John Lee's house, hoping to get there early enough to beat John Lee home so he could talk to Irene. He knocked on the door. Sure enough, Miss Irene was home alone.

Once she saw it was Alvin she smiled, saying, "Come on in Alvin."

He stepped inside, asking, "Where is John Lee?"

"He hasn't made it home yet," Miss Irene answered. "But he should be here shortly. So why don't you have a seat and tell me what has happened to you since the last time I saw you?" "Are you sure about that?" he asked her.

"Oh, come on in here so I can close the door, you handsome boy. I'm not worried about you anymore, I figure as often as you like doing it you'd have yourself two or three girlfriend by now and probably raped the last one just before you decided to come to my house."

"You're right not to worry about being raped again," Alvin said, "I may not have three girlfriends, but I have one that can't do the job of three girlfriends. This is why I came here, to invite John Lee to have dinner with us on Friday night. You may've noticed that I didn't mention your name – I can't invite you to meet her and keep a clear conscience. And I couldn't invite John Lee and tell him that he can't bring you or anyone he choose as his guest – preferably you, if all possible. So when I invite John lee, he'll assume that I've already invited you so there will be no reason for me to mention your name when he gets here."

"I understand Alvin" she said "and I feel bad about messing up our relationship. We were friends until I coerced you into having an affair with me."

"We are still friends," he answered. "That happened before I met this girl. Don't you feel bad about what we did, because I sure don't! The reason I'm doing it this way; I don't think it would be right to invite someone to meet my woman – who has made me scream to high heaven the way you made me do – not once but two times in one day."

Miss Irene chuckled, saying, "How well do I remember that day – especially the second time around, when you picked me up and laid me on the kitchen floor. After you left that day I relived those moments and thought about what you did to me – that was nothing short of being a master at your own trade. I'll bet it took me at least six months to finally stop trying to figure out ways to ask you to move back in with me – without arousing John Lee's suspicious. The same thing that had you worried the day I asked you to go to bed with me, had me feeling the same way – what John Lee would say and do if he knew you had slept with his mother: That's when I decided that I'd be better off to leave that thought along."

"You could have fooled me," Alvin answered, "what happened to the so-called rape me theory you're accused me of doing? You had me believing that I was some kind of out-of-control perverted sex-offender. Although I distinctly detected a touch of wildness in your action when I was so-called raping you. I couldn't be sure as to whether you had secretly accepted my invasion of your privacy, or maybe it another one of your involuntary attacks, which brought tears to both of our eyes, after the performance you gave in the bedroom?"

Miss Irene grinned widely, admitting, "Now that I think of it, I'd say it was both. I accepted your invasion of my privacy and yes my involuntary muscles went on the attack, fighting off her invader – especially where you penned her to the kitchen floor."

"Bobbie Jean was right when she told me that some women are so masterful at complaining about one thing and in the same breath they exclaim ecstasy." Alvin remarked.

"I knew what I was doing," Miss Irene said. "I had to do that because I was more worried about me becoming addicted to yours than I was about you being addicting to mine." he stood there looking at her with regret, as she continued, "I shouldn't have brought that up, but I guess when you mention the fact that I made you scream to high heaven, I immediately zeroed in on the second time we did it: which got me excited all over again and I slipped up and told you my well-kept secret. "Nevertheless – that's old stuff now. Like I told you then, I'm telling you now we'll never do that again, since all it does is ignite an old flame that neither one of us dare to extinguish. But I really do appreciate you inviting me to your home for dinner – you don't have to worry about a thing, regarding that secret of ours;

it happened so long ago that I've already convinced myself that it never happened at all."

"Good," Alvin said, with an interior sigh of relief. "That matches exactly the way I feel, so I'll just have a seat and wait until John Lee comes home."

Within a few minutes, John Lee came walking in, saying, "When I saw your car parked outside, the first thing come to mind that you were back with Bobbie Jean. Now that I've seen you face to face, I'd say I thought wrong because I haven seen you wear a smile on your face like this since the morning after you went dancing with Bobbie Jean, or so you say."

Alvin answered, "You know a lot more about me than I thought you did, which is why I'm here to invite you over for dinner Friday night. John Lee, did you already tell mama that we were invited to your house to have dinner with you on Friday night? Ask her," Alvin said and let her tell you whether I invited her."

"Mama!" John Lee called, "Did you hear that we've been invited over to Alvin's house for dinner on Friday night?"

Irene appeared from the other room, "He sure did, – that was the first thing he said, the instant he walked through the door." John Lee chuckled. "She must be something special, Alvin – that you're inviting us to meet the new girlfriend."

"Here's my new address," Alvin told them, "And remember, we'll be serving some of your favorite foods; catfish, coleslaw, hush puppies, lots of cold Falstaff beer and a few bottles of chilled wine – all offered under one condition – you can't mention the name Bobbie Jean. I've never heard that name before and either have you."

John Lee asked curiously, "What do this girl of your look like that has you so worried about us mentioning the name Bobbie Jean?"

"You'll be able to answer that question yourself at seven on Friday night – all right?"   "We'll be there," Miss Irene promised."

On Wednesday evening Alvin and Grace were invited to Maggie's house for dinner and a few drinks to celebrate the ending of her old job and the beginning of her new one as an apartment manager. The first thing out of Alvin's mouth to Maggie was, "These little afternoon celebrations of yours are going to get Grace and I killed if we keep riding around in broad daylight together."

"Oh," Maggie answered, "those old boys you saw out there are as harmless as a toothless bulldog. At first, they and their wives wanted to know who was that nigger they keep seeing coming and going in and out of my apartment with the beautiful brunette gal – and I told them the truth – that y'all belong to each other, and Grace was my daughter. I also told them that y'all have a lot of money. One of the fellow's wives said to me, 'They has to have a lot of money to dress the way they do!' I've often wondered who in their right mind would think about harming two people that look as handsome as you two always do." She handed Alvin his beer and Grace her half-glass of wine. "Drink this and stop worryin' about these nosy white people – they're just as curious about you as you are about them. This little celebration that I've invited y'all over to take part in, is more about me telling y'all that my sister Myrtle and her husband Ed are coming out for Thanksgiving, than it is about me telling you about the expression on my boss's face when I told him that I was quitting to work for my daughter as an apartment manager. He looked all out of sorts, when I told him what my last day would be. But the main thing I wanted to talk to y'all about – if it's all right with you and Alvin – is for them to stay at your house, rather then squeeze them in here. I need to let them know before they get on the road . . . and if y'all approve of them coming and staying at your house . . . y'all won't have to feel like you're living amongst strangers. You know, I'm not one to keep secrets – especially when it comes to blabbing off at the mouth about my daughter's marriage to Alvin. How will they know if I don't tell them?"

"Either way," Grace answered, "Aunt Myrtle is your sister and I don't have any objection at all for them staying with Alvin and I."

"That's settles it, of course I'll have to pay their way." Maggie looked relieved. "Myrtle and Ed haven't been doing so well here lately. Your Uncle Ed was forced into retirement because of a bad back, and Myrtle is too old to hold down a good-paying full-time job. Instead, she takes in ironing once a week, and cleans houses for people that can afford to pay her. Even when they add what she makes to the little Ed gets from his retirement, they still barely make ends meet. Ed has gone past sixty-five and Myrtle is nearly about sixty, which means things will get worst for them before they get better. Myrtle is the oldest of the four of us; twenty years

258

older than me. My Mama always told me that I got here by accident. She thought that she was finished with having children, until one day she said to my father, 'Milton, if I didn't know better I'd say I'm caring another one of your young'uns in my belly.' Sure enough, Mama said – nine months later and there I was."

"Unless they were using storks to deliver babies in those days," J.D. drawled, "there isn't any such thing as an accidental pregnancy. It's more like your daddy didn't bother to put the old mitten on the night you were conceived." Everybody chuckled, although Maggie just kept right on talking. It appeared she was accustoming to hearing J.D speak out of turn when he was drinking too much. Maggie herself wasn't feeling any pain, either, when she asked Alvin to dance with Grace to a Nat King Cole's version of 'non-de mint tee cal' – she claimed this was a reminder of the way they looked while waltzing around their hotel room on their wedding night.

After that visit, Grace decided to heed Alvin's advice, which was to take an old-fashioned bonnet when they went out together, something that would hide her face from the side, and minimize her exposure to some passerby who would go ape if they would've seen a white woman riding in a car at night with a colored man. They drove back home, and once safe there, Grace called her mother to tell her that they were back home safe and sound.

The next day Maggie went out and bought fresh catfish as well as the ingredients for the dishes they would serve to the guests which Alvin had invited over for Friday night's dinner. Late in the afternoon Maggie asked Alvin to ice down the beer and wine, before he took a seat in the living room with J.D. and John, watching westerns on the television.

Maggie and Grace were busy in the kitchen. A little after seven, there was a knock on the back door. Maggie answered it promptly, knowing it would be John Lee and his mother, Miss Irene. John Lee and Miss Irene weren't expecting to see a white woman answer the door.   "Excuse me, ma'am," John Lee asked, in a timid voice, "This is the third door I've knocked on tonight, and I still haven't found the fellow whom I'm looking for, by the name of Alvin Jackson. And it seems that I've made another mistake!"

Grace went to the door, saying, "Come right on in – Alvin is expecting y'all. I'm Alvin's wife, Grace. Alvin honey,' she called towards the living room, "Your guests have arrived."

John Lee and Miss Irene looked as if they had been slapped at the dinner table for farting and too shamed to cry. Alvin got up from watching his western, and came into the kitchen, drawling, "It's about time y'all got here." John Lee and Miss Irene looked around in disbelief, as they came into the kitchen.

"This has got be a joke!" John Lee exclaimed, at which everyone else chorused, "Surprise!" and Alvin explained, still laughing, "I purposely withheld something about my Grace, when I invited y'all over the other day. Otherwise you and your mama would be on your way back to Snyder by now." He reached into the tub of iced-down beer and gave John Lee one. "Here, John Lee – something to settle your nerves. Miss Irene, I'm gonna hold off on giving you something to calm your verves, until I introduce you to my wife Grace, and her mother Maggie, her brother John and her stepfather J.D." Maggie instantly saw how uncomfortable Miss Irene was, and handed her a glass of wine, saying, "Never mind, Miss Irene – this should settle your nerves. I know how you must feel. I've felt the same way a few month ago when I traveled to California with my daughter and Alvin for their wedding. I found myself surrounded with so many people of color, that I felt every bit as intimated as you're feeling. Grace and I were the only white women there but it didn't take long for us to feel like we belonged there, which is the way I want you to feel. Anyway you shouldn't feel uncomfortable since you're well-acquainted with at least one of the residents . . . and he just happens to be the owner of the house as well as your best friend."

Following a couple of drinks and a few of Alvin's corny jokes, everybody had begun to relax. Then John Lee asked Alvin to walk with him out onto the back porch for a smoke.

As soon as the door closed behind them, John Lee grabbed Alvin by his shirt, and demanded, "Look here nigger – what do you mean, bringing me and my mama out here amongst all of these unpredictable crazy-ass white folks. Are you trying to get us killed?"

Alvin only laughed. "We are married and we have a license to prove it!"

"Don't you know those white folks don't give a damn about some dumb-ass niggers with a license that's supposed to be married to a white woman? They'll take that piece of paper and wipe your dead black ass with it! Man, you had better hurry up an' get your ass out of this white neighborhood – or else you'll soon realize that you're a small fish swimming amongst big-ass alligators, and white ones at that. This'll be your last warning from me! When I finish smoking this cigarette, I'm gonna get my mama and we're gonna get the hell out of here, before somebody get themselves hung!" He flipped his cigarette out on the grass, as they walked back into the house.

While Alvin still laughing, J. D. asked, "What did you tell him, that you were having a luau and he was the designated pig?"

"That's about what it amounted to" Alvin said, "He told me he's gonna get his coat, hat, his mama and get out of here. But I've got news for him – he's not going nowhere until he drinks twelve more beers and eats his share of the catfish that my wife and mother-n-law spent all afternoon preparing for him and his mother."

"Just to put your mind at ease – I'm going to kiss my wife, standing right here next to her mother, and that way y'all stop thinking you've been lured into a trap."

"That's even more of a reason why mama and I should get out of here," John Lee said. "All you're doing is giving them more time to decide what tree is best suited for hanging three colored people from, all at once." Everybody laughed and was beginning to feel the same about John Lee as Alvin did, when he told them that he was a natural comic. After that, even John Lee felt brave enough to throw in a joke or two, just to keep the party alive. After dinner the women cleared the table, and continued to carry on small talk, while Grace kept everybody's glass filled with the wine that she had served with their meal. Finally the three ladies left the kitchen and Maggie focused her attention on the soft music that she was playing on the record player.

She looked over at John Lee and said, "I would ask you to dance with me if I wasn't afraid that you would run off and leave your mother and cause me to drive home tonight."

John Lee said, "It couldn't have been said any better if I had of said it myself." Everybody laughed. "Come on Alvin," Maggie said, "Help your mother-in-law to set an example for your Buddy John Lee. He needs to know that we don't hang colored people anymore for dancing with white women." The music that Maggie had selected was a ballet but Alvin whirled her around in a waltz, because he didn't want her innocently stabbing him with her boobs and embarrassing him like the last time they danced to gather. The next dance was with Irene, who was somewhat embarrassed to get out on the floor at first. But Alvin kept after her so she finally gave in, saying, "I'll only dance with you to a slow beat and you've got to promise you won't let me finish up face down on y'alls' living room floor, because I think I've had too much wine.   After he whirled her around the living room a few times, she asked him to excuse her because she claimed that she was too dizzy to continue. Finally Alvin and Grace took the floor, not doing too much of anything except turning around in one spot squeezing and kissing and priming themselves for their bedtime treat. At eleven o'clock John Lee and Irene decided to leave; so Alvin and John Lee walked out ahead of everyone else.

At once John Lee said to Alvin, "Boy, you are the luckiest Negro in all of state of Texas. She is about the most beautiful white woman I've ever seen. How did you get away with doing something like that? Is she color-blind or crazy or maybe both? I can't see what a pretty woman like her wants with a dumb-ass Negro like you. That woman is pretty enough to be a movie star!"

Throughout the evening, Alvin never got around to telling John Lee about all of his accomplishments, and he wanted to keep it that way. Alvin felt just like most of John Lee's friends did; they resented the fact that John would tell a few jokes to put their minds at ease, and then nickel and dime them all the way to the poor house. After they sent John Lee and Irene on their way, the three of then went back into the house and began to describe the expressions on John Lee and Miss Irene's faces, when they knocked on the door expecting a colored man named Alvin Jackson to answer and got themselves frightened right out of their minds at seeing two white women answer the door instead. They become even shakier, Grace said, "When I called out to Alvin and said 'Alvin honey, your guest have arrived,' I was afraid that poor Miss Irene would faint clean away!"

The next morning was Saturday and everybody slept late except Maggie. According to her she was up at six, and had already served her family breakfast by seven. Then, she read the paper while sipping on her morning coffee, waiting until ten o'clock so she could go shopping with Grace. Alvin suggested to Grace that he'd go out back and offer his car to Maurine, in case she needed an excuse to leave the house, or maybe buy the kids an ice cream cone, pick up a bottle of milk, or just take a joyride through the city.

"I'll take the bus over to John Lee's house to see if I could say something amusing to cheer them up from the heck of a fright we gave them last night."

"Alvin," Grace said, "I don't wont you to have to take the bus, just so you can joke around with John Lee. You keep the car and offer it to Maurine this afternoon, when you get back from visiting with John Lee."

"Oh no," Alvin answered, "Riding the bus isn't any problem at all for me – in fact, it'll probably do me good to ride the bus for a change."

"If that's what you want, then it won't bother me if it doesn't bother you. Just be very careful and don't get yourself run over, please for my sake?"

Alvin walked out to Maurine's apartment, asking first if she could she drive.

"Of course I can drive a car," she answered.

"Would you like to borrow mine, just in case you and the kids want to get out of the house and get a breath of fresh air?" Maurine happily accepted, after he assured her that it wasn't any inconvenient to him. He gave her the keys, and then walked back into the house to wait for Grace to finish dressing, so he could kiss her good-bye. He noticed it didn't take Maurine long to get herself and the kids ready and left the apartment. Finally Grace came out, dressed and made-up, every hair in place, and kissed him goodbye. After she left to collect her mother, Alvin walked out the back way, through the alley towards the bus stop when he heard a loud whisper

"Alvin!" He stopped – the whisper came from the direction of Mrs. Nichols house, and saw that it was Miss Cassie. Seeing her reminded him that it was a Saturday and Miss Cassie had to be home alone; Saturday was the day that her mother and her mother's best friend would go do their weekend grocery shopping, the same as Grace and her mother. He remembered those Saturday mornings as when he and Miss Cassie would create some of their most memorable moments together. She was standing behind the screen out on the back porch; she barely cracked the door wide enough for him to squeeze pass her. At once she closed the door, wrapped him in her arms, pinned him to the wall, and began to knead her pelvis against his. She tried to penetrate his mouth with her tongue, except that he firmly closed his lips, preventing her.

"What's the matter Alvin," she asked, sadly. "Didn't you miss me, honey?" Accepting her pain he lifted the hem of her gown, wiping her tears away with it. Taking her into his arms, he answered, half-heartedly," I missed you too."

"You certainly aren't acting like it." Alvin began to kiss her, allowing her to reach into his clothing and stroke him, while she sat on his knee, her housecoat opened from top to bottom. She was stroking him with one hand, and vigorously massaging herself until she reached her pinnacle. He allowed her to kiss and fondle his appendage, but never once did he let his make contact with hers, no matters how inspired he felt watching how hard she worked at achieving her satisfaction. Otherwise she wouldn't have had any reason to complain about how crummy she thought he was being; that he refused to penetrate her with his genitals instead of aiding her with his fingers. Alvin reminded her then, that he was married and she had as much business asking him to go into her as he would asking an undomesticated female lion to indulge in tame copulation.

Miss Cassie became indignant. "You could've, if you didn't think she was younger and prettier than I am?"

"So far," Alvin answered, "I haven't met anyone that is as pretty as you are, and I think you know that."

"I think you're lying to me," she answered. "I've seen her lots of times with a woman who I assume is her mother– and she's very pretty. But that shouldn't have anything to do with you making real love to me. Instead, you sat me on your knee and let me do all the work while you kept interrupting me every time I came close to making you come with your wife's reserves in me."

"Truer words have never been spoken," Alvin confessed. "But since you know that I'm married, you should also know it wouldn't be right for me to betray a woman that has nothing on her mind except me. She has completely dedicated her whole life to me, and she would die an awful death if she knew that I had unzipped my pants and let this naked woman straddle my knee and holding on to my genitals like a saddle horn. And you were absolutely right; just ten more seconds and I would've been guilty of breaking my marriage vows. And you're absolutely wrong about Grace being prettier than you, like I said so far I haven't seen anyone as prettier than you are. But the things we did last summer – that was all fun and games. We were innocent. We were both single and we didn't have a care in the world. The only worry we had was your mother – and later I found out that we didn't have any problem at all. She knew all along what was going on between you and me. Here we were trying to be so careful – and she knew practically every night you came to my apartment."

"Now how do you know all of that, and who told you that she knew about us?"

"Your mother did," he reluctantly admitted. "She also told me that she was glad for the time we spent together, and you couldn't have spent it with a nicer person."

Miss Cassie was shocked, but at the same time pleasantly surprised. "So, my mama really said those things to you about us?"

"She did," Alvin answered. "But please don't say a word about this to her."

"Oh, don't you worry yourself any – I'll never mention a word about my sex life to her. The only regret I have is that neither one of us knew she didn't care. Otherwise we could've spent my entire vacation in your apartment without worrying about Mother catching me in the act. If that were the case, I doubt that you would've been so eager to go out and get yourself married to some little chick who's too selfish to share you with your original partner."

"That was the first thing that crossed my mind," he said, "when your mother told me she knew and didn't mind because she thought I was a very nice person. I wanted so much to write and tell you, except that I was already too involved with Grace, by then. I had to dismiss you from my thoughts and go on with my life. I just wished you'd taken me seriously, when I first asked about spending the rest of our lives together."

"I'm sorry too," she answered. "Fate has it's own way of dealing with us individuals, so apparently it wasn't meant for us to spend the rest of our lives together."

"You're probably right about that – else we'd be living next door and you'd be pregnant by now." Alvin hastily kissed her goodbye, telling her he still loved her, and rushed towards the door, still trying to reposition his staff so it wouldn't show in front of all of those people standing at the bus stop. Before he reached the alley, Miss Cassie called out, "This is the second time you've said that to me. Why you don't say it as sweet as you did, the last night we spent together in your apartment?"

He looked all around. "Bye, Miss Cassie. I love you"

"You see?" she said. "You haven't forgotten about me – otherwise you would've remembered the last thing you said to me, the night I left your apartment. I love you too, honey." She said in a whisper.

After spending so much time with Miss Cassie, Alvin lost all interest in going to visit with John Lee. But he had to go; if Grace asked about Irene or John Lee, he wanted to be truthful with her. He didn't want to make up some cock-n-bullshit story instead of telling the truth – that is, if she were curious enough to ask. Even he might not have technically copulated with Miss Cassie, he didn't feel triumphant either. He did mildly regret that he didn't ignore his vows to Grace just that once, and slam into Miss Cassie, as if he was in a churning contest and working to make a whole lot of butter. When it was all set and done, though, he knew he had made the right choice. He could just imagine how guilty he would've felt even to the point of not being happy to see Grace when she came home.

Even so he still felt a cloud of guilt hovering over him, as he walked to the bus stop. He began checking himself all over to see if Miss Cassie had left any trace of evidence on his clothing. He licked his lips several times, trying to erase any trace of her lipstick. The only thing he found was a wet spot just below his zipper. Alvin thought to himself, 'This should disappear by the time Grace sees me.' The more he thought about what he had done with Miss Cassie, the more awful he felt. It didn't seem so bad when she was sitting on his knee, and they were stroking and kissing each other until she reached a climax. Remorse after-the-fact led him to convince himself that their interlude was just a favor that Miss Cassie claimed he owed her, in return for allowing that easy access, which he had taken delight in doing, those few days last summer. Apart from lending her his hand to facilitate her efforts to achieve satisfaction, he carried no other guilt save letting her penetrate his lips with her tongue. The bus finally came; he climbed aboard and rode to Rosedale and Crawford, walking the rest of the way to John Lee's house, still burdened with guilt. 'I let her reach in my fly and stroke what I swore to Grace on our wedding night belonged only to her.' By the time Alvin got to John Lee's house and knocked on the door, his body may've been there but his mind out there, wrestling with his sense of ethics.

"Well," John Lee said when he opened the door, "if it ain't the executioner! Boy, I thought for sure you were out of your cotton-picking mind, when me and Mama finally came to the right house. All I could see was this one black face, amongst all of those white faces, grinning like a jackass gnawing on yellow jackets! I must admit, once everything fell into place, I felt pretty good, being with a few civilized people for a change. Those white folks that you're mixed up with, they waited on Mama and me, like they been our friends forever. Now, that so- called wife of yours was me and mama's conversation topic, the instant we left your house until we went to bed last night – and the last thing we talked about until Mama went off to church this morning! No matter how many times Mama tried to convince me that y'all was equal because you was just as handsome as she is pretty, I can't get over how a pretty woman like her with so many better opportunities could fall for someone like you; I'm not talking about looks, I'm talking about moneywise. One thing about it I can think my fool head off trying to understand why, but the fact remains; not only do y'all have each other, but y'all have her family on your sides, too. I bet if you were to compare her to Bobbie Jean, it'd be like going from eating   hotdogs to eating filet mignon. So, tell me how did y'all get together in the first place?"

"We met each other at work," Alvin answered. "And before they knew about us, we had fallen in love. We had to live together for a while before going to California and getting married."

"Why do you say that you were forced to live together?" John Lee asked.

"Grace and I were secretly seeing each other until a misunderstanding broke out between us." Alvin explained. "She ran away without listening to my side of the story. So I went to her folk's house, got her, and took her home with me, since I believed she wouldn't be welcome at there anymore, once they knew she dad been involved a colored man."

"So, you are telling me you were crazy enough to go into some white folk's house and take their daughter away?"

"That's right," Alvin said, and John Lee shook his head.

"Damn, boy – I thought Hitler was crazy when he tried to rule the world, but he wasn't so crazy that he didn't reserve enough sense to know when he had himself in a no-win situation. Even Hitler had sense enough to gather millions of followers before he tried to take over the world! But you were one lone crazy black-ass colored boy, going up against the whole city of Fort Worth, because you actually believe you are within your rights to have their daughter as your live-in girlfriend." John Lee shook his head, and blew out his breath, saying, "An idiot stupid enough to pull a stunt like that has got to have balls the size of a male chimpanzee!"

Alvin finally got around asking about Miss Irene. John Lee answered, "I haven't seen her since she's left with Elmo who's supposed to be taking her shopping – provided she's finished telling him all about her and me setting around eating and drinking with those white folks that you call family. I hope that along about now, she's making that old bastard buy her groceries and things that she don't really need, but he buys it for her anyway. Sometimes I can't help but feel sorry for him; the way Mama takes his money, and then I think she should make him pay. He doesn't have to be here – he has his own family. Given that Mama knows that she doesn't have any future with him – except for being his old lady's bedroom surrogate – who would blame her for taken as much as she can get away with? I ain't never let no woman get that kind of hold on me. They want you to give them all of your money, as if the men are the only one that having a good time. You and I know better, they're the ones that are screaming, 'Keep going baby, in case we just happen to finish before they do.'"

Alvin finally decided that he had enough of laughing and listening to John Lee's non-stop line of bullshit. John Lee walked with him to the sidewalk and said their goodbyes. Alvin walked down to the bus stop and caught the bus home. As always during daylight, he'd use the alley-way and enter his home through the back door. This time, though, he debated whether he should use the front entry, to avoid a possible second run-in with Miss Cassie. At the last minute he decided against using the front door, in order to avoid attracting attention from the neighbors. He was sure that his presence wouldn't be an immediate priority for her – it had been less than three hours since she last at on his knee, dampening it with her juices. Alvin told himself, 'With a bit of luck and a lot's of hope she'll be lounging around on her divan fanning her crouch with one hand, and holding a book with the other.' When he approached the corner of her mother's back yard, he crouched down and hurried past the Nichols's place and entered his own house through the alleyway. Grace and her mother hadn't made it back from shopping yet and neither had Maurine and the girls. It was only two-thirty in the afternoon and they usually came home not earlier than four-thirty. In the bathroom, he washed up with plenty of soap and water, and grabbed himself a beer to wash away any trace of Miss Cassie's breath she may've left in his mouth. He turned on the television, feeling a little guilty but not much – and soon fell asleep watching a love story. When Grace got home she tip-toed over to where he was sleeping; she bent down to kiss him, which startled him awake. She sat down beside him on the divan, and whispered an apology.

"Honey," he answered, softly. "There is no need for an apology I'm glad you woke me so I could tell you how happy I am to see you. Darling, I've missed you so much today, that I could hardly wait to tell you."

"I know you do, honey, and I've missed you too." She kissed his lips and placed her hand over his eyes to close them, hoping that he would go back to sleep. She went back to the kitchen, talking to her mother, and helping put the groceries away. Alvin lay there, thinking how glad he was that he and Miss Cassie had not gone all the way, in her rage of passion, even though it had been nearly unbearable for him to abstain while she sat on his knee, fondling him. Retracing his encounter today with Miss Cassie, the only thing that he was guilty of was to let her put her tongue in his mouth. Really, all he had done was lend her his knee to sit on and his lips to kiss and his accessory to fondle; why he should continue to punish himself with guilt? Weighing the positive against the negative, he found himself innocent of all charges, whereupon he folded his arms and went back to sleep. He slept soundly, until one of Grace's little sisters came to the door to return Alvin's car keys.

He heard them as they raced noisily back to their house, shouting with excitement. "Mama, look what Grace bought us; a new toy!" A few minutes later he heard Maggie pick up the phone, to call J.D., asking if he wanted to come over for supper. After she hung up the phone he heard her tell Grace that he wasn't coming. John had gone off with some of his friends, and since J.D. was comfortable where he was, he asked Maggie just to bring him a plate of leftovers when she came home."

Around seven o'clock that evening, Maggie asked Grace to drive her home, in order to feed him before he went off to bed. As soon as Grace dropped Maggie off, she turned around and came right back home. No sooner had she changed out of her street clothes and into her housecoat, Walter arrived from Oklahoma, driving his old car, loaded down with all of his family belongings. Maurine and the children, and Alvin and Grace went out to greet him. They all came back to Alvin and Grace's house.

Grace handed her father a beer, telling him, "While you're drinking it, I'll fix you a plate of food – you must be starved half to death by now?" Before he could answer, Maurine said, "The beer he can have, but I've already cooked supper; it's waiting for him so we can all have supper together. After his first beer he reached out and took his little girls, and sitting them on each knee, as he began to tell everyone about his trip and how he managed to squeeze all of his possessions into that forty-nine Ford. He also told them how he had almost wrecked his car when he blew out the right-rear tire. He told them how discouraged he felt when he had to change a flat tire, and to find out that it was in such bad shape that he barely made it to a service station.

"I sure am glad you handed me that hundred-dollar bill," he said to Grace. "That was the thing that saved my bacon. Otherwise you just might be on your way to Oklahoma along about now to pick up me and my belongings."

"Either that, or you could've called me," Maurine said. "Alvin was nice enough to lend the girls and I his car, which we've had nearly all day. It apparent that he felt sorry for us knowing that we've been cooped up in this house, practically every day since you've been gone."

"Yes," Walter asked. "And where did you go?"

"Oh," Maurine answered, "I took the children, and treated ourselves to an ice-cream cone and some other little things. After that, we rode around town sightseeing . . . and you know – doing things like parking, watching people go by and whatever."

"How much money did you spend buying all of that stuff that they didn't need?" Walter demanded, and Maurine answered, "Five or six dollars."

"Damn woman don't go spending that kind of money on those kids!" Walter was angry. "You shouldn't have spent no more than seventy-five cents on ice cream between the three of you – and maybe that much on the other treats you bought – and that should have been enough! Six dollars is pretty near a half-day's wedges. I guess it's not safe to leave you with my money – hell, you are liable to spend it all on foolishness."

Grace and Alvin felt bad for Maurine and Maurine looked as if she felt badly for herself also. Grace got out her handbag, and handed Maurine six dollars, saying, "I offered to buy their treats – I just haven't got around to paying her yet."

"Now," Walter said, still riled. "Don't go trying to clean up her mess by giving her a few dollars. She don't need a handout. What she needs is a lesson in how to manage her money! Go on, girls, tell your big sister 'bye' – it's about time I had me some of that good home cooking."

The girls chorused, "Bye, big sister Grace!" as they walked out the door.

Grace closed the door after them, saying, "Wasn't that rude of my Daddy to chew her out in front of the children – not to mention you and I standing there, listening to him embarrass her?"

"I noticed it myself," Alvin said. "Was he that grumpy when he lived at home with you?"

"Oh yes," Grace answered. "I've witnessed my share of his edgy moments. He used to treat Mama the same way, whenever the least little thing went wrong. He would get all cross and cantankerous with Mama – and he'd take it out on John and me. Even so," Grace added, "I'm sure some of it can be blamed on him being tired, driving all the way to Oklahoma and back to Fort Worth, in that old car loaded down with all of that junk. The six dollars she spent – amongst everything else that went wrong – was probably just enough to send him over the edge."

That little which Alvin knew about Walter, in comparison to J.D. – made him think that Maggie was attracted to the same kind of men. They both suffered from a lack of self-esteem, which wasn't saying very much about Maggie's own self-esteem. 'One would think that a woman with a face, body and personally like hers would have done so much better for herself than hanging out with a couple of losers like those two guys. On the other hand, Maggie and Walter undoubtedly produced one of the best-rounded daughters I've seen in my short lifetime. Even, if her parents did have low self-esteem, she seems to have a good notion of her own worth, along with her mother's looks and personality. Alternatively, maybe her own self-esteem is no difference than her mother's. Maybe it'll take a little time for her lack of self-esteem to kick-in and drag her down to her parents' level. And my believing that my irresistible charm was what turned her head – maybe it was all my imagination. Any ne'er-do-well could've done the same thing. I did sleep with her one time – and the next time you ask, she'll move in with you. And perhaps maybe I was wrong to think I had totally monopolistic power over her. I hope, for my sake what I'm preoccupied with is nothing more than an illusion, and she'll be anything but a person with low self-esteem. Maybe Maggie isn't any of those things that I just described, either. Her problem could be that she's not a very good judge of character when it comes to choosing men.'

By the time he had finished analyzing her family; Grace came out of the bathroom, got in bed and found herself in a whole lot of trouble. She wasn't aware that she had been designated to minimize an extension, resulting from a naked woman, bouncing on his knee while he used every fiber in his body to abstain from diving in and deal with his guilty conscience after the fact.

Ten days after Walter had moved from Oklahoma to Forth Worth, Grace happened to walk out back to say hi to her little sisters. Walter told her all about him searching diligently for work, and had finally landed himself a job as a heavy-equipment operator. He praised Grace for all the good things she had done for him. However, those few friendly days he spent with Alvin were short-lived. It seemed that the more he saw of Alvin, the less he wanted to be around him. When he wanted to talk to Grace, he would ask the girls to tell her to come over, but never Alvin. Being the proud person that Alvin was, he would always decline to volunteer his presence, especially if he wasn't invited. When it was impossible for him to avoid coming face to face with Alvin, he would ether divert has attention to a beautiful flower that grew in the back yard, or stare straight ahead until he walked passed Alvin. As far as speaking to Alvin – elaboration just wasn't in Walter's vocabulary. Alvin and Grace discussed this Walter's rather churlish behavior, and eventually concluded that no matter how hard Walter tried, he couldn't bring himself to accept the fact that his daughter married a colored man. Being the relatively peaceful person that Alvin was, he didn't want to see Grace estranged from her father. Despite Walter's disrespectful outlook, he was able to brush it off and attributed it to Walter's fundamental beliefs and low self esteem. Alvin told Grace it didn't matter to him, as long as it didn't affect the two people he loved; herself and her mother Maggie. "I'm very much protective toward you and your mother – the same way I know how the both of your feel about me too. Walter's dislike for mixed marriages is like a dog in a haystack, he can't eat the hay – but he doesn't want the cow to eat it either. Sometime, I would like to ask your father, 'Why is it such a nothing when a white man sleeps with a colored woman, but potentially a death sentence for the colored man. if he's caught sleeping with a white woman?'"

Alvin never stopped Grace from mingling with her father's second family, especially the little girls. In late October of that year, Alvin and Grace looked over their bank account and saw that it had begun to recover from their last investment; it was time to contact the real estate broker that they had dealt with, when they bought the first apartment building. Right away, the real estate agent took the information that Grace gave and went to work. A couple of days later she called back, telling Grace that she had found a twenty-unit apartment building in a different neighborhood but for a higher price than the first building. And there was also another apartment building available in the same neighborhood as the first, for the same price. Alvin and Grace decided, before making any real commitment, they needed to make sure that they didn't overlook anything. They weighed all of the facts, counted their money twice, and saw that they could afford the more expensive building. One final thought came to mind; they should talk the choice of buildings over with Walter, and see whether or not he would accept living six blocks away from his ex-wife Maggie. Or would he prefer to move to the other side of town in order to avoid coming in contact with her? When they finally approached him to tell him that he would have the last word in choosing between the two buildings, Walter told Grace that he had intended to talk to her about managing the apartment.

"I've given this apartment-management crap a lot of thought." He said to Grace, "I think if I'm gonna have to pay rent for managing an apartment building, it might as well be one of my own choosing – without the hassle of administrations' duties?"

Grace felt somewhat sad, "What if I only charged you half the rent – what would you say?"

"My answer would still be the same!"

"Daddy," Grace exclaimed, "Tell me why you have managed to disappoint me over this, just when I was all excited about you and me becoming reacquainted, the way we were five years ago. But if that's not one of your priorities – if it was, you would've accepted my offer – if for nothing more than doing it for me! I was all set to come over some weekend, once you got settled in to your new apartment. And watch the kids while you and Maurine have a night out on the town.

"You and I can do all of that, after I move to the right neighborhood." Walter answered, and Grace finally understood what he was trying to tell her. She said her goodnights, and walked back to her own house. She was crushingly disappointed – she had thought Walter would be pleased to be the manager of an apartment building.

"You know, I wonder if I should have ever trusted him." She said to Alvin. "I thought he had begun to get used to seeing us together, and to be civil to you . . . but when he said that about moving to the right neighborhood . . . when I was so excited? That was a cruel thing for him to do. Be that as it may," she continued, "I don't need him either; not this time anyway. The first time he pulled a stunt like this I was fourteen. I was devastated – I was almost out of my mind, just as Mama was. But this time, she won't have to cry, and neither will I. We both have someone to lean on, and that someone is you. Mama knows how much she can depend on you for security – even more than she does on J.D. I do believe the reason she got with J.D, as soon as she did – he was halfway decent – and she needed security. Her only worry about him was that he might get drunk and doing something stupid – like running over somebody and going to prison. It's not a secret to any of us, and that includes J.D – we all look to you as our leader. We know you wouldn't hesitate to put your life on the line for all of us, the way you did out of love for me." Grace smiled, reminiscently. "Oh, when I think about you standing in the middle of my Mama's living room floor, and crying, telling her that you had come to take her daughter. You must've been frightened out of your mind. I know I was and I wasn't in nearly as much trouble as you were. But you persevered until you got what you came for. Sometimes, I used to ask myself –why me, when there must've been thousands of girls you could've took home without all the drama?"

Alvin smiled, lazily, "I've asked myself a few questions about you, too. What if someone had come onto you the way I did, when we first met? Would you have been as careful in choosing him, as you were as choosing me? I would hate to think that any need-to-do-well could've got your attention, and here I was thinking that I was this person called Mr. Invincible? I would be so disappointed if I knew that were the reason why you came to live with me in the first place."

"Alvin, honey, don't you remember me telling you about all of those boys that use to come to our house with their parents, and tried to persuade me to lay with them? The same way they tried to do to me at school? I'm surprised that you'd ask me such silly question?"

"I apologize for letting jealous thoughts get the best of me – I had no reason to compare you to your mothers' judgment of men. Beside, what I think you have something that your mother doesn't have. Both of you has all of this beauty – and yet she didn't value herself enough to hold out for the highest bidder. She shouldn't have settled with a man like J.D. – she should be with a man who's financially able to reward her with luxury – just the same as he's rewarded with the company of a smart and beautiful woman. That's why you see me working as hard as I do – because I'm wanting to accumulate enough wealth to put it at your disposal so you'll feel that you're being compensated for giving me access to your beautiful self. So far, darlin' Grace, we've both been rewarded. I'll keep giving and you keep looking like a movie star, and watch how effortlessly we can spoil each other."

She grinned and said, "Whatever it is of mine that makes you say what you say about me – I'm sorry to say that I don't see it. I know very well that I'm not an ugly girl – but I really don't think there is anything special about me. As far as I'm concerned I'm just another person that happened to be born female, which fitted right into your category."

"While we're off the subject of flattery," Alvin mused, "We need to be thinking about sweet-talking someone into manage the new apartment building. We're no longer obligated to buy the most expensive building, now that your father is out of the picture. We can buy that one in the same neighborhood as your mother's building – we'll be spending less on a down payment, and keep more money in our pockets at the close of escrow. Since Mrs. Maggie is managing the first building so well, why not have her manage both, since they're in the same neighborhood. We'll save on labor, and increase our revenue by renting the manager's apartment. Her job is to sit around all day, answer the phone, and deal with complaints – if any. So, why not have her listen to twice as many complaints?"

The next day, Grace called Maggie to tell her to get with the realtor and start the paperwork on the new apartment building. Three weeks later, Maggie called to let them know that the broker had told her all was needed to close escrow was a check for the required amount and both participants' signatures. She and J.D were on their way with the paperwork, and a couple of bottles of wine.

Maggie took it on her own to celebrate any event that she thought would pay homage to her beloved daughter. When everyone had finished off a couple of glasses of wine, with Maggie and J.D. praising Alvin and Grace about all they had accomplished so far, Alvin said to Grace,   "Our next investment will be in a small farm for my father and mother. While I was home back in the summer, my daddy mention to me about a small farm he'd like to own somewhere around a small town called McCauley – that's about forty miles due east of Snyder. He said it would be the ideal place for me to bring my white wife to visit – the place is about two miles from the main road and a mile back in the woods. People using that road are mostly farmers, and hardly ever pass through it after dark. After twelve hours of hard work those farm folk, lays down when the sun goes down. I think that my father was trying to tell me – if we're that far back in the woods, we wouldn't have to worry about being harassed by someone who hates interracial mixing."

"That sounds like a wonderful idea, honey," Grace agreed. "Why didn't you talk about it before we bought our second building? It'll take some time to raise enough for a down payment on a farm, since we've spent a large sum of our money on that last building."

"I don't know about all of that," Alvin answered. "The land in that part of the country is pretty cheap. We might have just enough or we will have – provided we get sixty days to close escrow, and preferably immediately get tenants for the old house and all of the apartment units. From what my father says, land in that part of the country isn't that expensive; the amount of acreage that we're talking about shouldn't cost more than five thousand dollars – if that much."

"What kind of farm are we talking about," Grace asked. "It sounds to me like it couldn't be more than twenty acres or so."

"The way Daddy described it to me; it's about two hundred acres of land that doesn't grow much of anything except a lot of underbrush. It won't grow wheat – maybe cotton if it was fertilized. It'll grow cattle feed and all kinds of produce, not to mention being a place where jackrabbits, coyote and squirrels thrive. Daddy told me, if I decide to do something like that he would get the name of the landowner from a reliable source and let me know. At that point, I'll let Maggie take over . . . going down to whoever owns the land, do all of the negotiating and give us a little feed-back every once and awhile."

Maggie asked, "Do you think that I can do something like that?

"As much as you talk," Alvin grinned broadly. "Why would you even doubt yourself? Stop and listen to the sound of your voice – and maybe you can hear how hard it would be for the prey to outsmart the predator." Maggie laughed, "I'm assuming you're picturing me as the predator and not the prey?" She thanked them both for trusting her with so much responsibility. "I'll do my best to bargain y'all the very best deal possible. Y'all just let me know when I'm supposed to leave, and tell me what price I should start with and I'll be on my way."

"I'll tell you right now, I'd like to start at no more than twenty dollars an acre."

"All right then," Maggie answered, "that's what it'll be!"

After a few trips from Snyder to Anson, Alvin's father Allan got the information that Alvin needed to start the transaction. Two weeks had passed from the time Alvin's father begin his search, until he finally contacted the heir of the long-deceased owners of the farm property. Alvin gave Maggie the name of the heir, her address, and phone number, cautioning her not to invoke his father's name during the transaction. Alvin had good reasons to believe once they knew it was a colored man involved, they'd refuse to sell to him, or hike the price so high that he couldn't afford it. After hearing that, Maggie and Grace put their heads together and wrote a letter, tendering an offer of twenty dollars an acre. Two weeks later they had not received a response. Alvin asked Maggie to do a follow-up by making a phone call. When she did, she got an old-sounding voice on the other end, saying that she had gotten Maggie's offer by mail. She also told Maggie that she was thinking alone the lines of twenty-five dollars an acre. By the time Maggie had finished talking, the old lady accepted a compromise offer of twenty-two-fifty an acre.

The next couple of days, Maggie spent getting ready to travel to Abilene to set up escrow. Once that happened, Alvin wasted no time getting the message to his parents, telling them that they were about to become the owners of their own farm. Alvin parents let him know that the old farmhouse needed quite a bit of repair. Even so they eagerly accepted it in its present condition because it was something that his parents had longed for, for years. They well understood that repairs of the farmhouse must wait until Alvin and Grace could reinvigorate some of their almost-depleted bank account. But they were not so strapped that they couldn't keep up the tradition of celebration, after they'd sealed the deal on one of their latest achievement.

Saturday night he and Grace invited J.D, and Maggie, John Lee and his mother Irene, to come and commemorate their most recent accomplishment. Unlike the time before, John Lee and Irene didn't need to saturate their brains with alcohol in order to act civilly around their white counterparts. As soon as everyone was comfortable and with a drink in their hands, Alvin told John Lee and Irene that the celebration was about two things. He and Grace had bought his parents their own farm, and the other was that they had just recently acquired an additional apartment building. At hearing what Alvin had did for his parents, Irene became astounded with what she heard coming out of his mouth. She began to question Alvin as to how he could've come so far in such a short time and make the things he does seem so unproblematic?

"I bet your father and Jessie May must be very proud of you along about now. I know I would be, if I had a son that loved me enough to get off his behind, and buy his mama a home like you have for your parents." She stared at him momentarily, saying, "Who would've thought this two-year-old snot-nosed boy that I use to see running half-naked, would grow up to be what he is today?"

Maggie ventured, "Irene, you say that as if you knew Alvin's parents."

"I sure do," Irene said. "I use to lived just right down the road from where Allen and Jessie May lived. You mean to tell me – Alvin didn't tell y'all I knew him when he was just a little thing running around barefoot with his older sisters and brother? That's how far back I go with him and his family. Not only have I changed this boy's diapers more than I can remember – and I've changed his sister's diapers as well. I hear he has two younger brothers, which I've never met. They came along after my husband, our children and I decided that there was nothing out in them fields but cotton. Since my family's name is Bailey, we figure us and those cotton fields had nothing in common. We moved to Fort Worth pert-near seventeen years ago, and been here ever since. Of course," Miss Irene added sadly, "my John Lee senior passed on, a little over five years ago . . . back to knowing this boy's family; yes, me and this child's mama cleaned a lot of mustard greens together, and in the fall of the year we all prayed for a cold northerly wind to blow in, so we all could kill hogs. You know in those days, most colored folks didn't have refrigeration and freezers like those that have them today. That's the reason why all of us coloreds prayed for cold weather, to keep the meat from spoiling." Miss Irene smiled, reminiscently. "Alvin, does your daddy still have that old smokehouse, out behind the chicken house? He sure did know how to cure those hams and smoke them sausages! I remember when I couldn't wait to watch him rub them hams with his own special seasoning, then he'd lay them aside to marinate. He'd start his fire and let it smolder until the temperature was just right. As the smoke begin to circulate though out his little smokehouse and hover to a plateau of perfection. After that he'd hang that meat and let them boogers smoke until they was just so nice and tasty. While he was doing all of that, me and your mama would clean them chitt'lins then we'd season them with a little garlic, onions and a few hot peppers. After that, we'd boil the daylights out of them until they were nice and tender. We would serve our families greens, cornbread and chitt'lins; sometimes boiled rice when we had it. That was some of the best eating I think I'd ever had in those days."

Grace nudged Alvin and asked, "What in the world is chitt'lins?"

He laughed, replying, "Actually the correct pronunciation is chitterling. But you know us colored folk, and how we mess up the English language! Chitterlings are pig's intestines that's been cleaned – and just like Mrs. Irene said, you boiled them until they are done."

Grace exclaimed, "Oh! Yuck!" Then she covered her face and broke into a laugh, before demanding, "Did you ever eat that stuff?" Alvin couldn't answer at first; everyone was laughing so hard from her reaction to Irene's description of chitterlings. Alvin finally stop laughing just long enough to tell her that yes, he had, before everyone started laughing all over again.

"Alvin" she said, "I thought I knew everything about you – until Miss Irene said you had eaten pig intestines? What other disgusting things have you eaten that you haven't told me about?"

After dinner, everyone continued to drink and discuss things that went on in each others lives from childhood until the present, which lasted until close to ten that evening, when John Lee and Miss Irene decided to pack up and go home. The next morning over breakfast, Maggie brought up to Grace her suggestion about everyone gathering at her house for Thanksgiving, including her sister Myrtle and Myrtle's husband Ed. "After I thought about it," Maggie said, "Your father and his family had already showed upon at your doorstep, before I talked about bringing Myrtle and Ed here for Thanksgiving. I don't know if y'all want to include him and his family in this Thanksgiving celebration or not. If that's the case then I'll make other arrangements about how I'm going to feed and sleep two extra peoples. I don't mind if you go ahead and asked him, but I got my doubts about him showing up, with as much a grudge as he has against Alvin. From what you said about how he's been avoiding Alvin here lately, he might not come within a mile of this house on Thanksgiving Day. If I'm wrong about him, let me know in plenty of time and the five of us will have Thanksgiving dinner at my house."

"I'll ask," Grace said "but I won't invite him. Either way it'll get me off the hook. I'll let you know as soon as I know what his answer will be."

"And if his answer is 'yes'" Maggie asked, "That's when I'll have to tell him that he and his family will be eating with his ex-wife, her boyfriend, his ex-sister-in-law and her husband Ed. If that doesn't deter him, then we'll all be eating Thanksgiving dinner at my house."

After Maggie and J. D. left that evening, Grace decided to walk out back to Walter's house to pay him and his family an unannounced visit. Alvin went with her, as far as the door, and waited in the twilight outside. Grace saw her father sitting at the kitchen table playing solitaire. She stooped down and picked up her youngest little sister and waited patiently until he suffered defeat at a hand he dealt himself. Only then did he turn his attention to Grace.

"What possessed you to leave your mother and her gang waiting in the wings and come to my house?"

"I don't remember whether or not I told you that Aunt Myrtle and Uncle Ed are coming in for Thanksgiving in the next few days. And I'm sure you've figured out by now that everyone will be coming to my house to celebrate the event. Alvin and I are wondering what you have planned for you and your family on this Thanksgiving Day."

"Well," he answered, "Yes and no. Yes, I'd love to have Thanksgiving with my lovely daughter, and no, not under these circumstances. I'm not about to bring my wife and daughters and let them be looked down on by your spiteful Mama."

Grace thought, 'He may not have known it, but his answer was exactly the one I wanted to hear.' Since she was on a roll, she might as well take it a step further and said, "If you change your mind, you know you and Maurine are always welcome to come and have Thanksgiving dinner with us – anytime after two that afternoon."

"Like I said," he said, "Not under these circumstances. Maybe some other time, when just the girls and we four adults can be alone together."

Grace hugged and squeezed her little sisters and said, "I wouldn't be in such a hurry to leave, except I was up late last night entertaining guests. I'm so sleepy now that even those dirty dishes of mine will have to wait until I finish my nap before they can get washed."

As she started out the door, her father asked, "Am I the only one around here that doesn't get a hug and a kiss goodnight?" Grace was startled, yet she leaned down to kiss her father. "Night darling," he said. Flabbergasted was the only word to describe Grace and Alvin's state of mind, hearing Walter speak to Grace with such affection; compared to the moody way in which he had been treating them for the last couple of months. As soon as they had crossed the garden, and were back in their house, Grace spoke. "I cannot imagine what brought all that on? Do you think his new conduct is any indication that he's changed his mind about moving as far away from you and me as he once did? Has he finally realized that no matter how badly he treats us, it wouldn't ever be enough to amend our feelings for each other?"

Alvin answered, "You and I have known all along where his problem stemmed from, which is he can't fathom the idea of this colored man to sleep with his white daughter."

"His other problem," Grace said, "is that he can't grasp the idea that I can allow Mama to live rent-free and not him. Never mind; he abandoned Mama and John and I to be with Maurine. This means mine and John's only contributor was our Mama. And now he thinks because I'm his daughter, he can treat my husband like crap, and expect me to give him the same preferential treatment as I have given Mama."

The next morning Grace called her mother to tell her that Walter wouldn't be having Thanksgiving dinner with her after all, which did not surprise Grace the least bit. What did surprise her was that he had offered to visit with Alvin and her at a time when just the six of them could be alone together. He even went so far as to remind her as she was leaving, "Am I the only one around here that doesn't get a goodnight kiss?"

"Oh," Maggie said, "he's just resents the fact that he has to pay rent, while you let your mother live rent-free. Another thing that could've send his tail in a downward spin, was when he realized that I were being paid a salary for doing nothing, except to sit on my butt. Like I've always told you, he's your father, so be nice to him. But don't go chasing after him and watch him come looking for you like a lost child looking to find its mama."

Chapter 11 – Thanksgiving

Two days after, Grace and Maggie had scrutinized Walter's reasons for going from bad behavior to propriety. Maggie's sister, Myrtle, and her husband, Ed, called Maggie from the Greyhound bus station and she was on her way to pick them up. In the meantime she wanted to know—being that it was on such short notice—would it still be feasible for her to bring them from the bus station straight to her house. Grace agreed; ninety minutes later, Maggie and her family, along with her sister, Myrtle, and her husband, Ed, all piled out of Maggie's car onto Grace's driveway. Everyone came carrying a piece of luggage, except J. D., who walked in carrying two six-packs of Falstaff. He went straight to Alvin and asked, "Are you about ready for one of these while they're still nice and cold? And if you don't mind, just put the rest in the refrigerator where they'll stay that way and we'll drink those buggers after supper."

"I know you remember my girl, Grace." Maggie said to her sister.

"Well my goodness," Myrtle exclaimed, as she met Grace halfway and began embracing each other. "Without a doubt, she's the prettiest and classiest young lady I've seen since your mother was a young lady your age." The instant they withdrew their arms for each other and stepped back away, Myrtle looked Grace up and down. "Yes-sir-ree," Myrtle continued, "excluding the age differences, you're the spitting image of you mother. It was hard for me to imagine me being related to Maggie back when she grew up to be about your age because she was so beautiful. And here I am tonight feeling the same way about her gorgeous daughter. And the both of you owe every bit of your beauty to our mama and Grace's grandmama."

Maggie could hardly wait for Myrtle to finish complimenting Grace so she could introduce her to Alvin. At that instant, Maggie said to Myrtle and Ed, "Now, y'all have heard me go on and on about the wonderful husband my Grace is married to. But there's one thing I didn't tell y'all about this brilliant man you see setting there relaxed and acting as if he's part of this family; he is part of this family because he's my daughter's legal husband. I'm sure you've noticed by now that I'd be wasting my time if I tried to explain to you what his nationality is. So since you've seen for yourselves, all I have left to do is for y'all to say hi to my one and only son-in-law, Alvin Jackson." Maggie went on to say, "This boy not only stole my daughter's heart but her mother's heart, as well the rest of my family. Alvin, this is my big sister, Myrtle, and her husband, Ed Gillespie."

"A pleasure meeting y'all," Alvin said.

"Well, well," Myrtle said, "this is a surprise." She extended her hand, adding, "When I saw you setting there, I thought you were a friend of J. D.'s. Never in a million years would I have guessed that you were my gorgeous little niece's husband."

Ed extended his hand, as he chuckled and said, "Maggie told us all about you and how seriously you take your responsibilities. She did leave out the part about you being colored. Other than that, it would've made us any different one way or another. If our little niece thinks you're good enough to marry, and her mama is just as agreeable, then what does it matter to the wife and me or anyone else as far as we're concern? We're just so much obliged to you and our little niece for the privilege of sharing your beautiful home with us. You just keep doing whatever it is you're doing for Grace, and you'll have old Maggie as a friend for years to come."

J. D. said to Ed, "I'm gonna have to interrupt your flattering bullshit story just long enough to ask you to continue this discussion over a couple of those cold five o'clock beers that went into effect about five minutes ago."

"Well, now hold on there, fellow," Ed said. "I gave up drinking years ago and haven't bothered to touch the stuff since. Nonetheless," he said, "out of respect for my sister-in-law, Maggie, who was charitable enough to pay our fare from Beaumont to Fort Worth – I'm placing my tradition on the back burner, at least while I'm amongst realities like these."

No sooner than it took the men to raise their cans of beers and the women their wine glasses and said cheers, Maggie and her sister went back and sat at the kitchen table, where they slipped back to the conversation that was already in progress. At that time, they continued to talk about events that took place years before either Alvin or Grace was born. Even though J. D. knew very little about either of their background, his curiosity finally got the best of him; he dragged up a chair and expanded on the chat by adding the little he knew about the family's history.

About an hour into their exchange of information, Grace called out to her mother and asked, "What are we supposed to do about Uncle Ed and Aunt Myrtle's supper for tonight?"

Maggie looked over and saw Grace resting her back on Alvin's chest and his arms clenched around her waist, while sitting on the divan watching television. "I'm assuming you don't have to do anything except to keep smothering Alvin with your affection. It was on the tip of my tongue a second before you spoke, that I was going to ask Myrtle to ride to the market with me to pick up a few items to start supper for everyone."

Ed stood and said to J. D. as he walked over to the refrigerator and took his second beer: "You know that first beer I just drunk seems to have been just what I needed to ease that recurring pain in my lower back. I figured a second one just might send that scandalous ache running out of my back, like a guilty fox from a chicken's house."

J. D. jokingly said, "Let's not get carried away with this beer made for medicine bullshit. I only brought two six-packs and I haven't got started yet."

At last Maggie and Myrtle came back with the groceries and made supper. Afterward they continued to be split into two groups. Alvin and Grace went back to the divan and watched television. The four older adults remained seated at the kitchen table and continued to evoke each other's nostalgic memories of things that happened long ago.

Finally, Ed asked Maggie to show him to his and Myrtle's bedroom. Following that, J. D. retired to his and Maggie's bedroom which had been reserved for them since the first night they spent there. Alvin and Grace had already gone to bed at nine o'clock, both of them being firm believers in having an adequate amount of sleep in order to perform well on their job the next day. Even though they had gone to bed, they didn't fall asleep immediately, because of all of the excitement about her uncle and aunt being there . . . and the time they spent doing other things. All of which kept them awake to hear practically every word that the four older adults spoke – right up until the two men went off to bed, at about eleven o'clock. This didn't include Maggie and her sister Myrtle. They carried on the conversation until only the two of them knew what time it ended, since everyone else was sound asleep.

When Alvin and Grace came home that afternoon, they teased Ed about having to make his own breakfast, since Maggie stayed up so late the night before entertaining her sister. However, Ed disputed their accusation and told them that Maggie may have stayed up until the wee, wee hours of the morning but nonetheless he claimed, "At seven o'clock sharp, she had breakfast on the table getting cold while she sit in front of the television sipping on her second cup of coffee." Ed and Alvin got into a discussion which eventually led to Ed asking Alvin all about his childhood and where he grew up. Alvin told him that he didn't have very much history of himself because of his age.

"As far back as I can remember, I grew up in a small town not too far from Sweetwater called Snyder." He went on to tell Ed about having three brothers and two sisters. Everyone had married except the two younger brothers who still lived at home. "I was seventeen when I decided to come to Fort Worth in search of a better life; one that just the opposite of the life I lived, living with my father. The poor man worked his children – as well as himself – half-to-death in those cotton fields. Always, at the end of the year, he had very little to show for his hard work except a lot of dirt that had adhere to his sweaty clothes, followed by a sad face. After his boss-man shows him his profit and lost statement, 'Oh, well' he'd say with an unhappy look on his face. 'I sure do hope next year's will be lots better than the previous year.' So like my father, we're both have a destiny with work, except mine is clean and I get paid every week. Plus the advantage of being paid every week, I don't have to wait until harvest time before I can afford to buy myself a juicy steak. Like the perfect job that I finally landed, I needed the perfect woman to fit in with my idea of having the two most important things in any man's life who had the desire to succeed abundantly. I allotted myself seven years from arriving in Fort Worth, which will put me at my twenty-fifth birthday."

"From what I hear," Ed said, "Boy, you sure do have a good start on it. It was no more than a couple of hours ago that I heard Maggie tell me and Myrtle that you and Grace had gone out and bought yourselves another apartment building. The thing that concerns me the most is how is it that a teenage colored boy like yourself managed to do all of the things you've done with no help from anyone other than your wife, Grace. I'll be the first to admit that the mythical saying, 'that colored people can't turn a corner without leaning on the white man's shoulder.' Well, as far as I'm concern

286

it's nothing but a myth, and may those of us who still believe that way should fall under the curse of mythical correction."

"There is no mystery to what I've done other than to have a made-up mind; at least that's the way it has been for me." Alvin answered. "All I did was plan and seek out the opportunity. Once it came within my reach, I latched on and took full control, and it appears now that all of what I've dream of becoming has just begun to become a reality. Even though my father had a reputation of being a failure, all the same, he was still my inspiration. So instead of me concentrating on his failures, I focused my attention on the good things I saw in him, and the words he spoke to me as to how I should live my life. One of which he told me that the most two important things in a young boy's life is that first he find himself a good job and obligate his self to take care of it. For instance, he said, 'let's say you see a calf stuck in the mud. If you know how to get it out all by yourself, why wait to be told? Take the initiate and your boss will notice and he'll reward you with money as well as with authority.' So I took my first job working for penny at the icehouse, and finally I landed my dream job working at the hotel, which is where I met my wonderful wife Grace.

"She was that missing link that was needed to bind the second most important thing which my father felt was necessary to shape my destiny. I concluded that she had all of the right qualifications, as far as I was concerned, but she had the wrong skin color as far as the public was concerned. So I thought of all kind of ways to find that same qualification that I saw in Grace in some colored girl. Little did I know that the two most important things in my life were being assembled under the same roof; my dream job and the perfect wife. One of many things I remember him telling me was, 'you must find and marry yourself a woman who'll understand the importance of committing herself to satisfying your manly needs. This way, your mind is free for constructive thought which leads to ambitious thinking, and optimistic people are the ones that create new ideas.' Those words of my father were fulfilled the night I finally persuaded Grace to leave her mother and father's house to come live in mine. Of course there were more to it than my asking her to drop everything and come live with me. It all stemmed from the one night as we were walking across the parking lot, which we'd did many nights before. Except this night was different – I finally got up the nerve to ask if she had seen a Humphrey Bogart movie called the Maltese Falcon. Apparently she was just excited about seeing the movie as I was. So we began to describe different part of the movie and what this character did, and what that character did to that fellow. Until this particular night when we had run out of things to say concerning the movie, Maltese Falcon, I decided to switch to a conversation about my plains for the future. I started by telling her that I had the perfect job, and all that was left for me to do was to find the perfect woman.

"After about two months on the subject of my plans for the future—as we walked to and from the storage room every night—I got the feeling that my words were more like entertainment to her, until I mention the fact that I wasn't willing to accept just any colored girl. I was looking for someone whose qualifications were equally as impressive to me as hers was. She gave me a tentative smile and ask, 'Why compare her to me, when you don't even know me'?

'I know lots more than you know,' I told her. To make a long story short, it took me another six weeks of merciless persuasion to make her feel that she had all of the qualification that was needed to be the colored woman's proxy. So there I was watching my dreams unfold right before my eyes. I had landed my dream job, which eventually led me to my beautiful and submissive wife – and now all that's left to do was to generate enough money to retire by the time I reach my twenty-fifth birthday. I have a habit of saying—whenever others want to know—what part Grace plays in all of what we've accumulated up to this point. I avoid going into so many details. I simply say, 'Fortitude' is how I describe my wife to other people. She assists me in making good decision whenever she's asked to do so. Plus she does it without deception; instead she takes delight in speaking out about being her husband's gofer."

"Well, its one thing about it," Ed said. "What you've told me ain't no cock-n-bull storie, because the things I've heard you say—most of it is tangible—including your darling wife. Furthermore, I'm inclining to believe a man not only needs an ambitious woman, or visa versa, but they must be receptive to each other's ideas. Or else, life could be a never-ending struggle, if one is going that way and the other is doing just the opposite. That is not the case with you and Grace; how else could y'all be in the shape you're in?"

By that time the phone rang; J. D. calling to remind Maggie that he wouldn't be coming over because the only car they owned, she had it. He also reminded her that she must not forget to bring home his supper when she came. As Maggie wasn't quite ready to go home, she volunteered Alvin and

Grace to take J. D. his food; providing John would agree to ride with them for security, just in case. Around eleven o'clock that evening, Ed decided to go off to bed, leaving Myrtle to stay up. Bedtime at eleven o'clock at night wasn't one of Maggie's first priorities, especially since she started to work for her daughter. All of which allowed her to pin a note to her apartment door with her daughter's phone number and where she could be reached in case of an emergency. Otherwise, Maggie had carte blanche to do as she pleased. She not only persuaded her sister, Myrtle, to sit up with her until she ran out of something to talk about, she even swayed Grace, to do likewise. Although Grace may've agreed to participate in their boring chitchat, she never told them that she wouldn't from time to time drift in and out of her much-needed sleep. Around two in the morning, though, Grace gave up on the two older women and went to crawl in bed with Alvin.

The next morning at seven o'clock when Maggie came and knocked on Grace's bedroom door, Grace felt somewhat swindled, especially after she had forfeited the major portion of what could been a good night's sleep, if she hadn't been swayed to sit up until early morning listening to the two older women talk about their history as children growing up in the town of Beaumont, Texas. Neither Alvin nor Grace answered the door, but it didn't matter to Maggie. She went away and came back with two cups of coffee, but this time she didn't bother to knock.

She came in just in time to see Grace stark-naked as she headed off to the bathroom to pee. "My Lord, Alvin," Maggie exclaimed to Alvin, "how much longer will it be before you've seen enough of her parading around the room naked and exposing everything she owns? Beside that – after you have your first cup of coffee, you agreed to go pick J. D. up and bring him here for breakfast, I promise you I'll dance at your next wedding."

Grace yelled out from the bathroom, "There is not gonna be a next wedding!"

After breakfast the two older men each took themselves a can of beer and struck up a casual conversation sitting on the divan, waiting for that big meal to be served. In the meantime, the women remained in the kitchen where they added their final touches to Thanksgiving supper, which was scheduled to be served no later than two o'clock that afternoon. At that point, John decided to go out back and visit with his father. Alvin wasn't interested in listening to the two old men lament their nostalgia about things that didn't concern him. He walked out on the back porch, to sit and think about insignificant things like halfheartedly wishing that he was with his own family on this special holiday. Alvin saw Walter had his front door open, and he could see Alvin from where he was. The next time Alvin looked up, he was surprised to see Walter's oldest little girl, Christina, standing in front of him with a beer in her hand.

"This is from my daddy and he told me to tell you 'Happy Thanksgiving.'" Alvin told her to thank her father for the beer, and tell him that he said Happy Thanksgiving to him, too. A little later Alvin leaned over toward Walter's front door and waved, in hopes he would see and accept it as a goodwill gesture. As it turned out, Alvin got no response from him, so he decided to walk over to Walter's house and thank him in person. Alvin knocked on the door and heard a voice saying, "Come on in, Alvin." Naturally, he knew it was Walter, who asked, "Did you come for that other bottle of beer, which I've sat aside for you?"

"I really came to thank you for the first one," Alvin said, "but since you mention another, well I don't mind if I do." He looked over and saw Maurine struggling in her small kitchen in her effort to prepare Thanksgiving dinner for her family.

"Set down and relax, Alvin," Walter said. Alvin cautiously sat down beside him on the divan. Walter told Christina to go to the refrigerator and bring back a beer for Alvin. "Are you having a good Thanksgiving so far?"

"The way things are being put together between the ladies, at my house, I'd say the only way it could be any better, is if I were back home having Thanksgiving with my mother and family."

"Mentioning family," Walter said, "I heard something about you buying your family a small farm somewhere down there around Abilene."

"Yeah, that's right," Alvin answered. "If you wonna call it that. The way Grace and I describe the place is two hundred acres of land with little value, and a run-down three-bedroom house on it. Grace and I bought it because it was something that we could afford without going over our budget. But to my father, it's a plantation, as well as a permanent place that he can call home. My father has always wanted his own little farm. His problem has always been that he didn't have the faith in himself to undertake such a venture as his own place."

"Whatever you paid for it, it's better than not having a farm at all," Walter said. "And I'm sure your father and mother must think the same way as I do. They must be very proud of you. I know I am, and I'm also especially proud of the contribution that my daughter has added to you're obtaining all of this. It's almost unbelievable what you two have managed to put together in the short time you've known each other. I've heard of white boys taking on projects and succeeding beyond anyone expectation – except they had their rich daddies behind them directing every step, but you're one in a million. Hell," he said, "I give up trying to figure you out, so why don't you go on and tell me. Because I want to know what motivated you to do what you've done and make it seem so effortless."

"Love and dedication with a desire to fulfill a promise I made to Grace. Actually," Alvin said, "in the beginning, she was the one who fixed on being able to entrust ourselves to each other. That's why I think the both of us do what we do with such simplicity."

"What was it that y'all commit to do for each other?"

"We made lots of promises that helped bring us to where we're today," Alvin said. "But the most important promise we made was the first we were alone together. She asked me for my assurance that I wouldn't ever allow another man to see her the way I had. And in turn she promised to never let another woman see me the way she had. Those words alone were more impressive to me than all the words she spoke that helped to bring us to that point. Faithfulness was her main objective. She didn't care about what kind of present I'd be able to give her in the short run. Her first concern was about securing her future with me for the long run. Her words proved to me that she wasn't some mischievous little girl, out looking to have a good time. Her first inclination was to secure a solid relationship with a boy who had promised to love her without end. Once she had done all she could to prove that she had trusted me to the fullest, well, then – it was all full speed ahead. We've been together going on two years now, and without a doubt, her unbending determination to trust me has been why I've achieved so much. One more thing, I believe has had a major effect on her eagerness to please me. And I don't take pleasure in saying in front of you. But the first conversations we had were all about how hurt she was, when you and her mother separated. And that estrangement between you and Mrs. Maggie – I believe that's what inspired her to ask for a foolproof marriage with me. That's not to say that we didn't live together before we were married, but she never condoned it and either did I. There was a misunderstanding between us . . . but my love for her overpowered my common sense, which caused me to showed up uninvited at her house that night. When that happened, it was obvious I had given away our secret. We had no other choice but to live together until she was out of school, and then we did what we had always planned – go to California and get married there. From the very first day we met until now, I can truly say that I love her to the point of feeling ridiculous about my obsession with her, and that's the only time in my marriage that I become bothersome. I'm afraid if I don't put some kind of control on my always saying 'I love you' she might get tired of hearing it and alienate herself from me."

Walter cleared his throat, "I think you are wrong about her alienating herself from you. I know enough about her to know that she doesn't make pledges to anyone unless she's thoroughly thought it through." Walter looked over at Alvin and saw that he had an empty can in front of him. He called to Maurine, "Bring two more beers for Alvin and me. And get one for you and join me in making a long overdue declaration of guilt, and to assure Alvin that my ridiculous transgression against him have ceased to be. From this moment forward, I refuse to allow my consciences to gnaw away at me, because I was encumbered with this stupid idea that you weren't fit to marry my daughter. I'm sorry for having treated you like someone who's not a part of what's considered to be the mainstream society. Let you and I remember this time as a day of reconciling our differences, acknowledged between the two of us with a stimulating beverage."

Then Walter added, "Wait just a minute. John, go get your sister so she can be in on this as well, since its concerns her as much as it does Alvin."

John went and came back leading Grace by the hand and launched her into a ceremony that she knew nothing about. When Maurine handed her an open bottle of beer, she knew something unusual was about to happen. Walter declared to her, "I've asked you to come here to hear me admit to you in front of my wife and children. I want you to know that I've laying down this burden of resentment concerning your marriage to Alvin. All of this been a dagger in my side since the first time I saw you standing with his arm around you. Like I told Alvin before you came; I need to stop resenting the fact that my daughter has fallen in love with a colored boy —who's obviously much more intelligent than me and my whole family put together, and a lots others that's part of my family. She has to have the means to function the same as any other couple that marries within their own race. I want to mention just one other thing. Your Mama isn't any better than I am about this racial thing. She'll make one believe she has no prejudice in her at all, and she's been this liberal-minded person all of her life. If you believe that about her, then believe me when I tell you that I have a commercial airplane for sale. She was just as prejudiced against colored folks as I was, if not more so. The only difference between her and me: she found out before I knew that there were prideful colored people like Alvin. So, just let me conclude by saying; if Maurine and I don't want to miss out on being a part of my daughter's family, we had better stop lurking in the shadows and accept Alvin as being part of my family. Or else another four years will pass while I'm living in denial at the same time I'm resenting the very one that has allowed me to live rent-free.

"Now," Walter continued, "I won't use the word son-in-law a lot around the girls, because they might tell other kids at school and hear about their sister's married to a colored boy and just liable to start teasing them. I don't want my little girls picked on because of some ignorant kid that been taught if it ain't white it ain't right." Walter gave John a coke, saying, "You've taken part in a salute to celebrate your sister's marriage to Alvin on your Mama's behalf. Now I ask you to join me in a salute on my behalf in accepting the fact that my firstborn's surname is no longer Adams, but Jackson."

After everyone raised and touched glasses and took their first a sip, Walter grabbed Alvin's hand and said, "On behalf of me and my wife, you've just been inducted into the Adams family via your wife – my daughter, Grace." Then he kissed Grace on the cheek, and said, "It took a little longer than I had anticipated saying what I needed to say. So I won't take up anymore of your time," he said. "I know you must have other matter to attend to that's more important than what Johnny-comes-late had to say."

"Why, what a surprise," as she thanked him, adding, "I wish you and your family was joining us, and we were having this discussion over Thanksgiving dinner. We sure are preparing a great feast for everyone today, and you and your family would fit in very well." She and Alvin walked back to their house and saw that J. D. had fallen asleep at one end of the divan, while Ed slept at the other. Instead of her and Alvin disturbing the two older men by watching television, Alvin and Grace took a seat at the far side of the living room and started a card game, during which they whispered to each other in regards to her father's change of heart.

"What did Daddy say to you before I got there that caused him to behave right, and suddenly become a peaceable and caring father again? I wonder – if he wasn't acting just like Mama told me he would, when he didn't get his way. His first defense was to pout. But ignore him, Mama said – and we did, and sure enough he did exactly what Mama said he'd do."

At two o'clock, Maggie called for everyone to gather around the table and hold hands. She invited Uncle Ed to bless the food. Afterward, she asked Alvin to carve the turkey and pass it around to each person. Everyone kept adding other assortments of food to their plates, which Maggie had prepared to complement the roasted turkey and dressing. Maggie was known amongst family and friends alike, to create sumptuous gourmet feasts for holidays and celebrations. Now and again, at such of those gatherings, she had been known to speak ill of her enemies whenever the opportunity presented itself. Unfortunately, it so happened, this event turned out to be one of those occasions. John gave her the perfect opportunity to make unflattering remarks about her ex-husband, in having walked out to the back to spend two hours at Walters' with his stepsisters and Maurine.

"What did you and your father talked about during those two hours you spent absent from your real family to be with him and Mrs. Jezebel?" Maggie asked, accusingly. "I mean, other than watching her stumbled around in her small kitchen trying hatch up a palatable Thanksgiving dinner for her and her warped-minded family?" Maggie asked John the question, but she came up with the answers, continuing, "I can hardly wait to see the day when Walter finally gets enough money to move her and their hatchlings as far away from this neighborhood as possible. That way I won't have to come face-to-face with a bunch of weirdoes every time I come to visit with my daughter."

Then she turned to Grace and demanded, "Have you heard him mention anything more about him taking his family and moving to the neighborhood where all of his extremist kinds of friends usually congregate? Or did he find out a little too late that people who think like him are not as easily found in Texas as they are in the hick town in Oklahoma where he grew up? If that is the case, then don't be surprised if he decides to put his resentment for Alvin on hold and tell you he changed his mind, and decided to stay after all."

"Mama," Grace said, "You sure seem to be always right on target when it comes to predicting Daddy's habits. It was just about an hour and a half ago that he sent John to ask me to come to his house. He wanted to announce to me in front of John and his family what he had already made known to Alvin; that he had set aside his hateful ways toward Alvin. He candidly apologized to me in front of Alvin and everyone else that his old habits was a thing of the past. He asked Maurine and John to join him in a deferred salute to his darling daughter and son-in-law."

"You mean to tell me he used beer and not a glass of wine," Maggie exclaimed.

"Yes," Grace said, "that's exactly what we did. First, he gave Alvin and me his benediction that lasted about two minutes. Then he raised his bottle of beer in the form of a salute, to prove that he had acknowledged my being married to Alvin. And the rest of us followed suit by raising our beverages to acknowledge his acceptance that my marriage to Alvin had been sanctioned by him."

"Well that just goes to show you the high of his intelligent," Maggie said. "I would of at least went and pick up a cheap bottle of wine before I'd inaugurate my daughter's matrimony with a bottle of beer! As far as I'm concern," Maggie said, "we can end this subject anytime you want!"

"With all due respect to Grace and John," Alvin said, "I would feel much more comfortable if they would move so I could see Maggie being her old self for a change. We won't suggest moving to him – we'll just let him take his time, and that way, no one gets his or her feeling hurt."

Ed took a napkin and wiped his mouth, grunted, and scooted his chair away from the table as he said to Maggie, "If I attempt to take another bite of this delicious food, I believe without a doubt I'd explode for sure. The true pleasure in life is to eat some of Maggie's mighty fine cooking, and today, I've had my share of it."

"Well thanks, Ed." Maggie answered. "You know me by now – if I make the effort to do something, why not give it your best?"

"You did that, all right," Ed said. "I've eaten so much I'm at the point of unbuttoning the top button on my trousers and lie down and sleep 'er off."

"Monkey see, monkey do," J.D. scooted his chair away from the table. "I'm going to follow suit, unbutton my top button, and go do like old Ed and sleep 'er off."

Maggie asked, "Alvin, you haven't said a word since you came to the table. Are you enjoying your food, darling?"

"Mama," Grace cautioned, "don't ask; just look at his plate. He has enough bones in front of him to start a turkey cemetery." Everyone laughed.

John asked Grace, "Where do you pick up that, Sis? You've never talked like that before. Alvin must be teaching you that cotton-field language they used down yonder in Snyder."

"Not Alvin, so much as I hear it coming from those people that are supposed to know the English language." She said, "I hear all kinds of slang and broken English that you can imagine right there in the dining room of this fancy hotel where I work."

"In addition to her putting up with all of the nasty jokes and slings," Maggie said. "She's constantly turning men down that's keep asking her to go out with them."

"Yes," Grace answered, "and I tell them all that I'm married to a man who sends me out to work all day while he stays home with our four children. As soon as they hear those kinds of remarks, they immediately lose interest in me and go on and tell the same lie to the next waitress. I remember telling that to a customer one day, and I looked over my shoulder, and there sat my boss chuckling about my lying to the man. I figured as long as I lie just enough to avoid hurting their feelings, they won't hold back on my tips."

"And about how much do you make in tips every day?" Myrtle asked.

"It depends on the number of customers I have, and sometimes it's me." Grace answers said. "If I can't get the food to the customer when they think I should, some of them will tip poorly, but overall, I average between six and eight hundred a month, including salary."

"My goodness," Myrtle said, "there is no wonder you can afford to buy all of this real estate, among other things. With you making that kind of money, who needed Alvin? You would have made enough money on your own to do whatever you want without enduring all of the racism you put up with by being with Alvin."

She then turned to Alvin and asked, "How much do you make?"

"About three hundred and twenty-five a month," he answered.

"So how is it that you're getting all of the credit for y'all success, when it's obvious that it is Grace' earnings that you're using to invest in all the real estate y'all own up to this point. As I said, she really doesn't need you to get to where she needs to go. She makes enough on her own to do what she needs too."

"Well, now," Alvin said, "I have a tendency to occasional overstate the facts in a situation like you just put me in. I'd rather you direct this particular question to Grace since she always tell it right the first time."

"Aunt Myrtle," Grace said. "When Alvin and I first got together I didn't have any money. I turned every penny I made over to Mama. The house we all seem to be so comfortable sitting and sleeping in – Alvin bought it. The first apartment building we owned? He bought it. The first car I ever owned; he bought. Even the nice dress you see me wearing: he bought it. And everything else we own before I had a dime – he bought it. To be fair with you, Aunt Myrtle, I have to admit the latest apartment building he bought, some of my earnings went toward the down payment. But most of the money we used for a down payment was a combination of Alvin's salary and rent from the first apartment building he'd purchased before I had any money. I've been making this kind of money for the last two months. So two months times six to eight hundred, less taxes and expenses, equal about twelve hundred; about what I've contributed. Mind you, he spent four thousand as a down payment for each building, which comes out to be eight thousand of his own money. Whereas, if Alvin had to depend on my money to buy this house, you may have had to postpone your visits until I could have afforded to pay my share. Either that or you could have wound up sleeping between Uncle Ed and John. Actually," she added, "Alvin doesn't really need my money to move ahead. If he did, he wouldn't have suggested that I start college this fall."

"Well, excuse me," Myrtle said, "I stand to be corrected. I should've known that a girl barely out of high school could've accomplished all of the things you have in three months."

"So, big sister," John asked. "When are you starting college? You know, if you wait too much longer, you'll be in the same class with me."

"I'll tell you like I've told Alvin," she said. "I appreciate your concern about me getting a college degree. The way I see it, if I started to school right now and went for four years, it would be a waste of time and money. By the time I get out of school we would have lost four years of my salary and tips, which would've gone against our plan to have enough money to retire by the time Alvin reaches twenty-five. The way I have it figured out," Grace explained, "I'd be going to school for four years, then afterward go out and find myself a job, then work four years to make up for what I lost going to school. Then two years of work would go to pay for my tuition, so by the time it's all over, I would've spent ten years worth of time and money trying to get a four-year college degree. If we stick with our plan, Alvin will be twenty-five and I'll be twenty-three and just about old enough to have a baby boy and dedicate it to Alvin's daddy."

Then she turned to John and said, "Now John, on the other hand, you should be thinking about getting yourself a college degree, because you are a man, and men need a good education in order to make a good living for his wife and family – unless you're fortunate enough to marry some woman with the same capabilities as Alvin has. Either way, you'll be out of high school in two years, and you'll need to start looking right away for that ambitious woman to help you as I'm helping Alvin, who doesn't need a college degree to be successful. Most importantly," she said, "whether you find this ambitious woman or not, the very first thought should come to mind is to find a job and save your money so when the time comes to go to college, you won't be running around in a state of confusion while trying to muster up enough money to pay your tuition." She drew in a deep breath, and added, "Now that we got all of that behind us, the next thing I need to know is: how long have Aunt Myrtle and Uncle Ed planned to stay and visit with us?"

Ed answered, "We don't have very many reasons for going back home, except to sit around and watch the time go by. For that reason, we are not in any hurry to do that. Unless we would've done what you and old Alvin did when we first were together as youngsters. Then we'd have plenty reasons to go home and reap the benefits of our labors like you two will in the very near future. But where us two whippersnapper made our mistake when we were young enough to do something about it, we had anticipated that things would stay pretty much the same. That's why we were satisfied with them few acres we bought back yonder, which we thought would be adequate to support us over into our senior years. But in today's world, all you have to do is have one bad crop and you're back to first base again. That sorter puts me in the class with the poorest of people I see walking the streets of Beaumont. So you can see why I'm in no hurry about going back home, except home is where you are out of everybody's way."

"You still didn't answer her question," Myrtle said. "When are we going home?"

"Questions like that should be directed to Maggie." Ed answered, "I reckon when she gets tired of me and my woman, she'll send us on our way, and the only way we'll go is if she send us."

"It's not my decision to make," Maggie said. "It's all up to Alvin and Grace as to whether or not they are tired of you and Myrtle. Although I don't thank that's the case and I think my babies will back me on that. Because they've assured me that y'all wouldn't be a bother to them at all."

"Absolutely," Grace said. "You'll stay as long as you want too. My reasons for asking was so I could estimate how much money I needed to give Mama to keep a supply of groceries for the duration of your and Aunt Myrtle's stay here in cow town."

"Now," Maggie said, "I wasn't expecting y'all to buy their food. I just wonted a place for them to stay while they were here in Fort Worth. And let the grocery-buying situation rest on my shoulders. Bear in mind that I'll be spending most of my time visiting and cooking for Myrtle and Ed anyway. So it stands to reason that my family will be eating here also."

The next morning, Alvin and Grace had to be back at work. The minute Alvin walked into the kitchen; Chef Rittenhouse approached him saying, "I need to talk to you before you go on line."

"Sure thing, Chef," Alvin said. Chef Rittenhouse told Alvin to just have a seat, and he'd be with him shortly. Effie came in right behind Alvin and took her seat at the opposite end of the table with a cup of coffee in her hand.

She said to Alvin, "I heard Chef Rittenhouse tell you that he wanted to talk to you. I suppose he's giving you Grady's old job."

"Why Grady's job," Alvin asked with a surprised look in his eyes. "Did something happen to him over the holidays?"

"Yes." Effie said, with relish. "You didn't hear about Grady shooting a man over some woman on Thanksgiving Day? They tell me that he was drinking awful heavy, and got into an argument with this man concerning a woman that wasn't Grady's wife. Grady wound up shooting the poor man and now his stupid ass is in jail – behind bars where he should be."

Alvin asked, "Did the man die?"

"No, not as far as I know," Effie answered. "The most I know, which is hearsay – Grady's argument with this other fellow heated to the point that Grady reaching for his pistol. The other man had no other choice but to run as fast as he could to avoid getting shot. As it turned out Grady fired, and the poor man took a bullet in his buttocks anyway. The other man is still in the hospital, getting the bullet picked out of his ass, and Grady is still in jail." Effie added very deliberately, "I guess if you hung out with the colored folks, I wouldn't have to tell you what you'd already know."

Alvin didn't answer her. Effie waited for a moment; then she asked with an amused and knowing look on her face, "So have you seen Miss Grace lately?"

"Yes." Alvin said, "It was just a few minutes ago that I saw her walk around the corner."

"I bet you saw her much earlier than a few minutes ago. I bet those panties she's wearing under that uniform are the same ones you pulled off her before y'all went to bed last night." Effie chuckled, "You think you're so slick – but not nearly as slick as you think you're. Most of us colored folks around here agree overwhelmingly that those goo-goo eyes y'all make at each other is more than just being polite. Contrary to what y'all think, we know y'all are either secretly living together in the maid's quarters in some white neighborhood, where you're unlikely to harassed by the authorities. If that be the case, then I bet y'all must be having yourselves an 'F' good time.

She's pretty and you're good-looking, which gives the both of you more of a reason to go at each other like two people in a wrestling match.

"I wish I was at liberty to prove to you that there're no dissimilarity between the white woman and the colored woman. Except for the color of the skin, I'll be willing to bet that there're not an ounce of differences between the white and the colored women." All the while she talked about what she thought she knew about white women, he thought about what she didn't know about white women; in particular the white women he knew. Because he had all but authoritative proof that Effie's chances of out-performing Grace would probably be next-to-nothing.

Chef Rittenhouse finally came and sat down beside Alvin with a cup of coffee in his hand, saying, "I guess you heard by now that old Grady won't be coming back to work here anymore?"

"Yes," Alvin said, "I just got the news from Effie about ten minutes ago. She told me something about Grady going to jail because he shot a man over some girl."

The chef said, "And that about what I heard also. However," he said, "Old Grady was a very good first cook, and since he won't be coming back, I'm offering you his job. The pay is twenty-five dollars more a week to start with. "Now," he said, "the gal named Evelyn, that I had working between helping Effie and Lee: I've already moved her into your old position as line cook. So I want you to report to my sous-chef, Maurice, and he'll get you situated on the duties that you'll be performing every day. Tomorrow I want you to come in at seven instead of six and you'll go back to having your Saturdays and Sundays off again, except for special event."

"Chef," Alvin said, "I want you to know how much I appreciate you giving me first choice at such a prestigious position. As always, I promise I won't let you down."

"I know you won't," he answered. "That's why I gave you the job in the first place. I'll grant you six months and you'll master it like you've mastered everything else I've assigned you to do."

Alvin immediately reported to Maurice—very anxious—but confident that he would surpass Grady's reputation any old day when it came to being good, fast, and sufficient. As it was Alvin's first day in his new position, Maurice systematically assisted him step-by-step to make sure that each entrée met his approval, emphasizing that there was no room for error in preparing the different kinds of food. As always, the first couple of hours on any new job that he undertook would normally turn into a tad bit hectic for Alvin. He didn't know that Maurice had strict instructions from the head chef to be very patient with Alvin so he wouldn't lose confidence in his first couple of days in his new position. However, once Maurice saw how eager Alvin was to learn and had the ability to learn well, Maurice told Alvin after the lunch rush that he had no worries about the quality of the food, since Alvin had natural talent to do things well.

While all of that was going on, Grace nearly panicked. "Where is Alvin?" she demanded, when she saw Evelyn cooking at Alvin's station. "What had happened to him?"

Evelyn replied, "I assume that the chef must've moved him into Grady's slot as first cook. Didn't you know? Grady went to jail over the holiday for shooting someone."

"Will he be working the morning shift or the evening shift," Grace asked.

"I can't honestly answer that question," Evelyn replied, "but it stands to reason – if Grady was working the morning shift as first cook, then I think I'd be justified in saying that Alvin will be working the morning shift as well."

"Oh thank goodness," she said as her color returned to her face. Suddenly she tried to minimize her excitement about knowing that her Alvin was all right by saying, "I guess I got so used to seeing him working where you're now working. And when I didn't, I thought something bad had happened to him over the holiday."

As Grace disappeared through the doors to the dining room, Evelyn turned to her co-workers and observed, "A good thing I told her that her man was in the back, cooking his ass off when I did. I swear, that white gal was on the threshold of hysterics – and all that could have been avoided if she'd stick to her kind and he'd patronize his own kind. But they both rather live in seclusion – and he believes this white woman has more to offer in bed because of the color of her skin. Likewise she thinks this colored man has something that's impossible for her to get from her own race of men. This just goes to show just how naive the both of them are. I say this – and

I'll comment no further – I know for a fact that there's no difference between the colored man and white man, and I say no more than that."

Mr. Lee told Alvin that Grace's panic attack was undoubtedly brought on when she didn't see Alvin on his station this morning. However, that only confirmed the rumor among the colored workers, that she was having an affair with him.

In any case, Evelyn could hardly wait until lunch was over, so she could remind Alvin that Grace's panic attack was a sure sign that he was having an intimate relationship with Grace. After Maurice came over and told him that he gave a fine performance out there today, and he also told Alvin, "You'll have this position mastered in no time, just the way you've mastered all the other that you were assigned to."

Alvin walked around the corner and waited until he caught sight of Grace. He motioned for her to come over, so he could explain to her why he wasn't working the line shift anymore. They walked around the corner and out of the view of the customers in order to avoid arousing their curiosity – and then Alvin saw that two other waitresses were standing there, with suspicious looks on their faces. He motioned for them to come over also to hear, while he pretended to be inquiring about the customer's reaction to his first day as first cook. He asked the three of them, "How did the customers like the food today?"

All three women answered, "Just fine. They loved it and don't think that anyone noticed any difference." The two other girls stared covertly at Alvin's face, with sheepish curiosity – as if they wondered, but did not actually want to ask if there was more to this than what meets the eye. The two girls walked away as they took quick peeks over their shoulders trying not to be caught looking.

Alvin was relieved that they left as soon as they did, and Grace stayed as long as she did. He needed the privacy to partially update her on what had happened to him this morning. They quickly touched lips and they returned to their workstations. He took all these precautions, not knowing that Evelyn had already explained to Grace what had happened. And Grace didn't have a chance to tell him that she already knew.

Just as Alvin had finished cleaning up his station and was about to leave, Evelyn approached him, in a rather secretive way. "Boy," she said, "you almost gave your little Miss Grace a miniature heart attack when she didn't see you on your station this morning. I wish it was cool for me to tell her not to worry – he'll be right out as soon as Effie finishing wiping this chalky substance off the front of his trousers." She grinned and said, "I bet you wish that part was true and don't try to deny it either. Because if I can see that you have a crush on her, I'm sure everybody else sees the same thing— except Ralph. Of course he wouldn't because as naïve as he is, he'd probably thinks the smile you flash at her is no different from the smile you give to everybody else you made eye contact with. You had better hope he doesn't find out that your smile for Effie was a signal aiming at arousing what's behind her underwear. Otherwise he will definitely confront you without restraint. I don't think you're nearly about ready to have your ass hauled off to the hospital and have the BBs picked out of your ass; the way Grady had his victim do Thanksgiving Day. Now I was just kidding about everything except for your white honey having herself a panicky attack, until I told her about you taking over Grady's old job as first cook."

"I don't know where you're getting information about Grace and me having an affair," Alvin said. "But whoever your nasty-ass informer is, tell them that I said to be sure it have the facts straight. Spreading lies about something as hazardous as a colored man as having an affair with a white woman could be a serious offense. I'd appreciate it if you'd tell your nasty-ass informer to find someone else to pick on so I don't start seeing them as a biting ol' horsefly in need of being swatted for minding everybody's ass but his own."

"You don't have to use that tone of voice when speaking to me," Evelyn said. "All I did was to answer her best I could without revealing any of y'all secret – especially with other people working in the same vicinity. You would've really been upset if I had of went into all the details and told you step by step and word by word as she worked herself into a state of panic. 'Where is Alvin? I haven't seen him all morning, and I'm anxious to know what could have happened to him?' Now you tell me what white woman in her right mind would go around worrying about what happened to some colored man if she isn't sleeping with him? You've gotten yourself into something that you can't talk your way out of, and you're madder than hell because I won't let you take your frustration out on me! You didn't have to go messing around with some white girl when there are so many colored girls just as pretty as she is. I'll be willing to bet that what she's got between her legs is no better than your ex-girlfriend Bobbie Jean has between her legs and maybe not as good. Otherwise, why is it that I see so many white men hanging out after dark holding on to those colored women when they got ten times as many white women to choose from?"

Alvin didn't answer her. She waited shortly and then she added, "I wish I could earnestly say that I don't care what you and your white chick does, but I can't – I wish it was me who were running around in a state of panic worrying about what happened to you, but I will say in all seriousness – if y'all love each other, I wish y'all well. Besides that, I just hope she don't finish up breaking your heart one day. It's not unlikely that she'll wake up one morning, look into the mirror, and figure out what she's got and what she could've had with all of her beauty. She'd finally ask herself, 'What would life be like if I had of married herself a rich white man, instead of a four-hundred-dollar-a-month colored cook.'"

Evelyn's words haunted Alvin for just a little bit, but he quickly dismissed it. He cleaned up and went home and found Grace waiting on the divan to tell him why she didn't interrupt while he was explaining to her what had happened to him this morning. At that, she clarified it by saying, "I kept silent was because the two servers were standing nearby. I didn't want them to hear about how frightened I was, when I didn't see you on your station this morning. But Evelyn had already told me just enough to put my mind at ease, but she didn't go into any details, which is why I didn't bother to interrupt. Alvin, honey, I may be smiling now, but I wasn't this morning. I was worried sick that someone had found out about us and an argument got out of control between you and whomever. I was afraid you'd take matters into your own hands, and do something unimaginable to that whomever, and got yourself fired. But Evelyn just said something about you taking over Grady's shift, because he had shot some man in the rear regarding some girl over the holiday. So," finished, "You tell me what happened to Grady?"

"Pretty much what Evelyn told me she told you – old Grady and some man got into an argument over some woman during the holiday, and he shot that man in the leg. The man is in the hospital and Grady is in jail. First thing this morning when Chef Rittenhouse saw me headed toward my station, he stopped and told me about Grady being in jail and offered me his job. The good thing about it, he told me, is that I would be getting a hundred more dollars a month – and the only difference is, I'll be going in an hour later. And you're not going to believe this, but I'll be getting my Saturdays and Sundays off again."

"Oh how wonderful Alvin, darling," she exclaimed. "This has turned out to be a very rewarding day for us, after all."

"Well," he said, "if you wonna hear more just listen to this. I thank someone had started a rumor about us. While I waited for the chef to get back with me, I grabbed myself a cup of coffee and took a seat at the table. Effie came in and took her seat with her cup of coffee also, which she usually as before going on duty. She asks about the last time I had saw you. When I told her that I had just seen you walking toward the dining room a few minutes ago, she laughed and said, 'I bet you've seen her much earlier than a few minutes ago. And I dare you to bet me that those panties she's wearing, you didn't put 'em on for her before y'all left for work this morning.' So as much as I know about what takes place on Thanksgiving Day, other than a lot of eating and drinking, I'd say this has to be one for the books when it comes to people meddling into other people business; no one does it like the kitchen crew at the Graystone. I suppose out of curiosity, old Grady shoots a man in the butt just to see how fast he'd run. And Evelyn was curious enough to question me about our relationship after she saw how boggled you were, when you didn't see me on my old station. This may sound crazy," Alvin said, "but I like it for people to think that I'm involved with the most beautiful woman that ever walked. Can you imagine how resentful some people must feel knowing that someone like me is being accused of having an affair with a woman as pretty as you are? Even if there wasn't any true in it—except it is true, isn't it baby—just think about all of the recognition I'm getting from those curious-minded people. Mind you that I don't condone any sort of assuming on either of our parts, so as to intentionally evoke narrow-minded people to wrath. But at the same time, I take pleasure in knowing that our uniqueness is so appealing that it cause other people to wonder about you and me. Even to the point of whispering amongst themselves without aggression or something even worst! I want them to believe without divisively that we are indissoluble in love with each other. You may have noticed me lately that I'm not nearly as afraid of the public as I was when I first met you. I believe it all stems from the teaching my parents gave me as a child. Do you remember me telling you one night while walking across the parking lot? All the while I kept begging you to marry me while we were young. Well, I was basing it on a couple of scriptures my mother use to read to us children. One of which was from Proverbs 5:18 where it said 'let your water source proved to be blessed with the wife of your youth, a lovable hind and a charming mountain goat. Let

306

her own breasts intoxicate you at all times and in an ecstasy constantly.' That scripture wasn't written for me. It was written for couples who have to work at doing those things. I've been intoxicated with your body since the first night you exposed it to me. Nevertheless, my dear," Alvin continued, "If we want the Lord's blessing to continue to be upon us, it's unfalteringly important that we do as we're told. There is also another scripture that I've clung to like the first one which is at Mark 11:24. It reads: 'All the things you pray and ask for, have faith that you have practically received, and you will have them.' And that's why we'll always be safe in a world of evil doers, because I love you and everything you are, and I will always trust in the Lord for our needs and our safe keeping."

"Whether it was your prayer that was being answered," Grace said, "or whether it was just plain old luck, but whatever you want to call it, I have to say, so far, we have been spared in most situations. So if things stay as they are until we have children of our own, I'll remind you to quote those same scriptures to our children—provided I can persuade you to stop planning for the future long enough to concentrate on how to get me pregnant. Or just simply discord that worrisome old condom, and I'll get pregnant for sure."

Maggie interrupted at that point, saying to Myrtle, "It's one thing about it: whether they were evil rumors or just innocent stares, they've got their boss's approval, and so far his word has prove to be a safe haven – as long as they're working at the hotel. According to Alvin, his boss has said every kind word of encouragement that one could imagine when he heard that he and Grace had gone to California and got themselves married. His finally word to Alvin on that subject was 'if you and Grace could somehow stay clear of the authority, then they should be quite safe living together right here in Fort Worth.'"

Grace remarked, "If I could change the pace and give you my deposition by adding to Alvin's statement that he just made about people and their curiosities. The waitresses that I work with – I just don't know if they know about us or not. But I have noticed there haven't been any changes in their attitude toward me since the rumor about Alvin and me started spreading. They seem to really like me; even more so now that I've become a waitress in the morning shift. So much so, that they've all agreed to change my name from Grace to the nickname 'Miss Graceful,' because of the way I handle my customers. Just a few days ago, June invited me to her home for a cocktail. She also told me to bring along my boyfriend. I told her that I didn't care for alcohol and didn't have a boyfriend. I didn't tell her that I was married to my boyfriend – but I really don't think she would've been surprised if I had shown up at her house locked in arms with Alvin. I've been thinking about inviting her to my house too; once I'm sure she's really open-minded."

"Now, you see," Myrtle said, "prejudice might've originated with the white race, but to hear Alvin talk, I'm led to believe that bigotry is ingrained in all kind of people. Before Grace gathered her thoughts and said what she did about how the white people at the Graystone reacted to her involvement with you, it certainly didn't have the same impact on me as Alvin's explanation did base on his observation of the colored reaction to his involvement with Grace. Grace's alleged suspicions where she felt that the white folks knew about your involvement with her had a positive effect. Whereas, Alvin's assumption—I'm guessing—came from coloreds; folks who he had alleged as being an evil perpetrator out to devour the both of you. So if I were Alvin, I'd be reluctant to pay too much attention to those colored people at the hotel. Otherwise, they just might have you mistaking harmless stares for a venomous rattle snake."

"Well now," Alvin said, "it's not unreasonably for people of color like me to think and feel the way we feel most of the time. Because if enough of the wrong kind of people stare the wrong kinds of stares, they're liable to get together and decide to wipe a person like me off the face of the earth; all because of my involvement with Grace. They'll do it first and ask questions later. So that's why I have to always think the worst and hope for the best."

"Aunt Myrtle," Grace said, "Alvin and I aren't angry at anyone. We knew what we were getting ourselves into when we decided to get together. We are just as curious as the people that are doing the staring. Whether they have bad intentions or good intentions, we don't know. Like those people, we also have a tendency to observe their reaction when we have been careless in showing our affection to each other, during the working day. When that happens, we immediately become apprehensive and check everyone's reactions."

Ed shook his head, at seeing J. D. already drinking a bottle of beer. Ed said to J. D., "I wasn't gonna have me one of those you're drinking until after supper. However, after I've sit here listening to the boring and insignificance story I just heard Alvin and Grace tell—as well as this severe pain that keeps recurring in my lower back—more than ever when I'm having my heaviest meal."

Alvin drawled, "Good idea. You should drink one now and one after you eat. That way, that heaviest meal is between two can of malt liquor and that pain won't dare show its face unless it wants to be attacked by two, big, bad bulldogs."

"Alvin, you sound just like a thousand other out-of-work comedians that's been seen roaming the streets at night." Ed answered.

"All right," Maggie said, "it's about time us two older ladies start making that something that makes our men appreciate us almost as much as what we give them for their bedtime treats."

Myrtle smiled, saying, "You must be talking about dessert. Otherwise," she said, "at our age, good food and a successful trip to the bathroom had become our main attractions, which takes priority over what use to be their bedtime treat." As she winked, she said, "I'm assuming that doesn't include Grace since she haven't been married long enough for Alvin to choose food over what she offers for his bedtime treats. And, oh yes," Myrtle said to Alvin, "may I use the name, 'Mr.-out-of-work-comedian'?"

"Maggie and I were discussing yours and Grace's trip down to see your family for New Years. We thought since Ed and I will stay through New Year anyway, Maggie and I were wondering if you and Grace could spend Christmas with your family in Snyder and celebrate New Years with Grace's family. If you can work that into your schedule, your mother-n-law and I would forever be grateful to you and Grace for doing that for us two old ladies."

"After that," she said as she did another wink—but this time it was at Maggie—"I promise to get out of y'all's way, and let you two get back to doing what y'all did before we came here. Like coming home after work, getting out of you cars, and racing through the door trying ripping each other's clothes off by the time you reach the divan. And kids your age are not going to tell me that we're not an inconvenient to y'all. I know if we weren't here, you'd be setting around with your clothes on doing nothing except waiting for time to go to bed."

Grace snickered and said, "If you're worried about interrupting our marriage duties, don't be. Because Alvin will never let that happen. He's just a little more discreet since y'all have been here, but like everything else that matters to him, he's always right on top of things."

"Ouch! That hurt," the two older women muttered simultaneously.

"That's nothing new to me," Myrtle said. "They're always the first to climb right on top of things. The reason is they know it's much easier to push downward then it is for us women to push upward. This proves that they're nothing but a bunch of lazy bums with a desire to sire their progeny – and make us women folks do all of the heavy lifting."

"That's it for me," Grace said. "I'm not saying another word tonight for the reason that I might have a slip of the tongue and embarrass myself all over again."

Ed said, "You don't have anything to be ashamed of; you just admitted to doing what every young hot-blooded teenager has done in our youthful years. We've all gone through that wonderful period in our lives. Most of us old-timers thought that we were man enough to burn the candle at both ends. Oh boy, until the morning after – which proved that I wasn't half the man I thought I was. I'd be so tired and worn out that I could barley muster up enough energy to get out of bed and go to work."

"Uncle Ed," Grace said, "You've just broken my code of silence and put me back in the conversation again. Now what you just mentioned about work ethic: that part isn't going to ever happen with Alvin. Since I know that it doesn't make any different how late we stay up at night, doing the thing that calls for him to be on top of things; the minute that clock goes off at five, he's out of that bed before I am – and he doesn't have to be at work for an hour later than I."

"If I may give a sensible answer to your remark," Alvin said, "if you folks think you're a bother to us, you are not. Me and Grace kind of like your company when we get home in the afternoons. As for as Grace and I changing our plans from New Year to Christmas, that's fine with me if it's all right with Grace."

"Now," Grace said, "all we have to do is write your parents and tell them we've had a change in plans, and they can expect us to be there for

Christmas instead of New Years." She asked Alvin, "How many bedrooms do your parents have?"

"As much as I know," he said, "there are three bedrooms, one living room, a kitchen – and a front and back porch."

"I bet if anyone has to sleep on the back porch," J.D said, "it'll probably be the white gal that you'll find coiled up out there, with icicles hanging off her butt."

"I'll definitely take that bet," Alvin said. "Knowing my parents, they're not about to let this white girl sleep outside and take a chance on exposing her to some hillbilly passerby that's looking for a stray cow. There're just one other thing that could be an inconvenience for Grace – she won't have indoor plumbing. Instead she'll have to use the old outhouse to do her business."

Myrtle said, "Don't bother me and Ed none. We have never had an indoor bathroom. I've used the outhouse for so long, I feel sorter out-of-place using you'll indoor toilet. But one good thing about having indoors toilet – you don't have to get all dressed up just to go to the bathroom."

"Using an outhouse," Grace said, "doesn't worry me the least bit. In addition to that, I think it's going to be a lot of fun strolling through the fields with Alvin at night. And it's too bad we can't do our walking during the daylight hours, but that's the way the cookie crumbles."

John said to his mother, Maggie, "I think I'll go visit with Daddy for awhile, so call me when you're ready to go." After John left to go visit his father, the three men scooted their chairs away from the table and congregated on the divan in front of the television while the three women stayed and cleaned the kitchen. Afterward they took their seats at the kitchen table and talked about what each one wanted for Christmas. When Maggie saw that forty minutes had passed since John left to go visit with his father, she asked Alvin to go and tell John that he had overstayed his time by about fifteen minutes.

As Alvin was about to leave, Grace extended her hand, and off they went together to her father's house. "Come on in you two and have a beer," Walter said. "I would offer you'll some of our leftovers, but I heard you'll just finish eating."

They did notice that Maurine looked very tired. Grace especially knew how tired she must've been; working all day at making Thanksgiving for her family, and constantly following after Walter and the girls, cleaning and putting things away in hopes that she would have time to sit and visit with Grace before she left. None of which seemed to bother Walter, the sight of his wife cleaning in soap suds up to her elbows. He just sat on his lazy ass and pointed his finger; like telling her to grab Alvin and Grace a couple of beers. And Maurine could never seem to remember that Grace didn't like drinking beer or anything with alcohol in it. Just to be companionable, Grace took a couple of swigs anyway and just nursed it until Alvin was ready for another.

As soon as John was told that his mother was waiting, he left and they rode home together. Alvin and Grace stayed behind where they conversed with Walter and his family, just to be sociable. A few minutes into their conversation, Maurine had done enough that she could stop and visit with Grace. Grace asked Maurine what she wanted for Christmas.

"Oh, a box full of money decorated with green ornaments and tied with a red ribbon if possible." Grace pretended to write this on a piece of paper.

Then she asked her father what he wanted for Christmas. "Since you're passing out boxes of money with red ribbon, just make that two boxes of money tied with red ribbons."

Grace asked, "Would y'all like those penny-sized match boxes filled with American pennies or Mexican nickels?"

"Just whatever is convenient for you." Maurine giggled, "I'm sure you must have at least enough uncounted change to fill a hundred penny-size matchboxes; not to mention the five gallons you've sat aside because you're too rich to count."

"OK," Grace said, "let's stop playing around and get serious."

"All right," Maurine said. "Would I sound too staid, if I ask you to take me and the girls Christmas shopping one evening, after you get off work?"

"Not really." Grace said. "In fact, that's a brilliant idea," she said as she crouched down, took and squeezed her little sisters and said, "The last two weeks before Christmas, me, Mama, and Aunt Myrtle have planned to spend those weekends buying Christmas presents for the families. So why don't you and I plan on taking the girls somewhere in between. That way, we'll let them pick out what they want, give them the Santa Claus story, and on Christmas Day they'll be convinced that Santa Claus really does exist."

Chapter 12 – Christmas

When the time came for the three women to do their Christmas shopping, Myrtle and Ed didn't have any money. Grace and Maggie decided to pitch in and give Myrtle money to buy Christmas presents for Ed and herself. Alvin agreed with Grace not to buy anything for his parents, as he was going to give them money and let them go to Hamlin or Abilene to buy their own presents. He knew how much his mother loved to shop, especially when she had cash to spend and not have to feel self-conscious about charging everything she bought. Grace chose to buy sport coats and two pairs of slacks for all of the men; Alvin, Walter, John, J. D., and her Uncle Ed; just in different sizes and colors.

Grace's Christmas present from Alvin was a surprise; a white-gold watch with diamonds and matching earrings and a necklace to go with an outfit that he had previously bought for her; the same one he had asked her to wear on Christmas day. He also bought a pair of shoes to match that dress. As a surprise, he wrapped and placed the jewelry inside the shoes, and then he wrapped the shoebox and placed it aside to be opened on Christmas Day at his father's house.

When Grace saw the box with her name on it, she said, "Oh, a pair of shoes from my husband – thank you, Alvin."

"Those shoes are not just any old pairs of shoes. They are a one-of-a-kind pairs of shoes." Alvin told her. Being the high-spirited woman that she was, she said, "If you bought it for me, you bought it with love, and that's all that matters."

It was about dusk-dark on the last Friday evening before Christmas Eve, when Alvin and Grace – with the help of her brother John – finished loading the back seat of Grace's car. On the very bottom, they placed a layer of a variety of booze, and everything else they stacked on top.

By that time they had finished, her father and his family, and her mother and her family were gathering to say their goodbyes. As usual, whenever Maurine and Maggie showed up in the same place at the same time, Maurine would be the one to stand and watch from a distance. She waved goodbye to Alvin and Grace as she stood outside her front door, while her old adversary, Maggie, came right up front to do her hugging, kissing, and waving – the same as Walter did when it came to farewells. It was obvious that a sense of competition with his former wife had driven him to stand within a few inches of her, just to prove that he wasn't intimidated when it came time to hug his daughter and send her on her way – just as her mother had done.

He also stood his ground while he took the time to warn them to be careful about accidents and flat tires. "The highway patrol will be there for sure with good intentions – until they see you riding with a Negro man; then their good intention will turn to bad ones."

"We'll do our best," Alvin said as he drove away very tensely, and he waved goodbye to everyone. By the time they'd driven out of Ft. Worth, they felt rather more relaxed, enough that Grace could ride with her head resting on his shoulder while listening to Christmas music on the radio. She rode that way between Fort Worth and Weatherford. When they came to the city limits of Weatherford, and then Abilene, Grace moved away, framed her face with her bonnet, and rode at attention until they reached the outer limits of each city. Once they reached Abilene and turned off Highway 80 and onto Highway 83 headed toward Anson, they began to breathe a sigh of relief.

Once they got to the town of Anson, then turned left on Highway 180, heading west toward Roby, they felt they were out of harm's way. As traffic was light, they figured the cops would be somewhere else, looking for speeders where the traffic was most congested. Grace tossed her bonnet over into the back seat, kissed Alvin, and leaned her head against his shoulder for a while, until they became serious about finding the farm road that had been described in a letter from Alvin's mother. Finally they recognized it from Jessie May's directions, and took a left turn going south, checking every mailbox along the way. Grace was leaning from one window to the other trying to read the names on the mailboxes. When she finally saw one that read Allan Jackson, she screamed with excitement.

"There it is!" Alvin hit his brakes, backed up about twenty feet and made another left turn going east. This brought them about one mile off the main road and into a wooded area. In the midst of a dark cluster of trees, they spotted an old house by the light of a dim kerosene lantern they saw, shining from a window.

When they arrived at his father's house, Alvin and Grace were so full of pee, that if they had been wearing false teeth, those teeth would have floated right out of their mouths. The worst of it was that Alvin's father didn't know that. He took his time assuring them that those four dogs that jumped off the porch, barking viciously, were completely harmless. As Allan Senior yelled at the dogs to be quiet, he assured Alvin and Grace, "Oh, they won't bite you. They're just curious about you as you are about them."

Alvin said, "Daddy, before I introduce you to my wife, I need you to show us the way to the bathroom." Once he saw how uncomfortable they were, he immediately escorted them through the house, Alvin holding his crotch with one hand and waving to his mother with the other. Grace came walking in as if she were cuffed at her ankles and using every muscle in her bottom to shut off her bladder.

A few minutes later, they both came back into the house – cold but relieved, and Alvin said to his father, "I want you and everyone else to meet your new daughter-in-law ... boys, your sister-in-law, Grace."

Grace gave her first hugs and kisses to Alvin's father, and then the two boys; then she hugged and kissed Alvin's mother last, and the family tried to pretend that there wasn't any apprehension among them, since their son showed up at their house in the middle of the night, latched onto this beautiful white woman. The tension was thick enough to cut with a dull knife and draw blood. Alvin's father got his gun and walked outside and scouted the premises to make sure some rowdy person hadn't followed them home. Twenty minutes later, he came back into the house and said, "I think we're safe for the night, so why don't we all relax and get to know one another."

"First of all," Alvin said, "if you'll give me a minute or so, I'll show you what I brought to celebrate this special event with." He motioned to his two brothers to help unload the car. The first item he brought back into the house was a bottle of gin and one of tonic, which he mixed and offered to his father as a cocktail.

"Well," Alvin's father said, "my motto has been to wait until Christmas Eve before I start to celebrate the event. However, being that you're asking your family to pay homage to your lovely lady Grace, I'll gladly forfeit my Christmas Eve tradition, and install her into the Jackson family by raising my drink in a salute to my new daughter-n-law."

Alvin gave his mother a beer and said, "I gave the strong drink to Daddy. I figured that as little as you drink, this gin and tonic might be too strong for you."

Jessie May replied, "And so is this beer you're trying to persuade me to drink. Aside from that, I'm inclined to agree with your father. Why wait until Christmas Eve to drink this nasty beer with the purpose of formally welcoming this beautiful lady into the Jackson's family?"

Alvin suggested to his father: "I know my brothers are still at the age where they shouldn't be allowed to indulge in alcohol. But it doesn't seem right out of five people, you and Mama are the only ones to take part in toasting this lovely wife of mine with a can of beer."

"Well," Allen Senior relented, "since you put it that way; you boys take one big gulp. Then me and Alvin will drink the rest." Everyone encircled Grace, their arms around her lovingly, while Alvin's father said a few words to the Lord in reference to Alvin and Grace's safe arrival, as well as a plea for their safe journey home to Fort Worth.

They all raised their glasses as a salute in order that she was officially inducted as a new member of the Jackson's family. Everyone hugged and kissed Grace for the second time. Alvin's father ordered the two younger brothers to hand over their beers. "I'm watching you boys, so I ask for them back, because I wanted to make sure that the boys didn't drink anymore than I had agreed to let you drink."

Very soon that combination of gin, tonic, and the can of beer that his father had consumed, made its way to his head in no time at all, which enabled him to say: "I thought I knew my boys pretty well, but Alvin, snuck one in on me, which got my thoughts running wild. Now I'm trying to comprehend something that beyond anything that I could imagine. Even with me being as modest as I can be, I'll still have to say that this young lady is as pretty as they come."

Grace smiled and said, "Well, thank you very much for those kind words."

Jessie May said, "Before I get into a long, drawn-out conversation with you, I'll tell you in advance that you can thank me too, young lady.

Since my husband has described you exactly the way I would've said – but I want to add something that he fail to say: that is, you have definitely exceeded anything that I could ever imagine my son bringing home as a wife to introduce to his mother and family. Now," she said, "beside all of the flattery about your beauty – which you well deserve – there is one thing about you that sorter troubles me to the degree of asking; what is my boy's guarantee that a beautiful and intelligent woman like you won't eventually wound up in the arms of some rich white man?"

"Doesn't Alvin get any credit for what you see me to be?" Grace asked, with a little touch of indignation. "With all due respect to my parents – especially my mother, whose love is immeasurable – when it comes to mother and daughter's feeling for each other... My family, we didn't ever see possibilities, or have any ambition for ourselves . . . and I was pretty much set on doing the same as we always had done. Not only was that a fact of life for me, but the people my family associated with – from the time I was a little girl until the time I met Alvin – they were anything but ambitious. I had no one to tell me that there was more to life than living in a run-down trailer park; the same as the people we associated with. The parents of the children, including me, looked forward to the weekend, when there was a tradition for six adults who play cards and drink down at least three cases of beer in one night. So all the kids were left unsupervised . . . my best friend wound up getting pregnant by a boy that knew her less than three hours. I've always had a saying as far back to the time that I was aware of our living conditions: I might be labeled as being trailer trash, but it doesn't mean I had to prove it by lying down for some ne'er-do-well. Alvin and I courted for at least six months and more, before I reluctantly gave in to his constant persuasion. Even to the point of forfeiting my innocence, which I'm happy to say; my carelessness got me my husband, who also made it possible for both sets of my parents to live rent-free. So if you think you have something to worry about, you should hear my parents tell me how fortunate they are that I married your son."

Jessie May said, "Not only did you give an intelligent answer, but you have your head on straight, for a girl your age. You understand that a pretty girl like you doesn't always walk away as first prize winner. You know that a girl could spend her whole life chasing after rich men and never catching herself nothing but a bad reputation. Most men are like animals, especially when a fight breaks out between two dogs. You'll see all of the other dogs in the neighborhood will come and join the dog on top and won't stop until the dog on the bottom is dead. Never min' that one on the bottom is being ripped apart by all of them on top. They don't care because they all want to be like the big dog. Once they've accomplish what they set out to do, they'll walk away and won't even remember your name anymore, provided they knew it in the first place. Now that I've heard from you what my boy has already told us, about the kind of person you're, I'm convinced that you're just as loyal to him on the inside as you're beautiful on the outside. So I said all of that, jut to get around to this – the minute I saw this woman walk through my door, I immediately said to myself: he can't go any higher than that; but what about her dedication? Does he have a solid relationship with her? Now I don't wonder anymore, because your conversation has just took all of the guesswork out of my what-if kind of attitude toward you. And to prove to you that I'm serious about getting to know you, I've set here and unconsciously gulping down half of this nasty tasting beer, which I've never developed a taste for."

"You're so nice to say that," Grace said, "but there is nothing extraordinary about me. Otherwise I wouldn't be constantly keeping myself in check in hopes that Alvin will love me even more than he says he already does."

"Well," Alvin's father said, "as much as I know, the both of you are even; he's told me pretty much the same thing about you. As for all of that reserve stuff, it ain't gonna do nothing but make you miss out on a lots of exciting things that you don't have the nerve to try at this point in your lives. I'm really enjoying this discussion," he said, "but not as much as I would if someone could make me another cocktail exactly the way you made the first one."

"Let me," Grace said. "I know precisely the way he likes it made." As she handed it to him, she asked, shyly, "Is it all right for me to call you Daddy Jackson? And you, Jessie May – Mother Jackson?"

"Of course you can," Jessie May said, as she hugged Grace. "I hope my drinking that half can of beer ain't causing me to make a fool of myself. Apart from I'm so excited that I'm gonna say it anyway; when my husband told me about our son being involved with a white girl, we expected her to be sorter on the trashy side. Having such a bad image about our new daughter-n-law, I was reluctant to write and tell my sister that Alvin had married a white woman. Now that 'I've finally got to met you, I can hardly wait to write and tell her—not only are you beautiful—but you're highly intelligent as well. The only bad part about all of this is I can't take you places and show you off as my pretty daughter-in-law!"

"Speaking of showing things off around here," Allan said, "I can't wait to show you and Miss Grace what y'all bought for me and your mama beside this house. As much as you know about farming, you should know that you can't plant cotton in the middle of summer and expect to harvest in the fall. By time escrow closed, it was too late to plant cotton, so I planted a few acres of maize, and believe it or not, we had a pretty darn good crop of the stuff. Even though the heads may've grown to maturity, but an early frost stopped its growth dead in its track, and they never got the chance to ripen."

"Oh boy, Grace," Alvin said. "Here is your chance to stroll through the fields at night like you told me a few days ago."

"If you think this cold weather is going to make me change my mind, you better think again," Grace answered. "I can hardly wait to take this opportunity to stroll through the fields as long as you're going with me." She turned to Mother Jackson and asked, "Are you going with us too?"

"No honey," Jessie May answered. "If only you knew how many times your father-n-law has persuaded me to follow him over every square inch of this property, you'd feel silly for asking. This man of mine is so proud of these acreages – nothing he's had in the past until now will ever measure to this house and farm. And if you're bent on going out in the cold, I don't think I need to remind you that you're gonna need a heavy coat – it can get cold enough out there to freeze the horns off a hairy billy-goat."

Grace put on a pair of Alvin's heavy socks, and everyone grabbed a heavy coat and took off walking through the fields, with the dogs trotting out front looking for a rabbit to chase – even in the dark. After a few minutes of walking facing the cold northern wind, everyone was ready to turn around and go back to the house, except Daddy Jackson; he was determined that they'd continue to walk with him as far as the dividing line between his property and the adjacent land. All the while, he sipped his gin and tonic out of a beer can.

Grace kept saying to Alvin, "I can't wait to see all of this in daylight. Better yet," she added, "I can't wait to go back to the house where it's warm and see all of this tomorrow when the sun is out."

Daddy Jackson heard, but he just kept right on walking and talking until they finally reached the first boundary. Grace looked over, and even in the dark, could see that it was not under cultivation.

She asked Allan, Sr. "Who owned this land?"

When he told her that he had no idea, Grace asked him if he would find out for her.

He answered, "Yeah, but why would you be concerned, when you've only seen a corner of the two hundred acres that you already own?"

"First of all," Grace explained, "if we negotiate the same deal as we did on this property, I have an idea that we could put together one of the biggest ranches in this part of Texas. And soon as I could afford to, I would start stocking it with all kind of farm animals – that could turn out to be a lucrative business for Alvin and me. Thirdly," she said, "before I get too keyed up about my idea, can you tell me about how many acres are in that plot I just mentioned?"

"I'm assuming it's probably about the same size as our farm; from my observation, it was most likely abandoned about the same time as this farm was. I suppose those people that owned the land were either too old to farm or it wasn't worth fooling with."

"Well," Grace said, "aren't you farming this land and growing grain?"

"Yes," Allan said, "but I'm fortune enough to have a family to do the labor for free. So everything we make we keep. Those farmers that abandon their land, most likely they couldn't afford to continue to wind up in the hole each year after harvest. Next year," he said, "I'll be planting only about fifty acres in cotton, since the rest of my so-call productive land is too poor to grow much of anything except weeds."

"What about the fifty acres of cotton?" Grace asked, "What kind of return do you expect to get on that many acres?"

"I'll be lucky if I harvest twelve, maybe fifteen bale of cotton," he said. "But you have to remember the return on that much cotton, which is about forty-five hundred. If all goes well, I have no doubt that will be enough to keep a family of four for a year and maybe a little extra."

321

After she and Daddy Jackson stood and talked for fifteen minutes, everyone except Daddy Jackson started to complain again about being too cold. At that, Allan, Sr. led his small entourage back into the house, and at once everyone gathered around the old freestanding propane heater. Jessie May observed, "If Allan showed y'all the entire farm, you had to be traveling in a car at high speed – or else y'all had to abandon the tour, because you were freezing y'all cans off."

Grace said, "I saw enough to start the wheels rolling in my brain. I have an idea, but I don't want to go into details with anyone until I talk it over with Alvin, when you go Christmas shopping tomorrow. Now, Mother Jackson – if you don't mind warming up some of that fried chicken I saw setting on the stove when I first came in, Alvin and I will forever be indebted to you."

"Don't mention it," Jessie May said. "The minute y'all walked out the door I put the chicken in the oven – I figured y'all would be hungry from walking around in all of that cold. It should be ready about now. Now about y'all going Christmas shopping tomorrow; I thank there has been a mistake. We've bought everything we need for our Christmas dinner. My turkey is lying on the shelf, thawing along with a nice ham; plus all the trimming that we'll be serving with our ham and turkey. So you see we got no other reason to be going Christmas shopping."

Grace asked, "What about presents for you and the boys? Don't you have a Christmas tree and all your presents underneath it?"

Jessie May explained, "With the kind of crop we harvested this fall, we can't afford presents. We feel blessed to have a nice ham and turkey for the holiday. Presents are for people that did a lot better than we did this year at harvest."

Grace reached in her purse, handed Jessie May and Allan each a hundred-dollar bill; then she gave Junior and Freddy fifty dollars each. She then said to Mother Jackson, "Now you can go Christmas shopping. All you gotta do is take our car and don't come back until you've spent the last penny."

"Whoopee! Thank you, especially for this much money!" Alvin's brothers chorused.

"Unh-huh," Mother Jackson said, "and that's what it probably take us all day to spend this much money."

By the time Alvin and Grace had finished eating, it was close to eleven o'clock. Jessie May showed Grace the room where she and Alvin would be sleeping. "Now," she said, "I must warn y'all this room is like sleeping in an icehouse; at least for the first fifteen minutes. That's about how much time it'll take for y'all bodies to generate enough heat to where y'all can settle in and have y'all selves a good night sleep. Unless of course, y'all want to speed things up a bit, then I suggest y'all do what I and your father-in-law did when we were young. We'd move into those old, cold houses, and on nights like tonight, we'd hug and vigorously massage each other as if we're preparing to do something naughty. We discovered it was better to briskly massage each other for ten minutes than to lay still for thirty minutes before we were warm enough to fall into a good night's sleep. The only heat we have in this house is in the living room and the kitchen. Like always, as soon as I finish cooking, I turn the fire off in the kitchen. The only heat we have to keep us warm until bedtime is in the living room."

"We'll manage just fine," Grace said, "but there is one thing I'll need to do before I go to bed tonight – I'm gonna have to use the bathroom."

"Oh, I'm sure you will at that," Jessie May said. "I hope you won't be surprised to know, not only do we not have continuing heat in this house, but we don't have running water either – we use the old outhouse."

Grace hugged her and said, "I know all of that. I was just saying that I'll need to use it again before I go to bed tonight. Otherwise, don't worry about your living conditions on my account, because yours is no worse than mine was when I lived with my parents. Except we had indoor plumbing, and there wasn't any need to put on shoes and an overcoat to go to the bathroom." At that Grace patted Jessie May's back and said, "When I finish talking to your son tomorrow, I think we are going to put an end to your bathroom problem."

Grace murmured to Alvin, "I think I'm warm enough to take that long, cold journey to the outhouse. Are you desperate enough to take it with me?" They walked out the back door and to the outhouse, and Grace observed, "Boy, I hope there aren't any poisonous snakes crawling around in the dark just waiting to take a bite of my butt."

"I'd kill it for sure," he said. "No one takes a bit out of your butt and live long enough to talk about it except me. Besides – you don't have to worry about snakes being out in this kind of weather. They're hibernating in some other animal's warm hole, presiding over a belly full of rats that need be digested in time for Christmas dinner." They walked back into the house and stood by the heater to warm up before going to their cold bedroom, and Daddy Jackson suggested,

"I know Miss Grace don't like drinking alcohol. However, I suggest you fix her a gin and tonic before she goes crawling between those cold covers. Otherwise, she's gonna spend a lot of time shivering before y'all bodies reaches a comfortable temperature to where y'all can get a good night's sleep. So here is my proposal: you must first fix yourself a gin and tonic, hold your nose with one hand, take this gin and tonic in the other hand, and drink it until the glass is empty. After that, give yourself five minutes and, me, I guarantee you those covers will feel as if you were sleeping in a 100-degree oven."

"Since this is a special occasion and the room is ice-cold, I'll try your concocted idea for just this one time only." She gritted her teeth and held her breath and drank the gin and tonic, leaving nothing but an empty glass. Afterward Alvin decided he would have the same as Grace, but with more gin, which equaled to three-plus beers. A few minutes later, she said to Alvin with glittery eyes, "I'm ready to go test Daddy Jackson's theory to see if that gin and tonic can transform a cold bed into an oven." She stood up and staggered shortly. "Oh Alvin, honey," she said, "Please take me out of here before I embarrass myself in front of your family." Everyone tittered except Daddy Jackson. He felt bad; because he thought she was going to be sick – with everyone else thinking that she was cute.

Alvin and Grace got between the covers and began vigorously massaging each other as they tried to generate enough heat to warm the bed, as well as themselves. After Grace continued to shiver for the first ten minutes, she whispered, "Where is the oven that your dad promised the gin and tonic would ignite once we got between the covers?" They shivered awhile longer until Alvin became acclimated, and shortly thereafter, he fell asleep. Except it was just the opposite with her. Once she started to thaw, she kept right on thawing to the point of overheating in a particular area of hers. The booze and all of the excitement Alvin had that night sent his metabolism into remission. After a few minutes of massaging, while trying to stimulate her unresponsive counterpart, she decided to climb on top and use her bottom instead of her hand. By doing so, she created enough friction to reverse her inconsistency. Little did she know she wasn't the only one who had an orgasm?

"How could he?" she thought, after she had finally slipped off, and curled up next to him. Her worry of being pregnant was of no consequences to her, because she knew he slept through the whole ordeal. She had no idea what piece of luggage the condoms were packed in, and she didn't bother to look; because she was under the impression – even if she had copulated – it was unlikely that he could ejaculate in his sleep and impregnate her. Afterward, she fell asleep and didn't awaken again until about seven-thirty the next morning.

When Mother Jackson called out to everyone that breakfast was going to be ready in about fifteen minutes, Grace turned to Alvin and asked, "Where do I go to wash up around here?"

"I'll take care of that," he said. He got out of bed, got dressed, and went into the kitchen where his mother had boiling water on the stove just for the purpose of washing up in the mornings. She gave Alvin a wash-pan of warm water, a bar of soap, and a clean towel. He took it back to the room so Grace could sponge-bathe. She quickly realized that bathing in a basin of warm water in a cold room was no different from bathing outside.

At that time, she suddenly stopped and hurried around the room, reaching for her clothes so she didn't get icicles. At that, he remembered to tell her what his family normally did on cold days like this one. If it was at night, the adults would wait until either everyone went to bed, or they'd close the door and bathe in the kitchen where it was warm. That's what he had planned to do after everyone went Christmas shopping. He left her to wash and dress, and went into the kitchen, where his father and two brothers were having their coffee at the kitchen table.

Finally Grace walked out of her room, neatly dressed in a pair of light gray slacks with a dark blue long-sleeved blouse. As always, she looked immaculately beautiful, which motivated Alvin to meet her halfway and escort her to the table and seat her in a chair next to where he sat. When everyone spoke they used the words "good morning, Miss Grace" and said how beautiful she looked.

At that she said, "I know Alvin's reason for calling me "Miss Grace," but I don't know your reasons for calling me that. I would hate to think your reasons are different from Alvin's reasons. But whatever your reasons are, I'd just as soon you call me plain old Grace. I'm your sister-in-law, your brother's wife; not your superior as some people would have you to believe, because I'm white."

"What are Alvin's reasons for calling you 'Miss Grace,'?" Mother Jackson asked.

"I believe it's just one of his ways of saying 'I love you' instead of actually saying it."

Alvin looked at his brothers. "Isn't she's about the most beautiful thing you've ever seen?"

"Now Alvin," Grace chided him. You shouldn't go putting them on the spot. If they have something nice to say about me, they'll either tell me decisively about the way they see me, or they'll indecisively tell you behind my back about their likes and dislikes, which is the normal thing to do when they're discussing their girlfriends."

"If he had asked me the same question," Mother Jackson said, "I would've agreed at once that she is a darling of a daughter-n-law. To think that I was surprised at how beautiful you were when you walked through my door, when I always knew Alvin has always been a magnet when it comes to mesmerizing the opposite sex. I don't know how long those little girls had been giving him the puppy-dog look, but when I started noticing them, he wasn't quite ten yet. And it wasn't all colored girls either. I caught a few of the little white girls competing for his attention as well. That part of him he got from his father. According to your father's mama, your father started as a youngster and somewhere along the way, it must've become ingrained in his head. He certainly surprised me my first day at my new junior high school. A bunch of us students was gathered in the hallway when him and a few of his buddies came and stood amongst us females. He topped me on the shoulder and said, 'Hi good-looking. May I have this kiss?' Before I could say no, he had me bent over his knee and kissed me right smack in my mouth. And to this very day, the old handsome devil is still going at it at full-throttle. I'll never forget my trying to get over how handsome he was compared to the way I thought I looked. But he chose to kiss me instead all of those other girls. After that, I felt he had just opened himself a big can of

326

worms. I got tired of waiting for him to come back for more. So I started to make myself visible by showing up at practically everywhere he went. He'd see me and say, 'You're too nice of a girl to be hanging around with us aimlessness-minded peoples. You need to go home and continue to stay that way. You'll prove to me that you're worthy of being my wife some day.' So one night after I had been stood up, like so many times before when he'd brush me off like I was this stupid little country girl. That particular night, I decided to go looking for him and give him a piece of my mind. And what I saw almost made me gag; because there he was hanging out with this little homely creature of a girl that everyone called Tillie. I told him 'If you don't leave that little gapped-tooth gal along and explain to me why he would choose that ugly creature over me. Boy!' I said to him, 'you had better have a darn good excuse for being with her or I'm liable to wound up going to prison over killing the both of you.' He didn't walk away from her at that instant, but the point is, I got my man and married that handsome Creole devil. Oh," she said as she looked at the clock. "I need to stop talking and get dressed so we can go do our Christmas shopping. I also need to start something cooking for y'all's lunch, because it'll probably be late when we get back home."

"Don't go to any trouble for me and Alvin," Grace said. "We'll find something for ourselves to eat."

"You'll still have to cook whatever y'all find around here to eat." Mother Jackson said, "We don't have cold cuts lying around in the refrigerator like most of the white people I've cleaned house for. Thanks to the Lord and you two, I don't have to clean other people's houses anymore."

"Well," Alvin said, "I'll solve that problem. I'll jump in my car and drive to the store to pick up cold cuts to make sandwiches for mine and Grace's lunch."

He asked his two brothers to ride with him in order to show him the way to the store. The twelve-mile round trip to the store took about thirty minutes. Upon returning from the store, Alvin couldn't help but noticed that Daddy Jackson had started and left his car's engine running and gone back into the house. When Alvin asked him why, Allan told him that he did it to have it warm by the time they were ready to ride to Hamlin to finish doing their Christmas shopping.

Alvin said to his father, "I thought it was understood that you were driving Grace's car."

"There's nothing wrong with my car that a good washing won't cure," Father Jackson replied. "Beside that – we're not going to Fort Worth, you know. We're only going to Hamlin, which is only a thirty-mile round trip drive from here."

Just as everyone started walking out the door and to their car, Alvin took his mother's hand and placed a hundred-dollar bill in it, telling her to buy a small Christmas tree. "Oh honey," Jessie May protested. "That much money could buy a very big Christmas tree, but I get your meaning, so thank you again, son – for the extra."

Alvin and Grace stood on the front porch and watched the four of them drove away. Afterwards, they went back into the house, at which time Alvin said to Grace: "I don't know why you went to all of the trouble to fix yourself up the way you did. As you well know how difficult it is for me to behave myself when I'm left along with you, especially when you're looking as sexy as you are right now."

She smiled half-embarrassed, saying, "And I can't be trusted to behave myself, especially when you've had so much to drink you couldn't respond to my demands."

"Why do you say that?" he asked.

"Well," she said, "after you fell asleep last night, I lay there wondering why my instrument was keeping me awake. Normally, when you're asleep and I have those recurring flare-ups, I give my little lady a quick massage – just enough to take the edge off and wait until morning. Then I hand her over to you and let you put on the finishing touches. But when I realized that it wasn't going to go away, I tried to awaken you. After about the third try and I still couldn't get it to respond, I took your matter and smothered it in my little lady and finally finished up feeling very victorious."

"Why didn't you awake me so we both could've finished up feeling triumphal?"

"Like I told you," she said, "I tried at least twice to wake you, but I couldn't. So I did what I had to do all by myself."

328

"I don't understand how you manage to do all of that and not wake me?"

"It wasn't easy." she said, "It took a few tries. It was like trying to shove a wet noodle into an upside-down catsup bottle. So out of desperation, I straddled you, and apparently the heat from my little lady must've struck a nerve, which gave her the friction she needed to alleviate that worrisome old itch."

Alvin shook his head, laughing in disbelief, "How could you do something like that? I've never known you to act like that before – or maybe you did and you never told me."

"No," she said, "I'm surprised myself that I could do something that was so unlike me – and then I thought it had to have been your father persuading me to drink that double shot of gin and tonic. Now that I think about it, I bet he purposely persuaded me to drink, because he knew that it would ignite the tigress in me. Perhaps he'd hear us doing it and incite him to give Mother Jackson what he assumed you were giving me. The next time he offers me one of his bullshit stories about gin and tonic made for medicine, I'll tell him to make one for him and give one to Mother Jackson and see how he feels the next morning when she tells him that she spent half the night trying to force a rope up a hollow tree."

Afterward, they bathed, got dressed, and went to keep warm by the fire, and discuss the condition of the farmhouse, and the vacant property adjoining Daddy Allen's farm. Their plans included remodeling the house, drilling water well, and adding electricity and telephone service. "After this trip," Alvin insisted, "we'll never visit my parents under these conditions again. We need to get busy – get your mother on this project and see if we can afford these ideals of ours without going overboard." They talked back and forth until both of them got hungry.

Grace made sandwiches and they ate. Around three that afternoon, Alvin decided to take Grace for a walk in the woods. Before he left, he thought it was best to go outside and check to see if anyone was prowling around the property that could possibly be a threat. He came back inside and told Grace as far as he could see, the coast was clear. So she slipped into her jeans and grabbed her heavy coat, while Alvin got his father's twenty-two rifle and a box of ammunition.

Then they took off walking through the woods with the dogs walking out in front of them anxious and eager to hunt. They followed the fences from one corner of the property to the other corners. Then, they felt they were being a little too bold, by walking in the open fields. At that, they aborted the walk in the field and took to concealing themselves amongst the trees and continued to walk inside their borderlines until they came to a certain cluster of trees when Grace stopped and leaned back against the tallest one. At that time, she asked Alvin to come and stand next to her. She then placed his arms around her waist and hers around his neck.

At that time, she looked up at the tree and began to recite a poem to him with these words: "Old tree, old tree / you've lost your leaves / as you stand tall and shivering in the breeze. / Your leaves have dried withered / and gone to return in the spring at the break of dawn. / Exquisitely, more beautiful and luscious than before, / with a fragrance so sweet that I adore / with knotted arms and sugary lips / I'll stay the course as a cruise ship / these avid moments must come and go / but not my love I'm sure you know. / Consummate this love / as you stand tall and be my witness / but that ain't all. / My love, my faith, my vows / I'll keep no storm / no rain shall make me weak. / My love is strong and planted / so deep with tenderness and mildness I'll give so sweet. / In the winter, in the spring, in the summer and fall, my vow I'll keep / but that ain't all. / You're mine, and all, / but most of all you're mine in all and in the fall. / Fear not dearest, marvelous oh man of mine / my love for you is truly divine. / In the good times, the bad times and even in ecstasy, / I'm yours forever in solidarity."

"Astoundingly beautifully," he said, "I can't believe what I just heard came out of the mouth of a woman that I've known more than a year. I never knew you could recite poetry as you just did for me."

"Are you sure you're pleased with what I just recited to you, honey?"

"I'm so honored to know that you think so highly of me. For the most part, you constructed a poem – cobbled out of your imagination. And without a doubt, I know for sure you recited it to me with love that came from the depths of your heart."

As she smiled, she said, "What kind of impact did my recital make on you?

"Let us not move an inch until we inaugurate this place as our tree of dedication. And let it be certified by way of touching our genitals together."

Afterward, he picked up his rifle and they began to walk back toward the house when she mused,, "Out of all of the gifts you've given me so far, I've chosen the land over everything else, because it's nature at its best. Think about it here: we are just me and you strolling through the trees, as free as the birds that I see flying from tree to tree; unlike the city that's filled with people who dwell on hatred, like the fumes from automobile that poison the air—the same way they're interfering with our freedom to be ourselves."

"Enough of the talk about love," he said. "I need to pick up the pace and hurry back to the house. I'm sure Mama and Daddy must be worried sick about us by now."

When they got home, Alvin's family was already back from shopping. His older sister Rose, and her husband, Jake, were there along with their two boys, J. J. and Marvin. Even though the boys' mother had already told them that their Uncle Alvin was married to their white Aunt Grace, they were still too young to understand, until they actually got to see her in person. Then everybody was anxious to converse with her. Rose even stopped helping Mother Jackson decorate the small Christmas tree just so they could visit with Grace and get to know her.

At last, Mother Jackson said, "I'm happy to know that I finished just in time to start those chili dogs, or else I was gonna have a bunch of hungry people that's too angry to eat."

Rose said to Mother Jackson, "Why don't you let me make the chili hot dogs while you and Grace rearrange the presents beneath the Christmas tree?" Eventually Grace worked her way into the kitchen and continued her conversation with Rose.

By that time, Daddy Jackson, Junior, and Freddy came in from feeding the animals. "Boy!" Daddy Jackson said to Alvin, "You had me worried there for awhile until I saw that my rifle was gone and I didn't see any dead dogs lying around. That's when I realized that nothing was wrong except you two had gone got yourselves bored and went for a walk in the woods. Even at that," he said, "you can't be too careful around here. There is a lot of vacant land in Jones County, and since there are no fences to keep out dangerous trespassers, you could wound up being a victim of circumstances. I tell you the truth," he added, jokingly, "I'm not really worried about anyone shooting Alvin, because I have three other boys. Now, if Miss Grace were to be shot, that's a different story. Because there're no way you'd have the courage to do what you endured the first time around in order to have a woman as pretty as Miss Grace."

Mother Jackson said, "Alvin, you and your darling wife started something when y'all bought your father that bottle of gin. He's already had his first nip and the sun hasn't gone down yet. Ordinary Christian people don't drink in broad daylight. Even if they do, they normally have very little to say. Unlike those who go around making jokes and calling attention to themselves? I knew he must've had something up his sleeve when he came to me around two and told me he'd be back shortly. Now I know where he went when he said he'd be back shortly; he headed over to Stanford to Pinkie's liquor store."

Allan said, "I bought that bottle of bourbon to toast my new daughter-n-law when the rest of the family gets here. Since Benny and Mildred are taking longer than I expected, I decided to break the rule and pour myself a small one just to tide me over until they get here."

"Miss Grace'"" Mother Jackson said. "If you believe that, then I want you to believe me when I tell you that I'm playing baseball at Dodgers' Stadium tomorrow."

"Come on, Miss Grace," Daddy Jackson coaxed her. "You and your husband need to join me in a round of cocktails – that way my wife won't keep accusing me of being a one-man drunk."

"Not on your life." Grace answered, "That potion you made me drink last night should last me until this time next year. That stuff made me do strange things after I went to bed last night."

When Alvin chuckled, she changed the subject and said to Alvin, "Is it too early to start discussing our plans concerning Daddy and Mother Jackson's living conditions, do you think?"

Alvin nodded, with a very sobering air. "Daddy, Grace and I spent the biggest part of the day going over our budget trying to figure whether or not we can afford to buy the farm flanking yours, fix up this house, and drill a well – all at the same time, without going over budget."

"Now son," Daddy Jackson answered, "that's mighty nice of you and Miss Grace to think about us in that way, but we'll be fine just as we are. It normally doesn't get this cold around here very often – and when it does, it only lasts a day or two. Already I've noticed it's starting to warm up, and I'll bet you right now that it's twenty-five degrees warmer than it was last night. Don't worry about us and this old house; the boys and I will do a little fixing up around here after the holidays. About the land," he continued. "That's another story. It's always nice to own a lot of land if one can afford it along with the equipment and labor that it'll take to maintain it. At the pace I'm going, it'll take me quite awhile to scrap up enough money to buy the things I need to operate that many acres – let along the acreages that I already have."

"Well," Grace ventured, "what about the water situation and your boys' education?"

"What about it," Daddy Jackson asked.

"If you had running water, you wouldn't have to use the outhouse on cold nights like last night. With running water you could install a toilet . . . and secondly, I hear that your boys can barely read and write. Those two things should be a must in the eyes of a father who loves his children and wants to see them do well in life."

"How am I going to afford to pay somebody to come and work my fields while these boys are in school? I didn't go very far in school and look at me; I'm doing all right. What them boys need more than an education is how to work hard, and learn to manage the money they make."

"Who's going to read, calculate, and sign documents for them if they can't read or write?" Daddy Jackson scratched his head but didn't answer, and Grace pursued her advantage. "How much do you pay a field hand for a day's work?"

"About seven-fifty for a ten hour day's work," he said. That's for chopping cotton and two dollars for every hundred pounds of cotton they pick."

"Now," she said, "overall, how many days does it take to complete the cotton-chopping part of it?"

"Well, let see." Daddy Jackson mused, "For the amount of acreage that the government allots me for cotton: once – sometimes twice a month – using four people, paying them seven-fifty a day."

She turned to Allan Junior, handing him the paper and pencil. "The numbers your daddy gave me: would you like to tell him what all of this is going to cost?"

Junior smiled sheepishly. "I'm not that good with math."

"Sure, you're not," she said, "and I'm not surprised, either."

She handed the pen and paper to Alvin, and in a couple of minutes he told her: "Give or take a few dollars, the minimum would be no more than three-fifty, and the maximum would be no more than five-hundred, give or take a few dollars here and there."

She then turned to Daddy Jackson and said, "According to what Alvin, told me, the bus he rode in on had barely reached the city limits of Fort Worth before he was off and champing at the bit to execute his plans he had fantasized about for years. Besides finding a good job, he made education his first priority. He proved it by coming home each evening after work, and spending at least two hours on furthering his education. I'm sure you have noticed the difference in his and Junior's ability to solve a simple math problem. With all due respect, Daddy Jackson – just let me say again what Alvin told me in the beginning of our relationship. 'Anyone,'" he said, "'can afford what he wants to afford. All you need to do is want it bad enough and you will have it.' Apparently, your boys' education is not a priority with you. If it were, you could afford it. Now," she continued, "I think I can raise the stakes in your favor and make it easy on you, and I think I can speak for Alvin – we're willing to pay the field hands their salary in exchange for your boys' education."

"Praise the Lord," Mother Jackson exclaimed, as she rushed to Grace and gave her a hug. "Do you know how long I've been begging and trying to get this man of mine to educate those boys?" Jessie May turned to her husband, saying, "You better listening to your white daughter-in-law. She's making you an offer that you ain't gonna ever get again. Take them up on it, because we need their help at this point. These boys of ours are so far behind, they'll have to go to school year-around for the next three years, just graduating with students their own age. That's why I want to hear you promise me and these boys – in front of all of these peoples – that you are going to take Miss Grace up on her offer and never go back on your word."

Allan said to Grace, "Well, I don't want to be too much of a burden on you and Alvin, but if y'all think you can afford it, I promise to keep them in school."

Again, Mother Jackson rushed, but this time it was into his arms and said, "You old devil; it took a white person to convince you the important of getting those boys their education." She kissed him in the mouth, which was unusual for them to do in front of people. She walked back to the kitchen saying, "Praise the Lord!"

As she and Rose begin putting the food on the table, everyone was already gathered waiting to eat their chilidogs with Pepsi and potato salad. Everyone ate to their hearts' delight. Grace and Rose commenced to cleaning the kitchen in slow motion as they pried their way into each other's personal life. That continued until Alvin's baby sister Mildred, and her husband, Benny, drove up with their little girl, Sue Ana. From that point forward, the house became noisy all over again. The children were running and screaming and yelling, and the women, talking, laughing, and telling stories. Whereas, the men went spiking their cokes with bourbon, and telling Alvin how fortunate he was to have a woman as pretty as his Miss Grace.

Mildred finally got her brother, Alvin's attention. "So," she said to him, "this is the pretty girl that everyone's been writing me about. Boy, no one told me that you were practicing voodoo."

"Why do you say that?" he asked.

"How else could you have gotten yourself a girl as pretty as your Miss Grace without casting some kind of spell on her? The only way that I can describe her beauty is to say the girl is definitely a gorgeous little white heifer, even if I have to say so myself." She turned to Grace and said, "Don't min' me none. That's just one of the ways I convey myself when I'm genuinely impressed with someone as elegant as you are."

Grace uttered her gratitude in a tentative manner. "Thank you very much."

At that, the two girls took Grace aside and began to question her about everything imaginable. Even more than that, they were curious to know how she and their brother could be married as a mixed couple and stay out of trouble with the law. "Y'all have to be half-insane," Mildred insisted, "to live in a state where hatred is anything but unheard of. And I wanna know what possessed you two to even think about riding together, all the way from Fort Worth to here and going back the same way."

"All I can say at this point," Rose said, "that we should all start praying in hope that y'all's drive back home together will be as safe as it was driving down here together.

"Other than that," Rose added. "I want to know when y'all going to make one of those pretty little mixed babies and add a little class to the Jackson family?"

"If you had asked me five minutes ago, I may have given you a definite answer," Grace said. "But since you feel that Alvin and my life depend on your prayers to get us back home, you may have to wait and see whether we make it back to Fort Worth alive – then I would be able to tell you when!"

"Oh girl," Mildred said, "don't pay too much attention to what Rose, says. She's just like Mama. She'll scare the socks off you, if you pay any mind to her prophecy about what could go wrong between here and Fort Worth."

The three ladies gravitated back to the kitchen and continued to make small talk in the company of Mother Jackson, where she sat reading the Bible and sipping on a Pepsi. There hadn't ever been a previous opportunity for three colored women and the one white woman to sit together and explore one another's culture. Each of them got their chance, by way of Grace entering into the family, and they took full advantage of it and talked until the wee, wee hours in the morning. Their yawning and scratching of their heads were clear evidence that everybody was exhausted and the only cure was a good night's sleep.

The next morning being Christmas, Mother Jackson and Rose got up at four o'clock in the morning to get an early start on preparing the ham and turkey with all of the trimmings, plus an assortment of pies. At seven-thirty, Rose came and knocked on everyone's door telling them "Merry Christmas," and that Santa Claus was there and about to eat their breakfast if they weren't at the table in fifteen minutes. With Alvin knowing the routine, he jumped out of bed and went into the kitchen where there was a pot of hot water on the stove. He filled a wash pan and took it back to Grace. She took her mini-bath, got dressed, and came to the table where everyone was sitting drinking coffee. Mildred got up and poured Grace her cup of coffee, while Sue Ana, kept squirming around in her seat, at once shy and curious about being seated at the table with a white person. Not only was it a first time for Sue Ana and the two other children, but a first time for their parents as well.

Grace took notice of the little girl rubbing her eyes out of shyness when she saw Grace looking at her. Grace said to the little girl, "Come, here Sue Ana and sit with your Auntie Grace." The little girl got off her mother's lap and in a snail's pace; she came to Grace, still rubbing her eyes. Grace picked her up, sat her on her lap, and asked, "Do you know who I am?"

Sue Ana whispered, "No ma'am."

Grace said, "I'm your Auntie Grace. I'm married to your mother's brother," as she pointed to Alvin. "This is your mother's brother, Uncle Alvin, who you've never seen before, and you've never seen me before either, have you. Now: I want you to repeat after me; OK? Say Uncle Alvin and Auntie Grace."

The girl was too shy to speak. Grace repeated herself. The little girl just kept rubbing her eyes. Rose's two boys saw the attention Sue Ana was getting, so they slowly dragged their little selves out of their seats, and the two of them walked around and stood, one on each side of Grace. She put her arms around both of them and asked them the same question as she did the girl. "Do you know who I am?"

J. J, the oldest boy said, "Huh-huh, you are my Auntie Grace."

"That's good, J. J.," Grace answered. She then turned to Martin and asked him the same question. He started pointing his finger at everyone with a spasmodic twitch, answering, "You're all of our Auntie Graces." After everyone had a good laugh, Grace squeezed and said, "That's close enough."

After breakfast, Grace asked Daddy Jackson if he thought it was safe for her to go out and visit the animals. "You won't see much," he answered. "I only own a few hens and a couple of roosters, two pregnant sows, and two milk cows; each of them had young calf. But you had better wait until me and Alvin scout around outside, to make sure no one is out there waiting to ambush you." They spent only a few minutes scouting the perimeters before Daddy Jackson told Alvin, "As far as I can see, I'd say y'all is free to do whatever as long as the both of you stay alert."

They come walking toward the house and saw Grace standing in the doorway, waiting to hear if it was OK to walk outside in daylight. Alvin called to her, from across the yard, letting her know that the coast was clear. Right away she jumped off the porch and followed him to the pens where the animals lived. As they went from pigpen to cow pens, Grace got to see each kind of animals in their natural habitat. The first pen she visited was the pigs; one was lying in the hay, while the other walked around picking up scraps of food. They visited the cattle and saw them doing pretty much the same as the pigs. Some were lying and chewing their cud while the others were walking around picking up scraps of food.

After they revisited each animal's habitat a couple of times, Grace said, "When we buy the adjacent farm to ours, we're gonna make our fortune in buying and selling animals just like these."

"People do make a decent living buying and selling livestock," Alvin said. "Of course, it won't happen overnight. If you start investing a little now, by the time I'm twenty-five, we should be well on our way to becoming the big-time ranchers you're dying to become."

"That's only five years from now," she said, "beginning January twelfth." Those few words of encouragement that he spoke inspired her to lock arms with Alvin. She was so interested in knowing about raising animals; Grace became lost in thought; they kept walking farther and farther away from the house, as she continued to collect information from Alvin about raising farm animals. In addition to her quest for knowledge about raising farm animals, she had another notion – to covertly work their way back to their tree of dedication. She planned for them to carry out a replica of the inauguration which they preformed yesterday, for good measure and via another roll in the grass. But Daddy Jackson was so concerned about their safety, noting that Alvin and Grace were headed towards the patch of woods, he called out, "Y'all have gone far enough now!" So much for revisiting the tree of dedication; Daddy Jackson continued, "my advice to y'all is to come on back to the house, and let us open our Christmas presents before we eat dinner."

They came back into the house just as Mother Jackson had begun handing out everyone's presents. When Grace opened the shoe box and saw the jewelry inside of the shoes, she screamed with excitement, "Oh, Alvin!" She rushed into his arms, almost knocking him off his feet. She held it high so everyone could see while she exclaimed, "I wouldn't be overstating the fact, if I said that this person that I'm married to is an amazing gentleman."

After everyone had paraded around the living room showing off their presents, they all went to their rooms and changed into their best clothes and returned to the living room. Mother Jackson was accustomed to say a word of praise, usher them to the dining table and seat then in a specific place. Since Mother Jackson and her Rose, had designated themselves as servers for the occasion, they were the only ones that didn't bother to change into their dress clothes. Finally, Alvin and Grace walked out of their room and into the living room where everybody was awestruck at the sight of seeing Alvin escorting Grace with all of her beauty.

After everyone gave them enthusiastic applause, Mildred asked Grace, "Honey, all I need to know from you is what does a girl have to do to have her man to buy her beautiful jewelry like your man did for you?"

Rose spoke up, "I'm guessing that same generous person must've bought you this beautiful dress you're wearing also."

"He did," Grace answered proudly. "He buys all of my stylish clothes, which I don't mind, since he spends more on my clothes than my conscience will allow me to spend." She smiled and said, "Remind me to tell you about the first dress he bought for me that almost got him killed."

"Uh-oh," Mother Jackson asked, "What happened?"

"It's a long, graphic story that might be too ugly to explain amongst the youngsters," Grace said. "Perhaps, when you come to visit me, I'll tell you all about it."

Finally Daddy Jackson insisted that everyone hold hands while he blessed the food. He prayed for Alvin's and Grace's safe return to Fort Worth, and mentioned a few words about the oldest son, Willie. He told how disappointed he was that Willie and his family had missed the chance to be part of the family gathering on such special occasion. Willie had no excuse; this was the third Christmas he'd missed in order to spend it with her family, instead of his. After dinner was finished, everyone remained seated at the table, relaxed, and focused most of their conversation on Grace and about her marriage with Alvin. When Alvin noticed that his family was asking the same questions, he asked his brother Allan to fill his five-gallon can with gasoline and put it in the trunk of the car.

He told Grace, "If you need to use the bathroom, now is the time to do so – in about an hour from now, we need to hit the road to Fort Worth, to our home, sweet home."

"There is still a lot of daylight left in the sky, y'all," Daddy Jackson pleaded. "As far as I'm concern, y'all are taking a risk you don't have to take."

"I think we'll be safe between here and Abilene," Alvin answered. "The dangerous stretch will be between Abilene and Fort Worth; if I were there at this time a day. By the time we reach Abilene, it'll be plenty dark enough to conceal our identity from anyone hunting for a mixed couple like us."

"Well," Daddy Jackson finally allowed, "My duty is to warn y'all of any possible danger you might encounter traveling this time of day. Other than that – I believe the Lord will protect two people like you who provide for their parents the way y'all do for each of your parents. But even so," he added, "we certainty don't wonna go putting the Lord to the test, now do we?"

Alvin thanked his daddy for giving them his blessing. He shook hands with all the men and boys and hugged all of the girls and women, while Grace hugged and kissed everyone. At that time, Grace got in her car, rolled down the window, and brandished her bonnet, telling Daddy Jackson, "I won't put this thing on unless it's absolutely necessary." She was right to say so, because she never once had to reach for her bonnet during the whole trip home.

At nearly nine that evening, they drove into their driveway. "Welcome home!" Myrtle said when she saw Alvin and Grace coming through the back door. "You just missed your Mama and family by fifteen minutes. So, do you want to first tell me about your trip, or would you rather save it until you've had your fill of these delicious leftovers? We certainly still have enough to choose from, even after Maggie took half the food home with her. We simply will not have to cook for all the rest of this week."

Grace said, "Maybe just a little bit of each." By the time she stopped scooping from each entrée, their plates were full. After a few bites of gorging themselves with Maggie's delicious leftovers, Myrtle commenced telling them about all of food that everyone ate and enjoyed over the holiday. "Besides all that," she said, "the food may've been enjoyable – as for the fun that everyone was supposed to be having – it wasn't fun for Maggie, because her two favorite children weren't in the midst of it all."

After those few words, Myrtle's conversation didn't get very much traction with Grace before she told her aunt that she and Alvin were so tired that the only thing worse than going to bed without a hot shower would be to fall face-first in her plate of food. "Meaning, if we don't end this talking shortly and get on with eating what's left on my plate, that's exactly what I'll do."

The next morning was almost as troublesome to them as it was before they went to bed the previous night. She and Alvin got out of bed and rushed between bathroom and bedroom, attempting desperately to wash up and dress and be at work on time. Both of them were still exhausted from the trip they'd taken to Alvin's parents. When they were laughing and drinking and staying up every night past midnight, they didn't know those good times were waiting for revenge.

Grace was so frazzled and hurried she was willing to suggest, "Alvin, honey. Since it's still dark at six o'clock in the morning, maybe you and me should consider riding to and from work together every day – just to see how long we can get away with it? Our main concern is to remember to keep our marriage license with us at all times, and be ready to present it in case of an emergency. Hopefully, once they've seen it, they'll accept the fact that we're married – and more than likely they'll let us go."

He smiled and said, "What makes you think they'll give it back, once they take it? I tell you the truth, Grace, honey – I don't like the idea of you being positive, when I'm feeling somewhat negative about your idea."

"It was just a stupid thought I woke up with this morning," she said. "I just happened to remember that we rode all the way to your father's house and back without incident. I thought to myself, 'why stop now when we're so far ahead.' You only stop when you are too far behind to catch up."

"Well," he said, "we'll never learn to swim standing on the bank . . . let's do it, baby."

"Yes," she said with excitement." Alvin pretended to be as cheerful as she was as he drove on his way to work. At the same time he prayed that he'd catch every green light, which he didn't, and became very nervous at every intersection where he caught red lights where other cars had stopped also. When he finally drove into the hotel parking lot, he breathed a sigh of release. Even then, he still felt fairly vulnerable; there were cars coming and going, and so many people that he felt that it was less hazardous to park around back, to avoid the heavy traffic in the main parking lot.

When they saw that the coast was clear, Grace got out and cheerfully said, "You see, honey, we made it just fine, didn't we." Alvin nodded and just sat there for a few minutes after she had gone inside. A few minutes later, he got out and made his way to the employee area and grabbed a cup of coffee. Then he walked over to the line cook's station for a visual inspection – just in time to see Grace hanging her first order. When she saw Alvin, she spoke as if she hadn't seen him since before the holidays. "Hi, Alvin," she said, "did you have a nice Christmas?"

He answered, "I can't ever remember when I've had a nicer one; did you?"

"I sure did," she answered, already walking away with her attention back to her customers, while Evelyn murmured to her co-workers: "Did y'all hear how casual she sounded when she asks 'did he have a nice Christmas.' I bet he did have a nice Christmas, and I bet she gave him his nice Christmas, the same as he gave her hers."

Evelyn turned to Alvin and said, "Everybody knows y'all is living together except her. Unless she meant to say 'boy did we have ourselves a nice Christmas those two days we spent together.'"

Alvin grinned and said to her, "I'll ignore your allegation and ask you the same question: did y'all have a nice Christmas?"

"What does it matter to you?" She said, "You're not concerned about what kind of Christmas I had. You're concern is how to cover up for her asking such dumb question in her attempt to overturn our curiosity about y'all living together. And this is a waste of both of your time. Because if y'all don't know by now that we all know that y'all is living together, the both of y'all is as stupid as the day is long. How can't we not know when all y'all ever do is make goo-goo eyes at each other when you think no one is looking?"

"Well," Alvin answered, "I'm guessing from the sound of the irritation I hear in your voice that you didn't have a very nice Christmas at all." He went to his station and started work an hour before he was scheduled to start, all because of Grace's big idea that they start riding together. When time came for them to go home in the evening after work, they did the same thing as they had that morning. Grace would walk out ahead of him and wait in the car for ten minutes before Alvin came out and rode home, similar to the way he rode to work that morning; nervously glancing at every car that drove near them. On a few occasions they might have caused a few heads to turn, but not for long. Since everyone was traveling at such high speeds, it was impossible for anyone to fix their gaze long enough to be certain about what they saw in the swiftly-moving traffic.

The minute he drove into the driveway, Alvin dragged the back of his hand across his brows. "Woman," he said, "If I don't stop listening to you, you're gonna be the death of me for sure." They got out of the car and began walking toward the house. Maggie stood there, holding the door open for them. She said to Alvin, "It's about time you showed these people around here that you have legal document that says this white gal you see me riding with belong to you. I assume y'all didn't have any trouble, so until you do, I suggest y'all keep it up until someone with authority tell you otherwise."

"Not the least bit," Grace said, "And this is just the beginning of the rides we plan to do together – until some fainthearted hypocrite with authority makes us stop."

"So," Maggie asked, "what kind of holiday did you have with your in-laws?"

"I loved everything about them, as well as the farm – but oh, that house! That is a different story. It's an old house that needs a lot of work in order to make it fit for human habitation. On a cold night, a person could easily freeze to death in either one of those so-called heated rooms. In addition to sleeping in an ice-cold bedroom, everyone had to go out into the freezing cold to use the bathroom. There is no running water. To take a hot bath, we had to boil water on top of the stove. The old house needed so many repairs, Alvin and I promised Daddy and Mother Jackson before we left, I was going to do something about those things before another winter comes and catches them in the same predicament. The first thing," Grace continued, "is running water, inside the house. Secondly, we'll have to install a furnace and radiators – some kind of heating system. The only heat comes from a propane heater in the living room, except when Mother Jackson is trying to cook a meal in the kitchen. When Alvin and I went to our bed that first night, it was like being in a freezer for about thirty minutes. It may have taken longer for our body to generate enough warmth to heat up the bed if Daddy Jackson hadn't made me drink that big shot of gin and tonic. The minute the bed warmed up, Alvin fell asleep. However," she said, "it had a different effect upon me. It had me doing all sorts of strange things."

"I bet it did, at that," Maggie said. "It probably had old Alvin wishing that you'd have a martini every night before going to bed."

"That's another story." Grace said, "I don't know why I went so far as to mention that part of our stay, but the point that I'm trying to make is that we want you to go and gather all the information you can on the land adjacent to the south of our farm. We'll also need a price on drilling a water well. We'll need a price on heaters, as well as the cost of installation, with the capacity to heat the entire house. Adding another bedroom is not a priority – but if it's possible to add an additional bedroom and stay within our budget, then do it. There are only three bedrooms –they'll need at least four with a family that's growing like Alvin's family. Lucky for them, there are three grandkids now – but even at that, people still had to sleep on the cold floor. I'm sure there are many more grandchildren just waiting to be born and they will need that extra bedroom."

"Wow," Myrtle spoke up and said, "That's an awful large order you're asking such a small lady to fulfill."

"Nevertheless," Ed said, "don't you wish we had a daughter that could give an order like that; and the money to back it up with?"

Alvin said, "Miss Maggie is no smaller than she is a stupid. I have come to believe that she is qualified to do just about anything she sets her mind to. That's why Grace and I have considered sending her to carry out this tall order of ours."

"Well," Maggie said, "I'll do whatever you want me to do. However," she said, "what about your daddy? Alvin, can he do all of the things you're asking me to do? I'm sure since he lives in the vicinity; it's much more convenient for him to do those things than it would be me."

"He could." Alvin said, "But I'm afraid that he's not qualified to negotiate with certain businessmen without getting himself cheated to the bone."

"When do you want me to start?"

"Not until after New Year's," Grace said, "because you're not going to accomplish very much between now and then, since everyone is off between Christmas and New Years – except restaurant workers."

At seven that evening, Grace's little sister Christina, came knocking on the door. "Grace," she said, "my daddy want to know if you and Alvin can come over and talk to him about your Christmases at Alvin father's house?"

Grace bent down and picked her little sister up, "Of course we can, honey." She carried her sister on her hip all the way across the back lawn and to her father's house.

"I'm sorry to have bothered y'all." Walter said, "But I was eager to know how well y'all faired on your trip to Alvin's family for Christmas. I'm well aware of the kind of people that live in those places . . . they know the law always looks the other way in the case of a couple like you and Alvin. There is more to this than what I just said – I asked y'all to come over, because I would just like to spend some time sitting and talking with my daughter in general conversation. Except when I need to talk to you about something that's important as you and Alvin traveling in that part of the country as a mixed couple. I want to hear about it as first-hand news and not ten days after the fact. If there were any other way to do it without taking you away from your mama, I'd do it; except I haven't figured that out yet, because she's always there. Even when you're at my house, I still feel like we're under some curfew. How am I going to talk to you if y'all don't come to my house? Like you're right now, we're relaxed with my wife while we're all talking back-n-forth between me, my wife, my daughter and son-in-law about things that happened to and from y'all trip to Alvin's father's house. Did y'all have any problem while riding around in those small backwoods country towns together?" He looked over his shoulder, calling into the kitchen. "Maurine – pour Alvin and me a shot of that bourbon that was left over from one of my Christmas presents. Go ahead. Don't be sparing with that whiskey . . . Grace, darling; would you like Maurine to pour you a small shot mixed with Coke or something soft like water? It'll sure make it taste better."

"Thanks, but no thanks," Grace answered, with a laugh, "especially after that drink I had at Alvin's father's house the first night we were there. That drink alone was enough to last me until this time next year. Besides that," she drew up a chair, and sat across from her father. "Alvin and I saw that farm we bought, for the very first time. I just fell in love with the idea of being an owner of my own land. Alvin and I have just finishing talking to Mama about buying the adjacent farm with the possibility of creating my own cattle ranch. And we'll also need money for all of the repairs that need to be done on the house. The very first night we spent there, no matter how hard we tried, I thought our bodies would never generate enough heat to where we could drift off into a peaceful sleep."

"It doesn't sound to me like y'all have very much fun at all," Walter observed.

"It was fun," Grace answered, wryly. "Except for those things that I've just complained about, but the rest of our stay was wonderful."

"Well," he said, "one of the reasons I asked y'all to come over, I wanted to thank you and Alvin for all of the presents y'all gave me and the family for Christmas. Maurine and I are especially grateful for the thing y'all buy us, mainly because they're very nice outfits."

"Good." Grace said, "I'm glad you like them – which means you won't mind wearing them to the New Year's Eve party the hotel gives its employees every year." She went on to say, "Me and Alvin have never attended the event, but our boss, Ray Davis, stopped Alvin in the hallway this morning and told him that he wanted to hear Monday morning that Alvin and I had attended the party. He also told Alvin that Earlene, the dining manager, will be there to make sure people don't drink so much that they don't start a ruckus over seeing us in close proximity to each other."

"I'm assuming your mama and J. D. will be there," he said.

"I haven't told them yet," she said, "but yes, they'll be there seated at a different table from y'all. Alvin and I will just have to take turns visiting between the two tables."

"Who's going to watch after the girls while we're out dancing," Maurine asked.

"Don't worry about that," Grace said. "I have it all figured out. John isn't going, so we'll have him stay with the girls until y'all return."

"Boy," Walter said, "she's got it all laid out for us doesn't she? Grace, darlin', I've been aiming to ask you what y'all are planning to do with this apartment. I know I told y'all that I was going to move out, and I'm guessing you're waiting for me to do just that. That way you can move your Aunt Myrtle and Uncle Ed in. Every time I turn around, I see them standing in your back door gazing at this apartment as to say 'I'm waiting!'"

"Aunt Myrtle isn't my mother and Uncle Ed is not my father – the instant their stay is up at my house, they'll have no alternative but to go back to their home in Beaumont. You and Mama take priority over Mama's sister and brother-in-law. Besides that – I assume you're asking me to let you stay?"

"Well," he said, "I haven't paid any rent since I've been here, and y'all would be well within your rights to kick me out."

"Daddy, you don't have to explain to me about you not paying rent." Grace said, patiently. "All I'm asking is: do you want to stay?"

Maurine spoke up, "Yes, we want to stay; just until we can save up enough money to move into a nice three-bedroom house. I want my girls to each have their own bedroom."

"Take as long as you want," Grace said. "Actually, you don't ever have to move. Now, Daddy – I'm sorry I have to go. Otherwise, Mama is going to be angry with me, because she wasn't finished talking when Christina came and got me."

"So! Let her be angry," Walter said. "Don't I deserve the right to spend the same amount of time with my daughter as she does?"

Grace kissed his cheek and said, "I know all about that, but I still must say goodnight." As she and Alvin walked back to their house, she picked up the part of conversation where she was in the process of telling her mother about their stay at the Jacksons' house for Christmas. However, she was interrupted to talk to her father about the very same subject she had been talking to her mother about. Nevertheless, Grace finally got around to telling Maggie that they were all invited to a New Year's Eve party that the hotel employees participate in every year.

"Well," Maggie said, "what brought all of this on? Y'all have never been invited before. Not only that, I thought we were all going to celebrate New Year's Eve together here in y'all's house."

"I'm sorry, Miss Maggie. I thought so too," Alvin answered, "until I met my boss in the hall this morning, telling me that he wanted to hear – come Monday morning – that I and Grace had attended the New Year's Eve party. When your boss tells you to do something like that," he explained," you can't rightly say no, especially if he's your boss as well as your only ally, in the situation such as we're in. More to the point, I'd guess that he is a secret supporter of integration and using Grace and me as his guinea pigs."

"Come on, Mama," Grace begged, "and show me a happy face. I'm just as disappointed as you are. Please say 'yes' so Alvin won't have to tell Ray Davis that his two favorite employees declined his invitation. I want you to wear the dress Alvin and I bought you for Christmas. Alvin wants me to wear the dress and jewelry he bought me for Christmas as well. He thinks everybody should see what he saw – and just maybe they too would go into convulsions the way he did when he saw me wear it on Christmas day."

"I just might go to your New Year's party," Maggie said, "but I'm still gonna have everyone gathered together at this table to a meal that's traditionally served on New Year's Day. I'll be dishing up what's supposed to be served on that day; black-eyed peas with fatback, crackling cornbread with a few minced jalapenos, and we'll have a lots of ice tea, too – that's the way my mama would've served it, because that's the way her mother served it, and I'm not changing their custom."